DEATH IN VEGAS

DEATH IN VEGAS

Margaret Goodman, MD

Win By KO Publications
Iowa City

Cover photography by Kim Nielson.
Model: Christine Unruh.
Design by Christina Gruppuso.

Win By KO Publications
Iowa City, Iowa
www.winbykopublications.com

ISBN 978-0-9903703-0-7 (50# acid-free paper)

Manufactured in the United States of America.

For the love of my life, best friend and mentor, Flip.

One

OLIVIA HAD JUST touched up her mascara and was tugging on the hem of her skin-tight Versace when she heard a soft knock on her open door.

"Dr. Norris, Bosch needs you in emergency," the unit secretary announced hesitantly.

"I'm off call and already late," she snapped. "O'Reilley is the neurology attending until Monday. Better yet, tell Dr. Bosch to call the chief resident."

"One of our research patients came in acutely confused."

"Who?"

"Mr. Simmons."

"That's impossible," Olivia muttered. She grabbed a lab coat and ran past the clerk, covering her attire with the considerably longer white coat.

Hastily yanking the Emergency Department (ED) door open, she somehow caught her spike heel in the bolt socket in the floor. "Bosch. What happened?" she yelled, cussing under her breath as she pulled the shoe free.

"No clue," Bosch said. "His chart says he had a benign glioma removed from his frontal lobe eight months ago. His head CT is clean." Bosch recited the lab results, all normal. "So it's unlikely he had a seizure," he said. "I gave him a B52 and he's just slowing down. He's in Bed 4."

She hurried to the bed as Bosch called after her, "Let me know if you want us to do a spinal tap."

Giving blood work and spinal fluid orders to her intern, who glared at Simmons in four-point restraints, Olivia began a detailed neurological exam.

Randall Simmons, 54, was in a longitudinal research study for grade 1 tumor patients. He'd been free of any cognitive deficits since hospital discharge eight months earlier. What could have happened?

Simmons's wife, Alisa, came into the room. She meekly said hello to Olivia. She answered no to Olivia's questions about recent head injuries, new medications, possible toxin exposure and travel.

"But over the last month, he was getting more and more depressed and angry," she added.

Randall had always been upbeat, even after everything he and Alisa had been through with his surgery and post-op recovery. "He's one of our favorite patients," Olivia said, reaching out and briefly taking Alisa's hand.

"I wanted to call, but he wouldn't allow it," Alisa told her, lowering her eyes. "I've never seen him fly off the handle so much. His outbursts were starting to scare me."

Reassuring Alisa that they would discover the cause, Olivia went back to her office and cancelled her date—another guy way too young in years and maturity that she'd met on Rush Street. Then she turned her attention to Simmons' chart.

•

Come Monday Grand Rounds, Simmons' condition remained unchanged. Olivia presented the case to interns, residents and attendings from the neurology departments of three affiliated hospitals. Each recommendation and potential diagnosis was something she had already investigated. Although spinal fluid cultures were pending, all the initial results were negative.

Olivia was still investigating scenarios that night at 11:30, when the Department Chair David Rogers cracked open the door and grinned at her. "I have Joint Commission coming to chew out my ass next week. What's your excuse, Red?"

"I know the answer is here somewhere," she blurted out, looking up from stacks of research articles and books. He was the only person in the world she had ever allowed to call her Red. She always felt the name was meant to be an insult, a comment on the hair color and complexion she had never found a way of liking. But she knew he didn't know he was insulting her. He called her that because he liked her, plain and simple.

She counted on David's high regard for her. She knew he was always happy to work with her, and normally she enjoyed being his favorite. But tonight she felt the pinch of time passing while she floundered for a solution. She had no idea how long they could keep Simmons stable.

"I even changed the Keppra dosage in case it was the culprit," she said, feeling her mind pulling her again into the endless loop of everything she had already thought of. "Any ideas?"

Still smiling, but toning down his natural ebullience, David came in and threw himself on her couch. "We have to remove him from the study," he said.

"I know. He's out. There are enough patients to complete the study." She took a deep breath and looked across her desk at him. He was a distinguished-looking man with thick silver hair and elegant features. He had piercing blue eyes behind very thin horn-rimmed glasses, which he would often take off so he could pinch the bridge of his nose, as if the glasses bothered him where they sat. Olivia knew he went through that series of actions just to gain time, to think or to formulate an answer or to find a diplomatic way of saying something. She watched him do it now and waited, as she always did, for him to be ready to go on.

"Let's review his data," he said when he had settled the glasses on his face and sat back on the sofa.

Calmly and thoroughly she presented everything she had heard, found or thought of so far. She kept all the emotion, the sense of emergency, out of her voice and out of her presentation but felt it, as always, in her shoulders and neck. David challenged her, prodded her, even teased her, as was his way, but at the end of three hours, when they were still nowhere, he quietly stopped. She felt it happen. She was looking up something, scrolling down the screen, and something in his energy, over there on the couch, changed. For a moment she kept scrolling, but she knew he was done.

"Get some sleep," he said softly, getting up and brushing the creases out of his trousers. At the door he turned and said it again. "Get some sleep, Red," and he was gone.

•

Olivia got up and closed her office door. She went to the file cabinet and took out a bottle of Dewar's—standard office issue as far as she was concerned, though she never drank while she was on duty. She poured what was left of the scotch into a paper cup and put the bottle back in the drawer. On the couch, she closed her eyes and felt the liquor loosen her shoulders and send a message of possibility to her brain.

She was awakened at 4:00 AM by Maintenance, then again at 6:15 by her chief resident on the phone, who needed to discuss a new case with her.

Olivia went down the hall and touched up her makeup, then headed to the emergency department (ED), turning her mind over to sideline the Simmons case. This mental exercise was something she had found she could do when she was a child, and as a doctor it meant she never lost the possibility of learning something from one case that might help her in analyzing another. It was what had made her reputation—she could always look at a blast of possibilities and come up with the best diagnosis.

The chief resident hailed her as she entered the ED. "Forty-five year-old female with acute Parkinsonian symptoms—"

"Clarify acute," she interrupted. "And what symptoms."

The patient had been working full time at a bank until a week ago, then developed stiffness, rigidity, hand tremors and gait instability. She wasn't on any meds, and all her tests were negative and normal. "Past history clean except she had an uneventful lumbar laminectomy 10 months ago."

"Here?"

"Yes. She recovered from that and has been off all pain meds."

"Has she responded to Parkinson meds?"

"A little…"

"Let's present the case to Grand Rounds tomorrow…get some fresh ideas. Remember it's at Community Hospital."

•

Olivia preferred Community Grand Rounds. Their budget included unlimited sweet rolls, bagels and fresh fruit—all foods she would never touch at home for fear of the pounds they would add to her difficult-to-maintain figure.

"Sit over here," she heard from across the room. Fran, her roommate during internship, was waving her over. Although they had completed separate neurology residencies and worked in different hospitals, they still sometimes shared tales of their failed romances and difficult cases.

"There's something weird about this one," Fran said, referring to a case that was new to Olivia. "He's a healthy 65-year-old who came in looking like he had stroke with cortical blindness. His MRI and heart studies are normal. His spinal fluid was normal except for a few white blood cells. He's got a negative history except for a cervical fusion."

"Why not present the case?"

"I did—the week you were in the Bahamas. No one had any good ideas."

Suddenly, something occurred to Olivia, a possible connection. Springing out of her seat, she hastily asked Fran to see if Community's lab had a few cc's of spinal fluid left from her patient. "If I'm right, we can't waste any time," she added. Heading back out the door, she ran smack into David Rogers, knocking his butter-slathered bagel out of his hand.

"Where're you heading?" he asked her, laughing over her confusion as she tried to clean up the butter on the floor with half a paper towel she happened to have in her pocket.

"Sorry," she said, standing up and tossing the bagel into the trash. "I'm off to order prion proteins—the 129 M/M variant, on Simmons."

She could imagine him thinking she was insane to consider Creutzfeldt-Jacob disease (CJD), but she didn't stick around to hear him say so. She had an idea, and if she was right, there was no time to spare.

There was no instance of CJD, a progressively fatal neuroinfectious disease, in the U.S., so it actually was a crazy idea. But she had remembered a *Lancet* abstract from a month ago on CJD transmission from surgical equipment in Europe. Classic sterilization methods had proved inadequate to remove prions, the infectious agents, from surgical instruments. A patient could present with stroke symptoms, blindness, Parkinsonism or even a psychiatric illness; the usually long incubation period could be shortened to as little as eight months; and often the EEG findings were absent early on. All three of the cases this week had had surgery either here or at Community using some of the same neurosurgical equipment. Simmons's surgery had been postponed, as she recalled, because the surgical brace it required was in use in another case at Community.

She headed on the run for OR 7, where a cerebral aneurysm clipping was in progress. They would be using the surgical brace, which they shared with Community. She had to stop them, if it wasn't too late.

•

A few weeks later, when the furor had died down, Olivia, on her way down the corridor from the Ladies Room and seeing her boss's light on, gave a knock on his door.

David looked up and smiled at her, inviting her in.

"It's been nuts around here," she said. "Hard to get anything done with all the TV and newspapers." They had barely seen each other since her discovery that morning.

"I think you might have saved a hundred people—maybe more," he said.

But she hadn't saved the three patients who had alerted them to the issue, and she couldn't shake the feeling it gave her. Losing Simmons had been particularly hard. If the others who were exposed had the prions, they might die, too.

"The liability issues are immense," David said, "but everyone is thankful." He paused, and looked at her as if to make sure she was listening. "Red, makes me proud I hired you."

"Ha, typical," she laughed, "taking the credit."

"I always knew you were a star. Here, have this on me." He winked, pulling out a Diet Coke from his coat pocket and handing it across his desk to her.

•

Thanksgiving was approaching, and David and his wife Adele were having their annual holiday bash. Olivia hated parties, but when the Chairman of the Neurology Department invited you, you showed up or you should never expect a weekend off, *ever*. Seriously, there was no way she could get out of going. She dressed to the nines, in self-defense, and arrived as late as she dared.

The Chicago suburb of Lake Forrest was a photographer's wonderland. David's sprawling colonial estate house lay safely nestled in a shroud of Christmas-decorated birch trees. David had published so many best-selling books on the coattails of NIH grant money that he could afford anything he wanted in this ritzy community. He was best known for demonstrating that women's brains shrink less with age than their male counterparts, and he had appeared on *Oprah* and CNN more than once. Hence, this picture-perfect *Gone with the Wind* residence.

For Olivia, a key to these shindigs was avoiding the parking valet. It wasn't to save a couple of bucks. Self-parking made for a swifter exit. Unfortunately, many others had the same idea, so valet it was. She saw the bored look of superiority on the sweaty, pubescent attendant's face, and watched it disappear as she opened the door of her '64 Mustang convertible. Swinging out her Victoria's Secret 5'10" frame that had tormented her in junior high, she flashed her best smile and flung back her shoulder-length auburn hair.

As she stepped onto the front stoop, Adele Rogers, an early '80s Miss Georgia, snatched Olivia's hand and swept her past the holly-lined staircase packed with red-faced carolers. "Dr. Norris, welcome dear. Did you come alone?"

She always came alone and that was partially by choice. Not that she had anyone to bring. Her rap sheet boasted a failed three-year relationship with a cardiologist she had seen so infrequently she could barely remember his face. This preceded a two-year stint with a general surgeon whom everyone knew cheated on her with the plentiful student nurses. Always slightly embarrassed at her resemblance to Jessica Chastain, with the freckles and the ruddy hair, Olivia blamed everything on not being classically pretty or model-thin.

Adele led her though the adorned *Architectural Digest* rooms filled with hospital administrators, residents, nurses and attending physicians. They were all networking as their significant others patiently sipped Adele's famous cider. Olivia couldn't help wondering what the point was of these parties.

Really, she saw these people day after day. It wasn't that she didn't like them. In many ways they were her only family. They'd shared countless horrifying moments while unable to prevent the crippling paralysis accompanying a stroke or nonstop seizures. These were the real ties that bound her to her peers.

"Adele, you're amazing," she said, raising her voice above the singers' six-part-harmony rendition of *Jingle Bell Rock*. "Everything is lovely."

"You're too kind, my dear." Adele's grip on her hand tightened as she continued to move Olivia through the rooms. "Giving parties is my hobby."

More like her life, Olivia thought.

Cruising by canapés and crudités-filled tables surrounded by medical students resembling a pride of lions who had taken down a zebra, Olivia waved hello. This lavishness made her flash back to nights on call where all you could do was scarf up stale broken potato chips.

On a mission, Adele finally dragged Olivia to her husband, ensconced in the den.

This was David's man cave. He was holding court, surrounded by his department minions while six plasma TV screens blared NCAA Conference Championships. He aimlessly changed the channels using a remote large enough to make up for any inadequacies a man might secretly feel. A 50-year-old child, Olivia thought.

"Now the party can start," David roared when he saw Olivia. He was the king, advising everyone surrounding him of the ground rules. He liked Olivia and lusted after her, though he kept the lust well hidden from all but a wife who had traveled that road before. Olivia never feared challenging his pompousness. Like most men, he took that as a friendly aphrodisiac. And then there was that other side of him, the side that joined her happily in serious work.

Olivia digested the male stares as the Louis xv clock chimed. There was already a lot of drink in these men—David not excepted.

"Red," David bellowed, patting the couch next to him to make sure she sat down. He winked at her. "You can still enter the pool," he said.

College football. The only thing that drove her crazier on the holidays than these inane gatherings was watching college football. But while most of her fellow female attendings were stroking Adele's ego or schmoozing hospital big-wigs, here she was, socializing with the men. It seemed to be her specialty—at least while the socializing was still in the acquaintance stage. It was after that that the trouble began.

"Dr. Norris, we need your help with this one," one of the group called to her. "Dr. Freedman wants to know if we can accumulate a big enough sample size of mild head trauma patients to determine susceptibility to chronic traumatic encephalopathy. Do you think we can get the funding?"

This question hovered dangerously close to Olivia's turf. She had published several articles on repeated head trauma. David encouraged his departmental "children" to play nice with one another. This might jerk Olivia's chain, because it might mean that she had to work with others less fortunate in obtaining financial backing. She was most comfortable working alone, and if she collaborated, she would rather it was with someone of her own choosing.

Just then, Michigan scored a field goal. The boys went wild and any thoughts of business flew out of their beer-filled heads.

It was a chance to escape, and she started to inch off the couch. But David wasn't about to let her go.

"Come on, Red, where you off to? The main event from Vegas is about to start."

It made her feel sick to think about it. "I don't care much for boxing, never follow the sport," she said. "I don't even know who's fighting."

"What?" David teased her, coyly poking her forearm and, she knew, wishing it was her backside. "You don't enjoy seeing men drop a few brain cells—for scientific purposes?"

Okay, okay, she got it, not time to make a getaway just yet. She half-smiled and leaned back again. "I'm famished," she mumbled, thinking she might excuse herself to get something to eat.

"Hold on a minute, you're in the right place," he responded. Muting the TVs, he yelled to a caterer. "We need some food in here. More beer and sausages." All he was missing was a toga.

Discussion quickly switched to boxing as the center flat screen filled with pugilists. Testosterone surged in the room, as the war stories about childhood fights, matches attended, and bets won (or more likely lost) began to flow. Guys who didn't know a right cross from a jab were suddenly expert judges, criticizing any move made by the referee.

Olivia knew how to joke around, be one of the guys, and handle crashing patients and overzealous students. But pugilistic violence horrified her. She finally slipped away unnoticed, never once looking at the screen, and with no idea who was in the ring.

Two

R ING-PHYSICIAN-TURNED-BOXING-JUDGE Bartolome Rossi, once Las Vegas's most respected emergency room physician, still worked a few hospital shifts a month. But now he mostly played poker for a living. He no longer needed the income from daily intubations on elderly respiratory-arrest patients or suturing drunks from bar fights. He was in a state of semiretirement at the ripe old age of 47, but for almost two decades he had been a fixture in the Vegas fight scene.

Bart considered himself an expert at most things in life, and he excelled in the nuances of boxing. Tonight he was working the undercard, the off-TV bouts. He should have been a judge for the headline fight, but the promoter loathed him and had excluded him from the plum assignment he deserved. Bart flaunted the exclusion like a badge of honor and showed up to piss off the bad guys.

He had a seat at the Nevada Boxing Commission's table for the main event. He was interested in the young white challenger, Curtis Montana, who was going up against heavyweight champion Samson Livingstone. As the fight got underway, the older, African-American Livingstone danced around the ring, throwing explosive punches to his opponent's chest and gut. The theory was "kill the body and the head will follow." Repetitive blows to the liver, spleen and kidneys had the ability to incapacitate the body and the very spirit of the fighter.

But Montana was more than holding his own, and he was giving it back to Livingstone. By round 4, the champion had a trickle of maroon blood from his left nostril, a deep cut underneath his right eye, and a puffy left eye limiting his depth perception. Bart thought, as he often did, how distorted that face was going to be tonight.

The packed 12,000-seat Mandalay Bay Hotel arena shook from the crowd's roars as roving spotlights scanned the faces of the rich and famous in the crowd: Mila and Ashton, Beyoncé and Jay-Z and Senators Harry Reid and John McCain. Celebrities and politicians were never in short supply at a Vegas heavyweight championship fight.

The fans screamed when a punch compressed the face of the boxer they were betting against. The fighters' heads barely moved despite the anvil blows. Being able to take a punch, not get hurt and absorb the pain—even enjoy the pain—moved the athletes to fight on. That was something Bart had taken from boxing, and he had applied it to everything he ever did in life. That is, he had once applied it. It had been a long time since he had felt anything but a healthy skepticism about the workings of the world. He let life come as it would and prided himself on being very good at rolling with whatever punches came his way.

Over the next four rounds, Livingstone took more and more punishment. By the end of round 9, he was beginning to look like he was close to being finished, while Montana went to his corner without so much as a mark on his face. The young fighter sat on the small stool that was brought in at each break with his arms leaning against the lower ring ropes. He wasn't tired. Bart could see that in the way he sat, in the obvious tensile strength of every muscle. But he might be a bit scared by the fanfare demanding he deliver a knockout.

Montana's cutman Lou Flannagan, an old, gruff soul, reached over the ring apron and rubbed Montana's face with an Enswell—flattened ice-cold metal intended to reduce facial swelling. Vincent Marquessa, the kid's long-time trainer, leapt inside the ropes, threw water on his fighter's face and squirted an ounce of water in his mouth.

"Kid, this is what we prepared for, the dream we chased," Marquessa said. His voice was steady and calm as he massaged blood back into Montana's legs.

"Remember how you handled your first fight? I could lie and tell you not to rush, like that night—to keep chipping away at this guy. I know you think you need to fight him on the inside. Sit down on your punches and use your jab. He's already exhausted and his mouth open. I couldn't be closer to you if you were my own flesh and blood. If you won't do this for yourself, do it for me. Both of us have a lot to prove. Now get out there and show the world. Most of all show yourself what you're really made of."

Montana looked ready, Bart thought. The young fighter, just shy of his thirtieth birthday, was looking at his opponent slouching on the stool across the ring gasping for air. "One-minute rest between rounds?" Bart said to himself. Hell, 30 minutes couldn't be enough to wipe away the blood oozing from Livingstone's facial cuts—or absolve him of years of trauma to his brain and body.

Marquessa grabbed Montana's face in his hands and yelled into the fighter's face. "Throw the damn right. Don't be a pussy with this guy. Stop looking at him, damn it. If you really care about what happens to this guy, go out and finish him off. That would be the humane thing!"

Bart was close enough to see and hear all of this and he was enjoying it tremendously. A boxing match could be a beautiful, bloody operetta with its own ebb and flow. He had seen some beauties. This fight hadn't had such back and forth extremes, but it was exciting to see a new champion emerging. The Vegas odds-makers had overwhelmingly picked the young "Great White Hope," and it appeared the experts were right.

But sometimes in boxing, for no apparent reason, the tide changes like a hot-air balloon deflating. Youthful exuberance gets overwhelmed by experience.

Not long after the start of the next round, Montana's defenses seemed to slow. He began to appear listless and tired, and his punches barely connected. The commentators wondered if it was the kid's right arm. There had been talk of a shoulder problem before the fight.

And now Livingstone came back. Even with a near empty tank, he had begun throwing wild left hooks, hoping something would land. Montana found it harder and harder to get out of the way. His legs were heavy, as if he was wading through quicksand.

At the end of round 10, the crowd quieted. The trainer jumped in the ring and pulled his fighter to the corner.

"I'm sorry, Vinnie," Montana said. "I know what I gotta do. I can't pop the right hand. It just isn't working for me."

Throwing water on the kid in an attempt to wake him up, Marquessa shouted, "Shut the fuck up! What's wrong with you? Go out and fight. If you don't take this guy out the next round, I'm gonna stop this fight. You hear me? Is there something wrong with you?"

Jason Mathers, the referee, leaned over the trainer. "If I don't see more from you, I'll stop this fight," he said.

Bart saw Gabe Gunderson, the executive director of the Nevada Boxing Commission (NBC), get up and quietly ask the chief physician, Mark Stewart, to see whether he thought the fight should be stopped. Stewart mounted the ring apron and tapped the boxer on the shoulder from behind. "Are you okay?"

When Gabe saw the kid nod, his eyes still clear, she sat back down and said no more. But Bart had a bad feeling about this one.

The doc nodded to the referee, indicating the boxer could go out for another round. "Keep an eye on him," he whispered to Mathers. "He doesn't have much left."

The bell rang as the cornermen took a few extra seconds rubbing Vaseline onto their boxer's faces to limit skin damage from the ripping power of the punches.

Livingstone gathered every bit of strength he had. Barely balanced on two feet, he repeatedly swung at his opponent. The kid's once-perfect skin became bloodied and misshapen, hued beneath with an unnatural pallor.

The fifteenth unanswered punch propelled Montana's head as if it was in a slingshot. Bart imagined he could hear his facial bones crack from the force. Already unconscious from the last blow, Montana crumpled to the ground. Mathers waved off the fight as the crowd stood in shocked, horrified silence.

Three

OLIVIA COMPLETED HER due diligence. She successfully flirted with every male, complimented the wives and bolstered the egos of her students and residents. Finally managing to get to the door to leave, she was just asking the housekeeper for her jacket when she heard gasps.

"Did you see that?" she heard David shout, at the same time as the TV's volume rose. "My God, Montana is out!"

Olivia ran to the den. She had to push through the crowd that had gathered there. Every screen was tuned to the same channel, replaying the scene of a defenseless young man incompetently fending off an onslaught of blows to his battered face.

David pounded his fist into his other hand. "Jesus, he's dead," he shouted. "I know he's dead. What a massacre. Why didn't they stop it?"

Onlookers couldn't move, stuck in a vortex of disbelief. Somebody sobbed. Curses rang out. Olivia was paralyzed.

Then Adele was beside her, asking her if she needed to sit down.

Drenched in sweat, Olivia caught herself as she swayed in the airless, crowded room. She grabbed the nearest table as tears streamed down her face. Adele helped her to the sofa.

David was leaning over her. "Red, boxing is a shit sport," he said. She felt his hand on her shoulder but she couldn't move. "I know why you hate it. Legalized murder," he went on, "like the Vatican says. But maybe we can use this."

Wait, what was he saying? She couldn't put it together. Probably grants, he was always thinking about research grants above all else.

Olivia stared at the floor. Someone offered her a glass of something. She took a sip and put it down. Finally, David turned off the television. "Come on, Olivia, cheer up. It's boxing."

Raising her head, trying to find breath, she whispered, "I'm sorry."

He knelt next to her, stroking her hair. "Nobody likes to see this sort of thing, especially when it might have been prevented. Real sad about Curtis Montana. Poor kid. Sadly, boxing was all he knew."

"Stop. You don't understand. *None* of you understand." She knew she was shouting. She tried to regain her composure but the shouting kept coming. "That 'poor kid', it's Curtis—my Curtis…"

A rush of energy swept her to her feet and, fending off all questions and concerned offers of help, she made her way to the front door and out to the stoop. Adele and David were quickly by her side, both pleading with her to stay until she felt calmer, but Olivia assured them she was okay and demanded that the valet get her car.

By the time she was behind the wheel, she had said a quiet and convincing goodbye to her host and hostess. She put all her concentration into her driving, pushing herself to use the same discipline she used when looking after patients in an emergency, distancing herself from the panic that was trying to submerge her. She found a parking space almost at her doorstep but knew immediately that she couldn't go inside. She couldn't bear to be alone right now. She would go to Jilly's, her favorite piano bar on Rush. She called a cab, but by the time it got there she had changed her mind about Jilly's. Too many people knew her there. She told the driver to take her to the Drake.

The Drake Hotel's bar never closed until all the patrons had left. When Olivia arrived, it was almost midnight. An illicit-looking couple shared a dark corner, and a smarmy, thirtyish stock broker-type, alone at the front of the bar, drooled over Olivia as she entered. She chose the opposite end of the bar, threw down her credit card and ordered a double scotch. A few minutes later, a similar drink arrived, then another—gifts from her admirer, who joined her eagerly. Needing to get shit-faced fast, she welcomed the endless supply. Soon Mr. Chicago Board and Trade looked pretty convenient. Playing with her wayward locks, he convinced her it would be a good idea for her to lie down in his suite. Out of the corner of her eye, she saw the bartender shake his head, as if he knew this scene all too well.

Just then she felt herself yanked off the stool, then she tripped and somehow her heel broke and she lost her balance.

Another guy who she had never seen before was holding her by the shoulders. He looked like a young Clint Eastwood. "Here you are, babe. Why didn't you call me?" he said. "We need to let the babysitter leave." He smiled, grabbing Olivia's waist and thanking her perturbed bar mate.

Her head was spinning. She wasn't entirely sure what was going on, but she accepted the change in partners and leaned into him as he guided her out of the bar. He was helping her into his car, which she recognized as a Maserati sedan, and then she passed out.

Four

BART ROSSI STOOD watching the chaos. People in the stands were shouting and fighting with each other. Cups of beer were being thrown. Two TV commentators, Tom Rush and Lawrence Hastings, were talking into their microphones, but it was difficult to hear them over the din. They stood with their backs against the ring as the cameraman moved in tighter. Security formed a circle around them to protect them from the crowd, which was pushing forward toward the ring.

Rush and Lawrence had both been with the network for over 20 years. They had seen it all, but covering tragedy was never easy, and today's event deeply affected them both. They were visibly shaken.

"I know for those of you at home this is tough to witness," he said to the camera. "Lawrence and I want answers, as do you. This is not a safe place right now."

"We're trying to stand here and tell you what's transpiring," Hastings came in. "Where is the ambulance crew? Curtis Montana is surrounded by Commission physicians working to revive him. Why is he still in the ring? They're *finally* placing oxygen on him. I've never witnessed this amount of disorganization."

The two reporters looked at each other, then Rush turned to see what was going on in the ring.

"Curtis Montana should be in surgery," he said, wiping traces of beer from his face and forcing a fan out of his view.

"Hey, man, we're filming here," he yelled at the fan. "Why don't you sit down and let them take care of Curtis?" Looking over the crew, Rush yelled into his microphone, "We need more security here. Lawrence, emergency personnel can't get close with this near riot."

The ring ropes were lined by Mandalay Bay Security and Vegas Metro Police. Fifty people stood inside the ring. Most didn't need to be there and were interfering with ring access.

As Hastings slipped between the ring ropes, some of the fighter's entourage shoved him aside. This further limited visibility of Montana, who lay motionless on the canvas, surrounded by people clutching one another in tears.

Hastings stabilized his footing with the help of a cameraman. His voice quivered in frustration as he spoke into his microphone. "Tom, I'm trying to get a better view. When are they going to do something? If someone had cared about stopping this fiasco, we wouldn't be in this situation. Where were the physicians when Curtis was getting pummeled?" He took a deep breath as his eyes darkened. "Oh, my God, is it too late?"

The telecast shot away from him as Tom Rush refocused.

"Twenty-nine year-old Curtis Montana came here tonight to fight for the United Boxing Association Heavyweight Championship," Rush began. "He *belonged* here. Unlike most boxers, Montana came from a strong upper-middle-class family, attending two years at the University of Illinois. He started boxing at age 14, won the Golden Gloves heavyweight title at age 15 and fought in the 2000 Olympics, unfairly losing due to suspect international judging. After turning pro, his meteoric rise to a top heavyweight contender was based on uncanny judgment, unending desire and pure talent.

"Tonight he could have had it all. Although he faced a formidable opponent in Samson Livingstone, he was clearly the favorite. Curtis's matinee-idol looks were matched by his charm and intellect. I can't think of a time when Lawrence and I didn't enjoy chatting with Curtis on everything from politics to his philanthropic efforts helping less fortunate boxers. In many ways, he was too good for a sport that caters to greed. We pray he will be safe. Lawrence, do you have anything to add?"

Bart, listening to the two seasoned commentators, kept his eye on the canvas. Emergency staff had started an IV with normal saline and drugs to stop the apparent seizures. They began CPR. The fact that Curtis was not on his way to the emergency department was not a good sign.

Vincent Marquessa stood behind the paramedics, looking at Curtis's limp body and sobbing in disbelief. Suffering from adult-onset diabetes and heart disease at 62, he was unable to catch his breath. Marquessa was not only the kid's manager, he was something like a father to him. Curtis had been a second chance at a boxing career for Marquessa, and he was his son in every way that counted.

Lawrence Hastings clutched the microphone. "Tom, for one reason or another, Curtis was hurt. Here you had a strong young man who never underestimated the danger. He never abused himself in or outside the ring. He had the best trainer around. We've seen him face opponents stronger than Samson.

Curtis had a brilliant future. Tom, we need answers, and there are none right now. The fight was tough. However, it suddenly stopped being competitive in the tenth round. The Commission or his trainer could have ended this sooner."

Hastings moved from the camera and grabbed the chair next to the one Bart was sitting in. Bart watched him wipe the sweat from his brow and guessed that the commentator was feeling his age. No one who had seen the fight could avoid the thought that the situation was more complex than a fighter who had taken too many punches.

Rush slammed his fist on the press table, shouting, "Can we speak to some-one in charge? Gabe, would you speak with us? We're on the air."

The cameras turned as Rush continued, "We have Gabe Gunderson, execu-tive director of the NBC, the Nevada Boxing Commission," he said, and he held out the microphone to her. Gabe had been commissioner for 10 years, and she had faced off with everyone at one time or another. She was the only woman ever to hold this position, and had been selected at age 35 following a grueling interview process against two dozen well-recognized male candidates. In Nevada, where boxing generated revenue second only to gaming, Gabe appeared to be a secure bet.

Bart was always interested to watch Gabe in action. She was the consum-mate politician, never ruffled, never taken by surprise. He watched her now. She was tough, but she seldom raised her voice unless she meant to. Tonight was no exception. She knew how to juggle the promoters, networks and sanc-tioning organizations that controlled the championship titles. She appeared to be an employee to the politically appointed commissioners. They did not quite recognize that she was *really* the boss.

Gabe assertively gripped the commentator's arm.

"Tom, I'd be happy to help you. Right now the well-being of Mr. Montana is foremost in all our minds. I ask for your patience in enabling us to do our job. We will speak to you as soon as the situation is stabilized."

Rush wouldn't back off. "When will Curtis be sent to the hospital? Why was the fight not ended sooner when you went to the ring physician and asked him to stop the carnage? Why'd you feel the need to do that if you didn't know something was very wrong?"

She never blinked. "Tom, that's too many questions," she said, with her party smile. She made a reach for the microphone but missed, as Rush was in her way.

"How are we to explain to the fans that boxing in your state is safe and that the fighters are protected?" he asked. "This isn't the first time Nevada has been questioned on such issues."

Finally managing to get hold of the microphone, Gabe placed it directly in front of her.

"Tom, we've worked together for a very long time. I know we're all devastated by the turn of events. However, this discussion in the heat of the moment serves no purpose. I ask you to allow us to do our job."

On that note, she turned abruptly and climbed the ring steps. "Clear the ring," she commanded, and everyone started to scurry.

Bart was chuckling to himself. Someone needed to take control, and she was the man for the job. She hadn't been on this earth 45 years to let these assholes in the press make a mess of things with their hunger for the truth.

Watching the monitor as the telecast concluded with a testimonial to Montana—including a clip of him sparring at age 16 with a much thinner and younger Vincent Marquessa—Bart felt tired. The kid was a natural, more at home in the ring than anywhere else. This was the life of a boxer, he thought, and this kid was no exception. His smile was full of hope and promise. His young face was unmarked by battle.

Ringside, the arena clean-up crew worked at lightning speed to remove any trace of boxing and prepare for tomorrow's sold-out Lady Gaga concert. TV techs hung from the rafters pulling down wires and lights, while the NBC officials huddled close by the ring apron waiting for instructions.

Bart hung around with the other officials for Gabe's standard review of the night's events, which was required before anyone could go home. Tonight, she would need to conduct an intervention for a distraught, demoralized group of referees, physicians, judges and inspectors. As she stood before the group, her hands on the back of a chair, she took a breath and everyone fell silent. "I want to thank you for your professionalism," she said. "Few can understand what we go through. People, especially the press, are going to want your comments. But as always, please refer them to the Commission. It makes us all look bad if one of us says something that contradicts what another of us has said. Statements are also easily misquoted and the next thing you know, they are front-page news or on Twitter."

Jason Mathers, the referee, slowly stood, his shirt covered in blood and sweat. "I want to say something."

Bart felt for the guy. Mathers was a good ref. Bart had watched him develop— it must be 10 years now since Jason had moved to Las Vegas from Pennsylvania looking to referee big bouts. His state had its share of boxing, but the fights were club shows with young kids starting out against older boxer who weren't that gifted and never had big money behind them. The bigger the fight, the more the judges and referee were compensated.

"I never saw it coming," Mathers continued. "I mean, Montana was alert during the entire fight. He never looked like he was in trouble."

Gabe interrupted what seemed to be the beginning of a confessional and pointed at some Internet press auditing their private meeting. "I'm sorry, guys," she said to the group at the back of the room. "This meeting is for the Commission. I'll address any questions you have at the press conference."

As soon as the disappointed young reporters left, Gabe praised the ref for a job well done, adding, "Let's review the tape and then we can talk."

Jerry Tyler, the newest of five governor-appointed commissioners, spoke up. "Everyone here tonight did the right thing. The press is only looking to find controversy. Don't give it to them."

Laughing inwardly at this horse's ass, Bart watched Gabe bite her lip, feigning respect. She had played this game with many a commissioner. Speaking to the officials was *her* job.

Tyler, the 35-year-old son of the owner of Nevada Construction who was proud of his dad's influence, was awaiting greener pastures in Washington, D.C. He still hoped to make a name for himself on the NBC. No doubt he was thinking tonight was the night.

Commissioners typically were businessmen or attorneys with little or no knowledge about boxing. Their mantra was "Don't embarrass the governor." Other than following that edict, they were superfluous. Gabe knew how to control all of them. Unfortunately, while the other four were already downing Kobe steaks and Grey Goose in the hotel's private dining room, Tyler seemed to believe he had a role.

One of the promoter's assistants called down to Gabe to come to the post-fight press conference. As she proceeded to leave the officials' meeting, Tyler yelled, "Gabe, dear, I should go with you."

That was Tyler all over, Bart thought, as he watched the executive director put on her best grin again and precede the commissioner up the aisle.

Five

A T THE PRESS conference, hundreds of national and international journalists were waiting to leverage the controversies of the fight into news flashes and columns all over the world. Despite the circumstance, Gabe would schmooze with the visiting journalists to make the NBC look good. Bart decided to miss some of that schmoozing and took a quick break to down a beer.

But he wasn't away long. He liked watching her. They went way back, and at one time had been close enough to swap war stories. He couldn't imagine doing her job the way she did it. She actually thrived on it. Irrespective of what happened in a fight, she owned the press room. Everyone looked to her, even if they didn't respect what she had to say. She understood which writers she could provide with inside information and which ones she could never trust. She played them all into thinking she would confide in them alone. These were attributes her predecessors, and the executive directors in other states, never understood.

Gabe's accessibility helped these guys finish their bylines in time, with a few extra special quotes. In turn, they usually gave her the benefit of the doubt in the midst of a controversy. The consummate spinmeister, she had learned to not let anyone throw her off balance and not to give in an inch to any insinuation of questionable behavior in her performance. If she was less than completely self-assured, she would end up road kill.

The pressroom was a cavernous ballroom off to the side of the arena. The secured entry had guards examining everyone's media credentials, while fans hovered outside hoping to get a glimpse of a fighter or two. Inside, satellite and radio DJs sporting nacho-stained T-shirts jabbered between their headphones. The banter was loud and filled with condemnation for the Commission. It was nothing personal—tragedies made for good radio speak.

Several press people tried to flag Gabe down. She ignored them. There would be time for this later.

At the front of the room, the usual dais with podium had been set up and lined with microphones, and water in brand name bottles had been placed at each chair. There were also diet sodas clustered along the table's center, all icy cold. Below, 50 rows of seats awaited reporters, although most stood taking notes, clutching coffee, cokes and Dove bars smartly provided by the hotel. A platform at the back of the room housed TV cameras and photographers perched in anticipation.

On a bad night like this, the conversation was filled with secretive speculation on the timeline to generate a follow-up story. There was always a pecking order for journalists, each appearing as if they had the scoop of the century.

Boxing officials rarely entered this room unless requested by the Commission. It was too easy for them to spill their guts and render absurd, meaningless quotes. However, Bart readily swam among the sharks. Only if he had been the judge for the main event would he have stayed away from the press conference.

Most of the newspaper journalists were his buddies. In fact, they had shared some sleepless nights smoking stogies in a dingy club at the corner of Paradise and Koval and trying to nail the best-looking broad in the room. Bart always took the prize, for whatever that was worth.

"Rossi, ol' man, aren't you going to the hospital?" his pal Stan from the *Boston Globe* demanded. "Any news on Montana? You think the kid'll make it?"

Immediately, a nest of reporters turned to see if they would learn something new. Bart didn't want to be part of this. He'd worked as ring physician at some of the biggest fights in Nevada and had presided at one where the fighter died. It had ripped his heart out. But he wasn't a ring physician anymore, and he was too seasoned to fall for the reporters' trap. "I don't do that job these days," he grunted. "However, I see Commissioner Tyler coming in with Gabe. Something tells me he'll be happy to discuss the subject."

Tyler heard his name as he walked by, and his ears perked up like a retriever waiting for a bird to land. Bart knew this would piss off Gabe. After all, this guy knew little or nothing except where to sit close to the ring.

Although Bart and Gabe had been confidants through many tough times with promoters and fighters, he knew she had too many masters and had long forgotten that the fights were about the boxers, not about TV exposure.

"Have you heard anything?" she called out to him.

He smiled and called back, "Gabriela, I try to stay out of these situations."

He was one of only a handful to call her by her full name. He used it to insult her—in a friendly way, of course—as if by using the girl's name she had not chosen he might cast doubt on her ability to do the job.

As Gabe swept through the crowd, Tyler trailed behind, nodding hello to anyone who would meet his glance.

Bart was still smiling, now in amazement, wondering if this asshole was running for office.

The talk ceased as the promoter Ed Rappaport stood in front of the podium.

"Gentlemen, please take your seats. This has been a long night. Could we have a moment of silence for the Montana family as Curtis fights for his life?"

One didn't need to know much more about Rappaport than that he was an attorney and the biggest promoter in boxing, and that he would sell his children to the network for a well-positioned fight date.

During the moment of silence, Tyler pulled Gabe off to the side, away from the dais, and holding her by the wrist said something inaudible.

Gabe gently removed his fingers with her other hand. Once free, she stepped back from him. He kept talking. No doubt he was giving her advice. What a dunce.

Now Rappaport had the mic, and he was shouting inanely about what a great boxer Montana was. As he went on and on, Gabe answered her phone and turned away to take the call.

Meanwhile Tyler was networking with hotel executives who wondered how the turn of events would affect their image. They understood that their hotel would be in every paper in America tomorrow, though even bad news could sometimes be good for business.

Everyone in the room, Bart guessed, wished they had ears on Gabe's call, which he presumed was from Mark Stewart. Stewart, the chief ring physician at tonight's fight, had been down this road before. Like many before him, he had become a ring physician on a whim, seduced by TV lights and the promise of recognition.

Fight officials, especially the ring physicians, were only supposed to deal with fighters during a fight, never outside of it. Otherwise it was considered a conflict of interest. You wouldn't want two athletes who were competing for millions of dollars to have a referee, a doctor or a judge who had a reason for one fighter to win over another.

But a few people—Bart among them—knew that Stewart had come to enjoy this life a bit too much. He was often called upon by promoters or managers to offer additional private medical assistance. He might inject a sore hand with cortisone or lidocaine too close to fight time or prescribe medications that could go undetected in a drug screen. He was closer to the promoters and matchmakers than to the fighters he was supposed to protect.

Stewart had a gig at the university hospital ED instructing the residents. Acute trauma carried greater risk. This brought the occasional lawsuit, which he always said reflected more on his poor bedside manner than his skill. The medical board made certain he was monitored by the hospitals.

Last year he also had a little run-in with the law. There had been no reporters casing the Clark County jail that night, and the story was missing from the news and the evening papers. It got back to Bart, though. You never knew when it might be useful to have this kind of information. Patients don't like seeing their doctor picked up for soliciting the services of a minor. Of course, the Commission never knew much about any of this.

Tonight Montana had sustained a beating while Stewart sat there and watched. What happened unavoidably called up the match with Omar Sharp, another Nevada boxer who had recently died on Stewart's watch.

Ed Rappaport was motioning for Gabe to come to the dais. Already seated were Samson Livingstone and his trainer. Livingstone retained the heavyweight title, but even though he beat Montana fair and square, it was as if he had blood on his hands. Guilt was always there when the other fighter was seriously injured. More often than not, the opponent was never the same after something like this.

Livingstone sat in silence, gazing away from the audience, his eyes welling with tears. Bart knew he would be praying there would be no questions. He had been close to Omar Sharp. Both had begun in the Detroit Golden Gloves. Samson was 12, Omar 14. They had the same trainer and grew up in the inner city without dads.

Rappaport might have been a sleaze, but he had shaped Livingstone's career (meaning he arranged plenty of low level opponents to produce a respectable winning record). This helped Livingstone secure a title shot through a sanctioning body. His rise was not meteoric, but it was respectable. He had a nice home, three beautiful children and, unlike most boxers, relatively sound investments.

Unfortunately, things hadn't ended this way for Sharp, who never had Samson's charisma. He wasn't marketable, though he held the title for a short time. The networks never once considered him main-event material until he fought last month—the bout where he collapsed. At one time, Rappaport wanted Sharp and Livingstone to fight each other. It would have been a Cain and Abel story. But the two would have none of it. They were as close as brothers, and now Sharp was dead. Samson had to be wishing he'd stayed in school and become a lawyer like his mom wanted…and now some might consider him a murderer.

Straightening her jacket and pushing her short, muddy blond hair off her forehead, Gabe went over to where Rappaport was standing.

"Gentlemen," the promoter said, "I'd like to introduce the brilliant executive director of the Nevada Commission, Gabe Gunderson." He turned toward her. "Gabe, honey, come on up. Oh, and we have Commissioner Tyler. This is the finest Commission in the world. I know they're doing everything possible for Curtis at a time like this."

He moved away from the podium and offered Gabe the spot.

"There isn't much to say at this time," she began, to catcalls.

The reporters shushed one another. Tom Rush and Lawrence Hastings strolled up the aisle glaring in her direction.

She continued in a strong and clear voice directly into the microphone. "Gentlemen, I've just spoken to Western Hospital. Curtis is in recovery. His mother, Sophie Montana, is by his side. He's in critical but stable condition."

"Gabe, tell us something we don't know," Hastings shouted up at her with contempt. "What else did the doctors say?"

"I guess we have similar reports," she answered, using her sincerest tone. "Curtis suffered a blood clot on the right side of his brain. It's very serious. We have to pray he'll make a full recovery."

The writers sensed her courteous evasiveness. Under normal circumstances, they would have obliged her and backed off. With this story, though, and with deadlines approaching, they needed something to chew on, even if it wasn't filet mignon.

Just then, the exuberant voice of Amanda Weekly, cub reporter for Channel 8, rang out. Bart couldn't help smiling, though he gave no other indication that he was listening.

Amanda was the most recent woman to grab Bart's attention. They had dated on and off for 18 months. Only 30, she hoped to land a spot with CBS national news. She had done a number of segments showcasing political malfeasance and complicit conflicts on the Gaming Commission. And she never missed a boxing story with political overtones.

Bart loved her aggressive career chase. He had every confidence she would get everything she wanted and, as a betting man, he would have put money on it. As it happened, her single-mindedness also gave him time to do his own thing.

"Ms. Gunderson, could you talk about tonight's officiating?"

Gabe knew Mandy. Everyone did. Mandy was a small force of nature.

"I'm willing to discuss anything you wish, Amanda, although Mr. Montana's condition takes precedence."

"I do understand," Amanda persisted. "You have to know there are questions. In fact, many of us were shouting for the fight to be stopped after the tenth round. And you yourself sent the ring doctor in at the end of the round. Have you spoken to the referee or the ring doctor? Are they here? Wasn't the physician the same one who worked the Omar Sharp fight? People want answers. Is this an unfortunate coincidence or is there a problem in Nevada? Why did it take so long to transport Montana from the ring? What time was he in surgery?"

From the back someone shouted, "Can you repeat the doctor's name?"

Mandy showed no intention of relinquishing the floor. Bart chuckled. She was such a delicious vision, all lanky slender limbs and golden hair shining like a helmet under the lights.

She kept at it. "Who were the other physicians working tonight? Did Commission doctors accompany Curtis to the hospital?"

While she held onto her platform, low-level chatter spread through the ballroom like a tidal wave.

Surveying the scene, Gabe caught sight of Bart reclining in the last row with his feet propped on the chair in front of him. He had an unlit cigar dangling from the side of his mouth.

"Let's save those issues for when we have our physicians here," Gabe said, "unless Dr. Rossi would be willing to comment on our protocols?"

Bart slumped further from view, waving his arm like a white flag in surrender. "You're doing fine," he called out. "I'm here to observe."

Tyler smiled at Bart's tennis lob.

Gabe held up her phone. "Gentlemen, I need to take this call." She turned to Rappaport. "Ed, please take over."

She got up and moved to the end of the dais, and turned her back to the crowd. After a few moments she returned to the podium.

Strong and clear, she gave them the update. "Montana arrested twice in recovery, but he's still with us," she said. "And his intracranial pressure is stable. At this point, it seems that there could be extensive damage if he survives."

Six

THE RINGTONE PENETRATED Olivia's sleep, then shook her awake. She reached out to pat the night table and opened her eyes with a start. She was on her sofa, fully dressed. The phone continued to ring as she scrambled to find out where it was. It turned out her purse was on the floor next to the sofa. She got the phone out and looked at the ID, trying to put together how she had gotten home and why she was on the sofa, not in her bed.

She saw her mother's name on the caller ID and let the call go to voicemail.

Very slowly she stood up, trying to concentrate as she willed her body to regain its equilibrium in a standing position.

Where had she been last night? All she could remember was leaving her car and getting into a taxi. She started going through her purse to make sure everything was there—a reflex action she had learned from earlier days. There was nothing missing. She had probably taken a cab home, but she would likely never find out.

Bending over had created a wave of nausea in her, and she bolted to the powder room, where she vomited. Filling her hands with cool water, she rinsed out her mouth and soothed her hot cheeks. She had better go up and get in the shower. She leaned both hands on the edge of the sink and peered at her face in the mirror. She saw her smeared mascara and bedhead locks and wondered how she had gotten home in one piece. She hadn't tied one on like this since... She didn't want to think about that.

Upstairs, she turned on the shower and stripped off her slept-in party clothes. She should be in an airport security line on her way to Curtis in Las Vegas instead of chasing a hangover.

Olivia hadn't communicated with her mother or her brother for two years. Her last conversation with Sophie had ended up with both of them snarling, then cutting the phone connection. Curtis had reached out to Olivia on many occasions, but she had rebuked him and lectured him and had numbed herself to his love.

Clean and warmly wrapped in her fleece bathrobe, she opened the front door and grabbed the *Chicago Tribune* covered in snowy sludge on her front stoop. Barely noticing where she was, she collapsed back on the sofa and started riffling through the paper. There was nothing about Curtis or the fight. Too soon, she knew. It would be there eventually.

She knew Sophie and Curtis were living in Las Vegas. They had been there for the past year, not much more. It was big news when he left Chicago.

Most people would have never lost touch with their family, she knew. *Most* people, hearing their family was in desperate trouble, would have headed for the first flight to offer assistance instead of getting drunk. This was a well-worn litany with her, the *most people* litany. *Most people* wouldn't have been able to breathe at this moment. But she wasn't most people, not even close. She was a cold, unfeeling bitch. She didn't wish to be this person, but she knew no other way. Maybe she could reclaim her roles as daughter and sister if she could just go there, and she could finally have a fresh start.

The phone rang again and she answered it. Sophie was sobbing, begging her to come.

·

Olivia had adored her father. A Chicago University-trained physician, Grant Norris specialized in forensic psychiatry, though given the turmoil in his marriage, Olivia wondered if he might have preferred family counseling or, better yet, personality disorders in women. His first love was the clarinet, and he had found solace and affection in too many jazz clubs. He and her mother divorced when Olivia was 12 and Curtis was 5, but he never was an absentee dad. She and Curtis had moved from Vancouver to Chicago with Sophie, but Grant telephoned them every week and relished bringing them out to Vancouver for holidays and vacations. Besides outings to the park or zoo, Grant would sit and talk to them about everything they liked and hated. He listened.

He never remarried. When Olivia was growing up, she somehow didn't question this. He never seemed to her to need anyone else. To her it seemed that marriage with Sophie had finished him for such things. But he was very affectionate with her and Curtis. Despite the long physical separations, father and daughter couldn't have been closer. When he died at 45 very quickly and painfully from alveolar cell lung carcinoma, she was left with a Grand Canyon-sized void.

As for her mother, Olivia never had much time for her. She blamed Sophie for the breakup of the marriage and steered as clear of her as she could. In contrast, Curtis rarely breathed without alerting his mother first. He desperately needed her approval. It seemed to Olivia that little else mattered to him. And no matter how many times he was suspended from school or picked up by the police, Sophie never flinched. She would stomp around the house and scream, then fix the problem. Nothing Curtis did displaced him in her heart.

Following the divorce, Sophie took back her maiden name, Montana, and pushed Olivia and Curtis to do the same. Olivia was glad she hadn't done it. Her father had given her more than her red hair and unusual height. He had given her an intellectual confidence that had allowed her to fend off the undermining comments her mother dealt out to her in subtle ways. Even now, so many years later, she felt the pride of being her father's daughter, a Norris, Olivia Norris.

She had been the perfect little girl and the perfect teenager. She made sure she did well in school, had the right friends, and always fit in. But even so, her mother would seemingly innocently suggest that she would be truly beautiful if she fixed the bump in her nose or wore more make-up or lost a few pounds. Olivia kept her weight down by discipline—and any other means she could find. No one ever knew it, but she was her own severest critic, and anything Sophie said just made her think less of her as a mother and as a person.

In her early years, Olivia lived in a fantasy world modeled on Fred Astaire movies and fuelled by the dream that one day she would become a successful singer. Her father had cultivated her appreciation of old standards by sneaking her into clubs past midnight during her Vancouver visits and having her sing with the band.

Curtis stopped going to Vancouver about the time Olivia went to high school. The divorce was already three years old, and he was used to being looked after and sheltered by his mother. He mistook his father's deep, quiet demeanor for indifference, and Curtis was not a child who thrived on indifference. Olivia was 15 by then; he was 8. It was about that time that his troubles escalated. It would be little things like talking in the middle of class, followed by tormenting the teacher. Eventually, he graduated to picking fights with classmates. His acting out was tolerated by many of his teachers due to his charm—he had movie star looks and could be funny and endearing. Their father had said to her a few times that he feared Curtis would never reach his potential because people excused his behavior. When Olivia foolishly brought this up to her mother, Sophie snapped back that it was because of the divorce, which she blamed completely on Grant. She said Curtis felt abandoned by him and that she had to make that up to him if she could.

Each time Curtis was sent home, Sophie bailed him out. By the time he turned 14, it was clear he wasn't going to be a scholar. He had been kicked out of two private schools geared to well-off mischievous children. And then their father died.

Olivia was a junior in college when it happened, and it stopped her in her tracks. In losing her father, she lost something she had never even questioned—the dream world where she became the glamorous, husky-throated singer, legendary for her surprise appearances at jazz clubs everywhere. She found herself so thoroughly bereft, it seemed the only thing she could do was drink. It was her main activity for several months of that year, as she left her student apartment only to go to bars and left bars often without having any idea how she had gotten home again. And then one day, in a state of wretched nausea, with the worst headache she could ever remember, she happened to pick up the phone when it rang. She hadn't spoken to anyone willingly in months, but the phone was so shrill, she had to stop it or it would kill her.

There was her baby brother at the other end of the line, talking about this new thing he was into that had changed his life. "Not religion I hope," she mocked. But he would not be deflated by her usual sarcastic manner. He had just turned 14 years old and he was working out in a gym downtown with Vincent Marquessa. The boy was on fire.

Olivia held onto the receiver as Curtis went on about how this time the judge had remanded him to Marquessa, a boxing trainer and former fighter who was a Chicago institution. Then she quietly hung up and turned over, praying for sleep.

But something happened. A way back into her life, whatever her life might turn out to be, began to come to her. A way to take hold of something and pull herself out of the dark hole she was in. The idea came to her to go to medical school, like her father. She had always lived by the strictest discipline. She could do it again, she was sure she could. She would have to work hard, not only to catch up on the months she had just squandered but to direct herself toward a goal she hadn't geared herself for until now. But she was sure, again, that she could do it if she wanted to. And magically, her determination flooded back into her.

At the same time, Curtis was working out in a seedy old boxing gym on the south side of Chicago with an old boxer who loved and lived for the sport. Marquessa, it seemed, had the perfect solution in redirecting wayward boys.

At first, Sophie was horrified. She'd never seen a boxing match, let alone thought of her Zeus-like son participating in such an endeavor. But even she was having trouble dealing with Curtis's constant behavioral issues. She rationalized that he'd found something that intrigued his curiosity and intellect.

Sophie would call her daughter just to talk about Curtis. "That angelic face," she said one evening when she had disturbed Olivia in the middle of studying. "He could be a model, and now he's going to end up looking like Jake LaMotta."

It seemed that Marquessa, or Vincent as Sophie called him, had a solid Chicago upbringing, much of it on the streets. He'd witnessed the best and the worst in people. Someone had helped him the way he was helping youngsters. And every now and then a real boxer would emerge.

One look at Curtis, Vincent had told her, and he knew he had something special. The boy was big and strong, could punch like a mule and had the agility to move well. He mostly admired that Curtis didn't enjoy hurting his opponents beyond the win.

In his own day Vincent had won every boxing amateur title except a failing bid for an Olympic medal. His professional career was cut short when faster challengers discovered his glass jaw—a jaw that wouldn't withstand punishment. Nevertheless, boxing was his life, his home and his savior, so he offered his expertise to young men and a few women.

•

They had a routine, Curtis and Sophie. Fearful of Chicago's south side, she would pick him up from school—ignoring his protests that nobody's mama picked them up—drop him off at the Lake Shore Boxing Gym and wait outside for him, clinging to her five-year-old Gucci purse with an eye on the door handle should anyone venture close to her leased Mercedes. Little by little, Vincent coaxed her inside and introduced her to the rest of the kids and assistant trainers.

Eventually, she permitted Curtis to take the "L" train every afternoon. In exchange, he had to improve his grades. Soon the altercations at school stopped completely.

After several years of local tournaments, Curtis developed a following among local boxing people. Many withdrew their kids from competition if they had to face Curtis. His photo in *The Chicago Tribune* and on local television made Sophie all the more elated.

She kept Olivia up to date on Curtis's accomplishments, and it was not unusual for Olivia to see his face on TV commercials when she turned on the set to put herself to sleep after a long day of studying and working. Olivia came to like hearing about Curtis's activities, and as long as mother and daughter stuck to that subject, their phone conversations were almost congenial.

Olivia knew Curtis well enough to guess that he never cared about the accolades. He loved Vincent, a substitute for a father he knew mostly from the negative things his mother had told him. Here was a male figure he could make proud. He strove to become everything he thought Vincent wanted, and he graduated from high school with a college scholarship.

Talking with Curtis in that period of her life consisted of listening to long paragraphs from him filled with delight and surprise at what he was able to do. She came to look forward to these conversations, though she didn't let on to Curtis. He usually called her late at night when she was in the midst of studying, and she would listen, no matter what she still had on her schedule to work on that night. But she was afraid to give in to him; she kept her distance.

With the Olympics' scoring system favoring someone who connected with multiple jabs rather than a hard puncher, Curtis qualified the first time out. He fought like a professional in the Olympics, intimidating the kids in his weight class or knocking out his opponents. His second to last fight, which could have secured him a medal, went to a bigger, older fighter from Uzbekistan.

The Olympic appearance catapulted him into the public eye, and the unfair circumstances made him look like a martyr. At that point, most people agreed that his legacy of success was already written. Along with this attention came the promise of gifts, private jet access and a chance at destiny.

The troubled kid had turned into a disciplined, hardworking young man. Going professional, he signed with Merle Perkins, former Wall Street legend and well-known boxing advisor, who was known to fight hard for each and every athlete he represented. Perkins was a genius in garnering lucrative advertising sponsorships for his clients. Although his tactics were ethically arguable, his roster was all high-profile world champions.

So there was Curtis with sponsors, Sophie joked, which made him the pugilistic version of Tiger Woods. Soon enough he withdrew from pre-law, choosing boxing because there was never enough time to do both. Sophie balked at first but quickly acquiesced, as Vincent explained to her that a boxer's career is historically shorter than a runway model's.

Moved along by Merle and Vincent, Curtis accumulated wins. All he wanted to do was be in the boxing life. Vincent made decisions for him, and that was just fine with him. When it was time to sign with a promoter, he signed with Ed Rappaport because Rappaport controlled most of the heavyweights and would be able to come up with opponents.

Sophie had big dreams for her boy. She had always fantasized about his fame and glory, but now some of it was beginning to happen. True, he wasn't in the movies, where she had pictured him. And true, he was getting his beautiful body and face beaten, but he seemed to come out of each fight with more glamour than before and, miraculously, without a scar.

Vincent acted as the counterweight to Sophie's influence, keeping his protégé grounded, always quietly cautioning him against his mother's grandiose ideas. From Vincent, Curtis learned about history's greatest fighters. They spent Saturday nights watching boxing on HBO, Showtime or ESPN. On the nights when there were no fights, Vincent gave Curtis boxing biographies and books about the sport. There were several by Thomas Hauser that Curtis especially enjoyed reading, books that delved into the good, the bad and the ugly of the sport.

Boxing was a business, Vincent told him again and again. A fighter shouldn't bring distractions to work. Women, money and drugs often presented themselves as boxers succeeded. Vincent was not going to allow his boy near temptations. Curtis never gave it another thought. He knew what was at stake, and that it could all disappear with a few losses or fights in which he looked ordinary. He committed himself to a life of training, eating and sleeping.

Seven

CURTIS AND VINCENT set out for Curtis's first professional fight at the Lucky Seven, a popular Indian casino outside Milwaukee. They had Lou Flanagan with them, a cutman who would look after any cuts or bruises to Curtis's face. A great cutman can save your skin and be the difference between winning and losing, and Lou was the best. His client roster included the best boxers in the business and stretched all the way back to the mid-'60s. He was gruff, had way too many pounds on him—especially at mid-line—from a love for good home cooking and, rumor had it, he had the soul of a saint. Besides, he loved Vincent Marquessa. It was natural that he would be the one to look after Curtis.

During the two-hour drive to Milwaukee, Lou sat in the back of Vinnie's banged up 10-year-old Ford, preparing items he would need in the ring. Vincent recited potential scenarios involving a cut or knockdown. Curtis listened intently, wishing Vincent would come up for air. No such luck!

"You hungry, kid? It's two o'clock, you might be hungry," Vinnie said. The fight was at six. "If you're hungry, have something light. Load up on water because it's a hot day, and I don't want you saying you're tired when you're really dry. Okay?"

"Sure, Vinnie. I had a good breakfast and a baked potato, pasta and fruit around noon."

"I want things to go well. You remember what we talked about? He ain't got stamina and he's gonna try to brawl."

Curtis had heard it so many times he knew it by heart. The guy would be okay for three rounds then be empty. He would want Curtis to drop his hands early so he could nail him with his left.

Vinnie was still talking. "He ain't smart, he's ring savvy. Remember the difference."

"Boss, we studied the tapes…"

"You have the wrong attitude," snarled Vinnie. "You'll get nowhere in this game with that smart talk."

"I wasn't. I only meant…" Curtis deflated a little into his seat.

"I don't want to hear what you meant. I'm not training someone who don't listen to my instructions. Every fight could be your last, and even though we're on some damn reservation, people will hear about this." Vincent paused, realizing that he might have been too strong. He looked over at Curtis.

The kid looked dismayed. "I won't let down my guard for an instant," he said without turning to look at his mentor.

Realizing it was *he* who was overly anxious and not Curtis, Vincent sat back in the driver's seat, grabbed his bottle of water and smiled. "No more caffeine for me today," he said, then took a big swig of water. "Sorry, kid."

Lou, who had seen this exchange a thousand times, knew part of his job was to keep the peace. He reached forward and gently squeezed Curtis's shoulder. "Come on, let's stop all this chatter and play some music."

"Okay, old man," Vincent said, grinning broadly around his unlit cigar. Glancing in the rearview mirror at Lou, he added, "I always was a bastard. Now the kid knows it too." He pinched his protégé's side. "You'll look back on this day as the best or the worst in your life. You choose."

Vincent popped a CD into the slot, and Curtis closed his eyes as Sarah Vaughn's mellow voice permeated the car. He'd heard this album hundreds of times. It reminded him of Olivia's singing. Today it took on a special significance—an opportunity to make something of his life.

Vincent settled into the music too, thinking about how much Curtis had already achieved and how much the kid meant to him. He had lost his whole family in a car crash when he was 6 and had spent most of his childhood feeling abandoned in the home of a strict, loving Italian grandmother who taught him the value of life. He never married and had always lived alone. It scared him how much he loved this kid, as if he truly was the son he had never known he wanted.

The soulful melody replaced anxiety with solace. It reminded him of the subtle elegance and beauty that can only happen in the loud silence of a boxing ring. No one spoke the rest of the way. Fresh pasture mixed with a hint of cow patties replenished their senses.

As they pulled up to the Lucky Seven, they caught a glimpse of the marquee: "BIG FIGHTS *TONIGHT*—ELIAS SAUNDERS VS. MARSHALL FREEMAN." There were other names, but Curtis's was conspicuously not one of them.

"Pay that no mind," said Vincent. "You don't want your name up there. That comes later. Earn your rewards. Truthfully, if you headline a place like this, I'll be nowhere in sight. This is a place to start or end, nothing else. You understand?"

Curtis shrugged. He really wasn't in it for fame and glory, more for the pure enjoyment of using his body well and of winning. He loved the feeling it gave him to win. It wiped out every negative thing that had filled up his life until boxing. He knew that Vinnie knew that, but still Vinnie had to make every speech and say every supposedly inspiring thing he had ever thought of. That was why Curtis shrugged. Let the old guy talk.

And Vinnie was talking, no question. Curtis tuned in again. "You'll witness a sport that can take every ounce of blood and respect from a man," said Vinnie. "Do your job; keep your eyes open and show no disrespect—even to Garner. None of this is about you or what you want. It's about what you will become inside and out. Your karma starts tonight. Arrogance can sell a few tickets, sure, but it's always a cover for a broken man."

"Except with Ali?" Curtis wondered, as Vinnie added, laughing, "Do some of that newfangled meditation stuff. You like that garbage."

Vinnie pretended yoga was for sissies. He was a purist and that meant omitting dieticians, conditioning experts and meditation. He respected yoga stretching even though he couldn't get beyond what he called the weird music. Privately, he admired Curtis for doing it because it was something that might set him apart and keep him safe in the hard times.

Vincent grabbed the bags. "Lou, park the car, will you? We'll get situated. It's been a few years, but I know that fights are held in the back ballroom. Kid, let's hustle. I want to make sure we grab some privacy."

The Lucky Seven reeked of cigarette butts and flat beer. A five-piece lounge band fronted by a 40-something bottled blonde chanteuse was barely audible above nickel slots and patrons yelling.

Nothing fazed Curtis. His iPod was locked on Tupac. He followed as Vincent zigzagged through the crowd until they were blocked by a Nathan Detroit look-alike who would have fit right in a *Guys and Dolls* backdrop.

"Curtis, glad to finally meet you," the guy said as he stuck out his hand. Curtis pulled the ear buds out of his ears. "I'm Sal Marino, the promoter." They shook hands. "The arena holds 2,500, and we're sold out," Marino said. "A lot of these folks are here to see you. This is perfect for your pro debut." He handed Curtis his credential. "Here are the buffet passes. It's open until midnight. You can grab something now or wait until after your fight. You're up around seven o'clock."

Vincent interrupted the patter. "I thought we'd be the first bout since we're a four-rounder," he muttered, not hiding his anger.

"Give me some credit, man. Your boy's got appeal." Pointing to the ballroom seats, Sal smiled. "See all those kids? They're from local amateur clubs. They have parents who buy tickets and drink. I got part of the bar tonight besides the gate."

Vincent was pissed, but he knew there wasn't much he could do. The last thing he wanted was to upset Curtis or make him think he didn't have enough faith in his winning. "Okay, I hear you," he said more mildly. "Let's not make too big a deal of this."

Sal slapped Vincent's shoulder as if that sealed the deal, then ran off to welcome some poker buddies.

Vincent wrapped an arm around Curtis's shoulders and pushed him toward the dressing rooms, muttering, "Once a club show promoter, always a club show promoter." He herded the kid into a dressing room and threw down their bags. "You're gonna hear a world of shit," he said. "Be polite. You never know where opportunities originate. Most of this is my job. No one goes far in this business by being inaccessible and unavailable."

The poorly lit makeshift dressing rooms were separated from the ballroom by a plywood wall. Privatized by curtains made of sheets, each was furnished with a folding table, two chairs, towels and a few water bottles.

"You've hit the big time, Curtis my boy," Lou laughed, appearing in the doorway. "This is your home for the next few hours."

Curtis had attended plenty of fights with Vinnie's other boxers, so this arrangement was nothing new to him. Facing *his* moment of truth was. The hustle and bustle of personnel gave them little privacy. A fiftyish corpulent guy wearing a worn crimson jacket burst in, introducing himself as the Commission inspector. He would be there to watch Curtis wrap his hands when the time came.

"We're short-handed tonight, typical for a club show." He sighed, scanning the list of fighters he was assigned to oversee as he walked back out of the cubicle.

Inspectors were paid by the Commission to make sure no illegal drugs or substances were used in the dressing room or between rounds. It was a part-time job. Most were diligent fight fans with day jobs ranging from teachers to businessmen. Despite the lousy pay, it gave them an opportunity to be part of the excitement.

They were the "eyes and ears of the Commission." If a boxer was injured during a fight, they were often the first to know and could report to the referee or ring physicians, though many were poorly trained and didn't know what signs to look for that suggested a boxer was hurt.

Almost immediately, Sal jogged in to check on his golden goose. "Lots of folks are asking about you," he chatted. "We even nabbed a couple of press guys who opted to show up here instead of Top Rank's Chicago card. That's because of your boy, Vinnie." Sal winked at Vincent, clapping his hands à la Eddie Cantor as he rushed out to bolster enthusiasm in the next cubicle.

Curtis quietly took off his black velour warm-up suit embroidered on the back with "Team Montana." He unsuccessfully rummaged through his bag for the trunks he had worn to the Olympic trials—his good luck trunks. But Vincent tossed him a black velvet pair.

"Here," he said. "I want you to wear these. They match the warm-ups."

"Boss, you said nothing fancy. You said I had to *earn* the right…"

Vincent was absorbed in methodically laying pieces of white tape and rolls of gauze on the table to be used as hand-wraps. He didn't lift his head or acknowledge Curtis's question. Curtis waited, watching.

Still not looking up, Vincent finally said, "I know this is hard to believe, but these trunks were mine when I was scheduled to fight Ray for the title."

"These are from that fight you walked away from?" Curtis looked down at the trunks he had put on.

They were short by today's standards. Despite the worn waistband you could clearly read "Marquessa" printed in gold letters. The front leg displayed an advertisement for a trucking company.

"Yeah, I was a light heavyweight. I still think you're about my size. I never wore them after that night." He stopped, as he always did when it came to talking about that night, then continued, telling Curtis the story he had always withheld until now. "My cousin was shot by a gang member who needed drug money. My uncle was nowhere to be found. My aunt needed me that night. I thought there would be other fights, other opportunities. I was wrong. I kept the trunks because they were all I had left to prove to myself I was worthy. Truth is, I never was. I was good, but I never had one-tenth of what you have." He paused, finally looking at Curtis standing there in the trunks. "You have a gift, son," he went on. "It's gone too quickly. Sometimes you even lose sight of the memories. I wanted you to wear these. Maybe it's for you, maybe for me. Hell, maybe it's for the trunks that never got their chance to show what they could do," he laughed.

The two didn't speak. Curtis sat, wishing Vincent's trunks held the key to everything he would face in life. At least they would serve as a reminder that boxing was about life. He vowed he would never forget his past, and he would make something of his future.

Vincent had forbidden Sophie to come to the fight. She would have been a distraction. Tonight her absence made Curtis miss Olivia more than usual. He hadn't seen her in four years, but at one time she had known him better than anyone. When he was little, she had always looked after him. Things would be rocky between their parents, but Olivia was there, beautiful and strong. He was never afraid in those days. But when the split came, and his mother made such a thing about him, it made him wild. He didn't want to be the hope of the family and all the other crazy things his mother had called him and said to him. He started to do everything he could to make her back off, but it backfired on him. Instead of his mother, it drove Olivia away. He had been sure she would understand, but she hadn't, and she wouldn't. He had tried to visit her a few times to let her know how he'd turned his life around. She listened, on the phone, but she refused to believe him. Why was she so angry with him? He knew he had failed her, but now he was making good. He believed one day she would come around.

Curtis watched Lou carefully laying out everything he would need, then packing it all into a doctor's bag—Vaseline, Q-tips, bottles of Thrombin and Avitene to stop bleeding, fresh water, a giant sponge, a clean towel and gauze to wipe blood.

Vincent told him to come on and have his hands massaged with the secret lotion to relax the digits and prevent inflammation. He called in the inspector and went through the familiar process of winding pristine gauze between Curtis's fingers and around his hand and wrist. No matter how many times he had wound his fingers, Curtis always marveled at the delicacy and precision of Vincent's technique.

No drug screen tonight. That was only required for the main event in this insignificant, two-bit club. State commissions had their own regulations, and most jurisdictions conducted no tests for anything, including anabolic steroids. They didn't want to take the chance of disqualifying a fighter at the last minute and having to cancel the match.

Vinnie laced up the boxing gloves and taped the tops to make sure the laces stayed tight. They went through the pre-fight routine—Vincent held the mitts while Curtis punched to warm up. Lou iced his face to constrict the skin's superficial small vessels to prevent bleeding and rubbed Vaseline around his eyes, nose and cheeks to deflect punches and prevent facial lacerations.

Sal's assistant stuck his head into the cubicle. It was time.

In his red satin robe with black velvet trim, labeled "Team Montana" on the back, Curtis breathed in the air of boxing. He looked at Lou and Vincent, wearing their black short-sleeved satin shirts with the same logo in red on the back, and he burst into a grin. He couldn't help it; he was a happy man tonight.

"Here son, take a sip," Lou said, pouring some water into Curtis's mouth, which was dry from nerves. "Between rounds you won't want to drink. You can swish and spit, but swallow some. The water will give you energy."

The Team Montana trio halted at the arena entryway waiting for the music they had chosen for the occasion. LL Cool J's "Mama Said Knock You Out" suddenly blared as the announcer stood in the center of the ring wearing a tattered black tuxedo that was a bit darker than his toupee. Curtis almost laughed with sheer energy.

"Ladies and gentlemen, the 2000 Olympian straight out of Chicago here for his pro debut, Currrrrrrrrrrrtis Montannnnnnnnna."

Vincent sternly advised him, "Don't speak to anyone in the crowd. Look straight ahead and visualize what you intend to do to your opponent."

Curtis's gaze didn't leave the ground. He felt Lou's hand on his shoulder for support and stability as he moved toward the ring. It was impossible to tune out the crowd's applause and taunts. Some wished him good luck. Others, out to have a good time, exercised their right to drink and shout. Eventually the voices were muffled, and all Curtis could hear was Vincent's words of support. He imagined moving around the ring and throwing punches. As he entered the ring he purposely didn't glance in the direction of his opponent, the man who would mark his career debut. He had never seen the guy in person, and he hadn't even given him a thought. At the moment he kept it that way, entering the ring and shadowboxing, throwing his weight against the ring ropes until Vincent grabbed his arm and shoved him to their corner.

"Cut this shit out," Vincent hissed. "You can do this sort of thing once you're champ. Now you're a kid listening to every word I tell you. You hear me?" He waited for Curtis to look at him, then went on. "I'm going to be in your head at all times. That's what all the months of preparation were for. Bad habits are hard to break and good ones are premium. You'll set your path tonight." Again he waited. Curtis nodded. He was listening, concentrating, absorbing.

Lou slapped more Vaseline around his eyes and cheeks, then vigorously rubbed his arms and shoulders while Vincent removed the robe. The ring announcer revved up the crowd and then, only then, did Curtis turn to see Garner. For an instant, he internalized his opponent's vacant look. It was without hope, dreams or passion. Garner was here to do a job, collect his pay and go home. Curtis thought it odd he knew so little about a man he would try to hurt or who could hurt him. One man is searching for his destiny and another looking simply to get by. For one second Curtis asked himself if this would be him one day.

But Vincent was on him, recognizing the look of compassion and sympathy. "STOP IT, damn it! This guy is going to use you to make a name for himself and get a few bucks. Stop thinking you're Gandhi and do your fucking job."

With that, he slapped Curtis's face. "This is reality. Don't go out there thinking you're gonna knock out this guy in one punch. That only happens in the movies and a few early Tyson bouts."

"Boss, I promise I won't let you down." He smiled, shrugging off his momentary lapse, and vowed to himself never to allow it again. He jabbed Vincent affectionately in the arm.

The balding referee, in his mid-forties with blood on his shirt from the previous fight, pulled both fighters to the center of the ring and gave them final instructions. "No hitting below the belt and obey my orders."

Curtis glared into his opponent's eyes. Vincent was right. Boxing was his salvation, too—what he strove for. He could prove his worth to everyone.

He thought of Olivia.

The bell rang.

At the start Garner stung him a few times, never landing anything flush. Curtis was traveling at lightning speed while it looked like his opponent was wading through mud to get to him. Curtis took his time, hearing nothing except Vincent's advice: "Stick and move, son. He can't handle your pace."

Although he barely had a mark on him, between rounds Lou reached over the ropes, sponged off his sweat and iced the areas around his eyes and cheeks. Vinnie breathed into his face. "You had your first pro round. Now I want you to get out there and make this next round your last; for tonight, that is." He winked and slapped Curtis on the butt, then pulled the stool out of the ring as the bell sounded.

At the start of the second round, Curtis landed an uppercut on the side of Garner's jaw, and the fighter fell back against the ropes. The referee looked closely to see the damage caused by the punch. Curtis stood motionless.

Vincent screamed, "Hey ref, it was a knockdown. Why the hell aren't you counting that? The ropes held him up."

Curtis wasn't worried. He was beginning to feel comfortable. Experiencing everything his opponent could dish out. He understood that Garner couldn't hurt him.

Although he didn't have his legs under him, Garner came back throwing punches. Vincent screamed, "Finish him. What are you waiting for?"

Curtis moved forward, planted his feet, feinted with the right and threw a devastating left hook that almost took off Garner's head. Garner collapsed. The referee waved off the fight. The crowd stood in silence as the ringside physician, Vincent and Lou all jumped between the ropes.

Vincent lifted Curtis by the waist, carrying him around the ring, as the patrons shouted "Montana." Curtis pushed Vincent away and ran to check on

Garner. Garner opened his eyes, wondering what hit him. Curtis relaxed once Garner was sitting on his stool answering questions from the doctor.

Vincent was beaming. "He was ripe for the taking," he nevertheless said. "They won't all be that easy. You need to be patient and get used to breaking down your opponent."

Lou just grabbed Curtis in an embrace. The three left in exultation with people rushing ringside, as they waded through the crowd to their cubicle. Young amateurs approached with programs for Curtis to autograph, and several scantily clad 20-somethings touched Curtis's robe.

Vincent wrapped his arm around his young charge. "Son, we need to get in the back. You did well, *real well.* Understand this is one fight. You still got a lot to learn. Hopefully, many more nights like this lie ahead."

And then, suddenly there was Sophie, overdressed in a bold print cocktail suit with a similarly floral hat, sprinting through a few inattentive security guards. Hoarse from yelling, she clutched Curtis. "You were beautiful, baby. How do you feel?"

"Mom, I'm glad you came," he said, wondering how anyone ever thought they could keep her away. "What an incredible rush. I looked good, huh?"

"Honey, you were wonderful. You should have seen the people. You would have thought you were a movie star."

Vincent understood the importance of timing. "Sophie, let's keep things in perspective. We have lots of work to do."

"Boss," said Curtis, "tomorrow at 6:30 AM?"

"No. When you fight, I don't give a shit if it's one round, 10 rounds or two punches, you will stay out of the gym for at least a week. You can do some cardio, but the less punishment you take, the better we'll all be and the longer career you'll have."

Curtis ran into the bathroom to check his face. No marks. Great. He threw cold water on his neck and took a deep breath. It finally sank in. He was a professional fighter and a pretty good one. He could measure up. It wasn't manufactured.

When he came out, Sophie was on the phone.

"Mom, is that Olivia?" He knew it was a long shot, but she was the one person who would understand his emotions.

"It's Aunt Lucy. She's so thrilled."

Curtis packed his gear. Vincent couldn't stop talking, Lou forced people outside, and Sophie called everyone on her speed dial as Curtis hid his disappointment. He had never considered inviting Olivia or writing her. Now she was the only one he wanted there.

As they left the dressing room, fans tried to grab a piece of something they sensed would represent future greatness.

Sophie understood when her welcome had expired, and she left them and headed for the valet, relaying to everyone she passed that she was the mother of a future champ.

Meanwhile, Curtis was ready to celebrate. "Boss, these buffet tickets are burning a hole in my pocket. I don't know about you, but I'm starving."

Sal Marino stormed through the fans. "Fantastic show, Curtis. Follow me to the press conference."

Both Vincent and Lou opened their eyes wide and stared at Sal. "What?"

"You guys think this is a schlock operation? I told you there were local guys and some Internet writers."

Vincent was not pleased. "Sal, the kid fought a pro debut."

"I promised them," Sal fast-talked, stepping in front, guiding them to a small ballroom where 20 guys sat munching on stale tortilla chips and pretzels.

The press conference wasn't bad. Curtis ate it up. And for a kid who was so quiet, Vincent had to pull him away from the microphone. Team Montana soon left and toasted with buffet fruit juice. Curtis was so excited he filled his plate three times. He felt like he hadn't eaten in a week.

"Vinnie and Lou, I know I don't thank you like I should. I appreciate every-thing." He lifted his glass to them each in turn.

In a low, gruff voice, Lou retorted, "Are you firing us? This sounds more like a kiss-off than a celebration. Let's get dessert or I'm gonna fuckin' cry." Excus-ing himself, he circled the oversized pie and cake table.

Vincent relished the moment alone with Curtis. "I've learned more from you than the other way around," he said. "Every fight, every success is a gift. You can make the most of it, or you can squander your time and live from fight to fight, dollar to dollar and woman to woman. Keep your goals in front of you and plan for the future. One day, I won't be around, and you'll have only yourself to rely on. When your career ends, have something to show for it, something to be proud of that will keep you warm when the public no longer wants to see you fight. Now get some dessert; you earned it by listening to all my crap."

Curtis grabbed a double portion of flan and started eating.

"That's it?" Vincent sneered. "Part of your vegetarian diet?"

"Yeah, something like that." Curtis let the flan melt in his mouth, savoring a taste of his childhood. Flan was one of the few things his mom could make well. Must be her Castilian blood. He and Olivia used to sneak flan into their rooms before bed.

Last thing that evening, as Vincent dropped him off at home, Curtis assured him he'd heard each piece of advice. "You'll see," he said, as he got out of the car. "My actions will prove I've listened well."

Eight

Thanks to plenty of booze and Aunt Lucy's incessant chatter, Olivia had little recollection of the drive to O'Hare or boarding the plane.

Sophie's older sister always materialized when Olivia was at her worst. Since her fifth Madrid divorce, 15 years ago, Chicago had been Lucy's home. Despite three grown children and six grandchildren, she treated Curtis and Olivia as her own. She had often been their go-between when it came to Sophie. She had supported Olivia through hospital tribulations and romantic breakups. Most important, she maintained an element of family unity even though Olivia scorned the idea of such a thing.

The United flight attendant passed by for drink orders, and Olivia signaled her and asked if she could have a blanket. She needed sleep, not another hangover. She was in a cocoon of loneliness. She finally had permission to be sad.

Falling asleep under the flimsy airline blanket, she dreamt about her childhood, about meandering for hours through Vancouver's Stanley Park where they lived. Curtis was just little, and they would play Knights of the Round Table. He was Sir Valiant—Valiente, in the mother tongue—challenging her to duels among the foliage. Sometimes they would watch the Sunday lawn bowlers or visit the zoo otters. Mostly they rode bikes and gazed endlessly at the harbor boats. He was so much fun, always up to mischief, but it was never anything that hurt anyone or caused any damage.

The bumpy McCarran Airport approach brought her back into consciousness with a groan, and she grabbed her makeup bag and got up to use the restroom. Waiting in line, she overheard the attendants talking.

The pert brunette was saying, "I heard he isn't doing well. Jesus, he was lying in the ring not moving for something like an hour."

"That's not true," the other attendant said. "He had surgery. I never heard if he's still alive. He was so gorgeous. What a shame. My boyfriend and I were supposed to go to the fight. I had to fly to Philly. I'm so glad I missed it. What a tragedy."

Olivia thankfully went into the bathroom and pushed the flush button, not wanting to hear what they said next. Standing in front of the mirror, she felt the weight of all her denials. How could she even look at her reflection?

All she wanted to do was cry, but she knew that road. She had gone down it before, and it never led anywhere except the abyss. She pushed the water spigot, cupped her hands under it and threw water on her face. Then she proceeded to refresh her makeup. She tied her hair in a ponytail, just to get it out of her way, and went back to her seat, concentrating on breathing, forcing herself not to think anything at all because thinking was too painful.

In baggage claim, she halted in front of a well-dressed bouncer type holding a card with her name on it. He took her Samsonite roller and asked if she had any other luggage.

"No. Who asked you to pick me up?"

"Ms. Montana. I'm Simon. The car is right outside."

Tracking behind the behemoth, she searched her bag for her phone. She listened to a half dozen messages from coworkers telling her how sorry they were. So, everyone knew. Well yes, since she had made such a scene at the party. Too bad the alcohol hadn't blacked out that part of the evening along with whatever had happened later.

As he held the limo door for her, Simon said, "We could go by Ms. Montana's and you could freshen up or change if you like."

Did she look that bad? "No, thank you," she said. "I'd like to get to the hospital as soon as I can." She wanted to ask for news of Curtis, but she couldn't get the question to come out of her throat.

"Your mother wanted to make sure I warned you there's press. If they see you in intensive care, there might be questions."

That meant he was still alive, she thought. Though as she knew too well from all her studies, there was a big difference between being alive and being the Curtis Montana everyone had grown to know and love. She wanted to cry and again forced herself to turn from the loss of control rather than be seduced by it. Instead, she settled against the sterile limo seat and watched the mammoth neon casinos appear and disappear as the car made its way through the heart of Las Vegas.

"I'm going to take you through the service entrance to avoid the media, if that's okay," Simon told her as he made a turn. Just then the sun passed between the mountains, illuminating the desert sky with tangerine and violet hues as they approached Western Hospital. The three-story facility bore a close resemblance to Chicago suburban hospitals, where specialty procedures were rarely performed. Through the limo's tinted windows, she caught an array of casually attired men holding recording equipment, perched to land on anyone they thought might be important. Five nearby TV trucks blocked the emergency parking entrance.

Could this be for Curtis?

"Not to worry, we'll bypass this ruckus," Simon grumbled.

She had learned how to survive tragedy, had trained herself in detachment. Even before her neurology residency, when she was interning at the county hospital, she had understood how to read what was going on, and to keep her own anxieties safely separate. She had a gift for medicine, but she also had the discipline, and she was depending on that regimen to get her through whatever lay ahead—minute by minute.

Who was looking after Curtis? Did this town have doctors who knew what they were doing? She recalled an underachiever from her residency who had moved to Vegas, a guy who had been at the very bottom of the skill scale. Was that the kind of physician she would find here?

Simon nosed the car into a loading dock, where uniformed workers were lifting boxes onto a freight elevator. He stopped the car and turned to speak to her.

"I can't park here or I'd walk you inside," he said. "You'll find Ms. Montana outside the ICU or in with Curtis. Look for Mirabelle, too. She's your brother's assistant and PR person. Here's my number if you need the car. I'll be waiting a block away. And you probably know Laurie?"

"Girlfriend?" she guessed.

He nodded.

She was embarrassed that he would know more about her brother's life than she did.

Maybe sensing her bewilderment, he added, "She's new. They've been dating a few months. I've been working for your family for a year, and this was the first time I saw her, too. She's on *Dancing with the Stars*."

What was *Dancing with the Stars*? Maybe a TV show. Olivia didn't watch much TV.

"Leave your bags with me," Simon said, and he got out of the car and opened her door for her.

For a moment she didn't move. She considered turning around and going right back to the airport. But she had come here for Curtis, and she would see this through, even though it meant dealing with her mother—and history.

Slowly, quietly, she got out of the car, straightened her clothing, thanked Simon and headed for the door.

She walked into an atmosphere she knew well, with scrub-attired women and men hustling gurneys and wheelchairs along the scuffed white linoleum floors. A large waiting area to the left was filled with anxious chitchat from exhausted visitors. Next to the area was the usual vending machine alcove. She could smell the bad coffee, along with the familiar antiseptic that made her feel more in control because it was part of the environment she dealt with every day. People were waiting by the call phone hung alongside large doors labeled "Intensive Care Unit."

Turning her back to the hallway, Olivia picked up the receiver and whispered, "I'm here to see Curtis Montana."

A unit clerk on the other end replied, "I'm sorry, I can't hear you. Who are you here to see?"

Clearing her throat, she said his name again.

"Are you family?"

"Sister."

"Hang on a moment."

Her knees were trembling. The clerk's silence gave her a moment to take a deep breath.

"Ma'am, we don't have a name for you on the list," the clerk absurdly said. "Have you seen Ms. Montana? She might be in the waiting area or the cafeteria."

Normally, Olivia would have argued. Why wouldn't her mother have put her on the list? Maybe Sophie had changed her mind about her visiting. Anything was possible with that woman, Olivia thought, but then she quickly stopped herself. She could not indulge paranoid theories now; Curtis needed her. She politely ended the call and scanned the waiting area.

A neatly attired brunette gently tapped her arm. "Dr. Norris?"

"Ah, Mirabelle, right?"

The Zoe Saldana look-alike smiled and brushed her bangs from her face. "We're so glad you're here."

"We?"

"Your mother and I."

Mirabelle couldn't have been more than 25, yet she exuded an air of confidence and experience of a woman a great deal older.

"Can you take me to see my brother?"

"Certainly. There's no update regarding his condition. One doctor tells us one thing, and then someone else says something different. Being a physician, perhaps you can help."

Olivia wondered if this angelic creature knew much about her family situation.

"Mirabelle, perhaps I can speak with my mother first?"

"She's grabbing coffee and should be back any moment. The press is swarming the hospital, and anything we say may be interpreted a thousand ways. May I suggest you not talk to them? That's why you have me." She half-smiled, straightening her fitted navy pantsuit, and flicked back her shoulder-length hair.

Olivia firmly took Mirabelle's arm and guided her away from the waiting area. "It's terrific you're here," she said, stopping just around the corner. "However, I wish to see my brother." Assuming her attending posture that worked well with the nurses, she added assertively, "Can we figure a way to get me in the ICU?"

Bordering on tears, Mirabelle whispered, "Forgive me. I'll arrange it immediately."

Olivia leaned against the wall as Mirabelle picked up the ICU phone. She watched the CNN ticker mention Curtis's fight and the outcome. It said he remained in critical condition.

Mirabelle hung up and pushed open the door. "Go right in," she said.

Inside the doors was another, deeper layer of the hospital, one that was instantly familiar to Olivia. This was the world she lived and breathed almost every day of her life. She was alive in here, she knew who she was as she stood for a moment absorbing the change. It looked like every ICU she had been in. The floors were strewn with tape and blood-stained gauze; the sound of ventilators manufacturing breathing added to the sounds of IV alarms and unit secretaries hailing staff to speak with family members and doctors. And the nurses ran back and forth, gathering medications. It was a world unto itself, and no one paid attention to someone coming in from the outside, until prompted.

Mirabelle pointed out a large cubicle at the far end of the 15-bed unit. A nurse sat at the foot of each bed charting vital signs. Despite the equipment cacophony, there was solace here.

"Curtis is in 12," Mirabelle told her. "Ron, his nurse, can tell you most of what you want to know. He's terrific."

"Can you give me the name of his doctor?"

"Sure." She sorted through a handful of business cards and found it. "Dr. Kalb. He was here an hour ago. Ron can page him."

Mirabelle appeared more and more frazzled.

"Please tell my mother I'll see her in a bit," Olivia said. "And why not take some time for yourself," she added, patting Mirabelle's arm.

Then she turned and walked over to where her baby brother lay motionless, a thick dressing covering his head. The monitor over the bed showed a normal blood pressure and pulse. His face was unrecognizable from swelling, another telltale sign of a craniotomy, the surgical opening cut into the skull for access to the brain. His eyelids were black and blue.

A man in his mid-thirties wearing a red bandana on his head and a scrub shirt with birds on it was adjusting the arterial line. Olivia found herself staring at the elaborate serpentine tattoos on his forearms. Removing his Latex gloves, he turned to her and suggested she sit. "I bet you're Olivia, aren't you? I'm Ron."

She nodded, fixated on Curtis. "How's he doing?"

"I'm guessing you haven't been told much yet, huh?"

She started to explain that she was a neurologist when Ron interrupted.

"Your mom hasn't stopped talking about you. She told me about your research and that you're an attending at the biggest university in Chicago. She sure is proud."

Proud? Olivia thought. She had a strange way of showing it.

Looking now at Curtis from every angle she could get, she tried to find something that would help her believe he might revive.

Ron was watching her. "It's different when it's family," he said. "A year ago, my brother was in a motorcycle accident and got pretty banged up. I was a basket case. It's tough knowing too much."

Olivia put a hand out to steady herself. This man had the kindest voice. She couldn't break down now.

"What can you tell me?" she asked, sounding stronger than she felt.

"His intracranial pressure is good, right around 14. Dr. Kalb was here, and the wound site looks good. Curtis's head CT from this morning showed resolution of the edema and midline shift. Of course we have him on paralytics."

For sure, she thought. You lowered the metabolic rate and cerebral blood flow to try to keep limit damage to the brain.

"Have they tried to lighten the sedation?" she asked.

"No, our neurosurgical protocol is to maintain a Phenobarbital coma until we're sure the ICP will remain low. We'll try to remove the sedatives in a few days."

"I'm sorry; I forgot it's only been 24 hours." She met Ron's eyes. She needed him to let her look at the scans. "Can I review the latest CT?" she asked, keeping her voice soft.

Although the circumstances were atypical, it was against regulations. She saw him look at her; she knew she had gotten to him.

"Sure, Doc, just don't mention it," he said. He handed her the radiograph.

"And do you have his original CT? I'd like to see the bleed."

Reviewing medical data would perpetuate her disconnect and allow her to bypass the anxiety and pain she was feeling in her whole body. She held the scan to the light. She had read thousands of scans, but this was Curtis's.

One by one she looked at the pictures of Curtis's injury. A post-op study looked considerably better than the original.

Handing the radiographs back to Ron, she took hold of Curtis's hand. She wanted to examine him. There wasn't much that could be gleaned since he was chemically paralyzed. Perhaps he could sense her presence. When Ron left to get a replacement IV bag, Olivia whispered in her brother's ear.

"I'm so sad that the first time we talk is like this," she said, and the tears rushed to her eyes. "I'm waiting for you to wake up and talk to me. This is your toughest fight, and I'm going to fight it right by your side." She wiped her eyes, forcing herself to keep breathing. She had to be able to speak coolly and with authority to anyone who might come through that door.

She had to face the facts. His scan showed extensive cerebral damage. Although it was his non-dominant right brain, which didn't control speech and language, his motor function on the left would likely be severely affected if he survived. That was a big *if*, and the odds were against it. She started talking, barely aware of what words were coming out of her, just needing to talk to him.

"There's so much to say that should have been said a long time ago. Nothing that happened before matters now." The tears twisted her mouth and strained her voice, but she had to tell him—even if he couldn't hear her, she had to say this to him. "I know you believe I never forgave you. I was too stupidly stubborn to tell you that I had. I've made a mess of my own life. Forgive me for not being here sooner. Let me try to make things right."

She raised her head from Curtis's chest, and there was her mother, standing in the doorway. Olivia was taken aback by her mother's beauty, heightened by worry and sorrow as it must be. Was it sadness, or had the years since they'd seen one another softened them both? All the resentment and anger between them dissolved. They fell into each other's arms and clung to each other for dear life.

When they pulled out of the hug, Sophie stroked Olivia's cheek. "You look tired," she said softly.

Olivia steeled herself for the typical barrage of negative commentary on an extra 10 pounds, her hair and wardrobe, but her mother just took her hand and led her back to the bed. "You're the only one who can help him, Livy," she whispered. "Is he going to return to us?"

Olivia started to speak, but Sophie, overcome by the unbearable truth of her inert son, began a diatribe about the fight, why it wasn't stopped, why they hadn't gotten him to the hospital faster, on and on through the loop of hopelessness they were all feeling.

Ron reappeared. Calmly he put an arm around Sophie's shoulders. "Why don't you ladies get some coffee while I change the bed?" he suggested, ushering her out the door. He turned back to Olivia.

"You're right," she said. "Come on, Mom. There's nothing we can do right this second." She stood out of the way so Ron could reenter the room. "When will Dr. Kalb be by again?" She asked him.

"I left him a message."

She smiled, truly grateful. "Seems like this hospital is lucky to have you," she said. "We'll be back in an hour. If Dr. Kalb is free sooner, call me?"

"Sure, Dr. Norris, will do."

Mirabelle was waiting right outside the ICU. "I got us a table in the back of the cafeteria. It'll be quiet."

Olivia was glad Mirabelle had ignored her advice to leave. Two gentlemen with notepads, trotting alongside them, barraged them with questions, and the young assistant intervened at every turn with the same answer: "Look, we appreciate you caring about Montana's condition. Please give the family privacy. I have your numbers."

Ed Rappaport, dressed in his standard three-piece pinstripe suit and eye-popping bling, yelled to Sophie and joined them as they neared the cafeteria. "How's our boy, Sophie? I'm at your disposal. Curtis is family to me. That makes *you* family."

Olivia didn't know what to make of Ed. She recollected seeing him on television and in the papers hyping a fight. He reminded her of a carousel barker crossed with Al Sharpton. No matter how low he spoke, people in the next building would hear his vibrato.

Sophie was muttering next to her the whole time Rappaport was talking. When he stopped, waiting for her response, she spoke without her usual acerbity. "Ed, we don't know anything more right now. The doctor is supposed to meet us soon."

"Curtis will beat this," Rappaport boomed. "He had such a great career ahead."

Sophie despised bullshit and wasn't about to start conceding to it now. She was about to call him on it when Mirabelle inserted herself between them.

"Ed, may I suggest you speak with the media?" she said, all sweetness. "I want to get the ladies some food."

Not backing off an inch, Rappaport turned his attention to Olivia. "And who may this lovely lady be?" he inquired, extending his hand to her.

Sophie introduced her, with real pride in her voice.

Rappaport chortled. "I feel like I already know this young woman," he declared. "My dear, your brother mentioned you a hundred times if he mentioned you once." He turned to the reporters—there were more of them now—as he continued to talk at Olivia. "Your presence will undoubtedly give him the inspiration to recover."

He was still holding onto Olivia's hand, and she pulled it away, hoping her gesture didn't show what she really felt. She couldn't get away from this man fast enough.

Skirting her and Sophie, Mirabelle intervened between them and Rappaport. "Ed," she said, batting her eyelashes at him, "We'll speak with you once we know more. Thank you for coming." She whisked Olivia and Sophie in front of her into the cafeteria as the booming voice followed them from afar.

●

On her second decaf, Olivia patiently listened to Mirabelle and Sophie detail boxing's major players—promoters, managers and trainers. She was glad to just listen. It spared her from having to answer questions about her own life and spared her from her own recriminations.

But where was Kalb? Curtis's CT showed three separate hemorrhages—two old. That was odd, given that he was reportedly in excellent health going into the fight.

Sophie's phone rang and she went to the window to talk to Lucy, which gave Olivia freedom to ask Mirabelle some questions.

"Did Curtis have any falls, out of the ring? Was he in any accidents lately? Do fighters get skull fractures?"

"I can't imagine that he was injured beforehand, Dr. Norris. We would've heard something. He collapsed on the canvas, although he almost fell through the ropes by the time the referee stopped the fight."

Olivia needed more. Moving over into her mother's seat, next to Mirabelle, she said, "Call me Olivia. I need your help. Sophie can't handle—"

"Olivia. Okay. They call me Mira. Anything you need, let me know." She was clearly pleased that Olivia had asked for her help. "This has got to be so hard for your mother."

"Doesn't Curtis have a girlfriend?"

"They haven't been close lately. She's always traveling back and forth to Los Angeles. I don't think it was serious. They argued all the time."

Olivia overheard Sophie's rapid-fire Spanish and remembered overhearing her mother on the phone with Lucy in endless conversations Olivia couldn't understand a word of. The two sisters were like orphans, with parents in

Madrid who were never well enough to make a trip and a brother who had died when they were children. Lucy was Sophie's mainstay, the older sister who always knew what to do and how to comfort her.

Mirabelle was still talking to her, but Olivia heard Dr. Kalb being paged to the ICU, and at that moment her phone rang. A chill ran up her spine. She caught her mother's eye as Sophie nervously looked in her direction.

"I'm heading back to ICU," she said to Mirabelle. "Please bring my mother with you soon. They just paged the surgeon."

"Okay. Don't worry. "I'll bring her in a bit."

Halfway to the ICU, when Dr. Kalb was paged again, Olivia quickened her gait. When she got there, this time she didn't bother using the ICU phone; she just moved quickly and with assurance past everyone standing around there. She couldn't get to Curtis fast enough. She broke into a slow jog.

Several nurses surrounded the bed. She knew this pattern and kept her distance.

The charge nurse held a cardiac rhythm strip. "Dr. Kalb, I've called cardiology. They're on the way. His ICP has increased and he's in atrial flutter. You want to order anything?"

Dr. Kalb looked a bit lost when asked what meds he wanted. Neurosurgeons weren't used to running an arrest, especially with an arrhythmia. Bart Rossi slipped in next to Kalb and the charge nurse announced, "Now we're in business. I was hoping someone from the ED would show."

Bart had a way of moving in unnoticeably. He spoke in an undertone—it almost sounded like he was telling a secret. But Olivia realized after a moment that it was something else. It was a regional accent, though she wasn't sure where it was from. She could see that he was in his element, asking to see the rhythm strip.

"What drugs have been administered?" he asked. "Tell me about his post-op course."

"Excuse me, Dr. Rossi," Kalb interrupted. "He had a fair amount of edema with a large midline shift. This morning's post-op scan looked good, and his ICP pressures were normal. We've maintained the barb-coma. He's close to 30 hours out from the injury, so it wouldn't be unusual for something like this to occur."

"If this is from cerebral edema, can you take him back to the OR?" Bart asked. Turning to Ron, he added, "Give him a 25 mg bolus of Cardizem."

"Sure doc. I'll start a drip."

Within a few minutes, the A-flutter returned to sinus rhythm and Curtis's pressures normalized. Even so, everyone recognized that this wasn't the best sign.

Kalb discussed possible courses of action. "We need to rescan him now and see what's changed. If there's more swelling, I can remove some of his right hemisphere. I should talk to the family." He turned to Olivia and introduced himself.

"Your mother mentioned you're a neurologist. Saying I'm sorry wouldn't be sufficient. Would you like to step outside?" He ushered her out to the hallway and a few paces away from the room, where there were some seats.

Olivia shook her head as he offered her a seat. She preferred that they stand so that they could face each other. She looked at him, the way he stood. He looked taller than he was because of his posture. Too many surgeons, especially cardiac and neurosurgeons, were aloof, with little or no personal skills. She looked at his face. He was probably somewhere in his early fifties. The lines around his eyes were no doubt carved from stress and too many hours in the OR.

"You're going to ask if I want you to continue to try to save Curtis's life and remove part of his frontal lobe," she said, meeting him eye to eye. "We have to hope he won't need it should he survive the next few weeks. He might arrest again, re-bleed, seize or have a whole host of neurological deficits." She was stating the obvious, making sure they were speaking from the same place.

He quietly agreed.

"There really isn't another choice," she said.

That stopped them both. He leaned slightly toward her as if he was going to argue, but they both knew she was right. He nodded, waited a bit longer as they stood somehow isolated there in the hallway, wrapped in a professional confidentiality that was comforting to her. Then with the slightest of movements, he gestured for her to precede him back into the room.

The monitors were showing a normal rhythm, and Bart and the staff left the area.

Kalb placed his hand on her forearm, as they stood facing the bed. "Dr. Norris, let me try to put it this way."

Interrupting, she said, "My mother isn't ready to lose him. Please do what you can. I understand the situation. He wouldn't have coded if the edema wasn't a problem."

She wondered if he knew much else about her family. It always brought an element of paranoia to the medical profession when they were faced with a physician patient or physician family member. Curtis's case was compounded by his celebrity.

Promising to call her as soon as his team was finished, he left the room to give orders and get an OR.

Now it was time to go find her mother. She would have to explain what was going to be done.

Sophie and Mirabelle stood glued to the ICU window.

"Liv, what happened? They won't let me inside."

Mirabelle stroked her shoulder. "Mrs. Montana," she said soothingly, "let's sit in the waiting area and hear what Olivia has to say."

They grabbed a sofa at the far end of the room, and Mirabelle went to the vending machine and came back with coffees.

Grateful for the hot black liquid, Olivia took a few sips, then began to explain to her mother the significance of Curtis arresting. She used her professional voice and didn't allow any interruption as she explained how they had resuscitated him and why he was returning to surgery. She knew her mother couldn't handle the details, and in any case she didn't wish to be the one to explain them to her. But she needed to prepare her. In truth, she was preparing herself.

When she finished talking, Sophie started right in, and as her commentary escalated, the thickness of her accent limited the clarity of her words. Mirabelle excused herself to answer a call. Olivia moved next to her mother. She knew she should comfort her. Somehow she couldn't.

"Mom, Dr. Kalb will telephone after the procedure. You must understand this is probably the last thing that can be done."

Sophie jumped up and tossed her cup in the trash. "There will be no such talk. You're always so negative."

There it was, the same old crap. She acted like it was Olivia's fault. Sophie pushed buttons that had eventually driven everyone away. Curtis was the only one left. Even Lucy could sometimes be a little bitter about her baby sister at this point.

Sophie suddenly stopped, looking over at Olivia woefully. "I don't think I can live through this..."

"Let's step back," Olivia said, trying to sound less icy than she felt. "When surgery is performed to remove the blood from the brain, it's natural for there to be swelling. There's only so much room inside the skull. The swelling itself may damage the brain. Curtis has been doing fairly well. Then again, it usually takes about two to three days for the greatest amount of swelling to develop. That's why he has that bandage on his head with a monitor to follow the brain pressure. His abnormal heart rhythm wasn't because there was something wrong with his heart. It was another way to tell us the brain swelling had increased. The only way for the doctor to take care of it is to take him back to surgery."

"I don't understand. Dr. Kalb said they have him on medications for that. They're not working?"

"There's a point where they can't do much more, so the doctor operates to remove a small part of the brain."

Sophie shouted. "They're removing part of his brain? He can't live like a vegetable. Why would you allow this?"

Olivia steadied her voice. "He has fought for everything his whole life, Mom. He's still fighting. I believe that we owe him the chance to survive."

Years of unwinnable confrontation taught her when to retreat. Olivia nodded to Mirabelle that she was stepping away as Lucy called, on her way from the airport.

"Olivia, are you okay?"

"Aunt Lucy, please come as soon as you can. Mom needs you."

•

An hour later, standing outside the hospital sucking on an unlit cigarette she had bummed off Ron, Olivia heard her phone ring.

It was Kalb.

"His pressures have normalized. I didn't remove much. He's back in ICU. We'll do a scan in the morning. I'll contact you immediately if his condition changes. Is the staff meeting your needs? I advised everyone you should be given explicit updates."

"Is there a trauma surgeon here?"

"No, but the emergency docs are less than five minutes away. We're used to caring for fighters because of so much boxing in Vegas. Everyone is on alert, so don't worry."

Not ready to hang up, she added, "In Chicago, there's no way this type of head trauma would be sent to a community hospital." She didn't mean it as criticism, and as soon as it was out of her mouth she hoped he wouldn't take it that way.

His voice was kind as he answered her.

"If I hadn't been finishing a case, they would have sent him to the university hospital. Sadly, I've operated on fighters before. Plus, the physician who attended to him ringside is an ED doc here."

"The physician who ran the code?"

"Not him. He's a judge with the Commission."

"I'd appreciate their names and information about what happened at the fight...and what they gave him in the field. I'm assuming he was intubated on the way to the ED and received boluses of Mannitol and Decadron? Did anything about his scans or condition look unusual to you?"

"Mark Stewart took care of Curtis ringside," Kalb said, but she heard something like a stammer. "The ED doc who ran the ICU code is Bart Rossi," he continued. "If you need anything, I'm on my mobile right now, so you'll have the number."

Wondering why he hadn't fully answered her questions, Olivia decided to hold off on her third degree for now and returned inside. She found Mirabelle and suggested she call Dr. Kalb. "He can fill you in on a few things you can relay to those bloodhounds outside."

Noticing Sophie manhandling the couch, she wondered if her mother had taken any sedatives. She'd been on antidepressants and anxiolytics for years.

"Mom, do you have your Xanax?" she asked, sitting down next to her and putting a hand on her shoulder.

"I'm afraid to take something and not have my wits about me," Sophie said as she dug in her purse and then shakily pulled out four prescription containers. "Dear, which would you suggest?" Her voice quivered, and she looked deep into Olivia's eyes. "If something should happen...Or if we have to make any decisions, I want us to be together."

"Mom, let me help. I came all this way. Lucy will be here soon."

Nine

Bart came in to take Mark Stewart's Monday afternoon shift in the emergency department. Stewart had been disheveled and distraught when he left Western Hospital Sunday morning and was in no condition to return the following day. Understandable, Bart thought, when Stewart had screwed up so unforgivably. This was as bad as the Omar Sharp debacle. Stewart should never be allowed near a ring again.

Normally, ED physicians visit the ICU only when summoned, but Bart felt compelled to go there to follow up on Montana. When he saw Curtis lying inert in his bed, he became upset all over again. Jesus, he thought, these young boxers look like child soldiers fighting an unjustified war. Why the hell wasn't the fight stopped in the tenth round?

He knew, however, that what had happened to Curtis could have started before this one bout. In boxing, serious injuries and deaths are often tied to previous undisclosed trauma. A fighter may have been dropped in the gym from a punch and never fully recovered. Maybe he developed a bleed on the surface of the brain that went unnoticed except as a minor headache. Once in a fight, the bleed became a deadly subdural, forcing pressure on the brain—second impact syndrome.

Is that what happened here? Cases like this were a rarity, and why this fate befell a specific athlete was seldom discovered. Was it Russian roulette? Bart left the ICU turning over the possibilities in his mind.

At one time, Bart had been director of the ED, working long, long hours. But he had made a deliberate change. Now he took only four shifts a month, which allowed him to indulge in his real loves: poker three nights a week and betting the horses, with women juggled in between.

He was still well known and highly regarded at the hospital, however, and he easily fell into its rhythms. Monday afternoons he always grabbed a sandwich in the physician's dining room. When he arrived there today, the TV was, as usual, turned to CNBC, while the doctors in the room exchanged poor financial advice and complained about Obamacare and Western's administrators.

Kalb, still in his scrubs and operating room booties, sat with his feet up, reviewing Friday's *Wall Street Journal*, an ice cream sandwich hanging from his mouth.

"Hey Rossi, thanks for your help yesterday," he said when he saw Bart. "What a sad case. I'm amazed you never left boxing altogether."

"Once it's in your blood, it's hard to run away," Bart answered, offhand. He had said it so many times it didn't even sound like anything to him. "You think Montana will make it?"

"I've done all I could," said Kalb. "He's in bad shape. Trauma cranies are hard on the arteries. It's why we brought more partners to the practice. Now I only take call twice a month." He gulped the last bite of the melting ice cream between the now soggy cookies. "I thought all serious bleeds like this would go to a Level 1 hospital," he said. His speech was purposely slightly slurred by the mouthful as he tried to pin Bart down. "Wasn't it obvious why he collapsed? Time is so precious in getting these guys into the OR."

"I don't have an answer," Bart responded, wondering if Stewart had brought Montana to Western to control the situation and help himself. Pulling over a chair, he said, "That ice cream looked pretty good. Chocolate?"

"In the fridge."

"Hmm, have to watch my girlish figure, or at least keep it nice."

"Rossi, you dawg. Not married, playing poker while the rest of us slave away putting food on the table."

"Bullshit, Kalb. Who are you trying to feed that line? I bet you make 10 times the amount us ED guys get."

"Sometimes the lack of marital responsibility looks nice. My wife and I are having our fourth kid. The bills add up. It's a nice fantasy, imagining you raking it in at the Bellagio tables until all hours, then running around with some model."

Bart changed his mind and grabbed an ice cream. "Give me a fucking break, Kalb." Checking his pager, he smiled. "Better get back to work. Hey, you saw his sister?"

"Not really."

"Quite a looker; smart, too." Bart snickered.

Kalb laughed outright. "Sorry, Rossi, this one's a Chicago neurologist—a nice leggy redhead. Way beyond your model types."

"Thought you hadn't checked her out," Bart said good-humoredly.

Bart Rossi came from a line of riverboat gamblers who had moved south to New Orleans for a more stable life. Gambling had given way to a more secure occupation when Bart's father reunited with relatives from Naples to start a group of restaurants that became renowned in the city and beyond. Rossi's specialized in Italian cuisine and seafood. Their oyster pie rivaled Mosca's, and they made the best *muffuletta* this side of Central Grocery.

The family became a fixture in the city, and Bart grew up to know everyone from the beat police who rode through the French Quarter on horseback to the elected officials and business owners. He always rode in the Mardi Gras Bacchus Parade. He had suffered a devastating loss at 15 when his parents died in a freak boating accident, but he was taken in by his uncle Gio, who continued his privileged upbringing. By the time Bart graduated from Tulane Medical School, anyone looking at his life would have said he had it made. Gio, a fun-loving bachelor, oversaw Rossi's Restaurant six days a week. On Saturdays he hosted lavish parties for celebrities, politicians and a bevy of Playboy Playmates at the family home, a three-story, 10,000-square foot residence off Toulouse Street in the French Quarter. Bart had a private loft at the top of the house. It was here he developed his affinity for poker, among other less intellectual pursuits. On weeknights he played the coronet at Tipitina's. His success at Tulane, one of the best medical schools in the country, gave him a ticket to an emergency residency at Big Charity Hospital. He could eventually have had the run of the town or held political office.

But Bart wanted to look around elsewhere.

After residency, he took a gambling vacation to Las Vegas during the Breeder's Cup. A new world presented itself to him, a world that suited his endeavors, especially emergency medicine. Vegas was evolving from small town to major metropolis, but its emergency facilities lacked organization and trained personnel. This was an opportunity for someone with skill and business savvy to elevate the standard of Las Vegas health care. Bart partnered with other doctors and established state-of-the-art emergency departments. Over the next 10 years, his group staffed the practices at most of the major hospitals.

At the end of a tough shift, Bart would head to the Hilton Sportsbook, a brand new place that offered every type of betting on every sports event anywhere in the world. Boxing closely followed gambling and casinos in his interest. Soon, he accumulated an eclectic group of doctors and attorneys who worked as officials for the Nevada Boxing Commission. Hanging out at fights, he quickly became friends with Doc Adams.

Adams, a family doctor in his sixties, never missed a fight. To many in boxing, he was more than a ring physician. If a kid needed a doctor for a cold, Doc Adams would prescribe his medicine. If a boxer with an upcoming fight had a tendon injury and no one wanted him to back out, Doc Adams injected his hand with a long-acting Novocain. If the good doctor was too close to certain fighters, promoters and managers, he was so well-intentioned that no one looked twice.

Bart made himself useful so that Doc Adams, who had always worked alone, would see he needed backup. Sometimes Vegas would have two or three fights a week. For a full-time physician with hundreds of patients, it was tough to attend every event. One weekend, Doc Adams had to leave town to attend a Geico board meeting. He was on the board of several big companies, which offered nice stipends. Bart filled in and became indispensable to the NBC. He brought a new kind of modernized medical care to boxing, increased safety regulations at ringside and improved medical tests to determine whether a fighter should even compete.

In the late '80s and the '90s, Las Vegas hosted great fights, and Bart was the man. He understood how to not cross the line. He knew when to stop a fight and when to let it go on. He became the best known and most highly respected ring physician in the world. If a mistake was made, whether it was his or some-one else's, he learned from it while perfecting his craft.

Bart always thought boxing was like riding a motorcycle; if you ride long enough, you'll regret the day you left your helmet at home. In boxing, deaths eventually happened, usually through no fault that could have been avoided. It wasn't always the toughest fight or one with the most head shots, and some-times, a fighter didn't collapse until two or three days after a match. But death, though not common, was part of the game. Bart worried about the fighters from beginning to end. Their lives were in his hands. But no one was more realistic about the sport than he was.

In 2002, Bart was the ring physician for a hotly contested middleweight championship bout between Alfred Santoro and Lawrence Foster that took place at the Hilton. Each boxer had more than 30 wins. The event was so big, it was impossible to get a ticket even to the neighboring casino's closed circuit showing.

Two days before the weigh-in, Bart received a call from a New York trainer who claimed that Foster was in no condition to fight safely. The trainer said

Foster had been knocked out in the gym by his sparring partner four days before and, in addition, had not eaten for three days so he could make his weight.

Bart had received calls like this in the past that never amounted to much. In the boxing world, jealousy reigned supreme, so the motivation behind such calls had to be acknowledged. A fighter's career was typically strewn with fired trainers, cutmen, promoters and managers, sometimes all four. But this call unsettled him, and so Bart checked around, calling in favors from friends, including a guy who worked at the gym where the knockout allegedly occurred. No confirmation.

Twenty-four hours before the fight, Bart took the fighter and his trainer aside to ask them point blank if he had been recently hurt. An obligatory "no" followed. Bart intuitively felt that Foster wasn't healthy. Nevertheless, this wasn't golf. Fighters were used to fighting through injuries, and no athlete ever came into a fight at 100 percent.

The fight went on as scheduled, and as the rounds progressed, the match certainly met expectations. Santoro and Foster traded blow after blow. Bart checked both boxers between the rounds to ensure they were okay. In the seventh round, Foster became tired. Bart listened intently to the cornermen. Nothing seemed out of the ordinary. Between the tenth and eleventh rounds, Bart looked at Foster again and asked if anything was wrong. Foster had lost the sparkle in his eye, and his look of defiance had turned to hesitancy. Bart knew that look, and it didn't bode well.

But to stop a fight at this level, there had to be a good reason, evidence of a serious problem with one of the fighters. Bart didn't have that. He sat there for the rest of the fight praying it would end without disaster.

In the twelfth round, with both fighters spitting blood from their mouth and nose and gasping for air, Foster was less able to escape his opponent's punches. Thirty seconds remained. The fans were on their feet when a punch from Santoro sent Foster down. His body lay in the middle of the ring. Knowing in his heart what he hoped was not true, Bart summoned the paramedics. Nothing they did made a difference. As emergency personnel rushed the fighter out of the arena into the ambulance, Bart felt more like a pallbearer than a ring physician. It wouldn't matter what they did or how fast they did it.

Foster's death was a blow, but Bart got right back on the horse. He became a fixture at every fight. He knew that some people thought he let a fight go too long, but others believed he stopped them too quickly. And he knew that whenever there was betting and gargantuan sums of money involved, no one was ever completely happy. From the get-go, he understood the political landscape and contradictions, and knew he needed to separate himself from the promoters and the fighters.

Bart trained others to do his job, but none of these new docs went the extra mile, and none seemed to have his sixth sense when it came to knowing if a boxer was in trouble. But Bart stayed in the game.

A few years later, he found himself working fights at a local casino, the Railway, which was hosting club matches on Fridays. The off-television card with no-name guys didn't deter diligent fans following future stars. The promoter had boxers he wanted to move up in the rankings. That meant getting them easy wins against respectable, moderately talented opponents who salivated over a trip to Las Vegas from the depths of Mexico. Sometimes the promoter searched the proverbial bottom of the barrel, meaning less-skilled and less-prepared athletes.

Every night, Bart touched base with these fighters in their dressing rooms. He accumulated a mental picture of the way each walked and talked so he'd have something to compare their performance to once they began taking punishment. He'd call upon the bilingual inspectors to translate between rounds. It was one of these fights that proved a turning point.

The card began much like any other.

More than half of the 1,500 seats were empty because most of the ticket-holders were finishing an afternoon of college basketball. For the fighters, this was their chance. They had hit the big time in Vegas, even if it never led to anything outside the Railway.

Roaming referees and judges waited their turn, discussing fights, bout assignments and one another. Bart was all business, inserting his trademark touch of humor to ease the stress. Working a fight was like going into battle. The ring physician needed a kinship with the referee, and vice versa.

In the fifth round, the stronger Mexican kid was stopped on a body shot. He cried in his corner that his dreams were lost. In the dressing room, Bart examined him and gave him medical clearance, and he left the Railway.

Two days later, Bart awoke to a call from an associate telling him that the same kid was brought in brain dead after collapsing in his hotel room. The coroner determined the cause of death as blunt force trauma to the head, a result of his fight. He had little bleeding in his brain. The cause of death was from severe brain swelling.

That second death was too much for Bart. This time, he hadn't even seen it coming. He lost his taste for ringside medicine in the time it took to hear the news about that poor young kid. Twenty-some years devoted to the profession, a career that nothing had ever interfered with, disappeared. He wasn't sure what to do. Boxing had been so much a part of his life for so long, but there had to be another way. He no longer felt he had it in him to be the one who bore the life and death responsibility of a ring physician. The realist had seen too much of reality. Time to move into another role and let someone less wounded carry on.

He completely left the sport for five years. He needed to take a long break and let the scar tissue form. But he knew, or at least hoped, that he would return to boxing at some point, and when the NBC approached him about becoming a fight judge, he took the plunge. This was a role he could perform. He enjoyed it from the start, and he quickly rose to the level of a respected world-class judge. When he saw ring physicians with poor understanding and limited compassion, he was frustrated, but being a judge resulted in less wear and tear on his heart.

·

Old habits die hard. Kalb's comments about Curtis's sister being out of his class drove Bart back to the ICU to take another look at Dr. Norris. Unfortunately, he not only didn't see her, but the gaggle of press and boxing people in the hall caused him to make a quick detour.

"Dr. Rossi."

Amanda's seductive tenor voice surprised him. He had failed to distinguish her in the group. She came up beside him, all business in front of her colleagues. He kept walking.

"Mandy, I'm working," he muttered. "Call the hospital operator and they can reach Montana's neurosurgeon."

Amanda took it without a flicker and fell in beside him. "I have a few questions about ringside protocol."

He quickened his pace, hoping she would give him a break. "It's not appropriate to ask me those questions. Call Gabe or Dr. Stewart."

"I think you're the one to speak to."

Bart felt his phone vibrate and took the call. They wanted him in a game at Mandalay tonight. "Not those Hong Kong guys," he said, but he agreed to come for a few hours. Hell, it was what he liked to do.

He turned back to Amanda. "I've got to finish my shift."

"How about afterwards?"

"I have a game."

"Doesn't it seem odd that Nevada is experiencing all these injuries? Montana should've been the last one at risk. Didn't he have an MRI going into the bout? Could he have been injured or ill beforehand?"

"Jeeze, Mandy, give you guys an inch and the next thing you know you're in a witness protection program." He stopped in his tracks. "These are valid questions, and there may be valid answers," he said, appreciating the look of hard-core insouciance she was able to muster in any situation where she thought it would help. "Right now I'm late. Talk to Gabe or Stewart."

They had reached the ED's doors. He turned to her with one hand on the door. "Call me later," he mouthed, and he threw open the doors and sprinted inside.

The ED secretary moved in front of him, handing him a handful of phone messages.

What a relief. The last thing he wanted was to be hounded with questions about the fight, especially by the woman who sometimes shared his bed.

The charge nurse flagged him down. "I think I saw Rosenblatt finishing an angiogram. Some guy came in earlier with a subarachnoid hemorrhage. Neurosurgery is waiting to take him to the OR."

In another 10 minutes, Bart was in the radiology reading room with Rosenblatt with the films in question mounted on the light box.

A neuroradiologist, Rosenblatt was a wiz at interventional procedures like coiling that stopped aneurysms from re-bleeding.

"I don't see a bleed," Bart said. "Do you?"

"Nope, looks good to me…maybe some pontine ischemia."

Bart noticed a series of head CTs lined up on the view box. "Those look nasty."

"They belong to your fighter. He had a terrible right frontal-parietal subdural. The shift was immediate. He was lucky he didn't herniate. Look at the left frontal area and left occipital lobe, looks like old injuries there, too."

Bart moved alongside Rosenblatt. It was déjà vu, the same as Foster's scan so many years ago. What the hell was Stewart doing? Come to think of it, what the hell was he, himself, doing here now? He had the game later.

The radiology reading room was always peaceful. No one sat in there at night except the on-call guy reading films and dictating reports. It was a solitary job that most radiologists loved—a way to avoid patient interaction. He and Rosenblatt had the place to themselves for the moment.

Starting to feel a migraine, Bart placed pressure on his temples. He popped a Treximet, which typically aborted his headache in an hour.

"Hot date tonight, Rossi? You single guys have it made. The women follow you around like you're giving something away for free."

"Stop whining and look at these areas of old injury," Bart grumbled, moving closer to Curtis's scans.

Their phones vibrated simultaneously.

"Maybe Montana had some kind of bleeding disorder that would explain the areas of prior injury?" he asked before answering his phone. It was Mandy. She was talking to someone on her end. It was part of her style, he knew, but he didn't like being the one waiting. He ended the call.

A moment later she called again. He said, "My place at 9:00 PM?" His game was around 10. "I can push that back a bit."

"Not tonight, Romeo. Meet me tomorrow."

"Do I need to prepare for an interview?"

"Very funny! Eleven tomorrow morning at the Coffee Joint. Think your game will be finished by then?"

He recognized the accusation in her voice. He had missed many of their engagements due to lengthy poker games.

"I'll be there. Will you give me the least little hint as to what I owe this scheduled meeting?"

"Don't be an ass. See you tomorrow."

As he hurried back to the ED, his mind wandered to the redheaded neurologist. Better to stay uninvolved, he advised himself.

Ten

"Liv, honey…," Lucy whispered above Olivia's head.

Olivia had crashed on two chairs that after several hours of fitful sleep felt like they had been designed in Abu Ghraib. Rubbing the sleep from her eyes, she gazed up into the fluorescent light to see Lucy hovering. She slowly sat up, then stood up and embraced her aunt. Sophie, still in REM, lay sprawled on the couch covered in her winter coat.

"Let your mother rest," Lucy said. "I don't think it will do us any good to wake her right now. Can we see Curtis?"

Olivia glanced at her watch. "It's change of shift. Let's get some coffee." She looked at Lucy and smiled, wondering why her aunt was wearing a fur coat. It wasn't that cold, and this wasn't the opera—though it sometimes felt like one.

Lucy had always had a flair for the dramatic, with Jackie O over-sized sunglasses and her jet-black straight hair in a bun. Lucy was a godsend. She'd buffer unavoidable conversations with Sophie and help Olivia weather the repercussions.

As the two strolled through a myriad of scrubs and white coats on an eternal quest for caffeine, Lucy mumbled, *"Pobre Curtis, qué dicen los doctores?"*

Once fluent, Olivia wasn't up for Lucy's Spanish right now. *"Inglés, por favor, tía,"* she pleaded. "Yes, Curtis's neurosurgeon seems terrific."

"I know your mother has a tough time with the truth. I don't." Removing a Hermès handkerchief from her bag, delicately blotting her eyes, she said, "Couldn't we transfer Curtis to Chicago? I—"

"I'm confident everything is being done. His intracranial pressure has stabilized. Although we're almost 60 hours out from the injury, more brain swelling can occur."

She told Lucy about the arrhythmia, about why they had taken Curtis back to surgery, and about the barb-coma. As she talked, she could feel Lucy next to her poised, waiting, wanting to break in, to say what she wanted, what she thought. It wasn't that she didn't want to know how Curtis was doing. Olivia knew Lucy. When her aunt had an idea, there was no changing her mind.

As they walked into the cafeteria, she heard Lucy take a breath to argue with her, and at the same time, she saw Ron heading for the coffee urns.

"Ron, join my aunt and me," she said, making the introductions.

He knew better than to get chummy with family members, except he was itching to talk. They grabbed a table, Olivia flashing a smile while Lucy held a chair for him, taking his coffee order.

He had to laugh. "How can I refuse, ladies," he said, sitting as Lucy went off to get the coffees.

Olivia sat next to Ron and leaned toward him. "What should I know about the emergency department or ambulance reports?" she quickly asked him. She guessed he might not want to say anything in front of Lucy, but he might, caught off-guard, speak to her. "The last thing I want to do is place you in a compromised position." Sincerely patting his forearm she whispered, "Please help."

"I don't have that information."

"What are the nurses in the ED saying?" She was insistent. She knew how to put an edge of urgency into her voice.

He murmured, unwilling to talk about something he maybe didn't know enough about. "The films are atypical. My friend Cyn, who was the ED charge nurse Saturday, said Curtis's scans showed three areas of injury, not only the one hemorrhage."

"Trauma can produce bleeding in more than one location. Did she say if any of the bleeding looked old?"

"The radiologist mentioned two of the areas looked old."

"He must have had an MRI before the fight, yes?" Olivia said. "They wouldn't have allowed him to fight with old injuries? Did the ED include skull films? I wonder what blood work he had beforehand. He must have had a toxicology or a drug screen on admission."

Ron stood as Lucy put down a tray with their three coffees and some Danish pastries.

"I need to head back," he said uncomfortably, nodding thanks to Lucy as she handed him his coffee and taking a few quick sips. "I'll look closer at the chart. You might want to ask Kalb those questions."

"Perhaps the ED doctor could help—the one who treated Curtis's arrhythmia. What's his name? He wasn't the doctor for the fight, was he?"

"Bart Rossi. No, the fight doctor was Mark Stewart. Curtis should be back from this morning's CT in about half an hour." Ron waved and walked away, sipping coffee as he went.

Olivia and Lucy sat in the cafeteria ingesting caffeine and sugar and arguing with each other—a mode they were both familiar with and which never worried either of them. After a while Olivia walked her aunt back to the waiting room, where the two sisters fell into each other's arms and wept.

Olivia went into the ICU. There was no one around who could tell her anything. She alternated pacing and sitting in the little row of chairs along the wall until Kalb arrived an hour later. He had little news except there'd been no change in Curtis's condition. Tomorrow they would lighten the sedation. He reminded Olivia that this might increase the intracranial pressure. If Curtis couldn't handle it, he'd never survive.

She understood this. But connecting this kind of information to her brother, whom she had loved her whole life and avoided for so long, made her dizzy.

Going back out to the waiting area, she ran into Mirabelle. The young assistant, phone earpiece affixed, attired in four-inch heels and a short-skirted dark brown business suit, politely acknowledged the sleepover throng of young journalists and went directly to Sophie. Behind her, several assistants dragged bags of fan letters to the waiting area. Mirabelle smiled, broadcasting optimism. "Sophie," she said brightly, "let's start working on these."

What a gift this girl was, Olivia thought. "Mom, why don't you sit in the cafeteria and go through these cards and letters with Lucy. It's nice to send responses. And you can read some to Curtis. I'm a strong believer in talking to comatose patients."

Sophie turned, hurling a dagger. "Curtis is *not* in a coma! How dare you say that?"

Everyone present knew this tone well. Lucy hugged her sister. "Sophie, *nada mas*. Olivia is trying to help."

Olivia pushed away a murderous thought and reminded herself of what she knew about her mother. Sophie was not ready to hear anything resembling the truth and didn't want anyone else to be the least bit realistic.

"We're all tense," Lucy said tearfully. "Olivia knows more than any of us. Right, Liv?"

Olivia excused herself to answer an imaginary call. Noticing all the people hovering in the lobby for news about Curtis, she began to get a feeling for just how well he had done. She had followed his arc of success from afar, but this was his home territory now, and seeing the way everyone gathered around him at this moment gave her a glimpse of what his world was like.

Standing slightly apart from her family group, she checked voicemails: the only messages were from David Rogers and an old boyfriend who had left her a couple years ago for someone with a stronger pulse and fewer brain cells.

Oh, but she had that pulse. She had suppressed it, but she could feel it now as her brother lay in limbo at the mercy of who knew what or whom.

Three-thirty, change of shift again.

Somehow, the day passed. Mostly she sat by Curtis's bed. At one point the library cart trundled by the ICU and Olivia flagged it down. There was a copy of *Pride and Prejudice*, and she grabbed it. She happened to know that Curtis loved Jane Austen, unlikely though it might seem. All that day, intermittently, she read to him about Jane and Elizabeth Bennett and their silly, silly mother. When she was too tired to read anymore, she jotted down questions for the doctors, then dozed in her chair.

She felt someone nudging her, and found Ron warmly smiling down at her. "I'll be back tomorrow," he said. She watched him put on a warm-up jacket that said *Nurses are better at everything.* He picked up his backpack and slung it over one shoulder. "I had lunch with Saturday's ED secretary," he said, so softly she almost didn't catch it. "She mentioned that several of the staff thought it strange Curtis was brought to Western instead of the trauma hospital. It could have been a blessing since Kalb was here, finishing another case." He reached out and gripped her shoulder for a second. "Get some rest. FYI, you're looking a bit green around the gills. Helen is your nurse on nights." He was on his way out the door as the ICU lights dimmed, but he turned, hesitated, then stepped back inside. "Maybe you have a greater purpose in Vegas than you think," he said. Then he was gone.

Their father had taught them to be their own saviors. They had each applied the lesson in their own way. Curtis, she thought, had gone out and put his whole heart into something he was truly gifted at, and it seemed he had never looked back. What had she done? She had put her whole mind and her seemingly endless self-discipline into trying to save others. Here she sat, a neurologist who had no authority in a hospital far from her own in Chicago, at the bedside of a fighter who would never fight again even if he did recover. She felt such a sense of oppression, for a moment all she could think was that they were both completely doomed. The next moment, the same pressure by some fluke translated itself into hope—something she had not felt for so long she was surprised she hadn't noticed its absence until now. She leaned forward and put a hand on her brother's foot, then rested her head on the bed and fell into a deep sleep.

Eleven

Situated in a row of one-story office buildings on West Sahara, the Coffee Joint was a Vegas staple. Framing the outside entryway were 10 tilted umbrellas deflecting the sun from munching locals. Inside, Vegas's elite movers and shakers, casino owners, politicians and corporate attorneys were either making deals or planning misdeeds.

Bart sat at a choice table at two minutes to eleven, waiting for Amanda to show up. He had a thick mug of steaming coffee in front of him, alongside a frosty glass of ice water that was mostly ice. Amanda was seldom on time. Of course it was never her fault. Her day typically imploded with serial news tips, story leads and arguments with her producer. Bart, on the other hand, made it a science to show up exactly on time. It wasn't so much from forethought, more from a conscious study of exactly how long it took to get anywhere.

Bart's all-night game had finished at eight that morning. Because Amanda detested his post-game fragrance—a result of Partagas cigars, garlic pizza and plenty of libations—he would hit the showers and change out of his lucky poker shirt and hat. He did this in a concerted effort to avoid needless debate over yet another reason their relationship had not progressed, and this morning was no different from others.

"Dr. Rossi, how is Curtis Montana?" asked a compassionate, nubile waitress as she brought him his coffee.

"It's been a rough night," he said. "I wish there was better news."

She was new. The Joint had quite a few waitresses rotate through. The tips couldn't be too strong. Nevertheless, the help was good-looking, seldom over 25, in short shorts barely crouching below the hem of their aprons.

"Tsk, tsk, Bart," Amanda called out in a joking voice from the doorway. "Always finding an excuse to eye a young girl."

He glanced over at her. She was wearing quite a bit lengthier skirt and black platform pumps, and she looked damn terrific.

Amanda's TV-ready natural shoulder-length blonde hair and inviting smile added dazzle to her whirlwind demeanor. Before taking her seat, she stopped to shake hands with several patrons who had either refused or agreed to interview on her show.

Bart slumped casually in his chair, paying no attention during Amanda's meet-and-greet, and perused the *New York Times*. The front page below the fold displayed an overhead photo of the event center ring that must have been from one of the CTV cameras. Curtis lay face up surrounded by emergency personnel and needless hangers-on. Metro lined the ring apron; all heads in the crowd were turned toward the ring. The headline read, "Death in Vegas *Again*: Is America's Fight Capital Unlucky or Just Can't Beat the Odds?"

Tossing down her oversized Jimmy Choo bag filled to the brim with newspaper clippings, Amanda slipped into the chair next to Bart.

"Okay, let's not waste time," she said. "I have a ton of stuff to ask you, and we go live at 5:30."

Without moving his feet from the neighboring chair, he grinned at the waitress, "Sorry, Ms. Weekly likes to make an entrance, and her business ethic often disregards politeness. Could you bring her some green tea? Now, my dear Mandy, what is it you want?"

His cavalier mien, nurtured and perfected over the years, was calculated to make him unattainable and irresistible. He was a great lay. He prided himself on it. If the time were right, she'd wonder if he was "the one." He was the one right now.

Rummaging through her bag, she glanced at the waitress. "Can you make sure the water is hot? And use those bigger cups. I'd like a bagel, dry with low-fat cream cheese on the side, strawberry preserves—not those little packets you guys put on the table. Oh, and half a grapefruit. Thank you very much. What's your name?"

Bart, who had already noticed the girl's nametag, gave her a meaningful smile. "Emily, thank you for your patience."

Amanda ignored him.

"5:30," he said to her. "That's network news. Are you filming something?"

"Bet you thought this gal was never destined for prime time."

Bart was curious, though he rarely watched any TV. Amanda's career rise to the CBS *Evening News* seemed inevitable to him.

"I'll bite. What ya' got going tonight?"

She pointed to his newspaper. "Curtis Montana is what we got going. Can you tell me what I need to know?"

"The network is covering boxing?"

After he spoke, he could have slapped himself for overlooking the obvious hypocrisy of the situation. "I got it now," he said. "'White boy suffers lethal injuries in Vegas showdown,'" he pretended to read out loud. "Oops, better yet, handsome white boy. You think you can use this as your stepping stone?" Without raising his voice, he allowed his anger to bubble into his words. "Montana is lying there with a fucking tube in his head. I thought you wanted to have breakfast, catch up and go back to my place. This is exactly why I got away from taking care of fighters."

Scooting her chair closer, she purred, "Honey, this is my job. This happens to be the biggest story today. Montana is news. Wouldn't it be better to have someone who cares about these kids discuss it?"

He considered her for a moment—not what she was saying but her presence. They had been less close for a couple of months, and this was why. Their conversation always ran on her obsession with work. She was beautiful and smart, with a killer body. Her zeal for the kill could be exciting, but more often it left him less than satisfied, irrespective of how good the sex was.

"Mandy, you're not chatting up your adoring public or your next studio guest," he said, without bothering to look her way. "I've been here before, and it never helps boxing to go into this stuff. Besides, I'm not the one to talk to. You need Gabe or the ring physician."

She was a bit taken aback by his fervor. Taking a different tack she asked, "How did the game go?"

"A game is a game. I know what you're trying to do. You want to soften me up." Characteristic of their most contentious discussions, he was ready to acquiesce. Years of living alone sometimes turned him into Grizzly Adams. Admiring her legs, he charmingly murmured, "Why don't we spend more time together?"

She ignored his flirting. "I want to know what's going on with the numbers. What do the fighters who've died have in common? Montana was a charmer. I watched a *GMA* segment this morning."

"*GMA?*"

"Yeah, *Good Morning America.*"

Bart was exhausted. "Okay, Mandy girl, let's head back to my house and we'll discuss it in depth. I've been up for 36 hours—the ED shift and then the game. Cut me some slack."

"I promise I'll come over tonight after the show," she purred, batting her eyes.

She spread her notes on the table, including features from the *LA Times, The Wall Street Journal* and *The Baltimore Sun.* "Are these accurate?" she asked. "Give me some direction. Come on baby, it'll only take a minute."

He read the articles and she texted her producer and assistant to check on other stories as Bart recommended them.

"First off, Montana isn't dead, and don't forget it," he said. "You could create sympathy by concentrating on the family, his girlfriend and his trainer. The guy's been with him since he was a kid. He has a mother, who is a piece of work, but articulate," he added. "And he has a sister, a neurologist. Now, these guys may not want to talk to you."

She leaned close to him. It was a trick of hers, he knew, to make sure he could inhale her Chanel No. 5. "Could you pave the way?" she all but whispered.

He inhaled. "Gabe is in the hot seat," he said as he nuzzled her ear. "Gabe, the Commission and the hotel are panicked. I bet Gabe and her posse will welcome a human-interest story instead of a condemnation-of-the-sport type expose."

Amanda pulled away, listening and taking notes as he continued.

"I'd schmooze Gabe. Tell her that the segment will be on network news. She'll beg you to set up the interviews."

Bart looked around for the waitress and pointed to his coffee mug. "I'd stand outside the hospital," he said to Mandy. "And please say nice things about Western. Remember when you covered the nursing strike? They wanted to tamper with the brakes on your car after that one." Playing with her ankle under the table, he winked. "Let's take a short break. Come home with me."

The waitress refilled his cup, and Amanda ignored his proposition as well as the thrill of his warm grasp on her knee.

"This could work," she said, excited. "What's Montana's condition?"

Bart felt an uncomfortable tug on his shoulder and turned around to see who would manhandle him this way.

"Commissioner Tyler," he said with mock joviality. "What brings you to our squalid watering hole?" He knew that Tyler showed up at the Joint almost every day. He noticed that the commissioner's confident demeanor had taken a hit since the other night.

"Ms. Weekly, how are you this morning?" Tyler beamed. "Here for a casual breakfast, or is today about business?" He pulled the chair out from under Bart's feet and sat down.

Bart was pissed. "What can we do for you, Jerry?"

"I got a call from my friend in New York. He's a producer for the CBS *Evening News*. Heard Ms. Weekly's doing a live remote with Scott Pelley. I thought you might have some questions for me."

Tyler was too obviously pleased that he had surprised them with his inside information. Bart couldn't have cared less, and if Amanda cared, she would never show it. Bart was sure the guy's real motive was to see if he could appear on the telecast.

Peering over Amanda's shoulder, Tyler perused her notes before she shoved everything inside her purse.

"Jerry, I'm concentrating on Montana's condition and how this has affected his family and friends. Is that acceptable?"

Not answering, he turned to Bart. "Is there any updated information?"

"No, except can you get Amanda an interview with Curtis's trainer, and maybe his mother or sister? Your connections could save a lot of time."

Tyler was practically salivating. Straightening his tie, he made a few calls away from the table. This gave Amanda time to pump Bart for details about Curtis. Five minutes later, Tyler returned.

"It's taken care of," he said with a smug grin, speaking to Amanda. "Gabe will meet you at Western at 1:00 PM along with Montana's assistant. How's that for fast work?"

Casually thanking him, Amanda turned to Bart. "Baby, let me use your phone, mine's lying dead at the bottom of my bag." Without waiting for an answer she picked up his phone from the table and excused herself to alert her production staff and talk to some people who had just walked in.

Tyler watched her walk away, then turned to Bart. "You think we're going to take a big hit on this one?" he asked. "I saw the *New York Times*. I got a few calls from D.C., including McAllen's office. This could stir up talk about the federal boxing bill."

Bart wanted to call him a weasel for only considering the Commission's image. For years the NBC had lobbied against the formation of a federal boxing commission that would take away state regulators' autonomy in policing the sport. Tyler was a prominent Republican, hosting celebrity political fundraisers.

"We have to handle this delicately," Tyler whispered, as if he had the secret to the Holy Grail. "We've had two recent deaths. Well, one death and another fighter gravely ill. It looks bad for the governor."

Bart took a minute to respond, perusing the *Times* sports section and making notes on games to bet. "The Bulls lost?" he said. "I can't believe it."

Ignoring the slight, Tyler shook hands with a couple of business associates passing the table. Each asked about Curtis. Once free he muttered, "Bart, I know we haven't been close—"

Bart waved to the waitress for his check. "We don't need to be friends," he said.

"I argued for several fight assignments you got this year. You're one of the best judges in the sport. We could use your advice on this one—how to play it."

"Play it?" Bart wasn't about to make this simple. He put down the newspaper. "This is beyond the governor reappointing the Commission and not looking like a jackass. It involves malpractice. It has to do with whether or not your physician screwed up Saturday *and* the month before. It involves figuring out if there's something wrong in the way Nevada handles fights. Are your referees stopping fights too late? Are your ring physicians not properly examining the fighters at the weigh-in or reluctant to recommend a fight stop? Are we unlucky like the *Times* says, or should boxing cease to exist? I don't have the answers." He was on a roll, and he kept going.

"If you came by my table to tell me how many fight assignments you've handed me on a silver platter or will hand me next year, and to then ask me to spin this in some direction to make you and the Four Horsemen of the Apocalypse look lily white, choose another table."

Tyler never lost his cool or his smile, and neither did Bart. Tyler had no bargaining power over him. He was a company man, a political animal, and wanted to keep his Commission appointment.

Appointments to the Nevada Boxing Commission were as good as gold. Although the five positions doled out by the governor paid no money, each commissioner received six tickets to every fight. Besides a position on the second-most prestigious commission in the State, everyone with money or a big Las Vegas business that benefited from tourism became your best friend.

Bart out-smiled the commissioner, and the latter stood up from the table. Bart handed him the *Times*. "This headline isn't good," he said. "Something tells me there may be more."

"You got something to say, say it. I despise innuendos," Tyler said indignantly. "Nothing alters the fact that we need to get past this crisis."

"You didn't hear a thing I said. These fighters need more than you assholes rushing to 'handle' the press every time there's a death or a positive drug test." Bart shoved back his chair to face Tyler. "They need you and your buddies to value them like they were your family. Damage control isn't the solution. Look within. Then again, you might come up empty."

Just then the waitress brought him the check. He handed it to a beet-red Tyler—a first, he knew, for the businessman who evaded every bill. Tearing Amanda away from a heated discussion with a state assemblyman, he told her they were leaving.

Nervously smiling, she followed. Bart seldom lost his temper, and never in public.

Shoving Amanda inside his Porsche, he slammed the door—another thing he never did. He climbed in behind the wheel. "You want to talk?" he said. "Let's talk."

For over an hour they sat in the parked car while Bart described ringside events and outlined how Curtis had come to fight Samson in the biggest fight of the year. She took voluminous notes, and her digital recorder was on the whole time.

"Why are you telling me this now?"

"I'm not sure," he said, stretching back in his bucket seat wishing he were asleep in his bed, preferably alongside his passenger. "Tyler made me want to slam my fist through a wall."

"More than normal?" she laughed.

"What happened to Montana isn't just because he's a boxer. There's something else...I haven't figured out what, yet."

"Don't take this the wrong way," she said cautiously. "Could it be that it reminds you of your past? Maybe you miss being a ring physician? Or maybe it drives you insane having Keystone Cop ring physicians."

"I don't know," he replied in a somber tone. "It's something to consider. I need some sleep. I promise to watch tonight, as long as you keep my name out of it. Don't worry about Tyler. He'll follow through on what he promised."

She leaned over and kissed him, murmuring a thank-you, then got out of the car. She did not slam the door. Bart watched her, long legged, walk to her car and fold herself in behind the wheel. His eyes panned to the Joint, and he saw Tyler angrily jabbering on his phone outside the front door. Thank God he had shot his mouth off only to Mandy, though he hated to think what he had handed her. Well, no doubt he would find out. What was wrong with him? He never let his ire get the better of him.

Right now, he was too wasted to care.

•

Standing in front of Western Hospital as the CBS *Nightly News* returned from commercial, Amanda removed her fleece-lined gloves and hat. The cameraman motioned for her to push her hair off her face as he adjusted the shot. Then they went live.

"Good evening, Scott. I'm in front of Las Vegas's Western Hospital, where Curtis Montana lies in a coma following injuries suffered in his fight last Saturday against Samson Livingstone. Montana has long since captured the hearts and minds of America after not medaling at the 2000 Olympics. Many credit

Montana with bringing fans back to a sport plagued by mediocrity and corruption—a sport desperately needing a hero with intelligence, charisma and good looks. Curtis Montana had all of that until his fateful fight last Saturday at Mandalay Bay."

Medical staff on their way home for the night stopped to listen before climbing into their cars, while Tyler and Gabe inched closer.

"Many questioned why this fate should have befallen such a vital and talented young man. Since his injury, the hospital has been besieged with thousands of cards, phone calls and flowers. America's heart continues to maintain a watchful eye on Montana who, like Ali and De La Hoya before him, is a hero to America's youth. Rather than concentrate on the origin of Curtis's injuries, we wish to talk about the man and his accomplishments. How is his family coping, and when will we know more about his future?"

While Amanda spoke, a video montage showed clips of Curtis as a teen competing in the Golden Gloves as well as his Olympic trials and early fights. There was a brief display of an early round against Samson and the knockout. There was no mention of the unending head blows, the referee's tardiness and the delay in emergency ringside care.

The interviews included Samson, Mirabelle and Vincent. Gabe detailed the Commission's efforts. The verbiage was undoubtedly written by the Attorney General's office and rehearsed in front of a public relations expert.

Amanda concluded with, "Scott, you're correct about the infrequency of these tragedies. However, Nevada has experienced other similar injuries in recent months. Another fighter died here less than 45 days ago. This is shocking. Yet, the NBC remains closed-mouthed in an attempt to make this seem just another part of an already dangerous sport. Only one Commission member returned this reporter's call.

"Will Curtis Montana recover? If he does, in what condition will he live out the rest of his life? More and more people here are asking for answers."

Pelley chimed in. "Seems as though you have serious questions. Do they include the origin of Montana's injury?"

She adjusted her earpiece and leaned in closer to the monitor.

"Scott, I've spoken with four boxing experts today who requested anonymity. They, too, have concerns. We can only pray that Curtis will recover."

"Thank you, Amanda," he said. "What a great young man. He's a credit to the sport."

•

Following the telecast, Amanda arrived at Bart's to find him asleep on the couch with UNLV basketball blaring on the 60-inch flat screen. An empty scotch glass, barely eaten pasta primavera and three shredded Palace Station sports book tickets littered the coffee table.

Turning off the TV, she softly kissed him on the lips. Eliciting no response, she repeatedly blew into his ear until he swatted away her efforts.

"How'd it go?" he mumbled.

"Good, good…Well, good for some."

"What?" he grumbled recognizing facetiousness when he heard it.

"Let's go to bed." She was playfully tugging at him to get off the couch.

He sat up, leaned back and looked her up and down. "Tell me what happened," he said. "On second thought, take off that skirt, first."

She unzipped the pencil skirt and let it drop to the floor, and he was up from the couch and hustling her into the bedroom in seconds. They fell upon his California king, which hadn't been made in days. She stripped him of his shirt, shoes and slacks, then slipped off her remaining clothes.

"I'll be right back. I want to wash my hair," she told him. "Don't fall asleep."

She hadn't been over in 10 days. Infrequency can mimic magic and mystery when there are no other options. Once he had thought he loved her. This was an acceptable alternative.

Lying on the bed, he yelled, "Mandy…"

Leaning out the shower door, "Jesus, a bit starved for affection, are we?"

"Want me to answer your phone?"

She ran out in a towel. "It hasn't stopped ringing since the broadcast. Can you check the number?"

"It's local. Some of your Commission fan club, no doubt."

"I tried to be nice, really I did. These guys were playing me all day. They had me do exactly what they wanted to get the desired results. Your buddy Gunderson, she's a piece of work. She didn't leave my side the entire time I was at Western."

"Maybe she was hitting on you."

"Cute!" Keenly aware of the sheets that had formed a tent over his abdomen, she approvingly said, "Hang on a second, Romeo. "At least let me comb out my hair."

"Don't take too long. I can't say how long this enthusiasm will last."

He watched her saunter back from the bathroom, her damp hair moistening her beautiful shoulders. The light from the bathroom accentuated the silhouette of her perfectly formed body.

Leaping onto her stomach next to him she grinned. "You always get your way, don't you?"

She turned off her phone, which listed seven voicemails. Bart turned toward her, motivating her to turn onto her back.

"So, did a 'Brazilian' originate in Brazil?"

Giggling, she said, "You're the Renaissance man, I'd have thought you'd know the answer to that one."

She stopped talking as he kissed the nape of her neck. They made love, and because it had been so long, tonight seemed more than a diversion. They fell asleep until Bart's phone rang.

10 PM. He glanced at the number and answered the call. It was an associate asking if he'd seen the *Evening News*.

At the same time, Amanda got her voicemails. Her producer said the network had loved the piece, though they had already heard from the NBC's attorney. Hmm, she said, poking him and letting him know. "Guess we struck a nerve," she said.

Disturbed by her news, Bart sat up trying to decide if he'd have another scotch. Amanda wasn't much of a drinker and thought he drank far too much. It was often the source of an argument.

"The Commission has powerful connections, all the way to Pennsylvania Avenue," Bart said. "You want the network job. I worry these guys could keep you from getting it."

"I've bypassed the fear stage," she said. She looked around the room. "How long have we known each other? Are you saving money on furnishings or do you hate clutter?"

"Don't change the subject. I admire a minimalist look. This room is for two things, and we did both tonight. I have pure thoughts, and that requires considerable space."

"It's a great place, but it's as if you just moved in—except for the kitchen. You have enough stuff in that kitchen to have your own Food Network show."

"Mandy, stop avoiding the issue; you need to be cautious. I know you want a Pulitzer Prize. This commission is not the way to get it, at least not unless there's something more untoward going on."

She turned on the CD player, perpetually set to play Professor Longhair, and snuggled close.

"Let's sleep before one of our phones goes off again," Bart said, inhaling the smell of fresh daffodils from her hair.

Twelve

FOLLOWING THE FINAL removal of sedatives, there was little improvement in Curtis's level of alertness. His intracranial pressure remained low for several consecutive days, and there was no re-bleeding. With his brain no longer snowed by drugs, an electroencephalogram showed five-cycle-per-second slowing. This was consistent with a moderate confusional state or an encephalopathy. In the area of acute bleeding, there was less brain activity.

Some people questioned why Curtis wasn't better. Others predicted his death, the outcome for most boxers suffering this type of injury. But soon he was able to breathe without the ventilator. Olivia permitted a trach placement to protect his airway while they waited to see what the next few days or weeks might bring. Curtis's pupils were equal and reactive. These were all good signs, though they didn't mean he could recognize people.

Olivia read to him for hours on end, graduating to her favorite: Russian literature.

Mirabelle played part sergeant, part missionary. The hordes of reporters thinned, as did the news.

Floral arrangements, not as many as before, lined Western's halls and the rooms of patients without family. Mirabelle introduced Olivia to Curtis's visitors and shielded her from the press. There were people who couldn't look her in the eye. Some cried. Olivia shook everyone's hand. She asked them what their relationship was to Curtis, and later she chose who she would permit entry. All the while she was haunted by the question of whether the injury could have been avoided. The answers were more frightening than the questions.

For her and her mother, Curtis became a bond offering absolution for years of misguided distance. In between bedside vigils, they shared dinners with Lucy at Il Mulino, a chic Greenwich Village restaurant that had migrated to the Caesar's Palace Forum shops. Swapping gossip with the maître d' and the waiters filled in for dinner conversation.

The respiratory infections that typically accompanied this sort of condition soon cleared, and Curtis regained some level of consciousness. He followed simple commands, though he wasn't able to speak. He was moved to a step-down unit with hourly neurological checks.

David Rogers kept giving Olivia more time off, always adding how much he looked forward to her return to his staff. As the weeks passed, the calls from her associates diminished from few to none, as did the newspaper and TV accounts of Curtis's survival.

One day it occurred to Olivia that there was no reason for her to go back to Chicago. It came to her simply. She felt no attachment there, never really had felt any except for Lucy. As soon as the idea came to her, she could think of nothing else. She looked up local neurologists and researched practices, clinics and hospital departments. She looked into who was here, who was known, whom she might know. Compared to other specialties, there were not that many neurologists practicing in Las Vegas. Maybe the move could provide new opportunities for her.

Sophie and Lucy both believed she could be happier in Las Vegas. She wasn't so sure. She wasn't convinced she could be happy, period. Was there something pushing her to settle here, or was it her need never to have to face anyone in her department in Chicago again, now that they knew all about her? For days, as she spoke to Curtis's nurses, doctors and guests, read to him and wrestled with her mother, the possibility of moving to Las Vegas began to take hold. At night she fell asleep thinking about it, and it showed up in many absurd ways in her dreams.

One afternoon, reading to Curtis about Anna Karenina's deep shame when she has lived through the birth of Vronsky's child in her husband's house, Olivia understood that her own dream of moving was the dream of change. True change. She didn't know if she could do it, but she knew she wanted to try.

That night, without having told anyone in Las Vegas, she called David and gave notice. He pleaded with her to think about it some more, pointing out how difficult the past weeks had been for her.

"You might not be thinking entirely straight," he said, and she could hear the urgency in his voice. "I don't want to lose you. You're the brightest doctor I have. I've always believed you were going to put this hospital on the map all over again."

She had expected him to be gruff with her. She had never known him to be anything but debonair, supremely confident that everyone would do exactly what he wanted them to do. She was disarmed by his genuine earnestness as he quietly laid out reason after reason for her to recant her decision.

As she sat listening to the sound of his voice, she knew he was right in every-thing he was saying to her. There was no good reason for her to walk away from her work in Chicago, her research, and the place she was beginning to make for herself in the field there. She had no idea what kind of practice she would have in Las Vegas or what kind of funding she might find for research. Going into medicine had saved her life. Why was she thinking of walking away from a highly funded, eminent department where she was excellently paid and where the department head was begging her to come back?

"Do me a favor," David was saying.

She waited, unable to make a sound lest it be the wrong sound and she found herself saying she would come back.

"Do me a favor," he repeated, "and take a leave of absence instead of resign-ing." He paused. She held her breath. "Take six months...or take as long as you need, but let me keep your job here for you."

It wasn't clean. Clean breaks were her forte. A complete break was what she longed for, but if this decision was really for change, maybe it was different from her history so far. Maybe it wasn't black versus white, flight from rather than flight to.

"Are you there?" David asked.

"I'm here."

"Will you consider it?"

"I'll take a leave of absence. I'd rather not specify for how long, but if you need me to, I'll say a year." She was feeling her way, making it up as she went along. "I think a year is long enough to get a sense of what there might be for me here."

"Good girl."

She could hear the relief in his voice. She knew it wasn't personal. That is, it wasn't intimately personal. She had been close to him for enough years to know that.

"Thank you," she said.

"You'll do well no matter where you are," he continued. "I just would rather have you as an asset to my department than let you bring glory to someone else's."

"Listen to what you just said," she laughed.

"Sorry. You know me." He was chuckling. "I'll be happy to make any calls you need me to make. Let me know what else I can do. And keep in touch, okay? We'll be waiting for you."

"Are you going to the hospital this afternoon?" Sophie asked her a few days later as Olivia entered the kitchen. The two sisters had already finished their breakfast and were sitting with coffee, peaceably reading the paper.

Although Sophie's 8,000-square-foot, newly built Tuscan home prevented much interaction, it was still too much interaction for Olivia—especially in the mornings.

"I'll work out at the athletic club first," she said. She and her mother almost never went to the hospital at the same time.

"Why don't you get a membership? You're wasting enough money on those day passes to total a yearly fee."

Here she goes, Olivia thought. Her plan to tell her mother about her decision to stay in Las Vegas instantly dissolved.

Lounging in a silk robe, Sophie sipped her New Orleans Community Chicory and went back to the paper as Lucy brightly greeted Olivia and invited her to join them.

"They still cover your brother," Sophie said. "It's been weeks and the articles don't stop. He'll improve, won't he? It has to be his will to live. It's you, too. You must know..." She trailed off, much to Olivia's relief.

Was her mother going to drag her along the ground of how she had deserted her and Curtis just at a time when they needed her? She couldn't take it.

She grabbed a low-fat scone and buttered it thoroughly, even though she knew her mother believed she had eight or 10 pounds to lose. Let her get on that subject rather than the real one. She poured herself some coffee, forcing herself to say nothing until she could open her mouth without saying something they would both regret.

"I'd like to visit Curtis's house," she said. "Lucy told me it's in the northwest." She looked from Lucy to her mother. "Someone needs to take care of his house."

Sensing a heated debate, Lucy excused herself.

Sophie got up too and cleared her and Lucy's plates. "I don't see why you can't live here," she muttered. "This place is a cavern. I've had people make certain his house is in order."

"I'm not arguing. I understand Lucy and you want me to remain in Vegas. I've decided to stay, but not here."

Hearing this, Lucy tiptoed back into the kitchen and threw her arms around Olivia. "I'm thrilled," she exclaimed. "Where will you set up your office?"

"Western has helped me locate office space close to Curtis's house and the hospital. A friend is renting my townhome in Chicago while she works with a realtor."

"You're selling your house?" Lucy said gleefully. "Oh goody, you're really staying."

Olivia couldn't help smiling at Lucy's delight. "Gold Coast real estate is still hot," she told her. "Lisa—the friend who's renting—will have my things shipped out here as soon as I can tell her where."

There was rejoicing in the kitchen that morning, and it was infectious enough to include Olivia. But just before she let herself be pulled into it, she thought of a line she had long ago memorized, from Edith Wharton: "They all lived in a world of hieroglyphics where the real thing was never said or done or even thought..." She would have to get *The Age of Innocence* out of the library to read to Curtis.

*

Aspen-sized evergreens and a 12-foot concrete wall surrounded Curtis's Jackson Hole-style wood-framed ranch house and property.

Buzzed in at the wrought-iron gate depicting a galloping horse, she thought, maybe Curtis wouldn't want her here. She guarded her own privacy; what if Curtis felt the same way?

The housekeeper, Luisa, a handsome middle-aged woman with kind eyes, already knew who she was. Sophie had called ahead. She welcomed Olivia, offered her coffee and left her to look around. A tumbled marble floor unfolded into embroidered maroon, gold and forest-green Ralph Lauren furnishings and a fireplace that could have doubled as a spare room. Plasma TVs accented every room, even the bathrooms. Ansel Adams black-and-white photographs alternated with Willem de Kooning and Lucian Freud lithographs.

Opening cathedral-sized glass doors, she stepped out into the garden. A 70-pound Golden Retriever, mistaking her for a long lost friend, leapt into her arms to greet her.

She hadn't nuzzled a dog in a long time. She breathed in her dog smell and rubbed her big floppy ears.

"What's your name, girl?" she asked her, kissing the top of her shiny golden head and then pushing her away as she became aware of someone standing in the garden watching her.

"*Lo siento, señorita.* Tyson, *ven aquí,*" yelled the handsome, toned young man, who was towing a bale of hay into the wood-paneled barn. The dog bounded over to him, and Olivia brushed herself off and took a good look around her. Behind the barn was a five-acre pasture. Another young man, also handsome and well toned, was walking a jet black Arabian horse out toward the paddock, while a nickering Tennessee Walker and a chestnut Quarter horse leaned out their Dutch doors.

Olivia was enchanted. She had not been near horses in years and years. She had left that part of her life behind.

"*Señorita*, can we help you?"

"I'm Olivia, Curtis's sister."

"*Mucho gusto*, I am Marco. This is Chui."

Petting the dapple-gray gelding in the last stall, she looked over at his nameplate "Sweetpea Won." Sweetpea was the name her father had for her as a child. She quickly blinked back tears.

"What a beautiful color. What kind of horse is he?"

"Hanoverian—a German Warmblood."

"I never understood the difference."

"A Warmblood is a cross between a thoroughbred and a draft horse. They're very strong." Marco looked at her for a quick moment. "If you wish to feel close to your brother," he said, "stand here with these animals. Toro Blanco loved them. I think more than fighting."

Why didn't I know this? she thought. "Toro?"

They laughed. Chui's English was a bit worse than Marco's. "*Sí*, we call Curtis Toro Blanco, White Bull. Your brother spoke of you often. In fact, this horse is named after you. He misses Toro."

After the weeks of pretending to be strong, she felt the tension leave her body as she petted Sweetpea Won and stood in the midst of the world her brother had put together for himself. She happily stood with the dog Tyson bumping against her legs as she watched Robinson and Jersey (named after Sugar Ray Robinson and Jersey Joe Walcott) munch on the pasture's plush greenery.

As they stood there, the two young men took turns telling her their story. Born in Mexico City, they were 7 and 5 when their father, a jockey, moved the family to Pennsylvania, where he had gotten a job working on a 500-acre horse farm. Preferring boxing to riding, the boys became friends with Curtis while competing in the Golden Gloves. Marco turned professional, but when he lost his first three fights by knockouts, he realized his lifespan would be shortened if he continued. Chui quit as an amateur. Horses were their only other love. Curtis had promised they would one day live together in style.

Curtis used Marco as a second. He carried a spit bucket and stool into the ring between rounds. Once Curtis was an established professional, he still invited the brothers to his fights. Three years ago, Curtis had bought this property in Gilcrease—a small untouched northwest area of Las Vegas. Here there were orchards and horse properties that used flood irrigation. Curtis had designed the house for himself. The boys assisted in construction and remained as caretakers and to work with the horses.

"These horses gave Curtis peace," Marco whispered. "He wouldn't have stayed in Vegas if it weren't for this home."

Still stroking Sweetpea Won's neck, she asked about the horses.

"Jersey is 4 and Ray is 2," Chui told her. "Ray's mother, Aspen, is the horse pacing in the barn."

"That gorgeous chestnut?"

"*Sí,*" Marco laughed. "She doesn't like having her baby out of her sight—like Ms. Sophie."

"This has been a difficult time," Olivia said. "I want to understand what happened."

"In my experience, we never have all the answers. Sometimes acceptance is the best medicine."

She sighed. "Marco, you should be a psychiatrist."

Marco hesitantly eyed Chui. He wanted to discuss the fight. It wasn't the time. Perhaps it would never be.

"I'd like to live here for a while," Olivia said hesitantly. "I hope that one day Curtis can return. Anyway, I brought some things with me."

Marco smiled. "The house has been so empty. Tyson needs a friend, too. She barely eats since…" He turned to his brother. "*Trae las cosas de* Olivia. *Están afuera.*"

"This won't interfere with where you sleep?" Olivia asked.

"We have an apartment behind the gym and pool. I'll let Luisa know you're staying. She can pick up some groceries for you."

"Yes, I met her, she let me in."

"Luisa is our cousin. She lost her husband and daughter in the hurricane of '85 and came here after that with her sons. Toro is also a son to her, though she doesn't get along with Miss Sophie."

Olivia felt an overwhelming fondness creep into her heart for these two men and Luisa…for the world Curtis had created.

Back in the house, she chose a guest room that overlooked the stable. The housekeeper was a small, stocky woman with deep golden skin and enough silver in her hair to make it sparkle like a halo around her face. Olivia immediately felt comfortable with her as the older woman made up the bed and helped her unpack her things, then invited her to come into the kitchen for something to eat.

The Cornue kitchen, an environment that would bring Joel Robuchon to his knees, made Olivia wish she liked to cook. Luisa made her two quesadillas from homemade flour tortillas and *queso fresco*, and then Olivia continued exploring.

The cold, darkened master bedroom, with its blinds drawn and curtains closed, said Curtis was never coming home. Next to the bed were photos of Tyson, the horses, Curtis's first professional fight and a framed publicity photo with his so-called girlfriend in a purple teddy. (Olivia hadn't met her. She had evidently fled.) The Spartan furnishings catered to the room's somber stillness.

In his closet, she lost count at 30 suits and 50 pairs of shoes, each arranged by color. Who knew he was such a metrosexual neat freak? She had never even thought about what his life was like and how he lived.

Off the bedroom she found a two-story library, filled from floor to ceiling with books. Almost dropping a first edition Winston Churchill biography when the phone broke the stillness, she waited for the call to go to the machine.

"Liv, are you there?"

Irritated, she pushed the speaker button. "I'm here, Mom."

"Come back to my house. Lucy and I will make dinner. We can discuss your moving tomorrow."

Olivia knew this trap. Before she could think, she blurted out, "I've made my decision. This place is just where I need to be for now. If there's a time when Curtis comes home, I can be here for him."

Sophie was silent. Olivia knew her mother was backing off just that tiny bit from her demanding stance because the last thing Sophie wanted was to give her a reason to leave Vegas.

"I have to go," Olivia said, then threw her mother a sop. "I have an appointment with Western's administrator in the morning."

"Is he single?"

"Jesus, give it a rest."

"I'll never stop being your mother. I'm learning how to temper my interference."

The daughter didn't laugh, but she wanted to. All she said was, "Old habits die hard. See you," and then she hung up.

She spent the rest of the day roaming around the property and took a drive to get a feel for the area. After a dinner much like her lunch, and just as delicious, she took a look around Curtis's study. DVDs from every great boxing champion in the last 50 years lined the shelves along with photos of Curtis and her in Vancouver. Next to the flat screen was a glass case holding Olympic boxing gloves and amateur awards. The empty top shelf, just waiting for a championship belt, sent a chill up her spine.

Frustrated, sorrowful, Olivia snatched a throw and headed to the stable. Making certain Chui and Marco were gone, she opened Sweetpea Won's stall and laid the blanket on a mound of straw. Who better to talk to than a horse?

Tomorrow, she'd ask Sherman Knight, the CEO of Western, to introduce her to referring physicians. She'd submitted her Nevada medical license application. David's Vegas connections would help her continue her research at a cognitive rehabilitation hospital.

Sweetpea Won nudged her shoulder with his pink nose. Feeding him a clump of leftover timothy, she told him about her limited riding experiences. He companionably rotated his ears to catch her mumbling. Equine chortles lulled her into a pleasant oblivion, and the next thing she knew, Tyson was crying outside the stall and it was 5:00 AM.

"Miss Olivia, you slept here?"

It was Marco. "I lost track of time," she said standing up and yawning as she wrapped the blanked around her shoulders. The early morning had a chill to it.

While sweeping the barn, Marco hesitantly asked, "Can we visit Toro?"

"Forgive us for not arranging that right away," she quickly said, thinking it was just typical of her mother not to have included them. "I'll make sure the nurse's station has your names. Tell Curtis about the horses and Tyson…and maybe boxing. Talk about the good times you shared."

"He's no better?" Chui asked.

"He's alive and alert. We have no idea what his quality of life will be if he survives."

"We'll bring pictures," Marco whispered emotionally.

Olivia went into the house and poured herself a cup of coffee. Sitting at the kitchen's center island sipping the coffee, she telephoned Mirabelle for the name of Curtis's attorney. She knew from Mira that Curtis had put her in charge of his trust, and that she was to handle his affairs should he become incapacitated. She scheduled a meeting with Mirabelle to make sure all employees were receiving compensation.

At noon, she was at the hospital lunching with Sherman Knight in Western's staff dining room. She met several physicians, all of whom seemed pleased to have her aboard. It had been a while since she had networked. Today, it was a nice distraction.

As they finished lunch, the balding 5'2" Knight shyly grinned as yet another of his doctors headed away after dropping by to say hello to Olivia.

"You're a bit of a celebrity," he said, "and you come from a great program. Plus—and we all really appreciate this—you're willing to take hospital consults. You can be as busy as you choose. These days most neurologists want to be in their offices making money."

He stood and pulled out Olivia's chair for her, inviting her to walk with him to the ED. "We hope to have a stroke center or, at the very least, we want to offer a state-of-the-art stroke protocol."

Olivia had experience handling community hospitals (nonacademic institutions) and administrators. The 65-year-old Knight broke the mold—half dressed for the golf course, half attired like a casino host. Shaking everyone's hand in the corridors, at the same time he talked to her about the hospital's ancillary services, including community outreach programs and medical student rotations.

"Western should make you feel right at home."

"Truthfully, I was looking forward to getting away from teaching. If you need me, I'll make time," she heard herself saying. What was it about this unlikely looking man that made her forget her trepidation?

Knight escorted her inside the ED. Patients spilled into the hallways. Ventilators inspired in unison, EKG monitors sounded an occasional arrhythmia. Nurses ran between the cubicles while the ED secretary called out telephone messages.

"Olivia, let me introduce Dr. Stewart."

Firmly shaking his hand she said, "We met when you visited my brother."

"Certainly, Dr. Norris. I heard you might be joining us. Welcome. How is Curtis?"

As she answered his question, she was thinking he must already know the answer. She peered at him, hoping he felt worse than he seemed to about what had happened. There had been no mention that she was aware of that he was considered legally to blame, though she had heard that the NBC still expected a suit to be filed on Omar Sharp.

They chatted about patient statistics and the need for a stroke rotation, and Knight excused himself for a moment while Stewart introduced the staff. Olivia was impressed. The ED was on par with any major metropolitan hospital.

A stocky, nurse in her thirties sporting black Goth hair came over. "Dr. Norris, I'm Ron's friend, Cyn," she said. "I'm the head nurse here." She snarled at Stewart, who had drifted away from Olivia and who now turned to look at the two of them from afar. "I'd be more than happy to speak with you," Cyn said pointedly. "I work days, but I filled in that night."

She took a small Post-it pad and a pencil from her pocket and scribbled her name and number. "We should meet for coffee," she said, handing the Post-it to Olivia. "Too many prying eyes here. Would that work?"

Olivia nodded, gladly pocketing the note.

Bart arrived for his shift at that moment. He went over to Stewart, who was on the phone at the admin desk, and poked him in his growing love handle. "Hey, who's the tall redhead?"

"Rossi, fuck-off. That's Montana's sister. I'm talking to the reading room about Bed 1. He has a subarachnoid hemorrhage…"

Bart shot an elbow into Stewart's ribs. "Shouldn't you make friends with our new neurologist?" he asked with mock innocence. "Cyn is bending her ear."

"And your point?"

"Cyn was working the night Montana came in."

"So?" Stewart grumbled, but he dropped the receiver and hustled back over to Olivia. "Dr. Norris, let us know if we can help you with anything. Cyn, please check Bed 4."

"Thank you Dr. Stewart," Olivia said coldly. If he could talk straight about what happened that night when he went into the ring to check on Curtis, that would help her. But that clearly wasn't going to happen.

Knight rejoined her and she followed him out of the ED.

Bart watched her move. Tauntingly, he whispered to Stewart, "You can't touch that. Plus, if she looks more closely, she'll realize you're the guy who almost killed her brother."

"You have no business saying that. I had nothing to do with what happened."

"You hold that thought, Stewart."

Bart went out to trail Olivia as Knight returned her to the medical staff office. He appreciated her class, and she had a fetching way of walking. Was she stuck up like most female doctors? Would she stick around if her brother died? She definitely had great legs. He didn't trust her for an instant.

Olivia was completing her paperwork when Kalb entered. Bart watched her greet him warmly.

"Curtis is following commands well," Kalb told her in his pleasant, authoritative voice, audible down the hall, where Bart stood. "More complicated tasks are tough. I'd like to say he's out of the woods; I'd like to say he'll continue to improve. We both know it's too soon. But he's a strong young man with a will to live. He has that going for him."

She asked him something Bart didn't catch, but judging by the answer, it was probably about rehab.

"Let's give it another few days. I'll have social services contact you about facilities."

Halfway through another sentence that Bart was unable to hear, Kalb's phone rang and Olivia broke off abruptly.

Kalb answered it, excusing himself for doing so, and told whomever it was to hold on a minute. He spotted Bart and waved him over. "What are you doing slumming up here?" he said. "Meal time so soon? Have you met Dr. Norris?"

Bart extended his other hand. "We met the night you got here, in Curtis's cubicle. I'm Bart Rossi, another emergency doc. Mark Stewart and I have nothing in common except we work in the ED. I promise."

Laughing on his way out to speak to his caller, Kalb yelled back, "Olivia, don't believe anything this guy says. He's a womanizer to the nth degree."

"I think I can take care of myself," she said to Bart, checking him out. "You treated Curtis's arrhythmia. Poor Sean here was more than happy to get the help. Right?"

"Okay, okay, I never said I was up on my ACLS," Kalb said, interrupting his call to get the last word in.

"Kalb, I think she's got your number, too. Olivia, how is your brother?"

Handing her paperwork to the staff secretary, she got herself a cup of water from the cooler, glad she looked especially good today in a black pantsuit that created an endless leg line.

"He wants to make it," she answered, sitting down to wait for the admin to process the papers. "I pray it will be for a life he can enjoy." She picked up the newspaper and started to thumb through it.

"Mind if I join you for a few minutes?" Bart asked, sitting down a couple of chairs over from her. "Have you staked out a place to live? No matter how big this town gets, it remains east and west separated by the Strip."

"I'm staying at Curtis's in the Gilcrease area."

"That's close to Floyd Lamb Park. Terrific view of the mountains."

"He has horses."

"You ride?"

"I did when I was a kid."

She wondered if she appeared to be the fraud she believed herself to be. How could she really like Las Vegas while her brother lie fighting for his life? She knew almost no one, and there was little academia or culture for that matter. Something told her to make amends and find a life she had never had and had never thought of wanting.

"You'll be staying?" Bart surprised himself by asking.

"I can't leave Curtis. And I wanted a change."

"You'd leave academia?"

She'd met plenty of his kind in Chicago: the classic McDreamy. He and everyone else thought he was God's gift to women since the day he entered medical school. This guy wasn't anything impressive, at least at first glance.

Pouting, she replied, "We've known each other five minutes, but I think you've already not been straight with me."

That surprised him, too.

"You work with the boxing commission, right?"

He was starting to regret that he had sat down with her. "I'm a judge."

"Weren't you a ring physician?"

Pleased and apprehensive that she had done her homework, he answered, "I was, then left the sport and returned as a judge. You might eventually find ringside medicine interesting. Your specialty and research would make you a natural."

"Oh, I couldn't." She jumped up, and replaced the newspaper on the shelf. It was the simplest exit.

"Dr. Norris, Olivia, I'm sorry. Of course, it would be idiocy for you to think about working in that capacity—"

Interrupting what she emphatically believed was a sexist remark and not an apology, she excused herself to run errands. "By the way," she shot over her shoulder as she walked out, "I could handle the job, don't fool yourself."

She considered apologizing for her tone, which historically had gotten her into as much trouble as her words. Rossi set her on edge. She would make it right the next time. Plus, after a few glances, he was pretty easy on the eyes.

•

Bart loved that Olivia wouldn't take any shit, and he didn't resist musing about her as he made his way back to the ED. As he came through the doors, Stewart motioned for him to chat, away from the nurse's station.

"Kalb said you were talking to Montana's sister. It's not good having her around."

Blowing off Stewart's paranoia, Bart greeted Roberta, the afternoon charge nurse. They'd dated for a month or two when she was fresh out of nursing school. Now she was married with three kids.

"Roberta, Dr. Stewart might need a shoulder to cry on. Afraid of a little old girl, are we, Stewart?"

Steward hissed. "Back off. She doesn't understand boxing and may be looking for answers to things that don't concern her."

Bart leaned right into Stewart's face. "I could tell you what I really think of you," he growled. "I could tell you how I thought you botched that fight. The truth: you and your buddies could have done a better job that night…and several other nights. Olivia Norris is trying to take care of her family right now. You're concerned with your reputation, which isn't much in my book."

With that, Bart grabbed the nearest chart. Glancing through a few pages he turned to Stewart. "Bed 4 should have been discharged an hour ago. Where are his labs? If you don't have your mind on work, you're no good to us. I could see it if you thought of Norris as a piece of ass. Instead, you're focused on your own neck. If you believe you acted correctly that night, why are you biting your nails?"

Although he no longer ran the ED, Bart still controlled the hiring and firing of ED medical staff, so Stewart shoved his hands in his white coat pockets and stormed off.

For the remainder of Stewart's shift, Bart stayed clear. He knew that if he didn't, he'd deck him. Sure, Stewart was a twerp, someone simple to dismantle, as he, too, had been dismantled some years ago as a ring physician. In this instance, his anger was more about frustration and guilt over not doing more to help the fighters.

"Dr. Rossi, Commission office for you on line three," yelled the unit secretary.

He reluctantly picked up the receiver and pressed four, only to hear the familiar squeaky voice of Carmen, the Commission secretary. She told him Gabe was asking if he could work the fight at the Orleans tonight.

"I'm beat. No one else is available?"

"Hang on, Gabe wants to talk to you."

Covering the receiver, Bart whispered, "Roberta, ask one of the nurses to start normal saline. Bed 2 is dry...Gabe, I'm wrecked and pulled an extra shift this week. I can't make the report time."

"I also need to talk to you."

"I don't want to hear it if it has to do with Montana."

"I'd owe you one," she said pleadingly.

"Your tally is already in the double digits." Frowning at the triage area filled with patients and family members, he groaned. "Let me see if I can get someone to cover. I'll call Carmen back in five."

What used to be his refuge had become his prison. He didn't know if it was Curtis Montana lying in a step-down unit, inadequate ringside care or apathy. Needing a break, he found coverage so he could make it to the Orleans. At least it was an off-TV card. There would be little press, no commissioners (they only attended big fights). Irrespective of his distaste for boxing politics, he loved the young fighters, who began with so much idealism and hope.

Thirteen

THE ORLEANS HOTEL-CASINO was packed with locals rushing to cash their paychecks. Close to the Strip, the hotel catered to mid-level consumers who relished cheap boxing tickets, enjoying a few beers and betting on a game. The fighters, some of whom were up-and-comers, might take home a few thousand. Many would get only $200 per round to risk their lives. This defined the quintessential "club show."

It was the first card since Montana's injury, and gossip ran high. As soon as he arrived, Bart remembered exactly why he shouldn't have come.

Boxing officials milled around the 1,200 seat ballroom discussing the media's portrayal of the Commission and Curtis's condition. No one knew the facts. A few had witnessed Amanda's direct assault on CBS and pontificated that there might be more to the story. Bart deflected their questions to Gabe or Tyler.

At 7:45 PM sharp, as Bart was taking a seat, he saw Amanda come down to the front and tap Gabe, who was talking to the ring physician. Behind Amanda was a cameraman, filming. Bart was floored she hadn't called him first.

"We're sorry, Gabe. We have a deadline," Amanda said demurely. "I wanted to showcase a smaller fight, demonstrate how fighters work their way up the ranks, and how the NBC is managing, after this nightmare."

Gabe was seldom speechless. She moved in front of Tyler, who rose to get a better look at the intrusion. The sound system blared Eminem's "8 Mile" while fighters entered the arena. One by one, they climbed through the ropes to scattered cheering from their fans. The trainers, much older than the fighters, slid through the ring ropes after them and fed their athletes encouraging words. As the referee checked the ropes for soundness and examined the fighters' gloves, the three judges took their seats alongside the ring apron.

Gabe steered Amanda and her cameraman away. "This isn't the time, and the NBC doesn't like revelations."

Looking past Gabe's shoulder, Amanda waved at Tyler. "Mr. Tyler, could we interview you?"

Tyler jumped in, moving Gabe aside. "Certainly," he exclaimed. "The chairman should represent the Commission, but unfortunately he isn't here tonight."

"How about shots of you in front of the ring?"

Traipsing behind Amanda and her cameraman, Tyler adjusted his tweed cashmere jacket, and smoothed his thinning, light brown hair.

Gabe had to let them get on with it, though Bart knew she would be cringing from what Tyler might say. She had too much to take care of right where she was. He waited for her to catch his eye and shrugged, smiling as if to say "She's gone rogue, I can't stop her now." Gabe shot a smile back to him, then turned and got back to work.

"Is this going to be on network news?" Tyler asked Amanda.

She pulled out her earpiece and shouted over the noise of the crowd, "Sure, Jerry. Matter of fact, I'm hoping *48 Hours* or *60 Minutes* will do an in-depth piece."

"Great," he shouted back, and Bart watched as he texted someone—probably his wife to alert everyone they had ever met.

Bart openly watched, amused. He could practically see Tyler's mind travel at warp speed over the thought of positive publicity.

After Mandy had gotten him to discuss the Commission's devastation over recent events, she asked without a pause, "Isn't Nevada concerned about two previously healthy fighters suffering tragic consequences in such a short time span? What kind of confidence can the public have in Nevada's care for its boxers?"

That's my girl, Bart chuckled to himself.

Tyler fidgeted with his tie. "I'm not certain I follow, Ms. Weekly."

Amanda wasn't going to play games. After all, the segment wouldn't be longer than two minutes. She needed to get a bite.

"Commissioner Tyler, you know exactly what I mean. The public has a right to know that Nevada boxers are safe."

"This is a blood sport. We host many fights a year. We can't protect every fighter every time."

"Are you saying that fighters aren't as protected as they should be all the time because there are too many?"

Tyler discretely wiped the sweat from his receding hairline and upper lip. "I meant this is a brutal sport. Every fighter faces the same dangers."

"Commissioner, are you supposed to guarantee the same safety standards for every fighter, no matter if he's a club-show kid earning $400 a round or, like Curtis, earning $10,000,000 a fight?" Amanda fired.

At that moment Gabe strolled over to the filming. Flashing her standard smile, she asked Amanda, "Can I offer some assistance?"

Tyler giggled nervously as Gabe pushed him out of camera range. "Amanda, we have no new information on Mr. Montana," she said, her posture expressing the adrenaline lift she must be feeling and enjoying. "I can tell you—"

"Hello, Gabe," Amanda interrupted her. "This is Gabe Gunderson, executive director of the Nevada Boxing Commission."

Gabe didn't acknowledge the interruption. "I can tell you," she repeated, "that Curtis Montana is a strong young man fighting to survive. We need to treat this situation with caution and allow the family to have their privacy."

As Tyler unhooked his microphone and returned to his ringside seat looking sufficiently shaken, Amanda leaned in with another question. Gabe quickly thanked her before she could get started, then made a show of storming off. For that one moment, Bart truly admired her love of power. She had saved Tyler's scrawny neck, and she had swerved yet again around the disastrous press that would have ensued.

As he took the judge's stool for the second fight, he glanced at the Commission table. Tyler was yelling on his cell about his fouled appearance. Once his fight was over, Bart stealthily crossed over to the officials' section, four rows from the ring.

Gabe sprang from behind. "Bart, you could have warned me the bitch was going to attack."

He couldn't help smiling. "Hold on a minute," he said, happily rubbing in her discomfort. "Did Amanda blame the NBC or Stewart?"

"She's salivating for a network job. I'm trying to handle PR and make sure things aren't manipulated. Our referee and physician did their best that night. Who knows why Montana was hurt."

He knew that what she was really thinking was that if she let Amanda blast the Commission, they would be facing a lawsuit for sure—not to mention the adverse public opinion that would ensue.

"Maybe your priorities are screwed up," he suggested. "Shouldn't the Commission be conducting the investigation? Stewart and his buddies have to be accountable when they screw up. Or..." He paused, making her wait.

"Or?" she asked.

"Or you need to hire a new group of doctors. You know what should be done for an injured fighter. You tell the referees when they make a mistake, you critique the judges. Why not the doctors?"

"I'm uncomfortable telling the physicians what to do."

"That's bull. This may be one time you pay for your complacency."

She let her temper show just a little, a little trick of hers that he knew well, to get people to back off her.

"You're welcome to come to my office Monday and offer any suggestions," she said sternly. "Matter of fact, I'll invite the chairman, and we can all talk. Tyler can come, too."

Bart felt himself get riled, but he couldn't stop himself. "The NBC needs to be proactive," he shouted. "To say that two serious injuries in less than two months is just part of boxing is hiding our heads in the sand while we wait for a third."

The crowd became silent as Emilio Vasquez collapsed after eating a solid right hand, and everyone who happened to be nearby could hear the last part of Bart's vituperative statement. Gabe scurried to the ring.

Bart checked to see if Amanda was still there. She was. Her cameraman was surreptitiously filming the scene, even though the crew had guaranteed they wouldn't record fight action.

Two paramedics plus two doctors carrying oxygen leaped into the ring. The referee cleared the area. Within 90 seconds, Vasquez was awake and responsive. The physicians slowly helped him to his stool. The cameraman captured the scene as Amanda narrated.

"Boxing continues in Las Vegas, Nevada. Little, if anything, has changed since Curtis Montana was gravely injured. Montana still lies in Western Hospital fighting for his life."

Gabe turned in Bart's direction out of earshot muttering, "Call off your bitch!"

Bart smiled at Amanda in her salivating mode. Her zeal still excited him. He considered texting her to meet him later. Like so many women who had come before her, she thought herself a worthy companion, but amidst the lustful, heated arguments and reconciliations, there was never a real connection. The more he pursued her, the more he was leading her on. He was never getting married. Why would he? It didn't matter how independent women like Amanda portrayed themselves, they still wanted the house, the man, the job and the kids. Though, come to think of it, pretty much all Amanda seemed to want was the star spot on prime time network news. He shook off of the idea of spending the night with her, saving himself.

Following the last bout, Bart heard someone call his name and recognized the high-pitched voice of Stu Rappaport, Ed's brother.

"Bart, they sure needed you the other night," Stu shouted.

Bart grinned and embraced his old boxing buddy. "I was at the fight."

"My God, I meant in the ring." Stu was chewing on the tail end of a dead cigar. He took it out of his mouth and threw it in the trash. "You know, I'm going to be 70. Ella has been yelling at me to quit smoking for 20 years. My doctor tells me to get one of those gastric band procedures. After these last few weeks with Sharp, then Montana, I'm finally ready to do both."

"What are you doing in Vegas?"

"We had Newton and the main event. I've been in the business for over 30 years and lost three fighters. Only three! King and Arum lost more. I pride myself on taking care of my kids. It never stops hurting."

Bart respected Stu. Unlike his brother Ed, Stu shot straight from the hip—a rarity in boxing. Unbeknownst to his brother, Stu would often pay out of his own pocket to get a fighter medical care. His wife and children came first; his fighters were a close second.

"Let's grab a cup of coffee," Stu suggested. "I'd love to get out of here."

Bart considered manufacturing an excuse, except Stu was a friend. The two had shared many tough nights determining the implications of a fighter's injuries. If a boxer had been cut in his last fight and Ed wanted to know when he could compete again, Stu called Bart. In the old days, less reputable people tried to muscle Bart, not knowing that he wouldn't allow an unhealthy boxer to return to the ring. Stu had a conscience.

Slinging an arm around Stu's shoulders, Bart led him up the aisle toward the exit. Outside, they ran into Amanda.

"Introduce me," she demanded.

Stu held out his hand. "Stu Rappaport," he said as they shook hands.

"This is Amanda Weekly," Bart said, none too pleased. Then again, maybe she would put some energy into what looked like it was going to be a desultory conversation about Curtis Montana.

"I saw you in there trying to get blood from a stone," Stu said, laughing.

"She's got guts," Bart agreed.

Amanda ignored him. "Good to meet you. I know your brother, of course. Excuse me for saying so, but I've never gotten a straight word out of his mouth."

Stu flashed an uncomfortable smile. "We're different. What can I say?" he countered.

"Let's play nice, Mandy," Bart interjected.

She shrugged. "You give provocation, you sometimes get interesting information in return," she said. She turned to Stu. "No offense."

"None taken. Listen, we're going to grab a bite, you want to join us?"

"Sure." She looped her arm through Bart's. "The Orleans?"

•

No sooner had they settled around a table at the far end of the Orleans coffee shop than Amanda started asking Stu about himself.

"Babe, Stu's our friend," Bart joked. "Let the guy eat in peace."

Stu shrugged. "No, I like her, Bart. She's got the fire in her. Remember when we used to talk about that? Your term—the sacred fire."

Bart waved him off. "You hear that, honey?" he said to Amanda. "Let's see what you can get out of this old reprobate."

Bart had told her over and over that she had to do her homework. He had told her to talk to the old guys. They loved to tell stories, and even if the stories were ancient history, she could learn plenty from them.

She liked talking to the old-timers. She sipped her iced tea and got out her pad. She had researched Ed, so she already knew that the boys grew up in Brooklyn—not rich, not poor.

"To quote the cliché," she said to Stu, "you and your brother grew up living, eating and breathing boxing, right?"

"Yup, from the time we could walk. Our father took us to every fight."

Their father, Max Rappaport, started in boxing doing public relations for Madison Square Garden. He promoted a little, losing every good fighter to someone with more to offer. "Boxing was our other parent, since our mother died when we were very young," Stu told her. Their mother had died from ovarian cancer soon after Stu was born.

Seven years older than Stu, Ed was a genius in picking out a fighter with a future and matching him with a stable of boxers he also controlled.

Amanda knew Ed's methods, and she knew that Curtis Montana was one of the ones he had picked out.

Stu warmed to his subject, alternating bites of delicious and completely forbidden hamburger with answering the questions Amanda was asking him. "Over a period of three or four years, Ed molds a fighter's persona so that the networks want to see him fight and the public recognizes his name. Along with this come deals, some fair, others shady. After all, it's boxing."

Networks wanted to televise championship fights. Even without a marquee name, there were at least five championship bouts on every Rappaport card with various meaningless title belts. This didn't mean the fights weren't competitive or exciting. On the contrary, they were slugfests, and even though the odds-on favorite was a Rappaport fighter, so was the opponent. People got their money's worth. Not many other promoters could offer that on a regular basis.

Amanda wasn't eating. She flagged the waitress and asked for another iced tea.

"Would you explain to me how it works?" she asked him as Bart, leaning over and borrowing the newspaper from a nearby table, settled in to read sports news. Amanda knew perfectly well how it worked, but he figured, let her hear it from a guy who could give it to her straight.

"Sure," Stu said. "First, a promoter gets his fighter rated." There were three main ratings sanctioning organizations—privately held companies that rated the fighters. A championship boxer had to defend his title against one of the top 10 to retain his belt.

"As you might expect, my brother has many of these guys. The others seldom get a shot at his fighters." Stu leveled his eyes with hers. "A bright girl like you," he mused, "surely you know all this already."

She smiled slowly. "I know some. The problem is always what you don't know you don't know." She lifted her glass to him and then took a sip. "Anything you can tell me might fill in that gap."

"Fair enough. One last thing. To be placed in the top 10, a promoter argues his fighter's worthiness with a so-called ratings committee. This means traveling to the sanctioning body's annual convention to wine and dine the organizers." He paused. "Many people believe the process is illegal," he continued. "Often it is."

Bart folded the paper and leaned into Amanda.

"Is she for real?" Stu asked him.

Bart rolled his eyes, and Amanda punched him in the arm.

He laughed, pretending to be hurt. "She's going to be a great reporter soon," he told Stu. "You watch." He turned to Amanda. "Stu here is the best matchmaker in the business."

She made him explain.

The matchmaker's job was two-fold. He would showcase the promoter's fighter in the best possible light while delivering the paying public a competitive fight. This was fraught with nail-biting anguish, as the promoter usually had the main attraction under contract and wanted to keep him winning.

"Imagine, then, the two Rappaport brothers in those two positions."

The opponent had to be competitive but unlikely to hurt the favorite. On a boxing card, there were anywhere from five to eight other fights. At least half were prospects fighting their way up the ranks. The others were there to fill up the card. More often than not, the promoter wanted one or the other boxer to win.

Stu finished his hamburger, wiped his mouth and took out his phone. "Got to make a quick call to Ella. 'Sweetheart, I'm with Bart Rossi. This son-of-a-gun hasn't visited us in two years. No, honey, I'm not eating anything I shouldn't," he said. "'No, I haven't been smoking.'" He smiled, taking out two cigars and handing one to Bart. "I'm leaving on the night flight. I should be in Jersey about 9:00 AM. I'll call when I arrive. Give Rachel a kiss. I'll give her a ride to school if the flight gets in on time. Get your beauty rest."

Amanda was processing everything she heard. "So you might say that people who still wonder if boxing is fixed don't understand the process," she began cautiously. "Sure, in the old days of mob connections, an outcome might be predestined. Nowadays, though…" she hesitated, as if she wanted to get it out just right. "In today's market, boxing is fixed through artful matchmaking—excuse me, Stu." She went right on talking. "The promoter wants to sell tickets, right? Unless you have the star power of a Manny Pacquiao, you need a well-stocked undercard of compelling bouts to capture the public's eye."

If she had understood this correctly, it meant that a talented matchmaker could make or break a boxing company. You didn't want your cash cow to lose or have no options on his future fights. He should know the capabilities of fighters in every country. This took a good eye and an understanding of a fighter's worth and potential.

Stu just looked at her, but Bart came in from the side. "A lot of matchmakers are heartless, concerned with the outcome," he said. "Fighters can become pieces of meat—not to Stu. Stu has a heart and loves the sport that gave so much to his family."

Amanda reached across the table and put her hand on Stu's pudgy one. "I've only known you an hour but I can feel that's true," she whispered. "And if Bart says it, I believe it. He doesn't fool me with his I-couldn't-care-less act. He cares more than anyone."

After that she excused herself.

Neither man said anything for a moment. Bart was thinking about Stu's stake in Montana. It was no surprise to him that Stu was taking the Montana injury so hard. He wondered if his friend had information that pertained to what had happened. Was he feeling a twinge of guilt, or was he just upset he had lost the most potentially lucrative boxer since Mike Tyson?

Bart's apple pie overflowing with vanilla ice cream—his favorite dessert—arrived at that moment. As he ate, savoring every bite, they shared old fight memories and debated boxing's future.

"That pie sure looks good."

"Have some. I don't know why I ordered it."

Stu's phone rang. "Ed," he said.

"Go ahead and answer it."

"No, he just wants to get me to ask you questions about Curtis." He let the call go to voicemail. "You've seen your share of these guys. What does your gut tell you?"

Bart wondered if Stu was still playing handball every morning in the park in South Jersey and taking the daily steam. Tonight he was unusually sweaty and pale.

"He'll have lots of problems if he makes it, probably be paralyzed on the left. If he's left brain dominant, his speech and comprehension might remain intact." Right-handed people were left brain dominant 98 percent of the time. "Curtis's bleed was on the right side, and though there was tremendous swelling, his left brain, which controls language, might be functioning."

"He might be able to talk soon?" Stu hesitantly asked.

"He's actually communicating—not speaking, yet. He's strong. Then again, I don't know if I'd want to live like that." He noticed Stu perspiring more. "Are you okay?"

"I'm tired, that's all."

"What meds do you take?"

Stu dabbed his sweaty forehead with a paper napkin as his phone vibrated for the second time. Bart grinned, thinking how lucky he was to not be at someone's beck and call.

Stu put the phone back in his pocket. "Anything Ed wants at this time of night, I don't want to do."

"I hear ya," Bart laughed.

"I asked Vincent if there was something wrong with Curtis before the fight. He said no, but it's almost as bad as having your dad in the corner. They're the last one to stop a fight, although I'm not blaming Vincent. He's a damn good trainer…"

Bart glanced at a text from Amanda. *Your team is pretty perturbed. Be at your place at 11.* "The kid even had an MRI the week of the fight," he said. "What do *you* think happened?"

"I saw Curtis arguing with Vinnie after the press conference."

"Do you know something?"

Stu shook his head.

All heads turned as Ed's bodyguard Lorenzo burst in. He marched over to their table, looking as formidable as could be in his funeral-ready midnight blue suit tailored to his 6'6" 350-pound, muscled frame. He stood over Stu and proclaimed, "Ed needs you."

"Sure, in an hour," Stu said, entranced with what was left of Bart's pie.

A one-time WWE contestant, Lorenzo bent over the table, casting an ominous shadow. "Ed needs you *now*. Listen to your voicemail. You'll get the picture."

Accepting that Lorenzo wasn't vacating his post until his mission was accomplished, Stu folded.

Morphing into the kid brother seven years younger than his hero, who just boxed his ears, Stu muttered, "Dinner next week? I'll be in town Friday."

Bart concealed his disappointment in the conversation's premature termination. "Give that bride of yours a kiss from me," he said.

Stu was already halfway to the door, with the goon right behind him.

*

As Bart made his way toward the parking lot, Gabe shouted after him, "I need a favor."

He knew that tone. "Yes, master," he grumbled, turning and waiting for her to catch up with him.

"We need a consult on Emilio Vasquez, the kid that got KO'd. Your girlfriend was filming while they took him from the ring."

"The ED doc will contact the neurologist."

"I told Channel 8 and the *Review Journal* that Dr. Norris will be seeing Vasquez."

He felt a flush of anger, and shoved his hands into his pockets, trying to remain calm. "Did you ask her? We have neurologists who see our boxers. Besides, Vasquez doesn't need a neurologist, just an ED visit, a head CT and observation for an hour or two. Was this your hair-brained scheme?"

Gabe knew she was out of line. However, bringing in Montana's sister would be a PR win. She hardened her tone, "I'm not the one with the girlfriend whose nose is up my ass. Can't you control her?"

Pranayama breathing came in handy, especially at a poker game or in dealing with boxing blowhards. Gabe always thought things through, and he understood her maneuvering. Would Olivia Norris?

"Dr. Norris isn't an idiot. The NBC should stop worrying about looking good on TV and focus on mishaps that are landing fighters in the hospital at the brink of death."

She tugged on Bart's sleeve to lower his voice. "The lead doc already called Dr. Norris to see the fighter. She's on her way. He said she sounded pleased."

"Yeah, she probably wants to get close enough to get a better shot at the Commission. She's not naïve, and she'll take the opportunity to assess the way your docs work, which will make the Commission more vulnerable, not less."

After sufficient groveling, Gabe knew she'd won, at least for now. Bart resumed heading towards his car, at the same time fielding a call from Amanda. As he was unlocking the car, Gordon Fletcher, the *Review Journal* boxing writer, came up behind him.

"I hear Montana's sister is seeing Vasquez. Is she working with the NBC?"

"Why does this always come down on me?" he grumbled to himself.

Staring at the cement, he replied, "Your guess is as good as mine. Call Gabe."

"It's your hospital, and you were talking to the executive director."

Bart smiled. "Trying to save a phone call?"

"Very funny, Rossi. You know I'm going to find out one way or another."

"No comment."

The 48-year-old Fletcher had been with the *RJ* for 15 years, and Bart had known him each and every one of those years. At one time, the paper had employed two boxing journalists, but these days boxing was eclipsed by basketball, football and mixed martial arts—a sport Fletcher made sure everyone knew he hated but was forced to cover.

The NBC used him to peddle their agenda. In exchange, he picked up tidbits before other journalists. He repeatedly tried to prove he wasn't a "kept man" of Nevada boxing, as opposed to someone "on the inside." Everyone knew the truth.

Bart reached for the door handle.

"Alright, play dumb," Gordon lamely replied.

"Look, as far as I know, the NBC hasn't hired anyone new."

"Okay, you guys need some positive PR. Even if Montana survives, this place is beginning to look like a death trap."

"That's a bit harsh."

"We both know there's a problem. When you worked ringside, these things seldom happened. Plus, people are talking."

Bart leaned against his car and faced Gordon, putting aside his distaste. "Have you heard that Montana was hurt beforehand?" He couldn't help asking.

"He wasn't getting along with Rappaport."

"Who does? But did you hear he was injured in the gym or had any medical problems in training?"

"No, I think he trained mostly at home, so I wouldn't know."

"Then who's saying he and Ed were having problems? Oh, I bet it was Joey Davolo. Who else would badmouth another promoter?"

Joey Davolo, former California resident and prominent attorney, moved to Vegas in the '80s, got himself several high-profile fighters to represent and turned to promoting. No one had a bigger mouth than Joey. Now 70, his furrowed facial landmarks made him look like a sea lion and told the story of too many hard-fought battles. It was common knowledge that Davolo loved manufacturing controversy with half-truths and innuendos that tarnished reputations in one fell swoop.

"Yeah, Joey's prolific," Fletcher responded, clumsily sidestepping Bart's question.

Bart looked at his watch and smoothed his in-need-of-a-trim hair. "Our discussion is off the record, okay?"

Gordon huddled closer. "Sure, sure, Bart."

Off the record had biblical significance. Even bad writers obeyed the rule.

•

Amanda called to confirm meeting Bart to burn off some calories. Instead, after telling Fletcher what he knew, Bart headed over to Western—as he'd done countless times to check on a fighter.

He missed the fighters. He hated being an observer, and he wasn't good at it. He was the best in preventing an injury and managing things ringside. His mere presence, whether silent or vocal, angered anyone less than confident. Tonight he went to prepare Dr. Norris and perhaps unburden his guilt, knowing she was being set up for something more high profile than she might be prepared for.

A few blocks from the hospital he called the ED. "Hey, Louise, how busy is it tonight?"

Louise ran the ED night shift. She was a buxom platinum blond in her early fifties, resembling early sixties in scrubs one size too small. A real looker in her day, before Gambler's Anonymous and a few stints in AA took their toll. Now she was Vegas hard.

Nothing that rolled into the ED fazed her. Bart and she had handled many a tragedy and many frustrated family members.

"Dr. Rossi, you never visit...always playing poker. Those day shifts are killing you. Come play with the grown-ups."

ED nights, he thought, so often they felt like being on a plane that was out of control. He loved the quiet, the limited number of personnel and the autonomy.

Bart had worked nights for his first few years following residency. Those were the times he drove out to Lake Mead to fish all morning, then headed back to the sports books to watch a couple games before it was time to return to the hospital.

"Louise, I was checking to see—"

"He's here, Dr. Rossi. And in case you're wondering, so is she."

"She?"

"Norris. And, all I can say is wow. No grass growing under those feet. My hair used to be naturally red…She asked about you, and I said I bet you were on your way."

Bart laughed. That was the mark of a truly great psychic-turned-emergency nurse. She anticipated everything, always sizing up the players before entering a game.

Sighing at his predictability, he chuckled. "Be right there."

Louise giggled, harboring her eternal crush. "Catch you soon good-lookin'."

Bart walked into the waiting room and looked around. It was Monday, a busy night for the ED. He stood for a moment feeling the atmosphere creep into his bones, feeling that strange, perverse comfort of being part of this. Every time the doors opened, the clamoring dissonance from the ED leaked into the waiting room. Western had 26 emergency beds, all full. Physician assistants triaged the worried roomful. Two doctors spewed a litany of orders for the nurses while visiting with each patient. They fired five basic questions: why are you here; where does it hurt; for how long; have you had this before; and if so, when? To save even more time, a brief hands-on exam accompanied the questioning.

Saturday and Monday nights were the two busiest shifts; so much so that doctors were paid extra for coverage. On Monday nights, EDs exploded with nursing home patients and the elderly compensating for a weekend of inattention and overeating. There was always a plethora of geriatric problems. Saturday night was a day of professional drunks, partiers and druggies, as well as those in training. The job of the doc was to stabilize critical patients and move others home or into hospital beds.

The thrill of being in the midst of the ED was something Bart would never get out of his blood, the thrill of simultaneously taking care of the 60-year-old bleeding from his rectum, the 41-year-old with chest pain and the 2-year-old with a sore throat. He would typically make a decision in 30 seconds, the standard time for emergency docs in the triage system. Gunshot wounds and major traffic accidents went to a trauma center.

On fight nights, like tonight, Western maintained an open room.

Emilio Vasquez patiently sat on the bed, one eye closed from his opponent's right hand—the other with a two-inch laceration under the brow. Close by, Olivia reviewed the ED notes.

Louise had officiously summarized protocols for her as she came on the shift. Olivia was aware she was being used by the Commission, but even so, she was pleased to be thinking about somebody other than her brother lying upstairs. When Bart arrived, she was more than happy to lay it on thick.

She was used to academia, which called for a cold demeanor in medical practice. Each patient became an interesting case for debate. Tonight, without residents, this fighter was her responsibility alone. She was surprised to find herself feeling good here, feeling like a real doctor.

"Dr. Norris?" Louise inquired as Olivia stepped over to the main desk.

"Call me Olivia, Louise."

"No, doctor, against policy."

"Understood," she said feeling sheepish. "Has Mr. Vasquez had his head CT? I was going to swing by radiology."

"The acute abdomen in Bed 3 took precedence. Vasquez will get his about 10:00 PM. According to the paramedics, he lost consciousness for 90 seconds, had no amnesia and came in with a mild headache, dizziness and nausea. A typical closed head injury."

"My thought exactly...The 'typical' part anyway," she sighed. Comfortable that Louise could be an ally, she added, "Why'd they consult me? Don't these knockouts happen all the time, and they send the kids for routine scans, observation and then home?"

"Could be an overreaction after your brother's injury. At least we had an opportunity to meet. I like to know all the new physicians on staff."

Vasquez's laser-white smile lit up his face when he saw Olivia. She reached for his hands, every bit as soft as a concert violinist's. He gazed at the floor and spoke in a soft monotone, answering Olivia's probing questions in broken English. Olivia declined a translator. She spoke her mother tongue to him, asking him about himself, liking the human contact.

Vasquez told her he was born in Valle De Bravo, a small affluent lakeside town outside Mexico City. He said that the villas—all modern—looked like they were carved into the rocks. It was a place like the Hamptons, where well-to-do Mexico City residents flocked on weekends. His uncle, four brothers and two sisters were professional fighters. They all worked in local restaurants, hoping one day to own a home there.

An invitation to fight in Vegas meant he hit the big time even though it was a club show. At home, he would now be a celebrity. He was 26, with a record of

16 wins, 10 losses and one draw. Plus his record didn't include several undocumented Mexican bouts. No one knew how many battles he'd fought in the gym.

Olivia took the time to listen and ended up with an invitation to his next fight.

Never had a patient been so thankful for her care. Was this true of all boxers, or was Vasquez trying to get back in the ring sooner than he belonged? It wasn't cynical of her to wonder this. It was her job. Vasquez's wife was about to deliver their first child, and he would need money to cover her hospital bills; then he could rest. He asked several times if Olivia could clear him to return to the ring sooner. To his disappointment, she clarified that it was the NBC's decision, not hers.

"How's Mr. Vasquez doing?" Bart whispered, coming up behind her.

Taking in his Clooney-esque half-grin, she responded smugly. "Dr. Rossi, so you know my fighter? He's doing very well." She turned back to Vasquez.

"Emilio, *espera. Nececito hablar un momento con el* Doctor Rossi. *Lo conoces?*" Telling the young fighter that she was going to discuss suspension rules with the doc, she moved Rossi out of earshot.

"What did Vasquez say?" Bart asked.

"He wants to fight sooner than the two month Commission suspension he was given. He mentioned something about 'Fightfax', Dr. Rossi. I explained—"

"Bart."

"What?" she asked confused.

"This is where I say, 'Call me Bart,' and I ask, 'May I call you Olivia?'" he said, unruffled. Fightfax maintains fighters' federal identification cards. It lists medical and disciplinary suspensions, such as when a boxer needed time off for an injury or cut. All U.S. commissions adhere to it. Ideally, it limits the boxer from sparring or scheduling another fight before he's fully recovered. U.S. commissions are required to follow the federal suspension list and use Fightfax as their reporting system."

She was intrigued by him. She was listening but she was also taking in his Cary Grant stature, with the right amount of age, experience and ruggedness.

"Something on your mind?"

"I'm not an idiot."

He seldom smiled truly, the kind of smile you allow to come from deep inside. One of the few times was when he won a game at Binion's World Series of Poker three years ago. Looking at Olivia, it was impossible not to flirt. He had to smile at her, but only just. He let her spew.

"I know everyone's concerned with the legal ramifications of my brother's injuries, so that's why I'm being included in your games."

"That's exactly what I thought when Gabe told me. I refrain from NBC politics. I work at Western and play poker, no less, no more. On the other hand, Vasquez is grateful for your expertise."

Bart got a text to join a game at Binion's. Grateful for the opportunity to split, he gladly accepted.

"My only advice is stay clear of ringside," he told Olivia. "Few have the stomach for it. You may not want to take on the pressure, and these kids take your soul. Gotta go," he said raising his hand. Why was he giving out free advice? It was something he conscientiously avoided doing. "Thanks for coming in so late. We can always use your expertise."

Olivia bit her lower lip in frustration and disgust. What an ass. Men manipulated everything, telling you the opposite of what they want to have you do. She wasn't contemplating working as a ring doctor. There couldn't be much to the job. She knew more than these bozos when someone was hurt. How could they not have a neurologist ringside? If she had been there for Curtis...

She pulled her attention back from that abyss and concentrated on completing her consult dictation.

Sophie called.

"Liv, something's wrong with your brother," Sophie shrieked. Olivia held the phone away from her ear. She heard her mother's voice, tiny but still clear. "I just woke up with a start—I heard him trying to cry out. I called and they said he's fine, nothing has changed. There's something they're not telling me. Check on your brother, now."

"The nurse would have called," she said calmly, reacting to a lifetime of hysteria from her mother.

"Someone could be dead on the night shift," Sophie shouted, "and the nurses still record the vitals."

"Mom, you've been watching too much *House*. I'm at the hospital seeing a patient. I'll go upstairs in a minute." She really could use a drink, she thought, recalling an unopened bottle of Patrón in Curtis's bar.

"Call me as soon as you see him," Sophie demanded. "If I don't hear from you I'm coming over there."

Olivia walked up the two flights to Curtis's floor. The night nurses were sitting at their work station munching on Capriotti sandwiches—brought in, they told her, by a patient's family.

The pervasive smell of merthiolate greeted her at the entrance to Curtis's room. The sterile ambiance was amplified in contrast to overflowing aging baskets of gladiolas, roses and tulips. He was sitting up with his eyes wide open, as if he were awaiting her arrival, and immediately tried to speak.

She hurried in and took hold of his hand. The monitor registered a stronger, more regular pulse than she had seen up to now. The BP cuff inflated as he tried to speak.

Stroking his forearm, she whispered, "You're off all sedatives. If you're in pain…" She had to stop herself from choking on tears as her throat closed up with emotion. Curtis had come back, and maybe she had a second chance.

She began to examine him. His pupils reacted normally to the penlight, and he followed commands such as *smile* and *stick out your tongue*. Suspecting his left side was paralyzed, she didn't ask him to move his extremities. There would be time for him to face that.

She leaned close to him and forced herself to speak softly. "Valiente, I've missed you and missed you, little brother. I hope you can forgive me, please forgive me." She stopped, unable speak for a moment. Finally she continued. "The past doesn't matter, as long as you can forgive me. I'll make it up to you, I promise."

He lay looking at her with his sweet eyes.

"I've been living in your wonderful house," she continued. "Curt, it's so real, and the brothers and Luisa are the best. You made a world for yourself." She felt her speech bubbling out of her as she went on, telling him that she had moved from Chicago, that she was working at Western now.

Curtis looked on intently, seeming to understand. As Olivia went to telephone Sophie, he lifted his right arm and motioned no.

"I have to call her, or she'll be here in her nightgown," Olivia laughed. "She already threatened me." She speed-dialed her mother, told her she was sitting beside Curtis's bed and that everything was fine.

"So go back to sleep, Mom. You'll see him in the morning."

As she put the phone back in her pocket she felt Curtis's touch on her hair. She looked up, startled.

He mouthed, "Livy."

She gestured for him to wait a minute and hurried out to the nurses' station to borrow a pad and pencil.

As she held the pad, he legibly scribbled the words "love" and "sad."

He pushed himself into a more upright position with the strength of one arm.

"Lie back," she said softly. "When you move like that it shoots up your blood pressure. Do you want some ice chips to suck on?"

He mouthed words she couldn't make out. His BP, now 200/110, triggered the alarm. She held the pad for him again and he scribbled "no."

"What do you mean?"

Curtis wrote, "u need no."

"I don't understand? I need to know something?"

She covered his trach site so he could speak.

"Sorry…Mom…not me." He blinked and motioned for water. His elevated pressure persisted.

Olivia rose to yell for the charge nurse, but Curtis forcefully motioned for her to remain.

"Livy…hurt."

"I don't understand? You're in pain now?"

"Hurt arm."

His systolic pressure jumped to 240.

Sophie's cell went to voicemail; Lucy's did the same. She left messages to come now.

Running to the front desk, she caught Curtis's nurse flirting with a man in a dark, blue suit—someone who shouldn't even have been on the ward. She ordered the nurse to administer sedation, then turned to address the man, who looked vaguely familiar. It was too late. He was out the door, getting into the elevator with another man similarly attired.

"Code 99" blared overhead. Olivia ran to Curtis's bedside while respiratory therapy checked for a mucous plug in his trach. Olivia knew better.

One nurse bagged him to deliver oxygen directly to his lungs, while others moved the crash cart next to the bed. They shocked him at 360, checked for a pulse and repeated the protocol two additional times.

No pulse, no rhythm.

The ICP monitor had been out for some time. Olivia deduced re-bleeding or cerebral edema.

An unfamiliar emergency doctor arrived on the scene, barking orders at the nurses as he approached. Olivia tried to call Lucy again. It went straight to voicemail.

Olivia stood helpless in the doorway as the staff continued the code for 40 minutes without a rhythm before they called the official time of death: 2:45 AM.

Fourteen

SOPHIE SPENT THE ensuing days medically numb on a cocktail of Xanax and Cymbalta, while Lucy and Mirabelle were Olivia's rocks. Mirabelle planned the service. Las Vegas Metro handled the press and on-lookers. The *Review Journal* reported that it was the largest memorial gathering since the death of Moe Dalitz in 1989.

The St. Mary's service, though a testament to her brother's accomplishments, didn't delve much below the surface. Olivia and Sophie didn't speak publicly—neither of them was able to do it. Lucy only made it through the start of her eulogy. Sophie sobbed, barely gazing at people who offered condolences. To the hundreds of mourners, Curtis was a celebrity, not a person filled with dreams and fears.

Whispered conversations moved to other topics: deals between promoters and managers for upcoming television dates, who was in attendance and, more important, who was not.

Vincent sent Olivia a long letter apologizing for not attending, insinuating that his presence would make it more difficult—which made Sophie furious. But Vincent wrote as if he had nothing left. He was completely heartbroken. Bart, too, stayed away, Olivia noticed. Someone told her Bart never "did" funerals.

After six weeks in Vegas, Olivia knew many of the attendees, if not their names. Some appeared guilty, while others embraced her as part of the "boxing family." Many fighters, including Emilio Vasquez, paid their respects.

The press waited for interviews from boxing luminaries, including Ed Rappaport, already walking alongside his new heavyweight contender in a concerted effort for free press.

The Desert View Cemetery burial was for family and close friends. Chui and Marco stayed by Olivia's side. Olivia fought Sophie against a fancy mausoleum, arguing a simple headstone out in the open would allow Curtis's fans to visit.

Every time Olivia glimpsed her grieving mother during the gravesite readings, Curtis's last words played in her head. She hadn't told anyone about the conversation or the scribbled notes, but she thought about them a lot. She lost track of the psalm being read as she asked herself over and over what Curtis had meant by "Mom, not me." There would be a time when she could ask Sophie. Today was not the day.

As she sat waiting for something to change, something to allow her to breathe, she stumbled on painful unresolved feelings of blame. Not only blame toward her mother but towards Curtis too. It surprised her. She had to stop herself from groaning. She couldn't shake off the feeling that they were at least partially responsible for what her life had become.

She tried not to think about it. She didn't want to go there. That part of her life was dead to her. That's what she had said to Curtis, and she had meant it. But it all came flooding into her, and she could feel it circulating poisonously, endlessly.

She was in her last year at Northwestern. The campus was the perfect home—close to Michigan Avenue, the lake and the heart of the Chicago social scene. She studied hard, frequently pulling all-nighters. After all, her goal was medical school. Despite her Spartan idealism, she appreciated the right amount of clubbing, drinking and dancing.

At an age when being slender automatically made you good-looking, she was striking. She flaunted it at the right time, without an air of superiority, and that made her approachable and exceedingly popular.

Living on campus kept her away from her dominating mother. It also prevented her from being a big sister to Curtis, who was beginning to make a name for himself at the high school principal's office. It didn't surprise her when she got a frantic call from her mother at midnight one Tuesday in January.

"*Dios mío*, Olivia, come home," Sophie screamed.

Olivia had fallen asleep earlier than normal. She had a biology final tomorrow and planned to cram in the morning.

"Mom, calm down," she muttered, exiting her dorm room so she wouldn't wake her roommates. "What's wrong?" She didn't keep the annoyance out of her voice.

All she could hear was her mother crying. Then Curtis must have grabbed the receiver.

"Livy, everything's okay. You know Mom…She gets crazy."

"I'm coming over."

"Let me handle this. There's nothing you can do. Mom will be fine. I gave her a—actually two—Valium."

"Tell me what's up or I'm coming."

Curtis spent the next five minutes talking her down, without ever really saying what had happened. She hated that he had to deal with their mother's craziness. Sophie exaggerated everything. He finally convinced her not to come, and she went back to sleep even though she felt uneasy, as though something was different in this particular hysteria. At 5:00 AM she woke up with a pang of fear in her gut. After a fitful further hour of lying awake and trying to convince herself not to worry, she got up and went home.

The Lincoln Park brownstone was still worth in the mid-$500s, part of a generous divorce settlement. Her once meticulous mother had ceased worrying about repainting or recovering the dilapidated upholstery.

Olivia arrived to discover every light on in the house and Sophie snoring on the living room sofa, her robe blanketed securely around her street clothes. Noticing facial bruises and dried blood on Sophie's scalp, Olivia started over to the sofa to rouse her. Hearing Curtis in the kitchen, she changed her mind and went in to talk to him.

"What happened?" she demanded "Is Mom okay?"

Reluctant to respond, he stared out at the snow-filled yard. He, too, was bruised, and had a two-inch gash above his right eye.

"Were you in a fight? Did someone break in?"

Sophie pushed open the kitchen door and cried, "Leave your brother alone. This has been a rough night."

Letting her anger get the better of her, Olivia stripped off her winter coat and threw it over a chair. "I have a biology final in a few hours, so make this quick," she shouted, crossing her arms and waiting for the usual blathering to start. She had already heard everything they would ever say. She was sure of it. It was sickeningly predictable. She watched her mother twist her hair into a French knot—something she did when she was anxious. Sophie went to the stove and poured some of yesterday's French roast into a saucepan. Turning the flame on under the saucepan, she commanded Curtis to get ready for school, and off he went without another word.

Olivia glared at her mother.

Sophie waved her away. "We're fine," she said, as if it were a joke. "There was a little fender-bender last night. I picked up your brother from the boxing gym. You know how he wants his driver's license? Well, I thought there wouldn't be any harm in letting him drive us home—"

"Mom, give me a break," she shouted.

"Don't shout at me. We were able to drive home and—"

"Mom, you're both hurt and need x-rays."

"I'm sorry I woke you up last night," Sophie said, looking genuinely sad. "I know you have your studies."

"It's okay. But please promise me you'll get Curtis, and yourself, to a doctor. You don't know what lasting injuries you might have." She put on her coat and headed toward Curtis's room, but her mother took her arm and hustled her outside. It made her angry all over again. The woman was impossible.

As she was unlocking her car, she noticed that the garage was shut tight. Even in winter, her mother never fully closed the garage door.

She went over to the door and bent to turn the handle. It didn't budge. She tried the door to the storage room that was attached to the carport. It was blocked with old toys her mother hoarded, hoping one day she'd have a grandchild.

Too bad she had never had a reason to own a remote for the garage, but there was only one, and it lived in the Mercedes. She put on her gloves to get a better grip. The door still didn't budge. She pushed with all her weight and it flew open, crashing into the wall behind.

She paused, expecting Sophie and Curtis to run outside. No one came. Cautiously she turned on the garage light, kicking aside plywood that had been used as a barrier to prevent the door from opening.

The car was parked head-in. The rear was in perfect condition. She peered through the back window and saw that the cabin was intact. Feeling her way along the driver's side of the car, she came to the front fender and gasped. The whole front end was completely shoved in and collapsed. He must have hit a tree or a light post.

Looking closely at the broken headlight, she saw a piece of blue material clinging to the jagged glass. She knelt on the cement floor and peeled off part of a bloodstained wool cap.

Banging on the entry to the kitchen, Olivia screamed, "Mother, open the damn door!"

Sophie must have been standing right at the door. It flew open. "Before you say a word, let me explain," she said, breathless.

Olivia stepped inside. Curtis was sitting in front of an uneaten bowl of oatmeal, which was his favorite breakfast since he was a toddler.

"Livy," he murmured.

Sophie yanked Curtis's arm, stepping between him and Olivia. "It was no one's fault. It was dark and slippery. We couldn't see with this damn Chicago wind and the snow fall."

"Mother," she growled. "It was your fault. Who would put a 14-year-old who doesn't know how to drive behind the wheel on a night like the one you've just described?" Her voice rose. "For God's sake, listen to what you're saying."

Sophie glared at her.

Olivia held up the piece of cap. "This is a piece of a woolen cap, and it has blood on it. Now tell me what happened." Curtis had been out of juvie for a year, and he had been doing better, concentrating on boxing and not getting himself into scrapes anymore—or so she thought. Now she wondered why she had believed anything her mother told her about him.

Sophie turned away as toast popped up from the toaster. She went over and methodically took the two pieces of toast out of their slots and reached into the cabinet for a plate.

Olivia screamed, "Tell me what happened. Who is the person whose cap was torn off his head by your headlight? What did the police say?"

Her mother was silent, but she stopped buttering the toast.

Finally, Olivia thought, she's going to tell me something. It only took another second for her to understand how deep they were. They hadn't called the police at all. Her mother planned to hide everything.

For a moment the kitchen was ominously quiet. When Olivia broke the silence, her fear forced her anger down into her throat, and her voice was controlled and dark.

"You know you could both go to prison," she said. "Where is the person he hit?"

"Olivia," Curtis exclaimed, but Sophie put her hand squarely on his shoulder before he could say anything.

"It was late. I picked up your brother from the gym. He wanted to drive. We turned off the highway. The streets were empty, I swear."

"Mom's telling the truth."

Sophie tightened her grip on his shoulder, shouting, "Go upstairs and lie down. You should miss school today. I'll tell Vincent you have the flu. Let me talk with your sister alone." She released him from her grasp and he stood up, then picked up the chair and slammed it against the wall. Then he went upstairs.

As soon as he left, Sophie locked the kitchen door.

"Now we can talk in private. I want you to listen, or you can leave."

They had butted heads countless times. There had been times when one or the other swore she'd never speak to the other again. Olivia saw that Sophie was trembling, needing help and planning to demand it.

"You know Cabrini Green, especially at midnight with two people in a Mercedes that don't belong. I thought we ran over a rock then we heard the loose bumper and felt the flat tire. Curtis pleaded with me to stop. I forced him to drive on, not even imagining we hit anyone."

"How did you know you hit someone if you didn't stop? You *did* stop! Quit lying."

"A boy came out of nowhere. I ran out and checked." Sophie's eyes welled up with tears. "Olivia, there was no need to stay at the scene. The teen was dead."

"He was dead and there was no reason to stay at the scene?" Olivia was having trouble getting the words to come out of her mouth. "What kind of a person are you? You killed someone and now you want me to keep quiet? I'm calling the police." She started pacing the room. Could she call the police? Her mother was right; they could have been in danger for their lives if they had stayed there. But they had killed a teenager—and who knew if they had even killed him outright. Maybe they could have saved him. She paced back and forth, arguing with herself.

Her mother glowered at her. "If you wish to turn your brother in to the police, I no longer have a daughter," she shouted, then added an old favorite of hers, "You were always much more Grant's than mine. Leave now," she demanded, and she left the kitchen.

Olivia heard her run up the stairs, and she heard a door slam. After that the house was quiet. She had no idea what to do. She felt like there were jackhammers inside her head. She couldn't think straight. After a while she poured herself some coffee, sat down and forced herself to focus. Sitting there, looking at the pieces of chair Curtis had left behind in his frustration, she began to understand how trapped he was. Even though he was the one who had caused the problem, her mother had laid the trap. You could never get out of that trap. Olivia herself was caught, again, after three years of staying away and keeping herself as clear of her mother and brother as she could.

Two hours had passed by the time Olivia left the house. Her hands were still shaking, and she had not come up with a workable plan. She didn't say to herself that she wasn't going to call the police, but she also couldn't see herself doing it, wrong though she knew that was.

On her way back to campus she stopped in front of a North Avenue liquor store. She sat in the car thinking about the bottle she would buy for after her test, knowing all too well the bottle wouldn't remain sealed. She had taken a drink before a test in the past. She looked at her hands, gripping the steering wheel even though she was parked because she couldn't stop them from shaking. She couldn't go into the store. She had better forgo the purchase. No matter how frightened she felt right now, she knew that the best thing for her to do would be to study. Studying was the only thing that took her mind off whatever else was going on with her. Reading, studying, working out cool-headed issues proposed by someone else—that had always saved her. She would sort this out later.

She put the car in reverse and got herself back out onto the street. Her phone rang. Seeing it was Sophie, she let it go to voicemail. Doctors had to compartmentalize. She'd never be accepted to med school if she didn't do well on this final.

A few minutes later, she pulled over at a hydrant and listened to her mother's message. It droned on for three minutes, most of it crying and apologizing in the usual way, "Olivia, I'm sorry...Please help us. We're depending on you to do the right thing."

The right thing? Olivia mused. The right thing would have been to rescue the boy by the side of the road. And what was the right thing now, considering that had not been done? Did it have to be silence? Every time she asked herself what to do, she went through the scenario. If she called the police, her brother would surely go to prison; probably her mother would, too. If she didn't call the police, this incident would fester in each of them until they died—that was, if they weren't found out. And if they were found out, she was as much to blame as they were.

She stopped in front of a newsstand to see if there were any headlines about the accident. It was too early. She scanned the Internet: nothing yet. There was only one way out of this, and that was to contact the police.

*

Days, weeks and months passed. Olivia remained silent. It was like a sickness inside her, the thick membrane that laid itself over her feelings and kept her from making any kind of decision about anything having to do with the thing that had happened. She found she couldn't stand the sound of their voices. She couldn't bear to see her mother's name on her caller ID. She blocked the calls. Every now and then her memory dredged up that she, too, was an accessory to a crime, and she buried it as quickly as she could.

Was it fair to blame Curtis for something that was surely their mother's fault? But she couldn't deal with Curtis either. He had already caused too much damage, even before this. When she got to that point in the endless tape, she stopped it, she shouted, shook herself, whatever she had to do to get her brain to veer from the nerve-shattering screech of that one fact.

She severed all ties with both of them. This seemed a fair exchange, if she even knew what fair was these days. If she had no connection to them, the thing that had happened would go away from her and she wouldn't have to keep agonizing over it, analyzing it, endlessly searching for the missing pieces.

At the beginning she spent hours trying to find out who the boy was and whether he had died. There was never any mention of a hit-and-run accident in Cabrini Green, a place where crime too often evaded compassion and media attention.

Despite multiple medical school acceptances, Olivia remained in Chicago. Partying on Rush Street with endless acquaintances evolved into an existence of studying, working out and drinking alone. No one learned her secrets or recognized her overzealous self-control regarding when and where to drink. When she couldn't drink, she binged on food.

She fooled herself into thinking that the occasional male hook-up was real, which only further advanced her sense of inadequacy and her fear that she could never be whole. This was the path she had chosen—and continued to choose—not the cards she was dealt. She had an emptiness she could never fill, no matter how many patients she saw or cured.

•

After the funeral, there was a Spanish buffet at Sophie's house that included Curtis's favorite foods. Olivia couldn't bear to look at them. She stayed near Lucy, and people kept coming over to her, telling her how much Curtis had meant to them. Among the group of admirers were several young boxers who had recently turned professional. Many people made a point of speaking to her, even if they just mumbled about the unpredictable ravages of boxing and uneasily looked away while they spoke.

After three hours of condolences, Olivia fled to Curtis's—a place where she had never seen him but where he was everywhere, in everything. Sobbing, she collapsed on her bed, unable to understand where to find comfort. She had never found it. She didn't believe it existed. But when Tyson jumped up on the bed and nuzzled in next to her, she breathed in her dog smell and held her tight until she fell into a deep sleep.

•

The phone vibrating in her pocket wakened her. She peered at the time as she took the call. It was 9:00 PM.

"This is Dr. Norris," she mumbled, stretching her cramped limbs and wrapping her shoulders in the blanket someone had put over her during the night.

She waited. No one responded. She was about to hang up when an unfamiliar female voice said, "Dr. Norris, I'm sorry about the loss of your brother. Could you comment on the death of Vincent Marquessa?"

"What? How did you get my number?"

"I'm Amanda Weekly from Channel 8 news. A few minutes ago, I got word from the AP that Vincent Marquessa was found unconscious at home, an apparent heart attack. Since he wasn't at the funeral, I wondered if you had heard from him."

"I can't discuss this right now," she barked, and she ended the call. Had Vincent committed suicide? Was that what the caller was implying? It made no sense.

She turned on the light and found her purse where she had flung it when she came in. Rifling through it for Vincent's number, which Mirabelle had scribbled on a piece of paper for her, she cursed herself for not putting it right on her phone, as Mira had suggested. She found it, along with several other numbers and notes, only when she dumped the bag out on the floor in frustration.

Sitting there on the floor, she pressed the number into her keypad.

An elderly male voice, barely able to form words, said hello.

"Excuse me," she said, "this is Olivia Norris. I'm calling for Vincent Marquessa."

"Livy. It's Lou, Curtis's cutman." Moaning, he sobbed out, "My dearest friend is gone. And Curtis is gone."

"What happened?" she asked, barely able to keep down a sob in her throat. "I got a note yesterday from Vincent that he couldn't attend the funeral. I assumed he was back in Chicago. Where are you?"

"We didn't leave. Vincent was a proud man. He was livid over what happened to Curtis. People grieve differently. I stayed here to comfort him and…"

"What?"

"We started drinking yesterday. Vincent hadn't touched the stuff in years. We've buried many friends." He paused to collect himself. "Curtis was ours, too, Livy. Vinnie was in no shape to go to a funeral, let alone have anyone see him. He fell asleep on the couch. I was afraid to leave him alone, he was so depressed. After a while I tried to get him to go to bed." He had to stop again. Then, out of a throat constricted with grief, he whispered, "Couldn't wake him." Another pause. "I called 911, but…"

"Where you are?"

"Vinnie rented us a place off Charleston Blvd. We'd stay here during training camp."

"No one blames Vincent. Come to Curtis's, and we can talk," she pleaded. "Please come."

Chui and Marco came to her doorway hearing her distraught on the phone. Pressing the mute, she asked them, "Would you mind picking up Lou?"

Marco snatched the Dodge keys. "*Sí*, Olivia, *ya me voy*," he said, and the two brothers were off.

"Sit tight," she told Lou. "Chui and Marco are on their way."

"I'm no burden to anyone," Lou answered, indignant.

"I need the company." It was the truth. "Please come. It would really help me." He was silent.

"You can tell me all about the years I missed," she said, and that made her weep. She ended the call.

Not wanting to sit and keep crying, she went looking for sheets and made up another guest room. The idea of having someone here who was close to Curtis gave her a sense of relief. She called University Hospital and confirmed that Vincent had been brought in, apparently in cardiac arrest. The paramedics coded him in the field to no avail. He had a few bottles of heart medication in his pockets. It was an easy assumption his death was from a heart attack.

•

Olivia opened the door when she heard the car pull into the drive. She watched Lou labor up the ranch front steps, his weather-beaten face contorted with grief. Chui carried a tattered suitcase with shirttails escaping through a torn zipper.

"Be careful with that trunk, Marco. It has all my equipment. Plus, I'm not sure I'm staying," Lou grumbled.

Cradling Olivia's face in his chapped hands he sighed, "Big sister, you look exactly like Curtis described...only prettier."

She took his hand and led him into the kitchen. "Would you like some strong green tea?"

"Sure, as long as it has a strong shot of whiskey in it." He took off his fedora and rubbed his thinning strands of Kris Kringle hair, then taking out his handkerchief, he blew his nose a few times. After that he stood fidgeting while she fixed them both big mugs of tea.

Olivia didn't know what to say. Lou was a big presence in the room, and his deep discomfort was nerve-wracking to her.

Chui and Marco were silent, too, hanging back but, maybe unable to leave.

The liquor was in Curtis's study. She went over to the boys. "We'll be okay," she said, hugging each of them in turn. "Give us a little while, okay?" Picking up one of the mugs and handing the other to Lou, she shepherded him down the hall.

In Curtis's study, Lou went from one photograph to the next, reciting magical tales about each. Olivia listened to every word.

"I've worked with a lot of champs," Lou told her. "Curtis was special. Vinnie knew it, too. We followed him on his journey to greatness." He put down the picture he was holding and turned away from her. "Then we got too distracted," he mumbled.

She touched his shoulder. "What do you mean?" she asked consolingly. "Was Curtis hurt in the gym? Did he take the fight when he wasn't ready, or do you think it was a fluke?"

He pulled away from her. "That's not what happened," he muttered as he poured more whiskey into his mug. He took a deep swallow and, putting the mug down, reached for a framed photo of Curtis, Vincent and himself in front of the Lucky Seven, all smiles and full of anticipation.

"Curtis didn't go into that fight the other night 100 percent," he said without looking at her. "His shoulder was bothering him, but that was nothing. Vincent and I knew there was more than that injury."

He put a hand out and leaned against the wall, forehead against the dark wood paneling. "Now my best friend is dead, too."

"Sometimes the heart can't take more. The hospital said—"

"Fuck the hospital." He turned on her, shouting for a second, then shook his head. "Vincent wasn't sick. I would have sure as hell known if he wasn't feeling well."

Olivia stood looking at him until he met her eyes. This was the ranting of a broken man. He had lost everything. She walked up to him and gently but firmly took his arm. "Let's put you to bed," she said softly. "Sleep will help in some way—though I'm not sure how," she added, knowing how hard it was waking up and finding everything the same as it was.

She escorted him to the room she had made up for him and took off his jacket. He let her look after him, never saying another word, and lay down docilely on the bed.

"I'll be here when you wake up," she told him. "See if you can get some sleep."

He looked longingly at her, and she understood that longing. She felt it too. It was the painful, heartbreaking wish to return to a time before that tragic Saturday night.

Fifteen

THE SOBERING DAWN brought more calls, unanswered questions and apprehension. Olivia scanned the numbers on her phone. None were familiar.

She checked on Lou, who was sprawled out on the bed fully clothed minus his tennis shoes. She scribbled a note with her phone number on it, asking him to call her when he woke up.

Feeling disheveled and exhausted even after a hot shower and a change of clothes, she drove to Western.

As she was getting out of her car in the parking lot, a tentative voice came up behind her. "Dr. Norris, is this a good time?"

Turning around she recognized Cyn from the ED. "I'm on my way to see a few patients," Olivia said. "Could we meet for coffee in a bit?"

Disappointed, Cyn returned an unaddressed Mandalay Bay envelope she had been holding to her leather jacket pocket. "I can do today at four—the Starbucks on West Sahara and Fort Apache?"

Olivia agreed, not sure why she had put Cyn off and wishing she had noticed the envelope before she said she couldn't stop to talk. Before she could recant, Cyn was on her 1980 Harley, and the next moment, she was off across the parking lot with a lot of noise, black and pink hair streaming out from under her helmet.

That was bizarre, Olivia thought. I must have seen *North by Northwest* too many times. What did Cyn want?

Inside the hospital, Olivia cruised by the ED. Eyeing Bart at the nurse's station, she made up an excuse to say hello.

Bart was happy to greet her. "I know yesterday was tough," he said.

"I heard you don't do funerals," she countered. "Yeah, it was tough, there were lots of people there to grab a photo-op or make a deal. But there were also people who knew and loved Curtis."

"You're starting to see the real side of boxing, an old Western with cowboys in white or black hats. The boxers are meat to most promoters. Promoters rationalize they're giving kids who'd otherwise be on the streets a shot at immortality. Bullshit."

Smiling for the first time in days, she interjected, "Please, tell me what you're really thinking."

"Sorry, I didn't mean to be a jerk."

She examined his face. Although not a typically handsome face, somehow it fit together perfectly.

"Having met Vasquez," she said, "I see how innocent these kids are. They deserve so much more—"

"You should consider working with the fighters."

She squinted at him. "The last time we spoke you told me the opposite. Now you're suggesting I work with the NBC? They'd rest easy knowing they weren't going to face litigation from my family?"

"Olivia, I didn't mean that. I walked away from this shit because it was never about the athletes. They're pawns. It's like with thoroughbreds—thirty thousand of them are born a year, and only a couple ever win Graded Stakes races. The rest are used up and tossed aside when they can't compete—a lot of them with crippling injuries or no breeding potential. Then they're transported to a slaughterhouse for meat that will be sent to France."

"And this is you in a good mood," she joked.

He looked sheepish, a look she thought suited him. "Sorry. I don't know what got into me."

Amanda suddenly appeared by the ED doors in a black Yves Saint Laurent suit, every strand of blonde hair perfectly in place, waving to get Bart's attention.

"Honey, I missed you last night," she called out. "I called the ED and they said you were filling in for a few hours. So I came by to see if you wanted to take an early lunch."

Bart grinned. How lucky could he get, standing between two attractive females? In this case, one was mad about him and the other, if he was correct, hadn't quite made up her mind.

Amanda's doe-eyed optimism poured over the desk with carefully disguised sexuality.

"Lunch?" he teased. "It's not even 10:00 AM. Maybe breakfast?"

Olivia slinked behind him. "Doing well, Dr. Rossi," she whispered with a carefully concocted smile designed to conceal her disapproval. And there she was, she thought, right back to the disapproving ice queen she had been for years. Hadn't Curtis's death changed anything? She thought it had. She moved away from Rossi, hoping he hadn't seen what really happened. She was embarrassed. She hadn't realized he was taken.

Bart moved toward Amanda to try to cut her off before she said anything embarrassing, but Amanda practically pushed him out of her way.

"How could you not tell me you knew Olivia Norris?" she exclaimed. She extended her hand. "I'm Amanda Weekly. Come and have a bite with us."

Bart knew there was no stopping his flaxen-haired bloodhound, and leaving these two alone would create a nightmare.

"Amanda Weekly," Olivia said, smelling the challenge. "So that's what you look like."

Bart flinched. What did she know about Amanda? Had she researched him?

Amanda was radiating sweetness, always a bad sign.

"Sorry about that," she said. "As a female reporter, I have to work harder than the others."

Olivia frowned. With a glance in Bart's direction, she was about to move away when Amanda caught her arm.

"I'm truly sorry about that call last night," she said. "I should have thought about how it would hit you." She paused. "Have lunch with us." She made it sound like a personal favor, hard to resist.

Almost convincing, Bart thought, as he took hold of Amanda's shoulders and physically moved her out of Olivia's path.

Olivia looked from one to the other. "Sure," she said, "in about an hour. I have to round on a couple of patients first. Let me know where you'll be, and I'll meet you."

Bart needed to intercede before Olivia thought it was an ambush. "Amanda is a journalist for the local CBS station," he told her. "She knows what's off-limits."

Olivia decided not to comment on that. "It might be fun," she said, meeting Bart's eyes.

•

Seated close to the entrance at Marche Bacchus, Amanda waved to Olivia coming through the door. Bart, in the middle of texting, didn't lift his head. At 11:00 AM, the restaurant was full, catering to brunch and lunch guests with light Mediterranean cuisine. The table was covered with crumbs from the baguettes and Brie the two of them were consuming.

"Cute place," Olivia heard herself saying. "The coffee smells great." She pulled the chair out from under Bart's feet, and he muttered under his breath as she sat down.

"This place doesn't have 'coffee,'" Amanda said. "They have the best espresso and cappuccino in the city."

Bart still hadn't put down his phone. He mumbled as he thumbed out the text, "Manny, dime on the Celtics."

Both women glared at him. He shrugged. "This is important."

"Well, looks like you need to housebreak this one a bit more," Olivia said.

Amanda giggled, obviously happy to flaunt her hold over Bart. She scooted closer to Olivia. "I'm sorry for your loss," she said, her hand on Olivia's. "If we can do anything to help you, let us know."

Bart heard "we" and mentally groaned. She was laying it on.

"Your suit is gorgeous," Olivia responded in kind. "I need clothes."

"Thanks. Neiman's. I have a great personal shopper there."

"Can I get an introduction?" Olivia had never used a personal shopper. It wouldn't have occurred to her.

Scrutinizing the ladies' nonstop chitchat, Bart saw he'd lost control. Women under 50 were either competition or a storyline to Amanda. Olivia was both. He'd wager his girlfriend's newfound friendship was not legit, or he'd give up his winnings from tonight's Bellagio game.

"Ladies, are we discussing horse racing?"

"Bart, you goof," Amanda said, poking him in the ribs. "Not everything in life is about a wager, my love."

Olivia looked around the café, which was lined with wine crates. Too bad it was before noon. This woman was gorgeous and so thin she made her want to fast.

But the food, when it came, was as delicious as the coffee, and she realized she hadn't eaten since last night.

She watched Amanda at work on all fronts, always conscious of everyone around her and quite obviously angling for something from each of them.

"You're good," she said. "I bet you never let a chance go by."

Amanda leaned toward her confidentially. "What a fascinating field, neurology," she said. "Do you plan to work at the hospital or open your own practice?"

Bart kicked Amanda under the table.

"Honey, I'm not conducting an interview." She turned right back to Olivia and kept on talking. "It was tough when I first moved from Fresno." She chatted on about the personal-interest stories at a local news station, working the desk, doing local news. "Bart thinks I should have stayed with that."

Olivia's attention drifted to Bart's hands as he seemingly continued to send and receive texts. Amanda tossed her hair back, and three or four people at nearby tables turned to look at her.

"My only point," she said, "is you have an opportunity to shape your career into what you want. Maybe you could do medical TV commentary? I can talk to my producer if you're—

"Whoa," Bart interrupted her. "The hospital is thrilled to have Dr. Norris. You're going to get me in big trouble with administration if you sway her."

"Don't worry," Olivia said, amused to be the object of their banter. "I like it where I am. No one is going to sway me, as you say."

Amanda's phone vibrated and she stood up, excusing herself and telling the caller to hold for a minute. She handed Olivia her card. "Call me," she said. "Let's go shopping."

Olivia rifled through her purse and came up with a business card of her own.

Holding the phone away from her, Amanda stroked Bart's cheek. "See you tonight?"

"I have a late game. Call you in the morning."

She blew him a kiss and left the table, phone to her ear.

Bart handed his Platinum card to the waiter before Olivia could take out her wallet. "Are you familiar with the origin of coffee and espresso?" he asked, angling his chair in her direction.

"Thank you for breakfast, and no, I don't know anything about coffee or espresso," she said averting her eyes from his steel-blue gaze that made her blush.

"Well, let's see," he answered sinking back against the metal chair frame. "The Ethiopians…"

Olivia watched him as he talked. His face was animated, belying the soft southern speech that came out of his mouth. It was a generous mouth with a lazy smile that made her heart nervously race as he stopped talking and apologized for going on.

"Not at all," she said with a laugh she couldn't suppress. "You left out espresso."

"Espresso is different," he said, suddenly distracted by her beauty. There was no other word for it. Her delight played in her green eyes. Her whole demeanor was alight. "Espresso depends on modern technology—" His phone vibrated and he rolled his eyes at the caller's ID. "I have to take this," he apologized, rising from the table.

"I should already be at my office," she hastily said, starting to gather her purse and jacket. He held up one finger, and mouthed "One minute."

He made her pleasingly uncomfortable. She wished there was more to discuss.

Bart finished his call, but he was not ready to leave. This was the banter he loved, innocent conversation he used to size a woman up. She made him nervous in a way that captivated him.

Olivia employed her personal version of biofeedback. The last thing she wanted was for him to see her jumpy.

"Vegas can use a good neurologist."

"I've been told many have left over the last few years. I'm not convinced I can maintain a solo practice."

Flashing his sexy grin he muttered, "Trust me, you'll do well."

"Trust you?" she exclaimed, baiting him. She inhaled and smiled. Two could play this game. "I'd be most appreciative of some referrals," she said, looking at him over the rim of her coffee cup as she took a last sip.

Bart looked at his watch. "Of course, hanging around the hospital or the ED will get you patients. I know in-patient consults are tedious and the reimbursements are low, but it will get you known."

That was sound advice. And yet, he had delivered it as if it were a proposition. She suppressed a laugh. Standing up from the table in order to be the first to leave, she held out her hand to say goodbye. He took hold of it in his own surprisingly strong, compact one, and only then did he rise, too, as gentlemen used to do. She knew the game, and she knew he knew it too. She wondered if he truly fit the womanizer profile.

As she went out of the restaurant, she shook off the spell. He was Amanda's. And the last thing she needed was a man who treated women as an afterthought, even with those captivating baby blues.

Sixteen

OLIVIA SPENT THE afternoon hiring an office manager and medical assistant and establishing office procedures while waiting to meet Cyn.

With her Mustang in Chicago, she was driving Curtis's brand new Range Rover—a dream of a car. As she headed for the Starbucks, she checked in with Marco and Lou by phone. A Chicago area code interrupted her conversation.

"Dr. Norris, your mother gave me your number. I'm Michael Brewster, Curtis's attorney. We met briefly at the funeral. We have matters to review. And then there is his will. I tried to speak with your mother, but she's so distraught. I thought it would be simpler for you and me."

Hurriedly pulling into a space in the Starbucks lot, she nervously replied, "Can you repeat…"

"I've represented Curtis since he was an amateur. He was a close friend."

Turning off the engine, she fretfully watched Cyn head inside Starbucks. "You're in Las Vegas?"

"I returned to Chicago that same day. I thought you might want a few days to yourself. I learned yesterday that Vincent passed. What a terrific man."

"Could you email me your information?" she asked, giving him her address as well. "I'm heading into a meeting. I can call tomorrow morning. When are you planning on returning to Vegas?"

"Let's chat tomorrow and firm up the details for a meeting next week. I'll email you a list of people who should attend."

Hanging up, she wondered why Curtis had needed an attorney as a teen. Maybe because of his run-ins with the law, or did Brewster know about the accident? The timing would fit. What did Curtis's words mean—"not my fault"—before he died? She shuddered. She hadn't thought about the accident for a long time, and now that Curtis was gone, that memory seldom evaded her. Did this secret die with Curtis? Was Brewster involved? "Please, let the calls stop for today," she muttered to herself, running in to Starbucks. Cyn was standing in the coffee line. She was wearing snug jeans that accentuated her ample J-Lo butt, with black high-heeled over-the-knee boots, a fitted eggplant-colored sweater and the same black leather aviator jacket. Seeing Olivia, she waved.

"What can I get you? I grabbed a table over there," she said, pointing to a table by the wall, where her ample black leather saddlebag took up most of the surface.

Olivia asked for a latte and went to wait at the table.

When Cyn finally came to the table, she put the coffees down and noisily pulled out her chair, never moving her bag. "I don't have much time," she said furtively as she pulled out the same rumpled envelope Olivia had seen her with before.

"Did you know my brother before he was admitted to Western?" Olivia asked, stopping herself from reaching out to grab the envelope as Cyn sat there holding it.

"No, although we attended several of the same horse shows."

"You have horses?"

"I have three thoroughbred rescues that I keep in Sandy Valley—it's on the way to Los Angeles." Fretfully averting her eyes, she continued. "This has nothing to do with horses. I know Ron told you I was in the ED when Curtis was brought in. He was already unconscious—"

"Did he regain consciousness?"

"No, I'm sorry. Before transferring him to the operating room, we removed his clothing to place a femoral line. I took off his socks and boxing shoes."

"My mother has his personal belongings."

Cyn paused. "She didn't get everything."

She handed Olivia the envelope. "I should have given this to your mother," she said. "I didn't want it to be misplaced. Truthfully, I forgot I had it for a day or so. Then I worried someone would question why I kept it so long."

"Is this why Ron suggested we speak?"

"No, I haven't mentioned this to anyone. I just suggested to Ron we should meet."

Opening the envelope, Olivia took out the tiny folded piece of paper it contained and unfolded it. All it said was "for Livy 10-25-68".

Cyn pushed out her chair. "I have to go. Please don't think I did anything wrong by keeping this."

"I understand," Olivia hastened to say. "You did the right thing giving this to me."

Cyn's punk biker persona momentarily switched to that of an empathetic nurse. She hugged Olivia so hard she couldn't catch her breath, then picked up her coffee and left. Olivia turned and watched her through the plate glass as she threw her leg over her bike, scrunched her hair into her helmet, zipped her Brando jacket and rode off.

Olivia sat for a long time staring at the piece of paper with Curtis's handwriting on it. The edges, where the folds were, were dark and worn thin, but the writing was perfectly legible. She had no idea what it meant. She couldn't ask Vincent. Would Lou know? Would her mother know? She somehow didn't want to expose this note to her mother, at least not yet.

She had no idea what to do next. Someone coming up to her table startled her by asking her if he could take the other chair.

"I'm leaving," she said, quickly tucking the envelope safely into the zip pocket inside her purse and getting up so abruptly the chair tipped over backwards.

"You okay?" the young man asked, coming close as she turned and fled.

A short while later, she pulled in beside Mirabelle's candy-apple red BMW convertible in Curtis's driveway. She joined Lou and Mira in the front room as they were eating Luisa's fajitas.

Trading happy remembrances, Mirabelle quoted condolence notes from fans. Lou suggested they watch films of Curtis as a pro. Olivia wasn't ready.

"Mira, what are you going to do now?" Olivia asked.

"I was planning to return home to Chicago until Ed Rappaport offered me a PR job last week."

"Rappaport seems like such a sleaze."

"Welcome to boxing," Mirabelle sighed.

"It's run by vipers," Lou put in. "Vinnie use to say..." He broke down. Immediately there was a stirring on the floor where Tyson lay as she got up and went over to him. She put her head on his thigh.

"Have you heard from Vincent's family?"

He shook his head. "His ex-wife passed a couple years ago, and they had no kids."

Olivia put her hand on Lou's arm. "Curtis's lawyer is flying out to read the will next week," she said. "Please stay here. I can use the company, and Tyson adores you."

Tyson was an adoring dog, though she was less cordial with Olivia than she was with Lou. Animals never took to her like they did to Curtis or her father. Maybe Tyson sensed her aloofness. Curtis was the one dragging home countless strays against Sophie's wishes.

"Tyson barely touches her food," Olivia sadly said. "Did Curtis bring her from Chicago?"

"Tyson has quite a story, don't ya girl?" Lou smiled at the dog, rough-housing her neck and ears. "From the day we met, Curtis talked about getting a dog. Your mother refused. Every night, Dave, a homeless guy, circled the neighborhood with a Golden Retriever named Daisy. She was a great dog—never left his side. I think she helped Dave get handouts. Curtis gave Daisy a treat every time he entered and exited the gym. It was the only time she ever left Dave.

One day Daisy was limping. Her back leg was covered with blood. Curtis dropped his gym bag, scooped her up and ran to a nearby vet. Her leg was broken in three places. They did surgery. It was extra dangerous because she was pregnant. Daisy didn't survive long. I think she had a broken heart."

"Dave?"

"He got run over trying to save Daisy. He was already in the hospital when Curtis found Daisy."

Olivia looked at Tyson. "This is one of her pups, right?" she said, marveling.

"Right before they put Daisy down, she delivered four pups. They thought none would make it. One did." Lou ruffled the dog's ears lovingly. "She was a fighter—and an ear nibbler, so Curtis named her Tyson."

She traveled everywhere with him and always lay next to the ring when he sparred. "She would have been in Curtis's corner during a fight if he'd let her." There had been articles written about the two of them. "If it's hard for us, imagine how it must be for her," Lou added, wiping a few tears.

Olivia knelt to pet Tyson, who snubbed the effort.

"She don't trust ya yet. You'll have to earn her respect."

"She slept with me, though, after the funeral. So maybe there's hope," Olivia said, trying to laugh it off. She sensed Lou was right about more than Tyson.

Seventeen

"WHAT ARE YOU wearing?"

"Jesus, Bart. I'm still at work. What do you want?" Amanda asked, glancing at her watch. It was 11:00 PM.

"Miss me? I'm in room 5507."

"Bellagio?"

"I have two hours between games. I showered and I'm lying here waiting for you. I ordered you two Kobe burgers."

She used to meet him on long poker nights. It was some of the best sex they ever had. He hadn't called like this in a while. She liked that he wanted her. She closed her eyes and could almost taste him.

"Babe, I have so much work and—"

"More important than me?"

"I can't stay long."

"Stay as short as you like."

⋅

He left the door to suite 5507 ajar for her and the room dark. Miles Davis and the steamy smell of soap and shampoo from his shower would greet her. Something like this was the routine between them.

"Bart, baby?"

He pulled her into the room and silently handed her a glass of Moët. He reached for the remote and upped the volume before kissing her, hard. He made it tough for her to breathe. She didn't resist. He pulled the band off her hair and buried his face in her neck, moving his lips along the nape. As her breathing deepened, he pivoted her to face away from him. He tossed off the hotel robe, grabbed her tight knee-length skirt and hiked it up to her hips.

She was wearing the seamed thigh-high stockings he loved. When he couldn't remove her panties, they tore easily.

Starting to speak and removing her blouse, he kissed her harder, restraining her hand and undoing her bra. Her clothes half off, he cupped her breasts. Harshly forcing her against the couch, he kept the kiss going, thrusting until they came simultaneously.

Gasping, she collapsed onto the couch and laughed. "Who spiked your Kool-Aid? And what's the second course?"

He couldn't help grinning. She was the ultimate sexpot, blonde and petite, with an intellect to match. He picked up her ruined clothes, including her torn panties and Hermès silk blouse now missing a button.

Pouring more champagne, he invited her to lie down with him for a few minutes before he had to be downstairs.

She didn't quite move. "Rough game?"

"No, I wanted to do that to you all day."

"Glad I was the one invited to your party," she giggled.

"Come lie down," he said, patting the bed as he drifted off to sleep. He was vaguely aware of the sound of the shower running, and then she got into bed and spooned up against him. Feeling her warmth and the wetness of her hair against his face, he began kissing her body. As he started to move on top she quickly turned to straddle him.

Neither said a word; it felt way too good for narration.

A short while later in the elevator, he amused himself by reminiscing about Amanda's flawless B-cup breasts, the erotic contour of her back and her firm alabaster thighs. He felt rejuvenated. It was a pure, physical sensation.

Eighteen

SATURDAY MORNING, Olivia got a text from Amanda asking if she wanted to meet at Neiman Marcus for some shopping. With only a brief hesitation, Olivia replied, "Yes." The idea of spending time with Amanda was intriguing to her because of her connection to Bart. Olivia knew it was insane to give in to this feeling, but that didn't quite stop her.

Neiman's on Saturday was its own kind of insanity, wall-to-wall people battling one another in an expensive shopping frenzy.

Olivia had dressed as she always did, in whatever her hand fell on first in the closet. She chuckled enviously to herself when she saw Amanda in form-fitting jeans, a tight white V-neck cashmere sweater and barely worn cowboy boots. Amanda pushed her way through the crowds, rolling her eyes.

"Las Vegas Neiman's has the highest sales per square foot in the country," she said.

Olivia wished, for a brief moment, that she had stayed in bed, but the next moment Amanda's sage professional shopper showed up, and they got started. After several hours in which the two women accumulated many clothes and added even more dollars to their charge cards, they headed for the store's Capital Grill, known for its 180-degree view of the strip. It had been fun trying on clothes and comparing looks with Amanda, even though she was so much thinner and tonier. They had lots of laughs, and the mood continued through lunch. Amanda chatted on, and Olivia joined in whenever it seemed necessary. She was used to this kind of surface interchange, and she had taught herself to do it well. While Amanda told stories of loves lost, Olivia gave out tidbits about her nightclub appearances as she worked her way through med school. She was never more envious than watching Amanda scarf down Wagyu beef carpaccio followed by the largest piece of cherry cheesecake she'd ever seen. How did she do it?

Amanda pushed the plate toward her. "Want any? You do need to eat."

If she only knew. Somewhere between last night's Pinot and sleep, she had inhaled two chocolate cupcakes, a pint of vanilla ice cream, Lucy's leftover pecan pie and a bag of potato chips.

Olivia seldom ate in front of people and hated herself for eating alone—more than drinking alone. She knew she had a warped view of her body, and that it warped her psyche, but she was good at keeping it hidden. She always thought that when she had a life that satisfied her and a successful relationship, these nasty "habits" would prove self-limiting. Or at least she hoped so.

"You okay?" Amanda asked, peering at her. "I can help. If you let me," placing her hand on Olivia's "Do you have more time today? Will you take me to see your brother's horses?"

"Sure," Olivia said, though something in her wasn't so sure. She couldn't quite dismiss the feeling of not wanting to let Amanda bubble into the private world Curtis had created for himself. Was it just Amanda? she asked herself. Would she feel that way about Bart coming to see the place? Maybe. And what did Amanda mean, that she could help her?

She couldn't figure out how to say no. That was what Amanda was so good at. Olivia made herself smile, picking up the check. "Might as well," she added, as if she meant to refer to her paying for lunch.

•

Walking into Curtis's place, Amanda exclaimed, "This is gorgeous. How long did Curtis live here?"

"A couple years. He designed and furnished everything himself. Hard to believe a boxer could do all this, huh?"

She watched Amanda perusing the photos and artwork, probably envisioning a TV segment.

The reporter turned to her. "I'm glad we hit it off. I don't have any female friends. If you need space, kick me out and I promise not to take offense."

Olivia pretended she hadn't heard her. She headed for the French doors off the living room. "Let's visit the horses," she said, throwing open the doors and breathing in the horse smell that greeted her.

Tyson followed them, thrilled to be one of the girls, wagging her tail with every step.

Standing there taking in the sight of nickering horses running in the pasture, Olivia immediately felt better.

"Sweetpea Won is a retired thoroughbred, Curtis's favorite," she said, pointing out the horse. "He earned a million and a half in his day." Curtis had sponsored horse rescues, Chui had told her. When they had called him about this horse, the poor animal was emaciated—which was what happened when horses couldn't run anymore or be used for breeding. Marco and Chui had transported him to Vegas and nursed him to health within six months.

Waving to the brothers, who were lunging horses on an exercise line in the middle of the dirt arena, she added, "Those young men protected Curtis like family."

Amanda suddenly turned to her. "I want you to know you're off-limits."

"Excuse me?"

"I'd never mention our conversations to anyone or infringe on our relationship or—"

Olivia was completely taken aback. Amanda had a fervor in her that hadn't showed itself before.

"I mean it," Amanda said.

"Okay," Olivia responded.

●

Later, as the two of them sat comfortably in the den sipping Glenfiddich, Olivia wondered if she dared confide in Amanda. Curtis's cryptic message that Cyn had given her was distracting her, as it had been ever since she first saw it.

"Do you have plans tonight with Bart?" she asked her.

"Are you kidding?" Amanda snickered. "Saturdays are the biggest poker games for newbies and out-of-towners."

Olivia excused herself and went out to get her purse. Sinking back down into the big easy chair whose twin Amanda occupied, she laid Cyn's envelope down on the coffee table.

"An emergency nurse gave me this yesterday. It's a small note that Curtis had tucked in his shoe during the fight. I know *how* Curtis died, but I don't know *why* he died. I've watched your news segments, and I believe you feel this, too. Am I right? Before he coded, Curtis told me something that made no sense —"

"You don't believe Curtis died because the fight was mishandled? You haven't relayed any of this to your mother or aunt?"

"I couldn't discuss this with them right now, but to not investigate further isn't fair to my brother's memory." She picked up the envelope, took out the piece of paper and handed it to Amanda.

"'For Livy. 10-25-68'? What does that mean? What happened on October 25, 1968?"

"I don't have a clue," sighed Olivia.

"Maybe it's not a date, maybe it's a combination, you know, for a lock box or something."

At that moment Lou aimlessly wandered into the room. Olivia jumped up and poured him a glass of Glenfiddich. She introduced Amanda and invited him to sit with them.

"Lou, do you recall Curtis slipping anything into his boxing shoe that night? Or, do you recognize these numbers?" She handed him the piece of paper.

Thrilled to receive an invite to drink with two lovely ladies, Lou settled comfortably on the sofa and put on his glasses to look at the paper. He shook his head and handed it back.

Olivia stared at it, as if looking hard enough would reveal its meaning. "Could there have been something Curtis kept hidden?"

Slamming the glass down, Lou snapped, "There was no one in better shape than your brother. He trained hard, never drank or used drugs. He was a purist."

Amanda interjected, "Let's get Bart's input. His game won't have started yet, and he always figures things out."

For a second Olivia wished everyone would go home, but she shrugged off the feeling and told Amanda to go ahead and call Bart. "He'd better come over, if he doesn't mind," she added. "He should look at the note himself rather than hear it read to him over the phone."

Amanda made a brief call just as Luisa came in with some quesadillas. Olivia substituted Lou's Scotch for ice tea after convincing herself to do the same.

Normally Olivia would have been frustrated having visitors. Throughout the six years in her townhome, she had hosted fewer guests than currently sat in this den. But tonight she found she was happy having everyone here. She desperately wanted to figure out what Curtis's note meant. And she found she was nervously delighted at the prospect of seeing Bart again.

Why was Bart coming over, why would he care? Was it because Amanda asked, or perhaps because he wanted to see her again, too? She remained keenly aware that Amanda had no intention of letting him out of her sight. From the brevity of the phone call, she guessed he had required no coaxing. And why would Amanda willingly put Bart in her path? Maybe she was really being a friend. Or maybe she wanted the story.

Luisa welcomed Bart into the foyer as Olivia came from the den smoothing her hair and tugging on her oversized sweater.

"Dr. Rossi, welcome." Seeing him eye her wool plaid socks, she shrugged. "As you can see we're a bit casual."

Bart scanned the 30-foot ceiling with disbelief and smiled approvingly at the paintings that somehow looked familiar. Approaching a greater than life-size overweight nude sculpture against the wall, he exclaimed, "That's a Botero."

She looked at the sculpture. "Yes," she said.

"Is this thing a reproduction?"

"A coffee expert *and* an art connoisseur?"

Amanda appeared at her elbow. "For good or for bad, Bart knows something about everything," she said. "Don't you, honey?" She kissed him and took his arm. "I haven't seen this jacket in years. You only dig it out for the rare congressional hearing."

Sneering back at her, he said, "I have a game, and besides, it's cold out." He unhooked her arm and spread his arms, looking around the space. "This place is wild. I had no idea this part of town even existed. I saw cows and a few bison next door."

"What can I get you to drink?" Olivia asked. "Luisa can also make you something to eat."

"My game isn't until eleven," he said, licking his lips. "I'll have what Mandy's having. Glenfiddich, right?"

"How did you—"

"Lips never lie." He winked at Amanda. "Of course, only if there's some left. I know how two ladies can, excuse the pun, 'soak up' an afternoon."

Amanda jokingly smacked him on his shoulder.

Olivia watched him stroll into the den. His eyes widened at the quintessential man-cave.

"By the way," Amanda said, right by his side, "you left this in the hotel." She handed him his watch.

Luisa asked him if he wanted to eat.

"*Muchas gracias. No me apetece comer ahora,*" he answered, as he buckled the watch onto his wrist above the one he was already wearing.

Olivia interjected. "You said you didn't understand Spanish," accusing him in a lighthearted way.

"Examining fighters, you have to know some. How else are you going to know if they're hurt? Every ring physician should speak it. Most don't even entertain the idea."

Olivia went to the cabinet and poured Bart a generous shot. "I doubt the numbers are for a lock," she said to Amanda, who had followed her. "Curtis didn't keep even a drawer locked in this place."

Amanda took Bart's drink and got a refill for herself. "I'll see what Bart thinks," she said soothingly.

The two women turned around to find Lou sitting, dreaming off in the distance somewhere, and no Bart in sight.

"Jesus Christ, Bart," Amanda yelled.

Smiling, beaming in fact, Bart came out of the kitchen with a bowl of peeled oranges and a white cotton napkin attached to his shirt collar, already spotted.

"Luisa is from Mexico City," he told them, putting the oranges down on the coffee table in the den and settling himself on the sofa. "She lost her husband and 12-year-old daughter in the 1985 earthquake. She met Curtis through Marco and Chui—cousins on their mother's side. She's in her late forties and misses your brother as if he was her son. Oh, and she's terrified of your mother."

"You forgot her social security number," Amanda grumbled. "I thought you weren't hungry."

Olivia thought he was endearing. She blurted out, "There are very few people careless enough *not* to be afraid of Sophie. I bet Rappaport quakes in his boots every time he runs into her."

Slouching on the sofa in front of the fire, Bart kicked off black suede loafers, revealing worn Argyle socks. He stretched backwards with an orange in his hand, then suddenly jumped forward as something snatched the fruit. "Whoa, what the fuck was that?"

"You need to be quicker around this house," Olivia laughed as Tyson trotted out of the room with the fruit.

"Okay, my cue to stop eating. On the other hand, I'll be happy to take another shot of Glenfiddich."

The laughter in the room seemed to wake Lou from his reverie. He got up, smiling shyly and excused himself to go and rest.

When he had gone, Bart asked if anyone had heard from the coroner about Marquessa. "It must have been a simple MI," he hazarded, more of a question than a statement.

Not wanting to betray any confidence Lou had shared with her, Olivia just said no, she hadn't heard from the coroner's office. Then she showed him Curtis's note.

He held it gingerly, as if it were evidence and he didn't want to interfere with it.

"Let me get this straight," he said handing the note back to her. He leaned back, hands folded behind his head and feet propped on the table. "Cyn found this paper in Curtis's shoe? You hadn't seen or spoken to your brother in five years. You weren't at the fight, yet he leaves you this cryptic message. But it's old, and the creases are worn. Chances are he wore this piece of paper to many a fight, just in case. But what?"

Olivia paced while downing her scotch in one swig.

He watched her take down the scotch, impressed. "The numbers aren't significant to you in any way?" he asked.

"There are other things that don't make sense." She searched his eyes. "I know the fight should have been stopped sooner, though that probably wouldn't have made a difference. The real egregious acts followed the stoppage. These doctors were incompetent, but I know there's more to the story."

Amanda plopped herself down next to Bart. "I can do a segment, show these people for what they are," she said, excited. "The media can make a difference."

"Bart, what's your opinion?" Olivia asked.

"I want to think this through. There've been more fighter deaths in Vegas than expected."

"We review what these deaths have in common," Amanda continued.

Olivia was looking straight at Bart. "Rossi," she said, to get his attention; it came out of her and it sounded right to her. "I went online. In the last few decades, only two heavyweights died from ring injuries—one had a stroke, and the other had a drug-related heart attack. It seems to be a popular opinion that ring deaths are from quickly dropping weight, and dehydration—like with jockeys. But heavyweights don't have to make weight. And the smaller fighters fight more often and absorb more head shots."

"We think that the ones who die come into the fight with a sparring injury," Bart replied.

"But they wear headgear in the gym."

"Headgear only protects against cuts. There hasn't been any research proving that headgear prevents concussive blows. That's why you also see fatalities in the amateurs. It's more likely that headgear gives fighters and trainers a false sense of security, so that in the gym they worry less about head shots."

Amanda exclaimed, "We need a plan of action."

"Texas Hold'em, ladies." Bart grinned, standing to leave. "Let me mull this over tonight."

To Olivia's relief, Amanda left with Bart. For a moment she fantasized about Bart coming back alone…She shook herself. Why was she flirting with someone else's man? Wantonly flirting. But there was something hugely compelling between her and Bart, she was sure of it, sure that it was mutual.

She went back into the den and poured herself what was left of the 'Fiddich to take to bed with her, but passing the hall mirror, she caught a glimpse of the puffy dark circles under her eyes. She left the glass on the hall table.

Calling softly to Tyson, she headed for bed. The Golden Retriever lay where she was, across the cold limestone doorway, waiting for Curtis. She had been a wonderful comfort that first afternoon when Olivia came back from the funeral. But with each day that Curtis didn't return, she became more distant and dispirited.

"I'm trying. Now it's your turn," she said leaving sufficient room for a dog nose to push open her bedroom door. It would have been nice to have some company.

Nineteen

THE FOLLOWING MORNING, Olivia stayed in bed, hung-over. She told herself it was expected after all she'd been through. Hey, she deserved a lie-in every now and then. Unfortunately, every now and then was becoming once too often. She remembered this syndrome.

Standing was worse than lying, especially under the bathroom skylight. Squinting in the mirror, she saw crow's feet and turned from her reflection. She put on sweatpants, a sweatshirt and sneakers. It was too bright to forgo her Ray-Bans.

She wished to smile at her four-legged visitor's calling card—a rubber replica of a chicken foot left next to her wool socks—but moving her facial muscles in any expression was excruciating.

In the kitchen, Luisa sang along with Shakira.

"*Buenos dias*, Luisa. *Gracias por lo de anoche.*"

"*No hay de que, señorita.*"

"Tyson?"

"*Afuera.*"

Tyson circled the pasture with a tennis ball while Marco hand-walked Sweetpea Won.

Heading outside gingerly to show the boys Curtis's note, Olivia walked right into her mother. She was on her way in trailed by Lucy, both carrying baskets of food.

"We're here to check on you, dear," her mother said, the sharp voice practically starting up sparks in Olivia's stressed head. "You don't look well," Sophie announced clutching the extra material in Olivia's sweatshirt and shaking her head in disgust. She peered at Olivia's face. "Look at your skin. Your hair color is awful. Let's schedule at my salon. They'll give you a fabulous facial and a make-up lesson. You could use a trim. Look at all these split ends."

Struggling out of her mother's death-grip, Olivia said with a smile, "Mom, why are you so mean?" She surprised herself, but her mother barely seemed to have heard.

"Now, Sophie," Lucy intervened. "Olivia looks wonderful. You know your mother. She would like to keep you under glass, like a pheasant."

"You know my mother, Aunt Lucy. She's a force of nature. There's no stopping her." Olivia stepped past the two sisters on her way to the pasture.

"Where are you going?" Sophie demanded as she marched up to Luisa with the baskets. "Please come back here, young lady. I need to talk to you."

Wishing she could just keep walking, Olivia turned back and stood in the doorway waiting.

"Come in here now," her mother said. "We need to talk." Luisa had taken the baskets and was setting out coffee for the two visitors. They sat down at the center island, both looking expectantly at Olivia. "Luisa, please give Olivia some coffee too," Sophie added, and like magic, another steaming mug appeared on the countertop.

Needing the caffeine, Olivia walked over and picked up the mug. She leaned back against the kitchen counter. "What's on your mind?" she said, trying not to seethe.

"Dear, I see no reason we need this big place, and who needs these horses?"

Olivia took a breath. We? She was not part of Sophie's life. "It might not have anything to do with you," she said. "By the way, Michael Brewster called. He's coming to town to read the will. Did he call you too?"

Sophie's rosy expression faded. "I had no idea he bothered you with such details. Let Lucy and me handle everything—"

"It doesn't work that way. Curtis wanted certain people to be present, and that's what's going to happen. When it comes time for your will, you can do things any way you wish." Olivia inhaled deeply, wishing the Dalai Lama would make a surprise visit.

Dramatically turning away, Sophie wiped her eyes and blew her nose.

Olivia knew the game. Next would be the sobbing. Curtis was Sophie's life. She never needed a husband—or anyone, as long as she had her son.

Olivia turned and opened the plantation shutters so the pastures, barn and guesthouse became visible. Then she calmly replied, "Mom, this is an exceptional place. Curtis couldn't have done this without the many gifts in judgment you gave him." She wasn't sure where that came from, but she found more in her, looking out at the pasture, and continued. "He knew you would follow his wishes. Let's hear the will first. Okay?"

Lucy slid a box of tissues over to Sophie and winked at Olivia.

Sophie blew hard. "What day?" she asked, dabbing at her eyes.

"Tuesday."

"Okay, I'll wait. Who knows how long ago your brother wrote this will."

Wait for what, she wanted to ask. "Mom, there's no point in speculation. We can discuss your ideas about the place afterwards."

Luisa brought in fresh *conchas*.

"*Tu es una artista. Muchas gracias,*" Lucy said, embracing Luisa.

"*Señoras, gracias,*" Luisa whispered before exiting to have a good cry.

With her fingers on Curtis's note in her pocket, Olivia said, "I found a piece of paper in one of Curtis's pockets with some numbers. Does 10-25-68 mean anything to you?"

"I have no idea," her mother said dismissively. "Now, on Tuesday, where's Michael coming—to my house?"

Olivia was surprised the note passed right over Sophie's head. "I'm assuming here," she said.

Her mother gave her one of her looks and—gathering her purse and keys from the countertop, where she had flung them when she entered—left without another word. Lucy hastily kissed Olivia and hurried after Sophie. "She's capable of leaving without me," she called over her shoulder with a laugh.

Olivia let out a sigh of relief.

"Coast clear?" grumbled Lou, sneaking his head inside the kitchen.

Olivia grinned. "Elvis has left the building."

"Livy, I'm gonna go to my apartment for my things."

"Marco will take you. Have you gotten any calls?"

"Stu Rappaport asked if I wanted to work for Ed."

"Aren't cutmen hired by the boxer or trainer, not the promoter?"

"True, plus I never got along with Ed."

"Did you accept the position?"

"I said I'd think about it. I'm not sure if I could work for those guys. They were good to Curtis. Vinnie didn't like them much. Ed did some crazy things getting his fighters rated, and who knows how he got all those dates on HBO."

"Wouldn't it be smart to stay independent?" she wondered aloud. "On the other hand, guaranteed work…"

Lou nodded. "I never did too well saving anything I made," he mumbled, sounding embarrassed. He put on his lucky fight hat and went out the back door. Olivia watched him head for the barn. He had an odd, slightly bow-legged strutting walk she found endearing.

*

Monday, Olivia spent the day at her office. She had no patients scheduled yet, but this was a quiet and neutral place for her and it calmed her to be here. In the humming atmosphere of central air and fluorescent lights, she laid Curtis's note in front of her on her desk. Think, think, think, she told herself. They couldn't be lottery numbers, because the piece of paper was too old—and anyway there weren't enough numbers for that. She couldn't think of anything she hadn't already come up with.

Almost 4:00 PM. She hadn't eaten anything other than a bagel. It was too early for a drink. She needed to keep busy. She dialed a familiar number.

"Hi stranger?"

"Red! Bet you're craving the snow and wind right about now," her former boss joked.

"I do miss it. How's Adele...and the department?"

"No one could replace you, though Goodson is trying. Is this a social call?"

More than anything, she wanted to hear a friendly voice. David was great at puzzles. They spent the next 15 minutes discussing the hospital, her office and Las Vegas.

"Bitch at me if I'm wrong," he said. "I hear something in your voice. Are those Nevadans not being nice to my girl?"

She knew he liked her way too much, but that was why their professional relationship was so strong—it was built on the tension between them, and on the trust going back years that neither had ever acted on that tension and taken advantage of the other.

"There's more to know out here."

"Can you be a bit more specific?'

"I've been reading statistics on boxing fatalities and the circumstances, like lower weight classes, dehydration and gym injuries. None of this fits Curtis."

"Everyone in the world knows that the NBC screwed up. I know you want justice. That Commission is filled with influential politicians. And from what I've been reading about Rappaport, he's renowned for working the NBC to get what he wants. Powerful people do disreputable things."

"No, I'm not considering litigation—at least not yet. David, I've got to go. Do me a favor?"

"Anything," he said, and she heard the basketball game he'd no doubt wagered too much on go mute.

"Think about risk factors for ring fatalities," she said. "More important, who would want a young athlete to die?"

"Red, it may be that only the sport itself is responsible. I know that isn't what you want to hear, except it may be the truth."

She ignored his speculation. "I'd appreciate you not mentioning my contacting you to anyone. I promise to touch base when I have more information."

When she ended the call, she would have bet he was saying to himself that some answers are better left undiscovered. Maybe that was true for some people, but not for her.

Twenty

OLIVIA ARRANGED FOR everyone mentioned in Curtis's will to be present, and all of them were there except for one unfamiliar person who, Brewster explained, seldom left Chicago.

"Where is everyone?" Sophie said, barging in 30 minutes early. Here to control events and move the furniture, Olivia thought. She asked her mother to answer the door.

"Michael Brewster is awfully late, isn't he?" Sophie said.

"He said eleven. You're awfully early. Have some tea. Where's Aunt Lucy?"

"She's visiting the horses. Why the extra chairs? Who else are we expecting?"

Lou shuffled into the room, rubbing his freshly-shaven face, proudly modeling a pressed Hawaiian shirt, new khaki Dockers slacks and white Nikes. Olivia grinned, impressed. He hesitantly extended his hand to greet Sophie, who immediately turned and beckoned Olivia to meet her in the hall. Lou tossed back a swig from the silver flask he kept in his pocket.

Acquiescing to her mother, Olivia mouthed to Lou, "Save me some" and rolled her eyes.

Lou gave a thumbs-up, opening the French doors for Marco, Chui and Lucy. Bathed and groomed for the occasion, Tyson sauntered in behind them.

By the time Olivia joined her mother in the hall, there was only time for a brief remark against "that man," as Sophie referred to Lou, and then the doorbell rang and she let Mirabelle in.

Sophie and Mirabelle wandered into Curtis's study, where everyone else was gathered. Luisa carried out trays of fresh fruit, *chilindrinas* and *bigotes* while Olivia made sure everyone had a place to sit.

Brewster, the last of the group, arrived precisely at eleven. Placing his briefcase on the floor, he embraced Olivia.

Why was he trying so hard, she wondered, hugging him back but feeling awkward about it? As soon as the embrace was over and she caught sight of his face, she realized his sentiment was genuine. He was stricken in the eyes, as if seeing her had been seeing Curtis's ghost. She watched him. He was a handsome man in his mid-sixties with a full head of pewter-colored hair, dark brown, piercing eyes and a chiseled face. He greeted each guest by their first name, offering condolences to each.

Before she could ask him what he would like to drink, Luisa presented him with coffee—two sugars and a dollop of half-and-half.

Olivia went over to Luisa. "Please, sit," she said, indicating a chair.

"*Perdón?*"

"Curtis asked you be here."

Luisa pulled out a hand-sewn handkerchief from her apron pocket and dabbed at her eyes. "Curtis gave me this *pañuelo,*" she said and, heaving a deep sigh, sat down.

Anxious for familiar faces, Tyson rubbed her fur all over the lawyer's brown pants and settled next to him as he sat down at the desk.

The lawyer reached down and gave Tyson a few pats. Then he sat up, cleared his throat and took a plain white envelope out of his briefcase.

Lucy was on the couch, holding Sophie's hand—her other hand clutching a moist Kleenex over her heart as she rocked slightly back and forth.

Clearing his throat, Brewster gently said, "I had two boys. One died last year in Afghanistan and the other died more recently, in a prize fight." Following a slow sip of coffee, he smiled at Olivia. "Everyone here knows me from my many visits," he continued. "I hope you and I can become friends. I loved and trusted Curtis."

Sophie stifled a sob, notifying all present of her devastation.

"I helped Curtis purchase this piece." The lawyer indicated the Botero sculpture. "Curtis was an unusually shrewd young man. I don't believe there's ever been a boxer as careful with his investments. Some might label art frivolous. He believed it was important to choose value with your heart." Gazing again at Olivia, he went on. "Before each purchase, he'd ask if I thought his sister would approve. It would make him very happy to know you're living in his home."

Curtis had set aside $200,000 each for Chui and Marco, $100,000 for Luisa, and $50,000 for Mirabelle—all to be monitored in a trust. The brothers were given the horses except Sweetpea Won, who was left to Olivia. Lou and Vincent were to receive modest homes in Las Vegas or Chicago, whichever they preferred. Vincent was to have money to open a boxing gym with all the trimmings, and Lou would have funds for a 30-foot retirement fishing boat. In the event of Lou or Vincent's death, the funds were to be distributed to Chicago Golden Gloves. Sophie was to retain her monthly stipend for home upkeep and reasonable shopping expenses. Lucy was left money to upgrade the family home in Madrid. Brewster and Olivia would remain the trustees of Curtis's estate, and in the event of Brewster's death, Olivia would assume control with Brewster's partner.

Everything else—Tyson, the house, cars, artwork, furnishings, real estate and stocks and bonds—went to Olivia.

Brewster read slowly and clearly, explaining the language and the clauses as he went along. Following the reading, he asked if there were any questions. There was absolute silence. Even Sophie said nothing. He stood up and replaced everything in his briefcase except a sealed business envelope with the name of his firm handwritten on the front. Olivia watched him come toward her with briefcase and envelope in hand.

Lucy stood up and pulled her sister to her feet. "Your mother and I are going home," she said. "Sophie needs to rest." She reached out and squeezed Olivia's cheek. "Are you okay?" she asked kindly.

"Yes," Olivia said, feeling anything but okay. "Please, take Mom."

As the two women made their way out of the house, the others followed suit, except for Brewster.

"I have a matter to discuss with you in private," he told her, nudging her with the envelope. "Can we go for a walk outside?"

The chilly Vegas winds felt more like Chicago. She bundled up in her pea-coat and gloves.

"Will you be warm enough?" she asked him. "I can loan you something of Curtis's."

"Only here a few months and already your blood has thinned? To me this is summer weather." He laughed, putting down the briefcase but keeping the envelope with him as he followed her out the kitchen door.

"I understand this wasn't easy for anyone, least of all you, Michael," she said, feeling tender toward this man who claimed Curtis as a son.

"Curtis and I had a unique relationship. I represented him since the Olympics. Actually, before—"

"I can't imagine it's common for a young man, even one with Curtis's success, to be so prepared. Was he always like that?"

"Back then, when he was training for the Olympics, he was the oldest 16-year-old I ever met. And by the way, he talked about your accomplishments all the time."

She looked away. "You must have known Curtis and I hadn't seen each other for some time?"

Brewster hesitated. "Yes, I knew. We have a need to be at peace before loved ones leave us. Life interferes with future goals."

She had no idea what he was talking about. She hadn't been at peace. Was he saying Curtis had that need? They walked along the gravel horse path surrounding the pasture.

"Matthew, my son, was career Air Force. He flew jets, something your brother envied. Curtis stayed with us for a while. I think you were finishing medical school at the time. He and Matthew became close. Laura, my wife, and I can't ever recover from his transport helicopter crash. After Matthew's death, I threw myself into my work. Laura's outlet became Curtis's career. His death was almost too much."

Olivia stopped to watch Jersey Joe gallop, and Brewster paused next to her.

"There's one person I didn't mention at the reading. Curtis left strict instructions that Bernard Champion continue to receive monthly checks in the amount of $2,500.00."

"Champion? Isn't that Mirabelle's last name?"

"Bernard was significant in Curtis's life. The money comes from a separate trust set up years ago. I just wanted to make you aware of this clause, as you will be reviewing the financial statements."

"Who are these people? Does my mother know?"

"I'm not in a position to answer questions."

"You can't answer because you don't know, or you've been asked not to discuss?"

Stammering, he said, "This is all I can disclose." He looked over at her. "Moving on. Four months ago, Curtis sent me this letter," he indicated the envelope, "and asked that it be included with his will. He said he'd be collecting a great deal of money for the Livingstone bout, so I didn't question his desire to secure future assets. And..."

"And what, Michael?" Olivia hesitantly asked.

"A fighter has to be prepared that something serious might happen. Sure, everyone—especially a young man like your brother—believes they're invincible. Curtis was different."

"You have other athlete clients?'

"Over the years, I've represented some Chicago Bears. Five years ago, Curtis became my only client. The longer I spent with him, the more I understood what a serious young man he was. He wanted to protect the people close to him."

Brewster took her arm, and they resumed walking as he told her about the first fight of Curtis's he had attended and how Laura kept a scrapbook of Curtis's newspaper clippings. The entire time he was talking, Olivia couldn't keep her eyes off the sealed envelope in his hand.

Stopping in front of the barn, he finally handed it to her.

"We should read this together," he said. "It may need clarification. And it does involve the estate. Shall we return to Curtis's study?"

•

Olivia was thinking about Curtis's cryptic note as she opened the envelope. She took out the papers and unfolded them, flattening the three-page document on Curtis's desk as Brewster closed the door of the study. Before her was a list of tasks, including looking after the horses, Chui, Marco and her mother. At first, she was angry that Curtis felt he had to mention such details. Then again, how could he not mention them, after their estrangement? The second and third pages were about boxing—things not typically part of a will.

She looked over at Brewster, who was sitting deep in one of the armchairs calmly waiting for her questions. Oh for one swallow of whiskey, she thought.

"Curtis wants me to set up a non-profit organization for boxers and work with Senator McAllen? The Texas senator? Why would Curtis take it upon himself to do this?"

"Boxing is state regulated. Each jurisdiction—that is, each state—has its own governor appointees who oversee the athletes and policies. People have been trying for years to push a national boxing commission through congress. Each time they've failed miserably. Even Senator McAllen."

She looked at the instructions again. Curtis had written that she needed to call the senator's office in Washington. He had to be kidding; no senator was going to talk to her. "Did Curtis know him?"

"I never got a chance to discuss any of this with him much. Right after the changes to his will, he went into training camp."

"No email? No telephone?" She knew she was being sharp with him but she felt cornered.

Brewster got up and went to the liquor cabinet. He poured two shots of whiskey, gave one to her and drank the other one down in one gulp. When she had done the same, he answered her question. "Championship-level boxers like Curtis may not fight more than a couple times a year. Eight weeks before a fight, he went into seclusion with Vincent—"

"Vincent!" she interrupted, suddenly remembering she still hadn't heard from the coroner. "Michael, can you wait and let me telephone the coroner's office?"

"I apologize about leaving today. Go right ahead. I can wait."

She made the call and was put on hold. "Want something to eat?" she asked while she waited. "I can ask Luisa to fix you something."

He nervously shook his head and momentarily stepped out of the room. Returning, he listened intently to Olivia's side of the phone conversation.

"Yes, Dr. Sorenson, I know it's late. Do you have results on Vincent Marquessa? An MI? I guess the toxicology screen will take a few weeks? Was there any indication of prior coronary insults? No, I promise to keep this confidential. I just don't want to be blindsided by any media inquiries. Yes, yes, doctor, thank you for taking the time. Please, if you come across anything else on the pathology or toxicology screen, will you let me know? Thank you."

Ending the call, she apologized to Brewster. "You knew Vincent, didn't you?"

"Yes. Very unexpected. He always ran with Curtis along the lakefront. Seemed in excellent shape. I'm convinced a piece of Vincent died the night Curtis fell."

"This doesn't tell us anything more, does it," she muttered, angry. She went over to the liquor cabinet and opened a can of diet Coke, though she would have loved to numb her racing mind with more alcohol. She felt she needed to keep hold of reality, even if only by her fingernails.

Pacing, waving the letter, she said, "Look, I'm not familiar with boxing, commissions, boxers, senators or any of this. I wouldn't know where to begin."

He took her hand and led her to the sofa. "Please sit down," he said emphatically. "I called my secretary to move my flight ahead while you were on the phone. Now let's discuss this as quietly as we can."

His voice was soothing. She knew she sounded hysterical. She could feel the edge of panic inside herself. She sat down, and he took a seat across from her.

Olivia asked herself why he would need to return home so quickly, as Curtis was his only client. Maybe it was as he said—his wife needed him. Hard to imagine the tragedy these two had had to live through in the last few years.

"I know this appears to be a highly unusual request," Brewster was saying. "I thought so at the time. Curtis probably believed it was his way to give back to a sport that gave him so much."

Committing seven figures to the effort and requesting that Olivia devote time to something that required government intervention didn't make sense. Was Curtis friends with the senator? She felt painfully wary of what Curtis seemed to be asking of her. She needed to think this through. Did Michael not have the answers, or was it that he wasn't going to provide them?

"My brain is fried. I can't think about this anymore tonight," she said, folding up the letter and getting up to retrieve the envelope. "I know you need to return to Chicago." She was thinking as she went along. "Why don't I call you after reaching McAllen? I'm guessing it could take a few days—if he returns my call at all. There's really nothing further you can offer on this, right?"

Gently touching her forearm, he sighed. "Please call with anything." He looked at her intently. "You know, when my son died, everyone said things would get easier. They didn't. Of course, it's worse for Laura. All I can suggest is to look at what you *do* have. You are where your brother wanted you to be. You can begin this new life—hopefully a life you want and will enjoy more than the one you left. Places and people can't fix us or our grief." He took her hand in both of his. "We go through this alone. What has helped me these last few weeks is to concentrate on the good Curtis and my son accomplished during their short lives. This letter may make the difference."

She kept her hand in his and walked with him out to the town car that had been waiting to take him to the airport. Before he got in, he embraced her, as he had when he arrived. "Something tells me you'll find what you're after."

Tearfully she murmured, "I hope so," and then, "Thank you, Michael."

•

Back inside she almost tripped over Tyson, who continued her front-door vigil, paying Olivia little attention.

"Want dinner?"

Raising her eyebrows, Tyson whimpered, transfixed on the door. Olivia went to the kitchen and put a generous helping of I-Vet dry food in her bowl. She stood in the kitchen doorway and waved the bowl, but Tyson remained motionless. She put the bowl down in its place by the pantry door and went back out to the dog. Squatting down, she petted the beautiful shiny head and smoothed down the velvety ears. "It's true, girl," she whispered through her tears, "there's no consolation."

She wiped her eyes, went back into the study and put the letter away in a drawer that locked. Pocketing the key, she headed for her room. What did Curtis mean, "'Call Senator McAllen's office, this will be the key'?" The key to what?

On her way to bed, she tapped on Lou's door. Answering from a sound sleep, he called for her to come on in.

"Sorry to wake you," she said.

"Everything okay?" He pulled himself to a sitting position and leaned back against the headboard. "Did you hear anything more about Vinnie?"

He looked five years older than the day before.

"Nope. All we know is that he died from a heart attack—nothing suspicious."

Squinting, "Why do you use that word?"

"I meant there wasn't anything sinister. Maybe he ignored the symptoms."

Lou sat in silence.

"Sorry to have woken you," she said. "I don't know why I knocked. Just... everything is so hard." She turned to leave.

"Livy?"

She turned back, expecting he might need comforting. Not that she had much to give. Instead, he pounded his fist on the bed so hard it shook the cherry-wood headboard.

"If you believe that shit, then you aren't your brother's sister," he shouted, at the same time muffling his voice. It sounded like he was suffocating. "I mean no disrespect. Vinnie saw his doc a few weeks ago. Sure, he was on medication. Who isn't at our age?"

Her eyes went to the small selection of pill bottles on the night table. "The last thing I want to do is upset you," she whispered. "Are you having any chest pain or shortness of breath?"

Standing up, pulling on his jeans, he huffed, "I need to walk. I do appreciate all you're doing, Livy."

Picking up a framed photo of Curtis with Vincent and Lou from the night table, she said, "Lou, wait."

"I don't have more to say," he angrily snapped, grabbing his jacket. Then, stopping short, he laid the jacket on the bed and sat down, shaking his head.

"I get it," she said, hesitantly putting a hand on his shoulder. "You think something untoward happened to Vincent. These are preliminary findings. Let's wait till the toxicology comes back."

He looked up at her balefully, and she felt the same way. "Meanwhile," she continued, "can I tell you about the letter Curtis left with Brewster for me?" Without waiting for a response, she sat down in the big armchair near the bed and started talking to him about the letter and Curtis's requests.

"Curtis never mentioned any of this crap," Lou said when she had finished. "I have nothing to go on, but suspicious sums it all up."

"Maybe neither of us is ready to let go, and we need someone or something to blame."

"I understand you feel guilty that you weren't close for some time. Your brother never held that against you."

Lou opened the drawer of the night table and took out his flask. He offered her a sip—which she gladly accepted. Half-smiling she said, "Glasses are a waste, aren't they?"

Taking a few more nips, Lou started telling her about growing up in the

Bronx, boxing as an amateur and a short-lived stint in the Navy during Korea. As the flask passed back and forth between him and her, he fondly discussed his marriage to Marilyn, her succumbing to ovarian cancer at 36 before having children and how Vincent and boxing rescued him.

Tipping over the drained vessel, Olivia faked a hiccup and said, "Guess we made good work of that whiskey. At least we don't have to drive." Searching every wrinkle on Lou's face, she took a chance and said, "I can see why you were indispensable to Curtis. You're helping me more than you know." She rose to go to bed.

"They were all I had," he said. "I'll put this to rest once we have answers. You still have questions too, right?" He grasped her arm, pulling her back. "I failed them," he cried out, again muffling his voice so no one else would hear. "I might even be responsible for—"

"This isn't getting us anywhere."

"Please sit down and let me talk," he begged. "I've done enough by my silence. No one ever starts out trying to do bad things. No one wants to cheat. Every kid Vinnie trained was important, but until Curtis, he handled mostly featherweights and lightweights."

She knew that heavyweights were the big-money fighters. What was he getting at?

"Everyone is taking something to make them stronger and give them greater endurance. Vinnie and Curt never believed in any of that shit. It's the truth."

She felt like shouting at him to shut up. She waited as he jumped up and started frantically rummaging through his suitcase.

"Was Curtis juicing on something—like an anabolic steroid?"

"He wasn't on that shit. At least not intentionally."

"What?"

"Listen, this is how it is. Everyone looks for something to get a kid through training. The smaller fighters coming up through the ranks might compete 10 times a year and take fights on short notice. They get injured—maybe a sore hand or shoulder, and they still need to prepare. There's pressure for them to fight more often because the money isn't there." He looked over at her, still half-bent over the suitcase. "If Vinnie caught one of his fighters taking drugs or supplements, he got rid of the guy and the drugs. Pushers are everywhere. They might come into a fighter's life as a conditioning guy. Vinnie ran a tight gym, but it was hard."

Lou gave up his search and sat back down on the bed.

"Now listen," he said. "A few years back, Vinnie almost lost the gym. He was bringing Curtis along slow, cherry-picking his fights. One day, a couple of his

Mexican kids came back from visiting their families with some vitamins and a protein shake."

Afraid of hearing any more, she quickly said, "Let's go over this tomorrow."

Lou shot up and threw his flask against the wall. He quickly apologized for his outburst, looking disgusted with himself. "Marilyn would have never forgiven my behavior. I'm sorry. But please, you have to hear this now. Tomorrow I might not be able to say it, like I wasn't able yesterday, or the day before or the day before that."

He went into the adjoining bathroom and threw water on his face. Coming out with a towel around his neck he mumbled, "I'm better now. Fear, and losing everything, makes people do things they wouldn't normally do."

"I'm not following."

"See, the Mexican kids started winning. We had three UBA champs. They filled Rappaport cards. They fought on HBO and Showtime. People touted Vinnie as one of the best trainers in the country. Nobody imagined the smaller fighters used drugs. I'm not saying it was bodybuilding shit, only that they were winning."

"Okay. Go on."

"We lost Miguel Noguiera. He was a terrific lightweight. Twenty-four years old." Taking a deep breath, he said, "No one escapes the risks. Sometimes it's like Russian roulette. Vinnie had never lost a fighter. Suddenly, we saw Vinnie boozing. We figured it was because he took Miguel's death so hard. Truthfully, I never thought much about it until later."

He took a photo out of his wallet and handed it to her, pointing out Noguiera. The boxer was standing with Vincent and an elderly heavyset man holding the UBA belt.

"Who's that guy?"

Annoyed he answered, "That's Raul Santiago, head of the United Boxing Association. The UBA is the largest sanctioning organization. This belt and the title meant the world to Noguiera. The fighters pay a sanctioning fee to compete for a title. Sometimes it's as much as three percent of his purse—the money he makes for the fight."

"These organizations are evil?"

"It's not that they're evil. They control the sport. If a promoter wants his boxer to fight for a title, he needs him rated by these organizations. At one time, the boxer had to be in the top 10, so the UBA increased the number of rated fighters to 20."

Beginning to follow Lou's flow, she guessed, "Boxers receive recognition for fighting tougher opponents?"

He laughed at her naiveté. "Things have never been like that. Promoters lobby sanctioning organizations to get their boxers rated. Even the networks feed into it. Ticket sales and TV viewership is higher with championship fights."

"So not always the best fights the best. But what does this have to do with Noguiera and drugs?"

"Although born in Chile, Santiago runs Mexican boxing. That includes the gyms. It's the gyms where many fighters start drugs."

"You believe Santiago handed out drugs?"

Lou nodded. "Noguiera went home to Mexico before his last fight. Vinnie went, too. I saw some of Noguiera's training on YouTube. He suddenly looked different."

"Bulked up?"

"He resembled a 135-pound Hulk Hogan."

"But aren't they drug tested?"

"Depends on where you compete. Sometimes the drugs are out of their system by the time a commission has them pee."

"How could Vincent, who you and Curtis loved and believed in, not have said anything to Noguiera?"

"You mean, how could *I* have not said anything," Lou growled. "I ask myself that every day. And I asked myself twice daily after Antonio Madrid died."

"Another of Vincent's fighters?"

"No, but he was from Tecate and so was Noguiera. The two sparred together. Madrid was a featherweight champion. He died a month after Noguiera. People said he used the same supplements as Noguiera. He died in Mexico City during a title defense. It wasn't a tough fight. Folks gossiped he was hurt in training.

"Although Madrid wasn't a UBA fighter, Santiago sent the family $20,000 for the funeral and money to support his wife and three children. You have to wonder if it was guilt. Or was Santiago trying to buy silence?"

"Hush money? Aren't the gyms monitored for injuries? And shouldn't drug tests to be universally implemented?"

"Madrid came to Vinnie after Noguiera died and told him he thought several fighters were taking dangerous supplements. Vinnie listened, but he didn't do anything."

"Was there something he could have done? It sounds like no one was listening."

Lou stood up abruptly. "I need some fresh air."

She grabbed his sleeve. "Goddamn it, if this relates to Curtis's death, you have to tell me."

"I wish I knew," he mumbled, head bowed.

"Whatever you say will stay between us. I give you my word." She put her arm across his shoulders and sat him down again. "We can't change the past. Didn't you just tell me that?" She sighed. "But we can try to make sure no one else gets hurt."

Looking at the photos, he told her, "Fighters were using this stuff. Noguiera was using it. Vincent knew, and..."

"Jesus Christ, Lou, are you saying Vincent gave this to Curtis after Noguiera died?"

"Vinnie didn't think it had anything to do with Noguiera's death, or he would have never let the stuff anywhere near another fighter."

"You're not answering," she insisted. "Did Curtis take this stuff?"

"No," he shouted. "Maybe. I don't know. But your brother never let anything go. He investigated on his own. He wanted answers about Noguiera's death—and Madrid's."

"What the hell do you mean *investigated*?"

Feebly shaking his head he murmured, "Please, no more. All I know is everyone close to me is gone."

She helped him lie down, wishing she could shake him but forcing herself to say goodnight quietly and soothingly. Once in her bed, she anxiously lay awake thinking about what he had said. Lots of athletes had been caught with performance-enhancing drugs. Then again, they weren't dead. Could this Santiago guy be involved? Was this part of a gym subculture? Did it relate to Curtis's last words?

Twenty-One

OLIVIA SNATCHED A scone from the kitchen and hurried to her car. It was her first day of patients in her new office. She threw her high-heeled Blahnik pumps and her purse over to the passenger side, slid in behind the wheel and then just sat there for a minute, thinking about what she had to do. Would contacting Senator McAllen ease her guilt? She had to do it. It was Curtis's wish. His death should count for something.

At work she was greeted happily by the two young women she had impulsively hired to look after her office. Seeing them this morning with their fresh, expectant faces, dressed in matching olive green scrubs, she thought they looked like puppy dogs—college-educated puppy dogs, granted, with husbands. Both had been thankful to be hired, given the slowing of the Las Vegas economy and Obamacare.

She had half an hour to make the call to the senator. Seated at her desk with a big mug of coffee from the office coffee machine, she looked over Curtis's letter one more time and dialed the Washington number. Fortunately it was three hours later on the east coast, well into office hours in D.C.

An efficient-sounding female voice with the hint of a Hispanic accent announced the senator's name. "How can I help you?"

"…uh, yes, my name is Olivia Norris. My brother Curtis Mont—"

"Dr. Norris?"

Anxiously clearing her throat, she answered, "Yes, I'm not exactly sure why I'm calling. My brother—"

"Dr. Norris, I'm Elena, the senator's assistant. The senator is a big boxing fan. Your brother visited a few times. The senator was horrified to hear about his passing."

Olivia tried to remember if she had heard from Senator McAllen after Curtis died. She was sure she would remember something from a senator.

"Excuse me," she said. "Curtis asked that I contact your office. He seemed interested in supporting a national boxing commission."

"Senator McAllen followed Curtis's career since the Olympics. He believes that fighters get a raw deal—I can vouch for that, too. He put together a proposal for a federal boxing commission. Curtis was helping him fine-tune it. Your brother's testimony, along with others', in front of the Senate Commerce Committee, helped the bill make it out of committee. Of course, it was voted down this last session. The Senator has no intention of giving up. It's too important."

Wary, Olivia asked, "Is it possible for me to talk to Senator McAllen?"

"He's in Qatar. I'll get him to call you when he gets back."

Olivia couldn't quite push through her reluctance to get involved in whatever all this would lead her into. "Are you a boxing fan?" she asked. "You said something about understanding their plight."

"Excuse me a moment," interrupted Elena. Olivia found herself listening to light classical music on hold, then Elena was back on the line. "Sorry about that. Yes, my brother Rodrigo was a champion." Elena's voice had turned dark. "He fought once on Showtime. Excuse me again, these phones." Again, a few measures of watered-down Mozart, then she was back, as if there had been no interruption. "We're from Tecate. Rodrigo lived and trained there until our parents moved to the States, once his career took off. I apologize for the phones. I need to take this. I'll be sure and have the senator call you next week."

Was there something strange about the call, Olivia wondered, sipping coffee and drawing arabesques on her yellow legal pad? Or was it just that it was so fragmented by the senator's incoming calls?

Then it was eight o'clock, and her receptionist called to let her know her first patient was in the examining room.

•

By 6:00 PM the office was quiet and the staff had gone home. As she was getting ready to leave for the day, she got a call from Amanda.

"Oh, I'm so glad I caught you," Amanda said a little breathlessly. "I'm going live in a few minutes and I need to get your okay on one thing."

"My okay?"

"Well, don't be mad at me, but I just thought I could say something about there being things we don't understand yet, just to get people questioning."

Olivia waited, wondering why this would require her okay.

"Olivia?"

"What? You don't need my okay for that."

"I'd like to have it, though."

"Fine," she said. "When are you on?"

"A few minutes." Amanda made a kissing sound, laughed and ended the call. Olivia turned on the TV in her office. After a few minutes, Amanda came on the screen standing outside the Mandalay Bay.

"Good evening," the reporter said in her chipper TV voice. "I'm standing outside the Mandalay Bay Hotel, where just a week ago Curtis Montana, a promising young fighter, was felled in the ring."

The Vegas wind played with Amanda's sparkly hair, pushing it away from her face and giving her an innocent look as she continued.

"Montana's untimely death has left many unanswered questions."

Olivia stood up and put on her coat. She was about to turn off the set and head out the door when she heard, "...including a cryptic note he left for his sister, a Chicago neurologist who has recently moved to Las Vegas."

"What!" Olivia screamed.

Amanda was wrapping it up. "We'll keep you updated as soon as we know more. There are growing demands for the Nevada Boxing Commission and even federal authorities to look further into the death of this gifted young man." Cut to an ad.

Enraged, Olivia turned off the TV and locked up the office. In the car, she calmed herself a little. How could she have let herself be had by Amanda? Why had she told her anything in the first place?

She grabbed her phone and started to text her "What happened to 'I'll never—'" But she saw how pathetic that was and deleted the text.

She sat there holding the phone, completely unable to know what to do next, when she felt the vibration of a text coming in and saw Amanda's name flash on the screen.

"Meet me at the CBS studio on Convention Center right away. I need your help."

"Are you kidding me?" Olivia railed.

Another text came in. "I forgot to say *please*."

Olivia had to laugh. This woman was irrepressible, and there was something perversely endearing in the way she charged into and through anything she set her mind on.

Against her better judgment, she headed for the studio, too curious to stay mad.

As she pulled into the lot, Amanda rushed out of the buildings, papers hanging from her Mark Cross briefcase, one arm struggling with her coat, the other hailing Olivia. She hustled over to the car, pulled open the door and jumped in. "Let's get out of this shithole before I say something I'll regret," she muttered.

A clean-cut, exuberant twentyish man ran after her, yelling, "Amanda, this is one story. Come back and let's talk. Corporate just wants you to concentrate on other things."

Amanda turned and lowered the window, seething. "That's bullshit, Ryan," she shouted. "I've paid my dues and turned down offers. Corporate expects me to do these asinine puff pieces while less talented journalists—"

She stopped abruptly as they pulled out of the lot, leaving Ryan way out of voice range. "You know I'm right," she said, as if to herself, "while less talented people take my stories. I'm not doing that anymore." She shot a glance at Olivia. "I took a chance and went on with that little tiny piece of information, built something around it and they slam me for it," she went on. Then pointing, "Turn here." She pulled out her phone and pressed a contact. "This is Amanda Weekly. Yes, I'll hold for Mr. Rosen."

On hold, Amanda put the call on mute and told her, "I'm calling the president at CNN. A month ago, he offered me a position. Me, idiot that I am, thought I was on my way to bigger and better things with CBS. Sorry you got caught in the crossfire." She waved toward a street coming up on the right. "Turn here. Duffy's is two blocks down. You'll absolutely love it. It's a real industry hangout, lots of reporters and TV folks."

"What, you got that segment on the air without authorization?" Olivia exclaimed. She wasn't sure if she was disgusted or awed. This woman could certainly be a liability, but with energy and guts like that, she might also be a huge help.

"Yes," Amanda said, "And I'd do it again."

Olivia had to laugh. "You sure you don't want to go back for more?" she said.

"I'm sure." Amanda pretended to pout. "They can think about what it will be like to not have me to kick around...Oh, hang on a second...Amanda Weekly for Mr. Rosen...I suddenly find I can leave my CBS position and Mr. Rosen mentioned...I know I was unable to accept the offer before..." Conjuring her passive-aggressive demeanor, "Excuse me, is Mr. Rosen there? Well, if you could give him the message?" She rattled off her phone number and ended the call.

In the sudden silence, Olivia took a quick look at her passenger. Amanda's eyes were welled with tears. This was not Olivia's forte, dealing with someone else in tears. And anyway, she reminded herself, Amanda was perfectly capable of taking care of herself. Olivia wondered why she had agreed to come. Then she thought about Amanda's hunger for a story. Why not use someone who would know how to investigate and how to follow leads? Whether or not she could trust her, Amanda was the most tenacious personality she had ever come in contact with.

Amanda took a deep breath and quickly dabbed at her eyes. Then, shaking herself as if she were shaking off what had just happened, she told Olivia where to pull in. "Valet will take the car. This isn't the best part of town." She started gathering her things to get out. "I'm so crazed I could scream," she laughed, examining her makeup in a pocket mirror. "Oops, guess I did some screaming back there. This isn't Ryan's fault. He does what he's told…I had to yell at someone."

Olivia got out of the car and handed the key to the valet. Amanda slung an arm across her shoulders. "I need a drink," she said. "I swear that once I get a drink—and something to eat—I'll be fine."

"You okay? You want to call Bart or anything?"

"Oh my God, he's so not good in a crisis. Besides, this isn't a *real* crisis. Its work theatrics." She guided Olivia inside Duffy's, where the strong odor of savory pub-grub hit their nostrils the minute the door swung open.

The eponymous owner, a rosy-cheeked Irish octogenarian, called out to Amanda. "Quit hanging around that gambling doctor, Mandy, and hook up with a real man," he shouted, and he ambled over and engulfed her in his arms. "And who's this lovely creature, new blood at the station?"

"Stop salivating, Duffy. Meet Dr. Olivia Norris. Don't frighten her. She's not used to Vegas hospitality. We need a booth in the back," she added, playfully slapping him.

The plum mahogany floors, tables and booths had seated all of Vegas royalty at one time or another. Regulars ranged from the Rat Pack to Bugsy Segal to Bill Clinton and his mother, who before she passed palled around with Elias Ghanem—physician to the powerful and famous, including Elvis. There was no Sin City place more exclusive yet more open to all comers. Over the last few years it had become more of a politician and newsman's hangout, the perfect setting to confirm a political story before going on air.

As Duffy was seating them, a bartender came over with the phone. Duffy listened, then pressed the mute button.

"Mandy honey, it's the station manager," he said, holding out the phone to her. "Go easy on these guys, though you do make them thirsty."

Amanda shook her head emphatically. She mouthed, "I'm not here."

He patted her cheek ever so gently. "I'll take care of it. Jimmy, bring these ladies two Mojitos. Or would you rather have something else?" he knowingly grinned.

Standing to gaze over at the on-tap beer section, Olivia asked, "How about a pitcher of Chimay Blue?"

"Mandy, you got a live one! My pleasure, lassie." Duffy gleefully yelled to the bartender, "We have a girl who knows beer." He put the phone to his ear and, with a finger to his lips and a wink at Amanda, pressed the mute button again and jovially told the station manager she wasn't there.

He returned with a pitcher and two glasses, overtly intrigued by his newest customer.

Olivia picked up the pitcher and, holding the glass at ever so slight an angle to limit the foam, gently poured the beer. She gave a glass to Amanda and offered the other to Duffy, who happily accepted while asking a waiter to produce another glass.

"You don't see Belgian Chimay Grande Reserve in Chicago," she said. "Too expensive to keep on tap."

Duffy lifted his glass to the two best-looking women in the establishment. Then the 5'8" Irish Burl Ives sprinted to greet a former Nevada governor arriving with a small entourage.

"Tell me what happened," Olivia said, as soon as they were alone." She still wasn't sure she wanted to talk about what Lou had told her, or about the Tecate connection. Hearing Amanda's story would give her time to think about it some more. "Start at the beginning."

"Wait a moment," Amanda said. "Chimay? You seemed like such a sweet naïve girl when we first met."

She had to laugh. She was a sweet naïve girl, but that wasn't always the way she acted. "I guess looks can be deceiving," she joked back, hoping her laugh didn't sound too hollow.

Over the next two hours, Amanda leisurely downed the Chimay while recanting professional war stories. "Paying dues for four years and putting on cutting-edge segments should have garnered a promotion, not a demotion," she finally said.

With her unintentional Veronica Lake hairstyle and Chanel red lipstick wavering off her lips, Amanda slouched on the booth bench, her shoeless feet propped across the way next to Olivia.

"Let's discuss you," she sighed, turning over the empty pitcher and flagging the bartender for another.

Olivia waved off the waiter. "I have to work in the morning, and so do you," she said gently.

"Screw that place. They can find me *here* if they want." She raised her voice so that all patrons knew there was a perturbed, tipsy blonde in the back.

Olivia summoned her solemn doctor voice to defuse Amanda's escalating annoyance. "So you pissed off someone important over a story that made people nervous," she said. "And they called you but you showed them, by not taking the call." She had the ability to do something like hypnotize hysterical or angry people. It almost didn't matter what she said, it was the tone of voice and the conviction she put into her words.

She motioned to the waiter and ordered two cups of chicory. They both needed to sober up, right away.

"Drink this," she said when the coffee came. "Slowly, it's probably hot."

Amanda did as she was told, still mumbling slightly. Two men materialized, heading toward the booth. A weathered Vegas gentleman in a navy pinstriped suit with a red tie and gold cufflinks extended his manicured hand.

"Ms. Weekly, we haven't seen each other in some time. You know Jerry Tyler, I think?"

Amanda sat up and shuffled her feet under the table, slipping them back into her pumps. "Governor Thompson, how are you? Commissioner Tyler and I are well acquainted." Olivia was impressed by the way Amanda pushed a TV smile onto her face and disguised the slightest slur in her speech.

Barry Thompson, now in his early seventies with a trim athletic frame, was revered by both parties. Nevada had been plagued with good-ole-boy Republicans the last few years. However, when it came to hot-button issues, the local news organizations interviewed Governor Thompson despite his being a Democrat.

Tyler never trailed far behind anyone of influence.

"Amanda and I are close," Tyler said facetiously. "She recently interviewed me on NBC issues. Are you working on any more boxing stories, my dear? Did I mention I'm great friends with Ralph Sorenson at CBS and Rosen at CNN?"

Olivia was ready to intervene, but Amanda let the remark pass, seeming not to have heard it.

The men offered condolences to Olivia regarding the loss of her brother and excused themselves, and Amanda motioned to the bartender that the coffee was not cutting it and to expedite a brandy chaser. Olivia soothingly touched her arm, nixing more alcohol.

She waited until the two men were safely out of earshot, then leaned toward Amanda and whispered, "I guess we have our answer."

Gulping her coffee, Amanda muttered, "Huh?"

"Listen, I still believe that Kennedy was shot by more than one gunman and that Benghazi was a cover-up. Isn't Tyler an NBC commissioner? Why would he conveniently throw out he knew the president of CBS and CNN? Haven't you been working on stories about the boxing Commission—stories besides Curtis's? And haven't you made a mockery of Tyler?"

Amanda sat up, pulled her hair into a neat ponytail and chimed, "Let's go."

This was one time Olivia was thrilled to see the valet. Amanda wasn't "fall-down-drunk," although walking a straight line was out of the question. Olivia plopped her into the passenger seat, secured her seatbelt and, getting in behind the wheel, asked her where she lived.

"I hate leaving my car in the station's parking lot," Amanda muttered.

"Like anyone in their right mind would let you behind the wheel of anything," Olivia laughed. Not that she was stone cold sober either, but she had drunk one to every three glasses of Amanda's. "We need to get you home. Maybe we call Bart?" Why did she have to keep saying that, she admonished herself.

Exhaling an inebriated giggle, Amanda replied, "Ha! He has no patience for me drunk unless scantily clothed in *his* bed."

"Got the visual." Olivia smiled.

"Besides, you're 100 percent right. Guys like Tyler do things like this all the time. Except..."

"Except what?"

"They're NOT doing this to me!"

Turnberry Place, where Amanda lived, was known for its luxury high-rise condominium towers with resort amenities. Amanda's place was one of the smaller villas—1,800 square feet, a corner unit on a high floor with a glass wrap-around balcony.

Olivia expected furnishings like the faux Louis XIV decor in the building entry, but Amanda had opted for utilitarian cement walls, granite flooring and gray, Scandinavian-inspired Roche Bobois furnishings. Brightly colored modern paintings livened three of the walls in the main room, and the fourth wall was taken up with eight plasma TVs perpetually set on different networks—mostly news. The spotless Gaggenau kitchen faced an outlandish view of the Strip.

Amanda dropped her things on the sofa and, opening one of the white-fronted cabinets in the kitchen, revealed a refrigerator stocked mostly with sodas and doggie bags from various Vegas restaurants. "I know it looks like no one lives here," she said, shrugging. "I'm not here that much, and Bart hates the place. Unfortunately, I still owe a fortune on it."

"It's gorgeous and suits you perfectly," Olivia told her, meaning it.

Kicking off her shoes and accidently hitting the wall, Amanda chuckled.

"Oops, guess I don't know my own strength. Let's make coffee with Bart's Christmas gift." She put a Roma capsule in the Nespresso maker. "Bart thinks I need more caffeine."

Olivia checked in with Marco. Lou and Tyson were tucked in for the night. She called the office answering service—nothing.

Taking the mug of coffee from Amanda, she had a thought. "Before we got out of the car, you said, 'They aren't doing this to me.' I thought you meant, just let them try, but now I wonder. What did you mean?"

"Long story. It's time to talk about you. I know last week was tough. Want something to eat?" Nervously looking around the kitchen, she cleared her throat. "How about something sweet? Wait, I have just the thing." Opening yet another of the sleek white cabinets, she reached into a freezer stocked with Häagen-Dazs. She tossed Olivia unopened containers of chocolate cookie dough, dulce de leche and chocolate peanut butter.

"These are my faves," Olivia said, laughing at the bizarreness of Amanda's move. Why wasn't she answering the question? What was she hiding?

"Guess we have more than one thing in common," Amanda grinned.

Olivia had been around the block one too many times to bite at that comment. She knew women and jealousy. She chose the dulce de leche. "Let's have a spoon," she demanded. She wriggled onto one of the stools at the counter pass-through and pried open the container. Regardless of Amanda's coyness, Olivia still believed she would be the one to talk to about Curtis and what she had learned so far. Amanda would go after a story no matter who or what tried to get in her way. Would she betray her? Would she have any reason to betray her? Well, yes, if she was involved with something or someone who had something to lose. Or, if Bart defected...

But enough—she needed help, and Amanda was the one who could give it to her. She parked the spoon into the ice cream and went over to her purse, where she had thrown it along with Amanda's things. She took out Curtis's letter and handed it to Amanda.

"What's this?"

"The lawyer gave it to me after the reading of the will yesterday."

Amanda took the letter out of the envelope and carefully unfolded it, flattening it on the countertop. Olivia watched her read the letter with rapt attention, her spoon poised and forgotten until a drop of ice cream fell onto the paper. Quickly she wiped it away and put the spoon into the ice cream container, barely noticing what she was doing as she read through to the end of the last page.

She looked across at Olivia. "Your brother was some guy, huh? Did you call McAllen, yet?"

"He's out of the country. His assistant said Curtis was helping McAllen with a federal boxing bill. I also had a long talk with Lou."

She related Lou's story. By the questions Amanda asked, Olivia could practically see her journalist's brain putting things together, connecting facts and ideas.

"It's a lot to digest," Amanda said, then laughed, noticing three empty ice cream containers on the counter between them.

Laughing with her, Olivia rose to leave. "I'm exhausted, I really have to go home," she said. "Can we work together on this? Will you help me?"

"Stay a bit longer."

Olivia hated intrigue and never liked to be up late unless she was alone—which meant drinking or gorging on sweets. Amanda was insistent. Not understanding why, Olivia reluctantly agreed and followed her onto the heated balcony.

Even on a Wednesday, the scintillating Strip lights covered the tourist-filled urban landscape. The Bellagio's fountains danced to a Strauss waltz while the Treasure Island pirate ship sank for the millionth time amidst pseudo-cannon fire.

The two sat in silence for a few minutes, side by side, looking. When Amanda spoke, the sound startled Olivia.

"I've had misgivings about the handling of your brother's fight from the start. But it's more than that. What if what happened ringside is a red herring?"

"Please, can we do this another time?" Olivia begged, feeling as if she was going to scream if she had to keep facing it right now.

Amanda reached over and stroked her face. Olivia kept herself from pulling away. She didn't want to appear frail in front of this woman, who had probably never felt frail in her life.

Withdrawing her hand, Amanda resettled herself in her chair. "What if we're looking in the wrong direction?" she asked. "Last night I charted serious boxing injuries over the last six years. Okay, I have insomnia, now you know." She got up and went inside the apartment, returning a minute later with her computer.

Olivia dragged her chaise close, and the two women looked at the screen together.

"At the top we have Curtis's death—the Saturday before Thanksgiving. In this column are all the fighters we know of who have died from boxing-related injuries since 2006—in a fight or during training. There are others. This will do for now."

At the top of the list was Omar Sharp, the heavyweight who had been knocked out at the MGM Grand Garden a few months ago. Olivia knew about him because the newspapers had been full of columns about Curtis's injuries coming so soon after Sharp's death. Then there was Miguel Noguiera and his friend Antonio Madrid.

"Can you think of anyone else?" Amanda asked her.

Olivia rubbed her eyes. "I don't know if Elena's brother Rodrigo sustained any injuries, but she talked about him in the past tense. And her family is from Tecate."

"Do we know his last name?"

"Nope. Though we could look up Elena's name—though it could be her married name."

"It's okay, I'll find it. In the meantime we'll put a question mark by Rodrigo. For the others, I've put in weight class, toughness of the fight, age, ring age, location of the fight, trainer, promoter and number of scheduled rounds. There're other factors, although I think they all died from brain injuries. Anyway, easy enough to get all that information and plug it in here."

Olivia asked her what ring age was. "And why does it matter how many rounds the fight was scheduled for?" she said. "I heard that most ring deaths occur in the later rounds. How am I ever going to learn enough to do whatever it is Curtis is asking me to do?"

"Ring age refers to what kind of career the fighter had—like how many losses and times he was knocked out. Fighters that have been knocked out or stopped from head shots age more quickly. It's more significant than their chronological age."

Olivia suddenly remembered something else she had read at the time Curtis was injured. "Wasn't there another Nevada death a couple of years ago? People blamed that Dr. Stewart, the doctor who worked Curtis's fight. The fighter's name was something like Pulaski."

Amanda Googled the name but at the same time exclaimed, "Yes, Pulaski. I covered that story. He was a Polish heavyweight with psychiatric and drug issues. The bout went 12 rounds. He checked out okay afterwards, but he was found two days later, collapsed in the shower. On autopsy, there was one small new hemorrhage, plus other areas demonstrating old trauma. He sure looks juiced in these pictures." He also had tons of acne on his back.

The two women sat staring at the names and data on Amanda's spreadsheet, trying to read something they hadn't thought of yet. The three heavyweights, including Curtis, had all fought and died in Las Vegas. Madrid and Pulaski's promoter was Joey Davalo. Noguiera's was Rappaport. Noguiera and Madrid's deaths were more typical—lighter-weighted boxers who absorbed a ton of blows and lost considerable weight before their bouts.

"I bet weight loss is frequently blamed," Olivia said.

"They have a day to rehydrate."

"Despite rehydrating, it's still a stress on their system. People argue the brain shrinks with dehydration. Then the subdural vessels, a tiny web of veins connecting the brain to its outer covering—the dura—undergo more tension. They tear and bleed when the skull is hit. Actually, that's what's commonly thought, but research demonstrates the brain is the last structure to experience dehydration. Instead, dehydration slows a fighter's reflexes. They take more shots that contribute to brain injury."

Amanda took it all in, making notes as she listened. "We know from Lou that the Mexican kids may have been given performance-enhancing drugs," she said, trying to put the pieces together and typing as she spoke. "Vincent knew that Curtis might have taken them or was investigating the issue. Then we have the bungling Nevada commission."

Olivia chuckled bitterly. "No one wishes to blame the NBC more than I do, but I know that once a brain suffers an acute bleed, there's little that can be done to intervene. The expanding blood puts pressure on the brain, triggering rapid cell death. It's virtually impossible to save anyone with an injury like that, irrespective of how quickly you transport the person to a trauma center and relieve the intracranial pressure."

"Hah," Amanda said, grinning, "you know your stuff. We'll make a great team. Uh, I know this is callous, and please forgive me for even asking..."

"Spit it out."

"You've never watched a tape of the fight, right?" She spoke quickly, as if she wished she had kept her mouth shut. "No one would expect you to *ever* see it."

Quietly shaking her head no, she timidly answered, "I despise the barbarism."

"Ah, but there's another way to look at this. We can assume that these boxers died because they were boxers. Or, we can concentrate on incompetence by the NBC. It happens. Then again, I lean towards suspicious circumstances."

"Suspicious? I told Lou there was nothing suspicious about Vincent's death, and he was enraged."

"That's right, we forgot about Marquessa," Amanda yelled. "Can we be certain Vincent's death wasn't a suicide or—"

"Amanda, you've definitely watched too many crime thrillers."

"No, no, didn't you just tell me Lou hit the ceiling when you mentioned the word suspicious? Marquessa was heartbroken over your brother's death. What if he was caught up in some bad stuff in Mexico? Or Curtis's death was the last straw? We have to look into Marquessa." She put his name in a separate column and noted that he had trained Noguiera as well as Curtis.

"And Madrid confided in him, and he did nothing. Guilt can be a powerful motivator."

"Or?"

"Maybe something else caused their deaths," Amanda said. She looked at her, her face half-lit by the computer screen. "Or, let's go one step further," she said cautiously, whispering as if someone might overhear her. "What if it wasn't something else, but some*one* else."

Olivia rolled her eyes. "Really, Amanda!"

"All I'm asking is that you consider it."

"We can't prove anything."

"Not yet." She closed the computer and got up to admire the fountains. Olivia, leaning back in her chaise, watched her brain churn.

"I have an idea," Amanda said excitedly, turning to face her.

"Something tells me I am not going to like this. Am I?"

"Well, it depends. It could be fun."

Olivia shook her head, annoyed. "Fun? Really? It's almost 2:00 AM. Fun right now could only involve a warm bed."

Amanda looked at her watch. "Okay, you're right," she said. "Meet Bart and me tomorrow morning at the Coffee Joint—on Sahara near Valley View. I promise to have this worked out by then."

Twenty-Two

O NE OF TWO Coffee Joint patrons at that hour, Bart finished reading *Barron's* and added raisins to his oatmeal before finishing his second double espresso.

"Catching up on some light reading?" Olivia teased, standing across the table and thumbing through the scattered pages.

Bart took his feet off the chair and pushed it out for her to sit. "Waiting for Amanda, who's never once been punctual. Want to join us?"

Still standing, she looked at the empty chair. "I guess your girlfriend forgot to mention one *tiny* detail." She sat down, averting her eyes from Bart's boyish grin. To her, few things looked sexier on a man than a snugly fitted starched white shirt. His folded tie lay close to his empty cup.

Olivia seldom primped, but today, against her better judgment, she had spent time styling her hair and carefully applying eye shadow and mascara that made her eyes pop. She didn't think Bart had ever seen her in a skirt. This black one had a tiny slit showing a hint of leg, culminating in knee-high black leather three-inch heel boots.

He smiled, deliberately ignoring her legs. "All Mandy said was to meet at the Joint. She never said—"

"Forget it," she said. "I suppose she told you she was demoted."

He nodded in a way that didn't allow her to tell if he knew about the demotion or not. She brought up Curtis's will, Lou's story of intrigue and Amanda's late-night musings. All the while Bart was equally glad he had a reason to stare at her. He ordered her a cappuccino with no whipped cream.

"Armani?"

"Excuse me?"

"Your suit. It is Armani, isn't it?" He knew the cut of the jacket.

"Amanda was right," she answered trying not to appear self-conscious. "You know everything."

He wrinkled his brow, as if he knew it made him look endearing. "What else did Christiane Amanpour-in-training say?"

"Don't get nervous. She said you knew a little, or a lot, about everything. And here you are commenting on Italian couture."

Nodding his head, "I'm right, huh?"

"What else do you know about women's designer wear...or women in general?"

If he thought she was flirting, she was. She felt a racing in her blood in his presence.

Coming behind Olivia, hugging her man, Amanda exclaimed, "Have you filled him in? I'm so sorry I'm late. I—"

"Mandy, you're always late," Bart grunted, moving the papers to the empty chair and motioning the waitress to bring a green tea and a sweet roll—hot icing on the side. "Yes, she has filled me in."

Amanda scowled. "Did someone get up on the wrong side of the bed?" Not waiting for a response, she handed him her notes. She had also printed out the spreadsheet.

"The one thing we failed to mention last night were the numbers in Curtis's shoe."

Olivia shook her head. "I've wracked my brain over that. I keep coming up empty."

Bart looked up from the sheaf of papers Amanda had handed him. "I get it. You're drooling over an investigation. For years, I've tried to find common denominators in boxing deaths," he muttered.

"Honey, you're not hearing me. This is more than boxing deaths. There's something else that results in dead fighters—deliberately or indirectly."

"Mandy, I can't start digging into the Commission office. Yes, these people have competency issues."

"This may exceed the NBC and their bozo doctors. We need a mole."

"I don't have time to—"

"Jesus, Bart, not you. Olivia."

"Mandy, that's insane. It'll never work."

"The NBC will accept her." She touched Olivia's arm. "I know this is rough to hear. They're worried about their reputation. Your brother's death destroyed them more than the others. Plus, Gabe is under the gun to demonstrate they've cleaned up their act."

Bart looked down at the table, shaking his head in disgust.

"You're just pissed because this wasn't your idea," Amanda said.

"I'm not letting them off the hook. Bringing in Olivia would most assuredly do that."

"Then let's nail their asses to the wall. We're in agreement they're hiding something. They won't buy you investigating. Olivia as a ring physician would solve all their problems. It would prove she wouldn't bring a suit. And, even better, it would absolve them from press accusations. Can't you see the story? 'Sister of deceased contender joins Commission.' How could they ask for better press?"

"But I know nothing about it," Olivia finally interrupted. "I don't have even a lick of experience."

"Bart can teach you everything you need to know." She turned back to Bart, her eyes vibrating with excitement. "You were the best ring doc they ever had. I bet if you had instructed the others…"

"It's a crazy idea," Olivia said, but she was beginning to catch some of Amanda's excitement.

"Look," Amanda said, "we have no clue what went wrong that night or before. But one thing seems certain: your brother didn't die just because of an incompetent Commission doctor. If someone as conscientious as you is taking care of these kids, and if you can find out whatever else is going on, other fighters might be saved."

Olivia silently stared at her cold cappuccino. "I'm not convinced I can stomach the violence," she said.

Amanda reached across the table and put her hand on Olivia's forearm. "There may be no other way to find out what happened to Curtis."

Tapping his foot, Bart angrily interjected, "It takes years to become a good ring doctor—and that's only if you have innate judgment and understanding." He glowered at Amanda, then switched his stare to Olivia. "It's easy to hate boxing, and impossible not to love the fighters." He held Olivia's gaze for what seemed like a full minute, then he got up and left the restaurant.

"He left?" Olivia growled. "We're in the middle of a discussion and he just walks out? What a jerk."

"He'll be back. See, he left his phone. He never intentionally goes more than a block without it. He's thinking. That's his M.O. He'll come to the right conclusion. I think this could be cathartic for him—for you, too. Bart gave everything to boxing. Most of the medical regulations in place, like cutting the championship fights down from fifteen to 12 rounds, are his."

The two of them started talking about how it would be done, how they could make it happen, who might be helpful, what questions they wanted answers to. They let their calls go to voicemail—including the ones for Amanda from the station.

"Screw them," she laughed, toasting her cup against Olivia's. "I have nothing to say. Plus, I have a couple of stories in the can they have yet to use."

Fifteen minutes later, Bart somberly returned and laid down a small piece of torn notebook paper.

"Okay, you guys want to play spy? It has to be done right. That means it'll be my way or not at all. I'm not eating the blame if this plan goes to hell."

"Whatever you say, I swear," Amanda said, saluting.

"I want your word."

He had traveled this road with Amanda before. He had worked with her on a couple of exposés on sports books and an illegal poker ring. The latter turned out well, although for a long time people mistrusted him as a whistle-blower. Once the Department of Justice released the case testimony, though, he became revered, and Amanda found herself one step closer to network news.

"I'll pave the way with Gabe," he said, looking at Olivia hard. "Mandy is correct that the NBC will drool. I need assurance you're ready. There's no turning back. It'd embarrass us all if you quit before you even began. We'll come up with some story why you want to be a ring physician—something credible."

He had done the thinking and come down on their side. Olivia felt a thrill listening to him as he drilled into her with his eyes. No flirting now. He was all business. She would have to prove her mettle.

"You're going to work hard," he said. "There's no clinical course for this. You'll learn by watching, spending time at fights and weigh-ins, trailing ring docs, and by becoming a student of the sport. I'll forward you a list of websites to review daily. Most important, watch fights. They can be televised or online. I'll sit with you and explain your duties."

Olivia looked nervously at Amanda. All she saw was the intense concentration she had felt from her the night before. No inkling of personal feelings among any two of them was evident.

"There are those who'll try to show you the ropes," Bart continued. "Listen to no one. The last thing ring doctors want to see is a good-looking broad stealing fight assignments. They'll want you to fail."

He pushed the piece of notebook paper across the table to Olivia. It was a checklist. She copied it onto her phone, and Amanda did the same.

"Ladies, I have a meeting with Gabe."

"Already?" Olivia exclaimed. Turning to Amanda, she said, "How can we not admire this man."

"I was heading to the Commission office anyway. If I'm going to do this, we do it now. That means you have no time to waste," he said pointing at Olivia.

Sensing Olivia's mind spinning at warp speed, he gathered up the newspaper, buttoned his jacket, and put his phone in his pocket. Then he leaned over Olivia's shoulder.

"I'm getting something out of this, too. Boxing is a cesspool of wrongdoing. We may have to face that it can't be fixed." Moving between the two women, he put a hand on each of their chairs and whispered, "Ladies, sadly it may turn out that we prove the corruption but can't get anyone to do anything about it."

Olivia turned and confronted him. "If Curtis died from boxing, I'll accept it. But if his death was no accident—if the deaths of all these fighters were from negligence or worse, then whatever we uncover is going to have to be stopped."

She hated displaying emotion, especially to these two. She took a breath and composed herself. Then she scheduled her first ring physician lesson after work with Bart.

Amanda recognized the chemistry between Bart and Olivia. She would see about that. But it wasn't just about Bart this time. Yes he meant more to her than any other man ever had. But she knew a good story. This was a *great* one.

Returning to the station, she dusted off her parking nameplate. She could lie low and be a good little girl. That's how she had achieved goals before. And there was more at stake this time.

No doubt Tyler had cut her off at the knees to keep her from the truth. This would be more than payback. She wasn't about to let it go. She would try to capture the story and bring down the man.

Twenty-Three

OTHER THAN THE Gaming Commission, the Nevada Boxing Commission generated more tax income than any other state agency. Their seventh-floor, 1,500 square-foot space had a million-dollar view of downtown from its corner windows. Inside, though, the tattered Naugahyde furniture and chipped, cream-colored walls resembled every other government office.

Every boxing star from Muhammad Ali to Mike Tyson had walked on the irrevocably scuffed linoleum floors. Posters of Julio Cesar Chavez versus Oscar De La Hoya, Sugar Ray Leonard versus Marvelous Marvin Hagler, and Manny Pacquiao versus Juan Manuel Marquez lined the walls.

For Bart, this place was familiar territory, and he greeted people as he made his way toward Gabe's office.

"Carmen, you're looking formidable," he said, stopping at Gabe's assistant's desk.

She shot him a look, but she was chuckling as she turned to grab the phone.

Carmen was one of three Commission assistants. It was her job to field calls from promoters, managers and press; maintain the scoring during fights; schedule referees, doctors and judges for fights; and handle medical documents for fighters seeking licensure.

On the latter side of 30 with a hardened appearance from 13 years as a government employee, Carmen still wore skirts a bit too short and blouses too fitted for her robust frame. Bart knew her well enough to know that "formidable" was just about the nicest thing he could say to her. He never missed a chance to joust with her, lavishing on her a kind of attention she seemed ready to respond to. He always enjoyed his encounters with her. They livened up these drab offices for him.

Officials knew to stay on Carmen's good side or they'd be slighted on fight assignments, and Bart was no exception. She thrived on power, and if she overestimated her position, it was potentially to Bart's advantage, as she knew he had a personal appreciation. Gabe, too busy to oversee a day-to-day office and in need of an effective buffer between herself and her calls, paid no attention to the fact that Carmen terrorized others.

Finishing her phone business, she went to Gabe's doorway.

"Bart Rossi is here," she said, then turned to Bart. "You free to work Rappaport's main event this Saturday?"

He couldn't refuse. Olivia needed all the counsel she could get. It would be an opportunity to introduce her to the press and the promotional end of things. They had to work fast.

"Sure, count me in," he said. "Can I have a credential for the fight? I'd like to bring someone."

"Hmm, new girlfriend on the horizon, or just the old one that everyone wants to eviscerate?"

"Funny, Carmen. No, Amanda has a press credential. I need one for a friend. Someone who might make a good ring physician."

"I have next week's agenda," Gabe announced as she waved him into her office. "We're forming an independent committee to review safety regulations. That should get the press off my ass." She stood up and went to the doorway. Leaning out, she advised Carmen, "Unless it's a commissioner, don't interrupt."

Bart watched Gabe move, thinking how professionally polished she was. She had long ago figured out how to show just enough vulgarity to fit into this world but not enough to make herself look anything but smooth and handsome.

She offered him coffee, and he declined. Closing the door, she went back around her desk and sat down. He watched her tuck in her loose white blouse, and he didn't miss the glance she cast at her daughter's college photo. "Who's this candidate?" she asked. "We can't bring in just anyone. We've been ridden hard by the press."

He shook his head. "It's not like they haven't had sufficient fodder."

"To expedite this discussion, let's admit you're correct. I asked you here because I want you to chair the safety committee."

"No."

"Christ, Bart. A hard *no*? At next week's meeting, we want to nominate you to head this committee. It can go in any direction you want. Of course, you'll have to clear—"

He slammed his hand on her desk. "There're always preconditions," he said, keeping his voice down. "I'll be *on* the committee. That's the best I can offer. We both know what'll happen. They'll deal with bullshit issues like weight, when to hold the weigh-in, medical tests, monitoring the gyms, blah, blah, blah. Nothing will come of the recommendations, and another kid will die.

Let's move on to another topic. I came bearing gifts." He gave her his ear-to-ear grin.

She raised her eyebrows. "I'll bite."

He had figured his angle before he came in. "The NBC needs good PR. I can deliver it."

"Why the hell would you care?"

"I don't give a flying F about your commissioners," he said, settling back in his chair and enjoying the deceit he was about to put into place. "But I live and work here, and I started most of the medical regulations you now follow. The mishandling of these fights reflects on me whether I like it or not." He paused for effect. "And I have an idea."

A knock on the door interrupted them. Bart turned to see a twentyish, neatly dressed brunette in a business suit standing in the doorway. "Ready to go to lunch?" she asked, all smiles for Gabe.

"Be there in fifteen. Meet me at the restaurant," Gabe said, flirtatiously returning the young woman's smiles. Waiting for the door to close again, she smoothed back her hair and picked up where they had left off. "Cut to the chase, Bart. I'm getting the distinct impression you want to add a ring physician."

He refused to be rushed. He was enjoying the moment too much. "Who's the brunette?" he asked. "Does she work in the building? I haven't seen her before."

"She's out of your league," Gabe said with a laugh. "And she would never associate with a womanizer."

"Aha! You do have a heart."

"Stay out of my personal life. If you're not finishing what you came to say, I'm off to lunch."

"Sorry, I shouldn't bust your chops. It's nice to see you smile again. By the way, I want to bring Olivia Norris on as a ring physician."

She stared at him, as if she was waiting for the punch line. When he said nothing more, she couldn't hold her tongue. "By the way? If this were April Fool's Day, I would laugh. Are you serious?"

"I don't know Dr. Norris well. I do know she's willing. She doesn't know much about working a fight yet, but she's a quick study, very bright, and I believe I can train her. Do I need to detail the positives?"

"This could be the answer to our prayers," she exclaimed. Then she looked at him skeptically.

He met her with a studied seriousness. "This is not meant to be the answer to *your* prayers. It's meant to be a start in the right direction to improve ring safety. If it helps PR, then so be it."

He was leaning heavily on that one-time friendship he and Gabe had shared. He watched her struggle with it.

"Trust me," he said, "it's a win-win."

"I'm not stupid. I know what you are doing," she sighed.

He used his poker face. "You unraveled my scheme? Let me tell you in my own words so you're not up late. It's time we improve things around here. I can't do this myself. I believe a highly trained neurologist is what the fighters need."

"Who do you think you're kidding? You like this girl, don't you? Are you already sleeping with her?"

"Fuck you," he shouted, jumping up from the barely held together wooden chair. It was a calculated explosion. "You want to be serious, call me. Until then, good luck with your absurd committee that will hold down headlines until someone else dies or you get sued by Olivia Norris." He pulled open the door, winked at Carmen and pinched her cheek and headed for the elevators.

Gabe, who never ran a mile in her life, scurried to the outer office, catching up with him halfway down the hall.

"Bart, I was just teasing you," she said, slightly breathless. "I'm putting Dr. Norris on Wednesday's agenda. Have her submit her CV to Carmen. Can she be on the phone? Or better yet, attend the meeting?"

"Sure," he said, and kept walking.

*

Gabe had contacted the five commissioners in advance of the meeting. While each maintained a healthy curiosity as to why Dr. Norris, the sister of a recently deceased boxer, should step so close to the scene of the event, it didn't seem to be an issue with any of them that she might have a conflict of interest. Bart knew that Gabe would count on their egos getting in the way of them questioning Olivia's motives—or Gabe's, for that matter—other than as an attempt to better the sport. And not one of them would have been blind to the public relations aspect of the appointment.

Olivia's 10-page résumé, including her cerebral injury research, impressed everyone at the meeting, not least of all Bart. Her modest but self-assured demeanor in speaking about herself and her qualifications, and the way she expressed her desire to make a difference, were so convincing most of the commissioners believed she could've "sold snow to the Eskimos," as one of them was overheard saying afterwards. Bart detailed how an additional ring physician with Olivia's experience could improve safety and help implement research.

•

"How did it go?" Amanda asked, meeting the two of them in Curtis's driveway.

Bart chortled. "She's a shoe-in."

"That's our girl," Amanda said, giving Olivia a hug.

Olivia uneasily moved away.

They set up in the den, and Bart outlined the structure of the sessions. Olivia worried that the spark between her and Bart would be hideously obvious, but as they got going, she found that the session was all business. The spark converted itself for the occasion into energy and concentration in this mutual endeavor. Watching fight DVDs was hard for her at first, but she took it as a point of pride not to let it show, and after a while she became absorbed in what was happening on the screen as she listened to Bart, and sometimes Lou, comment.

From that night forward, she and Bart reviewed fight DVDs in Curtis's den nightly, with Amanda always behind them quietly taking notes and Lou adding his two cents at every chance. They ate Luisa's vegetarian burritos, fried plantains and homemade salsa and anything else the housekeeper decided to prepare.

In Nevada, though the ring physician could make a recommendation, only the referee could stop the fight. Bart concentrated his lessons on when a fighter could continue after a knockdown or a tough round.

Lou educated her on trainers and cutmen: some kept the ring physician away from their fighter while others manipulated the doctor to stop a fight when their boxer was losing so they could demand a rematch. Both taught Olivia when a laceration stops a fight.

She jotted notes in her iPad, including idiosyncrasies of specific trainers, fighters, cutmen, referees and doctors. Boxing required incredible stamina, and she began to feel a real appreciation for what athletes endured.

Sophie, hearing that her daughter had joined the NBC, harangued her nightly about working alongside the people who had killed her brother. But Olivia also heard, in the way her mother was talking, that she loved the new purpose and attention it would bring to her own life.

"It's what Curtis would have wanted," she told her mother, giving her a media sound bite about how this was their family's way to prevent other boxers from suffering a similar fate. In typical Sophie fashion, her mother swept aside the inconvenient contradictions in the situation. She'd again have a ringside seat and remain a martyr for her loss.

The press gobbled up the figure of Dr. Olivia Norris and the story of Curtis's sister as ring physician. Boxing stories were romantic, and this one was no exception. All that remained was for her to play the role while exploring the truth wherever it led.

At the end of a week, Bart leaned back and lifted his glass of seltzer.

"Turns out you might have an aptitude for the job after all," he said, grinning broadly. "It's a gift shared by too few."

•

Her first fight came 10 days later.

Leaving her car in the parking structure at Mandalay Bay, Olivia checked her watch. It was almost 3:00 PM. She had better move it or she'd miss her first weigh-in.

Since Curtis's death, she seldom went anywhere except to her office or the hospital. She used free time to learn boxing history, how the sport was run and to reacquaint herself with the brother she'd deserted. Now she had something she had to do, and it meant being in the public eye. She overcame her reluctance for the tenth time and entered the building.

A roped-off area of the Tiki Lounge—a Polynesian-style bar in the middle of Mandalay Bay—was transformed into temporary Commission facilities.

Ten sports writers, mostly poorly dressed middle-aged men, stood around gossiping about which boxers were having difficulty making weight, how many tickets had been sold and whether there was food in the press room.

Forty feet away, Olivia leaned against a wall, feeling for a second completely out of place, as though someone might tell her to scram. Where was Bart? He had promised to meet her here. Should she leave? Searching for a friendly face, she spotted Gabe and timidly waved.

"Dr. Norris, can I call you Dr. Olivia?"

"Olivia is fine.'

"You're 'Dr.' here," Gabe said, wrapping her arm under Olivia's. "If this looks chaotic—it is."

With Olivia in tow, pushing through five guys dressed in chartreuse sweatsuits that read "Team Vasquez," she reached the plywood credentials table and asked Carmen to give Dr. Norris an all-access credential. Turning to Olivia, she explained, "I want to make sure you can visit the fighters' dressing rooms tomorrow."

Olivia listened intently through disorganized noise and confusion from five other registering entourages.

Outside the roped section, a hundred fans held notebooks, seeking an auto-graph from a famous boxer—or a future champion.

Gabe reintroduced her newfound star magnet to the commissioners and made sure she caught the attention of the hotel bigwigs showing up to see if the hoopla would stimulate foot traffic and ticket sales.

Olivia had learned a lot during her tutelage under Bart, Lou, and Amanda, and it hadn't all been about being the medic. Some of it was about how impor-tant boxing was in Vegas.

The sport was very big business in this city. A pay-per-view fight card would stimulate the economy and increase a gaming company's quarterly returns. CNBC always discussed potential revenues. On fight weekends, the airport, taxis, hotels, restaurants and shows were flooded to capacity with patrons and bursting with a buildup of excitement. Retail sales dramatically improved. Unlike concertgoers or vacationers, boxing fans spent money freely and tended to gamble excessively.

When she had tried to wave off further details about non-medical issues, all three of her teachers had come down on her. She needed to know what was at stake. It was big money all down the line, and the promoters were kings.

A promoter with a TV date, either on HBO, Showtime or pay-per-view, would offer a gaming corporation, like MGM, a fight card. The company asked boxing experts, perhaps even a former NBC Commissioner, if they should buy the fight. Depending on the notoriety of the main event, the promoter paid the site fee, which might be as high as ten million dollars.

It was this kind of money that she and her comrades in arms were proposing to mess with.

If the fight was not as attractive, there might be no site fee, but the hotel paid for advertising and provided rooms to the promotional staff and fighters along with meal vouchers. The promoter might "four-wall" it, which meant that the casino would pay nothing, while the promoter funded food vendors, and set up and took down the seats and ring. There were countless permutations for a contract. A contract for a million-dollar event could be 100 pages, including foreign TV rights, advertising on the ring mat and a long list of other items.

If the promoter had a deal with the network, it could amount to tens of mil-lions or a combination of money plus pay-per-view buys (what is spent by each cable viewer who purchases the fight). The promoter also paid the fighters, the amount ranging from a few thousand to millions, and often a percentage of the live gate (ticket sales) or pay-per-view buys. The boxer might also have a separate contract with a network.

Not only would Olivia need to be completely conscious at every moment while she was attending fights, she would have to understand this whole complicated set up—who gained what from whom—in order to make sense of what she might see. All of this was swimming through her mind as Gabe shepherded her through the crowd.

She saw an older, somewhat stocky man approaching them. "Stu Rappaport," the man said as he extended his hand. "It's a pleasure to see you here, doctor."

Many people had already shied away from her, not knowing what to say, but Stu marched right up to her. His comforting words, delivered with a crack in his voice, told her there was a real person behind the gruff demeanor.

Fifteen rows of press sat near the registration table. Photographers and TV cameras stood poised behind those seats. A makeshift stage, framed by a backdrop advertising the fight, was filled with Nathan Detroit types pacing around the weigh-in scale. Olivia felt almost giddy for a few minutes taking it all in. It seemed more like a movie than anything she would find herself involved in.

After many introductions, Gabe escorted her into a curtained area no larger than Curtis's tiniest closet. Inside, Mark Stewart and two other physicians patiently waited. The cubicle was too dark for a speakeasy, let alone an exam room.

"Dr. Norris, welcome to our humble office," laughed Stewart. The others nervously snickered. "This is Brian Mitchner and Bill Atherton." Brian was a general surgeon, and Bill was an ED doc. They had been with the Commission about eight years. "The NBC rarely adds physicians," he said pointedly. "These spots are highly sought after—until doctors see all the scut work we do."

Olivia had loathed Stewart on sight, and after working with Bart, she was in a position to recognize Stewart's incompetence. She tried to keep an open mind about the others.

Gabe periodically stuck her head between the full-length black curtains to make sure her "children," as she called them, were playing nice with the new student. Stewart offered Olivia the chance to examine a couple of boxers. Many boxers spoke only Spanish, so she translated for the other doctors.

Stewart gave her the rationale for the abbreviated physicals—checking the fighter's blood pressure, pulse, heart rhythm, lungs, eyes, ears, mouth and hands. The boxers were there to make weight, he told her. Their mandatory weigh-in attendance corralled the fighters into one place for physician access. Shortly afterward, the athletes would step on the scale and then immediately replenish their fluids. If the weigh-in was televised, the process moved even faster.

Olivia kept calm. Bart had impressed on her that nothing proved a ring physician's aptitude more than maintaining composure. This happened to be her forte.

Once the physicals were done, the boxers took the stage as their entourages clapped and cheered. Many of the boxers stripped to their briefs before hopping on the scale. Gabe joked with them as she called out their official weight.

Amanda was busy conducting celebrity fight fan interviews for the local evening news. Bart was a no-show.

As Olivia watched the activity with her fellow physicians, a gentleman in a bright green sweatsuit came up and embraced her.

"*Doctora*...Emilio Vasquez. *Me recuerda del hospital?*"

Finally recognizing him, she exclaimed, "*Oh Dios*, Emilio. *No tienes una pelea?*"

"*No, no doctora, mi hermano.*" He turned showing her Team Vasquez on his jacket. Grabbing his brother he announced, "Julio, *mi neuróloga.*"

"*Doctora*, Emilio could not stop talking about you. We watched Curtis train in Tecate. He was a great man."

"Your English is excellent," she said, truly happy to be talking to him and his brother.

"*Sí*, my wife is American; we live in Los Angeles. I'm happy to hear you're now with the NBC. They need a doctor in your *especialidad.*"

Olivia blushed. Her three medical associates were standing within earshot. They clearly weren't pleased.

Once the boxers made weight, Gabe stepped down from the stage and maneuvered close to Olivia, continuing introductions as if they were at a wedding reception. Olivia felt Gabe was milking the opportunity but bit her tongue, eying Amanda motioning for her to keep it together. If she was going to do this, she had to fit in—nothing new for her except this time it was personal, not business.

When there were no more hands to shake, Olivia left the building and headed for the safety and solitude of her car. This was one time she wished she still smoked. She got into Curtis's big, comfortable car and just sat there, eyes closed, happy to be alone.

She might have drifted off, but she was sharply startled by the passenger side door being pulled open. Before she had a heart attack, she saw that it was Amanda scrambling into the car. She quickly closed the door as if she was being chased.

Olivia glared at her. "You scared me to death," she said.

Amanda laughed. "Got something for you," she said. "But get us out of here. You're not supposed to be consorting with a reporter."

Olivia snorted, but she turned on the ignition and backed out of the space. "Don't be so mysterious," she said, relenting as she saw Amanda's dimpled smile out of the corner of her eye.

"Wait till we get out of here," Amanda said, blasting the radio and immediately singing along with "Bye, Bye, Miss American Pie." By the time they got to Curtis's, they were both singing at the top of their lungs, no matter what the song was.

Once they were inside the house, Amanda squatted over her bag and brought out a sheaf of worn documents and handwritten notes. Several papers fell to the floor, and Olivia knelt and helped her collect them. Some were medical tests in Spanish.

"These belong to fighters," she said. "How did you get them?"

Amanda was beaming. "I got them from a friend," she said. "And how I got them, you don't need to know."

"What, you stole them?"

"Nope. I was able to get them through FOIA—the Freedom of Information Act. Boxer medicals are not protected once they go through a public Commission meeting."

Olivia looked at the papers again. "Noguiera, is that Miguel Noguiera?" Nervously looking at the MRI report that was on top, she asked, "What's the first name here? It says 'Madrid'? I can't read his first name." Her heart was racing. "Antonio Madrid?"

Amanda was nodding her head *yes* as she brought her computer out of her bag.

Olivia headed for the kitchen. "Bring the computer in here. I'll make some espresso," she said.

Opening the computer on the kitchen table, Amanda said, "Now, let's see what hay we can make with this information."

•

Just as they settled down to fit the new information into the base spreadsheet they had made the first night, Olivia's phone vibrated with a call from Senator McAllen's office.

"This is Elena Escalone. I'm sorry it's been so hard getting you together with the senator," the assistant said. "He's been completely tied up in hearings. He wanted me to let you know you're number one on his list."

Putting Elena on speaker, Olivia asked, "Your brother was a fighter, right? Did he compete in the U.S. or only in Mexico?"

"He had several fights in the States."

"He knew Curtis?"

"They knew each other through Vincent."

There was that pounding in her head. "Your brother trained with Vincent Marquessa?" she asked.

"Vinnie worked with him for a year, in Mexico. Rodrigo got strong. He even moved up in weight. Curtis was giving him pointers on diet, too."

Terrified by what the response might be, Olivia mumbled, "Where's Rodrigo now?"

"He's in Tecate."

She breathed a sigh of thanks. "He's still boxing?"

"No. He has a job."

"In Tecate?"

"You've heard of Tecate beer?" Elena teased her.

Olivia laughed. "Oh, of course. So, he works in the factory now?"

"He's in charge of the entire factory."

"That's great." Thinking about Curtis, she wished he, too, had quit boxing and gone into something safe.

"My daughter-in-law has a great job there, too," Elena added, evidently happy to chat on. "She runs Rancho Cielo Azul."

"In Tecate?"

"One of the best spas in the world. You must go. The visitors are almost all American."

"I'd love to speak with your brother some time."

Elena's phone interrupted them, and promising to email her Rodrigo's contact information, she ended the call.

Olivia and Amanda looked at each other. "This is getting a little creepy," Olivia said. "Elena's brother knew Curtis?"

"Not to be patronizing, but boxing is a small world. In a month you'll know everyone—many of whom you'll wish you never met."

Ignoring her remark, Olivia kept thinking aloud. "Maybe he was there the same time as Noguiera and Madrid. There has to be a connection."

Amanda suddenly looked at her watch. "I can't believe it. Gotta run," she said. She was covering a premiere at the Palms Brendan theaters—the latest Scorsese. "By the way, did you play nice in the schoolyard today?" she asked as she packed up her things. "It can't have been easy hanging with Mark Stewart."

Olivia pretended to shudder. "What a creep."

"I'll call Bart on my way home," Amanda said. "He's got a game tonight, but he needs to know about all this new information. I'm tied up all evening. Leave me a message. What time tomorrow will you be at Mandalay?"

"The report time is 4:00 PM."

"I should be there then, too. Bart will take you around. You'll have fun."

"Fun? Are you out of your mind?" She started laughing. It was all too bizarre. "I have to see some hospital patients in the morning. Then I'm zoning out for a few hours."

"Olivia, you want to find out why Curtis died and why he left you those numbers. Every time you consider bolting, consider what we can accomplish. Worst case scenario, Nevada gets their second-best ring doctor."

•

The house felt completely empty. Lou had gone to dinner with friends; Chui and Marco had gone to Luisa's. They had left her notes on the hall table.

The big silence conjured uncomfortable Chicago memories. As soon as she turned on the hall light, Tyson slipped away.

She checked on the horses resting quietly in their stalls. As she petted Sweetpea Won's velvety gray nose, his nostrils flared in pleasured response.

Startled by a sound behind her, she turned to find Bart standing in the shadows.

"Rossi," she murmured. "Didn't hear you come in."

"I rang the bell."

Noting that he was as good-looking as she remembered, she said, "I appreciate...I mean, everyone has a life. And contrary to what you wish everyone to believe, you work hard. And..."

"And what?"

She strolled down the barn isle. "I want you to know I get that this is a life you walked away from."

He smiled, handing Sweetpea Won a carrot from a bucket outside the stall. "Even though I judge fights, I have a great deal of unresolved anger. You neuros do psychoanalysis, too?"

"Us neuros?" she giggled, wishing she had showered and fixed her makeup.

The sharp Vegas wind blew back her hair. Bart stared at her face. No matter how hard he tried, he couldn't escape Olivia's porcelain skin—skin that had lived in humidity and far from the sun.

"Here, take my jacket."

"If you wouldn't mind, can we head back inside? I'd like to clean up. I promise to be quick—years of practice rescuing terrified on-call residents."

Bart wanted to say that nothing could make Olivia look sexier than she did at this moment, but he caught himself.

"Sure, I'll get the clips ready. Tomorrow you'll be examining the boxers after they fight. I want you to learn to critically dissect other doctors' actions. In the ED and your office, you see everything *after* it happens. Here your decision is hugely more complex. Who can take another shot or who will be seriously injured if hit. The repercussions of your actions…" Stopping, he recognized his callousness. He touched her arm. "Sorry. Who knows the repercussions better than you do?"

Giving his forearm a gentle squeeze, she excused herself. He made her woozy—or was it an absence of food? Either way it was a blissful revelation that she didn't crave a drink or chocolate. Working side-by-side with him these last few weeks had produced an inexplicable calm. He made her feel safe. Odd that they knew only the minimum about each other. If he knew more, she thought, he would have an excuse to run.

Olivia stood naked in front of the bathroom mirror. She could hear Bart playing tug with Tyson in the den. Wondering whether her houseguest would find her appealing, she turned sideways. She thought she looked okay for her age. Some flabby areas…She laughed at herself, touching butt and thighs. Hell, those had been there when she was 18.

In the shower, she again found herself fantasizing. Stop it, she chastised herself. It had just been so long between men, she reasoned, that was all it was. But she knew better.

She pulled her wet hair into a ponytail, pulled on oversized blue jeans with holes at the knees and a loosely fitted white Team Montana sweatshirt. This has to be the least appealing I can look, she thought, admiring her image once again but dressing to remind herself Bart was Amanda's.

As she crossed the entryway on her way to the kitchen, she called out, "Be right there. Want a drink?"

He shouted back, "*Agua por favor.* I need to stay sharp for the game, and you need to be on your toes tomorrow."

She entered the den with two Evians with lemon. Bart was lying on the couch, feet on the table, with Tyson lying across his lap, panting. Olivia handed him one of the Evians and flopped onto the green velvet lounge chair perpendicular to the couch.

"You know, Norris, this dog doesn't like you."

Frowning, she angrily replied, "A lot you know."

"Wanna know how I know?" he said, grinning.

She took a gulp of Evian and lifted the glass as if she was going to empty it on his head. "Okay, lay it on me, Dog Whisperer."

Bart slid Tyson next to him and patted Olivia's thigh. "These jeans tell the story."

"Grow up."

"Hairless!"

"What?"

"I've been here with this dog for, what, 15 minutes? Look at me. I'm covered in hair. Either you have a wide selection of dog-hair removal systems or she never comes near you. I'm surmising the latter."

Olivia tried to think of some quip, but he was right. "Why doesn't she like me? I've tried to make friends."

Sensing he'd struck a nerve, he quickly backpedalled. "Whoa, whoa. I was joking."

As she rose to grab some paper and a pen, he noticed that even loose jeans couldn't camouflage her tight ass or how adorable she looked.

"We'll address the issue of Tyson on Sunday," he said. "Tonight we have work to do."

They shared popcorn, and Olivia told him about the physicians' disapproval of her knowing the Vasquez brothers. He relished staring at her without embarrassing himself as they discussed Amanda's latest coup.

At 11:00 PM, Bart got a text and abruptly stood up. Tucking in his shirt, he mumbled apologetically, "I have a game in an hour, and you need rest. Good work tonight."

She stood up and straightened her tousled clothing. She pulled the tie off her ponytail and let her hair fall around her face. She wasn't sure she was going to be able to let him walk out the door. The evening had passed with the two of them hard at work, but without the others there it had felt as if they were together. Even though she knew that wasn't the reality, the abruptness of his announcement jolted her.

"There's a lot to learn," she said. She started turning off lights and gathering the debris of their session.

The dark house left the room with a sultry amber halo from the barn lights.

"You'll call Amanda later, right?" She wondered if Amanda knew he was here, but she couldn't ask. "Give her a rundown of what we covered tonight." How could he not hear her pounding heart?

He didn't answer. He was turned away from her, not moving, seemingly looking at the floor. She put their empty glasses into the popcorn bowl and was about to pick up the bowl. He reached out and took her hand.

"None of us can appreciate what you've been through these last months," he whispered, putting his other hand over hers. "Are you nervous about tomorrow? Your hands are cold? It's okay. I'll be there the whole time. I'm hoping I can sit beside you for some of it. Let me research Noguiera, Madrid and Escalone." He was speaking these practical words, but they were coming out sweet. "There has to be something here besides the obvious. There has to be," he murmured.

Her breathing deepened. His sapphire eyes cut into her, right to the core. She pulled away from his grasp. "It's late. You have a game." She didn't do it for Amanda; she did it to save herself.

She picked up the bowl and led the way out of the room, flicking the wall switch as she went and leaving him, a few steps behind her, in the dark. Approaching the front door, she put the bowl on the hall table. Bart was putting on his coat, looking everywhere but at her. She had her hand on the front doorknob, but he didn't join her.

"Can't bear to leave me?" she taunted him, wishing it were true. She turned around and he was right there, reaching his index finger around the loop of her jeans, heatedly forcing her against his chest. He wrapped her right arm behind her back in an unbreakable grip, kissing her before she could say no or turn her face away. Molding to his frame and searing lips, she inhaled while his hands moved inside the back of her T-shirt.

And then they stood frozen as a taxi stopped outside. Breathless, Olivia propelled herself two feet away as a billion *Lifetime* network storylines shot through her brain.

Bart pulled open the front door and stood on the threshold, waiting for Lou to pay the taxi and amble up the walk. The two men greeted each other and gossiped a little about tomorrow's fights. Then Bart excused himself and went down the driveway to his car.

Olivia closed up, as she knew so well how to do, concealing her disappointment and shock. She stepped back into the house and hugged Lou goodnight, at the same time waiting for the sound of Rossi's car reversing out of the driveway.

She carried the popcorn bowl with the two glasses in it into the kitchen, still waiting. Finally, there it was, just as her phone vibrated. She looked at the text, from "Rossi, Bart": "Forgive me."

Lying in bed in the hushed darkness, her heart wouldn't let up. She didn't know what to feel. "Forgive me." For what? For kissing her and leaving immediately afterwards? For cheating on his girlfriend—a woman they both admired?

She turned onto her side, trying to shake herself loose from him. He probably goes around kissing women all the time, she told herself. His little game.

How was she to respond?

It was late. The house was dark. The man was a known womanizer.

"Ignore it," she said out loud. Should she apologize to Amanda? "No, ignore it," she said again.

She turned again just as her phone posted two texts. From "Weekly, Amanda":

"Got great stories. C U at Mandalay." And from "Rossi, Bart": "Sorry to leave in a hurry. C U at Mandalay."

Reality check, she thought. Amanda's text was the helpful cold water, and it drenched her. She laughed it off and fell into a deep sleep.

Twenty-Four

Her fight credential prominently displayed on a chain around her neck, Olivia parked behind the Event Center. She greeted HBO personnel running in and out of RVs housing the directorial staff. Stepping over gigantic cables, she went through a metal detector and flashed the credential to a burly security officer seated in front of the steel entry.

Except for Commission officials, TV crew and security staff, the arena was empty. Cameramen and their assistants were busy adjusting ringside equipment. There were women patting matte makeup onto the faces of Rush and Hastings while they prepared monologues on nearby monitors and spoke to the producer in the truck.

Gabe welcomed Olivia, and Carmen handed her a clipboard with physical forms to be completed on each boxer after his bout. She would have another physician with her for the post-fight exams. She asked an ambulance staffer to point out the ringside oxygen canisters and gurneys. If an athlete required transport, one paramedic would accompany her to the dressing rooms and radio the hospital.

As a ring physician, she would have to make decisions within seconds about what was and what was not life threatening—and do it in front of millions of people. Those decisions would have crucial implications for everyone involved, including her. Bart had drilled into her the far-reaching consequences of any action she took. The bettors would sometimes make their bets based on who the doctor was. The wrong choice could end a boxer's career or his life. If she stopped a fight too early, she could force a boxer into obscurity. He might never get another shot. And of course if she waited too long to stop it, she could cause a ring death or a punch-drunk syndrome.

"Are you in charge?" she asked Mark Stewart.

"No, Atherton is. He'll be in the red corner at the end of the Commission table; I'll be in the diagonal blue corner. He jumps in the ring if a boxer is KO'd.

We check our corner's boxer between rounds when needed."

"So I do the post-fight exams with Brian Mitchner?"

"Uh, Brian should be here somewhere." Stewart looked around. "Gabe," he shouted over the cameramen's instructions, "seen Brian?"

Gabe shook her head. "He hasn't checked in with me yet. I have to distribute these judge and referee assignments. Take Olivia in the back."

Following orders, Stewart escorted Olivia to the dressing rooms as he grumbled about the importance of physician punctuality.

"Once the card begins, it's bedlam," he told her. "You have to hustle between the TV staff, security and boxers' entourages. Our schedule is limited by the network. They often interview boxers in their dressing rooms before their ring walk, but sometimes the interview is in the ring afterwards. If there are quick stoppages or knockouts, TV may go right into the next fight. You have to complete your exam, decide if your guy needs stitches or a head CT and return ringside."

The championship fighters and some of the undercard guys were drug tested, he continued as Olivia took in her surroundings. There was a paper bag near Carmen's seat containing the drug test materials—each kit labeled with the boxer's name. There was a chain of custody. She was to hand them to the inspectors in the dressing room. "They'll observe the fighter urinate and complete the paperwork, and they'll return the sealed containers and bags to you. Quest picks up the urines from you at the end of the night."

Olivia knew about the chain of custody. Every time a high-profile boxer tested positive, they contested the results, and if the chain had been broken, the results had no credibility. Even though only a handful of cases made it to court, and there wasn't one that had been overturned, the chain of custody was important.

She nodded, wishing she didn't have to spend one more minute listening to the oily voice of this incompetent physician.

"Why do I have to be ringside? You and Atherton will be there. If a boxer needs more of our time, shouldn't I stay in the dressing room and monitor him?"

"If they need a head CT after a rough fight or a KO, it's best to get them to the hospital ASAP. After the bout, Atherton or myself will give you a heads-up regarding a fighter's condition."

"Couldn't you text me?"

Clearly annoyed, Stewart sighed heavily. "You can remain in the dressing room, but then you miss the fights," he said.

She stared at him, dumbfounded. If the physicians were hired to keep an eye on the fighters—especially following a knockout—surely they shouldn't be ringside schmoozing with the swells and watching fights. She kept her mouth shut. She would ask Bart about it later.

Stewart showed her around the dressing rooms. The ones for the main events, used for stars like McCartney and Bieber, were lavishly furnished with huge flat-screens, marshmallow-pillowed couches and plenty of cold water for the entourages and families.

The undercard dressing rooms were typical locker rooms with wooden benches, towels strewn on the floor and open gym bags. One room was designated "red corner" and the other "blue corner," each housing five athletes. There were trainers in each room holding mitts so their fighters could warm up. Others were in the process of methodically wrapping gauze and tape around their fighters' hands and giving last-minute instructions as the boxers fell into a focused trance. Bart had told her 10 times: hands had to be protected above all else. Commission inspectors monitored the cutmen and trainers so no illegal substances were administered and the correct amount of gauze and tape was used.

He had made sure she knew the parameters even though both she and Lou had argued that there were things she actually had to know, and this wasn't one of them. Bart made her memorize it—15 feet of soft gauze was permitted, no more than two inches wide, to be held in place by 10 feet of surgeon's adhesive tape, one inch wide. She watched one of the trainers carefully cross the back of the hand twice, which was permitted, and extend to cover and protect the knuckles of his fighter—also permitted. No one wanted to see a "loaded glove."

Olivia sat down next to each of the boxers she'd examined at the weigh-in. She asked how they were feeling and told them it was okay to be nervous. It was a technique of Bart's, to hear their speech and observe eye movements and facial symmetry.

Stewart hung his head, letting her know his disgust at her empathetic, motherly support. She knew he was thinking, *a female ring doctor, this will never work.* And she knew he wanted her to know that was the way he felt. The boxers, on the other hand, were thrilled. Most of them knew of Curtis and appreciated the TLC only a woman could provide.

Gabe popped in. "Doing okay?"

"Doing great. Dr. Stewart is showing me around." She flashed a thumbs-up and confidently squeezed Stewart's shoulder, further riling him.

Going back ringside, Stewart introduced her to judges and referees.

Why was the place so empty? "Don't these fights always sell out?" she asked Stewart.

"Yup, it's sold out. Most fans, especially the gamblers, don't show up until right before the main event."

She barely heard his answer as she caught sight of Bart on his way down to the ring apron, where he interrupted Gabe talking to one of the officials. Bart said something in Gabe's ear, she seemed to demur, and Olivia saw him grab her upper arm and pull her abruptly away.

•

Bart didn't let go of Gabe's arm until he had her out of earshot at the edge of the spotlight. He would have preferred to do this out of sight, but there was no time.

Gabe growled at him. "What's so important?" she demanded.

"I just learned that Stewart has been treating Vasquez for a sore hand," Bart said, turning his head away from the light so that no one could see what he was saying.

She made a face. "Where would you hear something like that?" she asked, half-scoffing, to brush it away.

"Don't be ridiculous," he said, practically snorting with scorn for her tactics. "He's been treating Vasquez for a sore hand for the past week and right up to tonight. You have to take Stewart off the card." Not only was it illegal for a ring physician to treat a fighter outside the ring except in an emergency, it was a clear conflict of interest.

"You have to give me more than that," Gabe insisted, then suddenly pretended to be entertained by something Bart had said, as two of the judges passed them heading for the ring.

Bart beamed his best smile at her and hissed between closed teeth, "You know damn well you have to take Stewart off the card." He had gotten a text from Stu Rappaport while he was stuck in traffic on his way over. When he called him to get more details, Stu was his usual completely calm self and gave him the information about Ed's fighter as though he was chatting about the weather. Bart had to laugh. Good old Stu, all kinds of chicanery going on around him and he remained straight as a die, with complete confidence.

Gabe looked at her watch, then turned to go. "Will do," she said brightly. Turning back, she added, "Let's not spread it around why, shall we? I'd prefer to keep it quiet."

Bart gave a short laugh and said, "Sure," and walked past her down to ringside seating. Taking a seat about 20 rows back, he caught Olivia's eye and saluted her. She was looking a little wild, he thought. He was considering whether to call her over when Mandy slipped into the seat next to him and nuzzled his ear.

"I need to borrow your phone," she said. "Mine's dead as a doornail."

He sighed and handed her the phone. That dizzy blonde act didn't fool him as it did others, but he liked the charade. It amused him to see how she got what she was after.

"I'll be right back," she said, jumping up and pushing in a series of numbers as she walked away.

He hated to think what she was up to, but he would bet it was going to annoy someone, sometime.

Olivia cast another glance in Bart's direction. He motioned to her and patted the seat next to him. Despising being beckoned like a 5-year-old, she dawdled over, keeping a grip on her belongings as if she were in the subway at rush hour.

"Wound a little tight, are we?"

Frowning, she sat down. "Maybe."

He looked at his watch. "The first set of boxers will enter the ring in about 10 minutes. Did you familiarize yourself with each fighter in the back?"

"Of course," she snapped.

"Whoa, Sweetpea Won. There're a million things happening for you right now, I get that. On the other hand, you have one priority when working."

"I know, keep the boxers safe."

"Correct. You want to leave Mandalay tonight knowing that every fighter you sent home will wake up healthy in the morning. Daunting, huh? You're not a mind reader, and you can't send each one in for a head CT. Their lives are in your hands from the weigh-in until they leave the arena. Be a doctor first and foremost. You're the boxers' advocate. If I'm pushing you, it's because I believe you can do better than your associates. The boxers deserve nothing less. If you can't give more, leave now."

She sat quietly next to him. Funny, his pep talk had relaxed her. Looking up, she saw that everyone associated with the Commission had their eyes on her and Bart. It made her feel strangely important.

He laughed. "You'd think we were Brangelina," he said. "Get used to it, Norris. You're the new kid in town. No one knows quite what to think. The docs will hope you make an idiot of yourself, and the commissioners hope you take the focus away from them—in a good way."

Handing her a rumpled thicket of papers from his jacket pocket, he said, "Here are the Fight Fax sheets." She knew that the Commission downloaded the sheets before a boxer competed in their jurisdiction. She took the sheets and scanned the top one: wins and losses; where the guy had fought, when, and with whom; weights; and medical suspensions.

"Next time ask for these at the weigh-in or have the NBC give you online access," Bart told her.

Good, she was glad to have all this information. She straightened the papers as he continued in his undertone drone.

"Most of these knuckleheads don't care about statistics. Every commission gives different suspensions—some commissions are less vigilant. If a guy was knocked out in his last fight and only got a 30-day suspension, maybe he shouldn't be fighting again so soon. And if his opponent tonight is stronger than he is, maybe the ref should stop the fight sooner rather than later if the guy gets in trouble."

She felt slightly embarrassed that she hadn't thought about the Fight Faxes earlier. He had taught her about how to use them before a fight. She would be making it a rule to go over each boxer's Fight Fax with the referee scheduled for his fight once she started working ringside.

Bart waved to someone ringside who had caught his attention, then leaned in, never missing a beat. "Some judges, refs and even the docs avoid knowing anything about the fighters beforehand, believing it makes them less conflicted. That's one approach—"

"I get that," she interrupted, indignant at the idea, as she had been when he mentioned it to her several training sessions ago. "If I'm seeing a patient in my office, wouldn't I review their medical records? History is everything." She stopped herself from putting a hand on his arm. "I'm not sure I get this advocate thing, though."

He took his time, sitting back in his seat and resting his feet up on the seat in front of him. It was such a typical pose, it made her smile. Slouching, with his hands behind his head, he said, "It can be hard if not impossible to read a kid—how's he really feeling, how much more punishment can he take, does he want to go back out. Their trainer won't know when to pull the plug. They're too close to the situation and need the win as much as the fighter."

She had already heard this. She needed to hear something that would give her more than she knew. She was the fighter's "independent" advocate, not compensated by anyone other than the Commission to do the right thing. If a fight needed to stop, she had to recommend it. If a boxer needed to go to the ED, she was the one who had to know that, and send him. And if he needed a longer suspension from fighting again, it was she who gave it to him.

She didn't interrupt Bart, but her impatience must have registered with him. He stopped talking for a moment until he was sure he had her attention. His look said, *I will repeat myself as often as I feel I need to, and I suggest you listen.*

She nodded, and he continued. "The pressures are immense, especially if the kid is looking at you with those big sad eyes asking to be sent out for another round. That's when you sink down deep inside yourself and ask what would you do if he were *your* kid? Stopping a fight will often make you unpopular, maybe even make you a pariah, but you'll be able to sleep at night. Can you handle the pressure?" he taunted her, smiling his sexiest smile.

Just then a Lil' John rap song blared overhead, and Bart stood up. Olivia rose as the cutman carrying a spit bucket mounted the ring apron, followed by the trainer and cheering supporters pumping up their guy. They formed a sea of bright red warm-up suits. Bart walked down with her and pointed out where she should sit. Turning to head for his own assigned seat, he whispered, "Go get 'em, Norris." It felt just like a pat on the backside, which he surely would not have hesitated to give her if there hadn't been so many eyes on them in that place. Slightly annoyed but more than slightly amused, she went down and found a seat a row behind the doctors working ringside.

The NBC table faced the main HBO camera. Gabe spent considerable time assigning these seats, and she liked to joke that it made wedding-reception seating look simple. With the mandatory seats for the commissioners, the lead physician, one judge, a sanctioning organization representative, Gabe and Carmen (who was keeping score), there was only room for one or two VIPs.

Olivia had sat a row back, as Bart had told her to do. Gabe turned and reached over the back of her seat. "We'd like you to sit next to Dr. Atherton," she said, tapping Olivia's knee with the pencil she rarely put down. "He can instruct you on policy and explain when he enters the ring to check a fighter, etc."

Eavesdropping, Bart rolled his eyes. Judging this bout, he sat at a right angle to the Commission on a barstool chair against the ring apron. Bart had his own system, as every judge did, for determining who won each round. He believed that most people's systems lacked consistency and thus lent themselves to poor decisions. Because of the individualistic—read "haphazard"—systems, the scores of many of the big fights just added to the carnival atmosphere of the sport itself. That the right fighter usually got the decision was a matter of statistics and not skill.

Bart's system was time-tested. He applied the same standards to each aspect of every fight he judged, and he made sure he knew who was ahead at any point in the fight. Effective aggression, great defense and fancy footwork were irrelevant to his system. If the fighter didn't throw and land a punch, he scored no points. He judged not only the punches landed but also the effectiveness of those punches on the opponent. A grazing jab had minimal relevance, whereas a straight right hand thrown to deliver its full power registered high in his system.

He was ready for this fight and happy to be down front for it. He cast a glance at Olivia, looked around for Amanda and didn't find her, and then sat uncomfortably listening to the small talk coming his way from the guy sitting next to him. He considered going out and returning in time for the main event even though he had told Olivia he would be there the whole time. But it was a pleasure for him to watch her move, so he stayed.

Besides a few die-hard fans, the Event Center was still empty as the referee motioned for the four-rounder boxers to touch gloves and return to their respective corners for the bell signaling round 1.

Olivia turned to Atherton. "There's no paperwork on these two?"

"It's their professional debut, so no Fight Fax statistics yet," he said. "The African-American kid is a Golden Gloves champ; I'm not sure about his opponent. Some have tons of amateur fights and others little or no experience before turning pro."

"Amateur bouts are still fights," she muttered, glancing at Bart, whose eyes never seemed to waver from the ring action. Olivia told herself she had better have some discipline and not keep looking over at him. She could play that detached allure card just as well as he could. Not to mention not wanting to blow her cover with everyone else. Who knew who was watching her for signs of something—incompetence, collusion, ignorance.

Atherton was telling her that Gabe approved the matches, so a promoter couldn't match a skilled boxer, with several wins, against someone with no experience.

The first round was competitive. During the one-minute rest period, the cornermen wiped the boxers' faces while giving instructions on how to destroy their opponents' aggression. Olivia felt an excitement in being so close—seeing the spray of water from the cornerman's bottle mix with sweat flying from the boxer's hopeful, determined face.

She glanced over at the HBO table where Rush and Hastings were getting ready to call the main event and saw Amanda. She was covering the mic and saying something to Rush. Amanda scampered off, and there was an interruption in the music that was blaring during the break. Rush announced that Mark Stewart had been taken off the card for the Vasquez fight because of a conflict of interest and went on to explain what the conflict was.

Olivia tried not to let the announcement affect her visibly, and she steeled herself not to look up and catch Bart's eye. The bell rang for the next round to start.

Watching the action, with the fighters trading blow after blow, Atherton leaned over to Olivia and whispered, "You never get used to it. In a way, you feel as if you're intruding on their privacy. These are intimate moments. We docs have to be this close—part of the process. It's important to listen to what takes place in the corner between the fighter, trainer and cutman. It will often be one of your best clues in assessing the boxer's condition."

At the end of four rounds, neither kid was hurt—one had a bloody nose and a small laceration above his eye. Warriors and competitors hugged one another after the final bell sounded.

While the judges' scores were being announced, Olivia checked her clipboard. There had been no drug test. She trotted to the dressing room alongside the red corner boxer, who was as jubilant as if he had won an Olympic medal. This was his pro debut. His win was equally significant.

"No suspension, unless he has complaints in the dressing room, Olivia," Atherton yelled.

Olivia sat the boxer down on the locker room bench. This face, which had risked permanent injury, resembled that of an altar boy barely old enough to shave. She asked if he felt well, had a headache or dizziness. Then she completed the paperwork.

By the time she returned ringside, the second of eight fights had concluded. Bart passed her down the arena isle whispering, "Told you things go fast."

No sooner had she pulled out her notepad of questions than Bart disappeared among an expanding, boisterous crowd. Her watch read 6:30 PM. She maneuvered her way to the dressing room and repeated the post-exam process.

Ed Rappaport and his entourage came out of Julio Vasquez's dressing room. Glimpsing her coming down the hall, he applauded her. "Dr. Norris, we're honored to have you aboard our ship of fools," he resoundingly called out. "There's no greater tribute you could have given Curtis."

Embarrassed by the loud attention, she thanked him and quickly excused herself to see Vasquez.

The dressing room was a Mexican Mardi Gras. An Elvis Crespo merengue shook the walls while supporters sang along and clapped. His trainer held the mitts as Julio punched. Emilio immediately embraced Olivia, thanking her for keeping an eye on his brother. When she had made sure Vasquez had no complaints, she moved to check his opponent.

The other dressing room was the antithesis of Vasquez's. Dante Verde had already worked up a sweat shadowboxing and listening to old Cuban tunes on his iPod. A priest blessed him as the room attendants held hands and prayed to keep Dante safe.

Did this dichotomy portend any significance other than the two fighters' traditions or preferences? She remembered Bart's description of Marvin Hagler alone in the corner before he fought Ray Leonard, and a famous heavyweight getting a blow job from his girlfriend in a side room before heading to the ring. Everyone had his own prefight style.

Running back ringside, she noticed Stu Rappaport carefully watching the ring entrances. Stu's eyes searched hers, and he was about to speak when Ed yelled for him to follow him and he obliged.

Bart passed by. "Don't embarrass me," he hissed.

"What an ass," she muttered to herself. Did he think she was his employee? It was as if last night had never happened. A ploy to control her, that was all. She stopped herself. She knew he was a ladies' man. What did she want from him? He was fun, a thrill to be around, but none of it meant anything. She would be a fool to think it did.

"Dr. Norris, I can't tell you how glad I was to know you'll be working with the Commission."

She recognized Mirabelle's voice and jumped up from her chair. The two women embraced. She hadn't seen Mira since the reading of the will. She had wanted to ask her about Bernard, but had been waiting for them to run into each other. "It's so good to see you, Mira," she said. "How's your job working out?"

Mirabelle happily babbled about her new duties with Ed Rappaport. Olivia stood half-listening as she enviously noticed how Mirabelle was one of the few to take a good credential photo.

"Is Bernard your brother?" she asked, hoping it sounded like an idle question in passing.

Interrupting, a Rappaport assistant asked Mirabelle to head to the dressing rooms.

Excusing herself, she turned and shouted, "He knew Curtis in Chicago."

As the evening went on, Olivia stopped noticing anything but the fights and the fighters she talked to after each bout. Three hours into the card, the main event was heralded by the Event Center bursting into thousands of cheering voices as Vasquez and Verde made their ring entrances. Rappaport climbed the ring apron with an assistant carrying the flag of Mexico. Vasquez's entourage displayed his three championship belts.

Soon the ring resembled an exploding sardine can. The crowd pounded their feet screaming "Julio" or "Dante." The referee checked the fighters' gloves. The ring announcer then introduced two exotically dressed female entertainers who sang the boxers' respective national anthems.

Atherton reviewed the two fighters' history with Olivia. The commissioners arrived and took their seats. Sensing the overcrowding, she offered to relocate. None would hear of it. They wanted her front and center.

She was amazed that the commissioners didn't bother showing up for any but the main event. She asked Atherton about it.

He smiled, discretely drawing her attention to a scantily clothed 30-something blonde. "Guess they have more important things to do," he said as the young lady, adjusting her pink flamingo-colored lip gloss, blew a kiss to Tyler, mouthing she'd meet him at Aureole later.

Olivia wished for one moment that she had stayed safely in Chicago, where she would never have had to know people like Tyler or Stewart. She blamed boxing. She blamed Curtis. And then she stopped herself, because she was here. She had to do this. It was for Curtis.

She watched Gabe, looking every inch the Commission Director, as she stood behind her chair keenly evaluating the ring activity. Directly opposite, Rush and Hastings spoke into the camera about what the fans could expect and speculated on Vasquez's hurt hand.

There was a blast on the air horn, and the referee cleared the ring. Only the boxers and their trainers remained, impatiently standing in the center. The announcer held the microphone close to the referee who asked the men in turn, "Any questions from the champion; any questions from the challenger? You heard my instructions in the dressing room. I expect a clean fight. Now touch gloves and let's get started."

A minute later, the two fighters were alone in the ring. Olivia's heart pounded from fear, but she felt an excitement and an anticipation she had never felt before.

The crowd went ballistic when Vasquez landed his first punch to Verde's jaw. Verde didn't flinch. The bout continued for a grueling 12 rounds. Each boxer was knocked down once. Atherton and Mitchner checked their corners twice between rounds. Blood repeatedly spattered onto Olivia from Verde's facial lacerations. Atherton gave her a running commentary of his assessment and what he was communicating to the referee.

At the final bell, the entourages jumped in the ring, each hoisting their fighter in the air. The scores were 113/111, 111/113 and 113/111—a split-decision. The announcer declared Verde the winner. If only one judge had given the twelfth round to Vasquez, it would have been a draw.

Olivia, who prided herself on emotional detachment from her patients, experienced a newfound heaviness in her chest.

She grabbed the drug-testing kit and followed the deflated Vasquez as he made his way to his dressing room. Hundreds of fans lining the pathway were yelling "robbery." He shook his head in defeat. What could she say to make him feel better after absorbing a terrible beating?

In his dressing room, the exuberant music had evaporated without a trace. The once rousing voices of his entourage were silent except for his 3-year-old daughter crying for daddy to pick her up. Sweaty and bloodied, he scooped her up, smiling, holding the love of his life. His wife kissed his cheek. The family priest replaced a delicate gold crucifix around Vasquez's neck. The fighter immediately clutched the cross and thanked God for keeping him safe.

Anxious to move onto the next dressing room, the inspector had Vasquez sign for his paycheck. The last 10 minutes had turned his soft clear skin into a bloodied, black-and-blue Halloween mask

Returning his daughter to his wife, Vasquez nodded to Olivia. "*Listo, doctora,*" he said.

"Julio, I'm so sorry," she murmured, holding his hand while she felt his pulse and examined his swollen fingers. "Do you have a headache?" she asked, thinking this was an idiotic question. How could he not?

Julio shook his head and pointed to his chest. "*Doctora, mi corazón.*"

"Your chest hurts? Maybe from the body shots?"

Smiling through a bloodied lip, patting Olivia's cheek, he replied in broken English, "No, *doctora*, I hurt my heart."

She was startled. He was trying to make her feel better. How could she have missed this with Curtis? And there it was. Boxing and the fighters had taken hold of her soul.

Completing her exam and the paperwork, she handed the drug kit to the inspector. Could she leave? Was he really okay? She sat quietly watching him. He had no neurological deficits, although too often nothing serious would be evident until later.

His brother, more saddened than Julio by the loss, assured her they would closely watch him tonight. She wanted him to get a precautionary head CT. Reluctantly they acquiesced.

As he waited for Julio to change, Emilio spoke of their childhood fights— brother fighting brother in their backyard—and how Julio grew stronger despite several minor career setbacks forcing him to take time off.

"I'm three years older than my brother," he told her. "We began our careers at 118 pounds. Julio became *mas fuerte*—bigger and stronger."

"Julio, *cómo?*" she asked.

"*No sé*, maybe the trainer *y vitaminas?* I never took anything to help me. Julio had to."

"I don't understand."

"His injuries—the *medicina* or *vitaminas* helped him."

Out of time to pursue the story, she stored it in her brain and took care of business—speaking to the paramedics and notifying the ED that Vasquez was coming. She texted Gabe, then escorted Vasquez to the ambulance.

Inside the rig, Julio sat with his daughter perched on his lap, his wife alongside.

"I'll check with the hospital," Olivia said, and she backed away as the EMS guy closed the door.

She went back inside. The crowds were gone, and the Event Center staff was deconstructing the ring in preparation for *Disney on Ice* the following night. Gabe stood in front of the officials seated in the first five rows and reviewed the bouts and the scoring.

When she saw her, Gabe pulled Olivia beside her before she could take a seat. "Looks like you came through tonight with flying colors," she said. "Not as easy as it looks, huh?"

Most people laughed indulgently. Olivia, embarrassed, took a seat next to Atherton.

Mirabelle swooped by and congratulated Olivia on her first fight night.

Mirabelle Champion, Olivia said to herself. What was the story here? It hit her suddenly. Could Bernard Champion possibly be the kid Curtis hit that stormy night when he shouldn't have been driving? Could the kid have survived?

Twenty-Five

FOLLOWING THE OFFICIALS' meeting, Olivia hurried out of the Event Center. She wanted to take another look at Curtis's requests. Bart tried to catch up with her, but she waved him off. She texted Amanda that she was too exhausted for a party; she would call her tomorrow. Lou, who had worked Verde's corner, had said he'd be home late.

Tyson looked up mournfully from her place on the threshold of the entryway. Olivia hurried past her, grabbed a diet Coke and a giant bag of Mrs. Field's and closed herself in Curtis's office. Dumping old checks and bank statements from a large desk drawer onto the floor, she sat down cross-legged and started wading through the contents, looking for the name Champion.

Come 2:00 AM, she was no closer to an answer.

She wasn't going to telephone Mirabelle at this hour. On the other hand, she wasn't going to bed, either. She changed into her PJs, went back into the dimly lit kitchen and inhaled a hefty piece of chocolate cake. Returning to the office, she found Tyson comfortably lying on the documents. The soulful dog eyes searched hers. Olivia curled up next to the retriever, who surprisingly didn't resist, and both fell asleep.

Awakening an hour later, Olivia stretched, achy from all the tension of the evening and sleeping on the floor. Grateful that Tyson hadn't left, she grinned at her. "I know you're stuck with me," she whispered, stroking her head. Tyson edged closer. "I miss him too," Olivia said. She hugged Tyson with every bit of her strength, sobbing.

Finally breathing again, she blew her nose and telephoned Western to confirm that Vasquez had been sent home with a negative head CT.

Tyson got to her feet. Stretching and then shaking herself, she tripped over the empty drawer. That was when Olivia noticed a printed letter, cryptically taped to the drawer's bottom.

September 24, 1998

Dear Mr. Champion,
We can't apologize enough for your misfortune. This notarized letter will serve to acknowledge our agreement. The first of every month, $2500.00 will be deposited into your account with First Chicago Bank and Trust. If there are any additional medical bills, please contact my office directly.

Acceptance of this arrangement will recognize the already agreed upon confidentiality clause dismissing any public or private discussion of the events that took place on January 30, 1998, as well as serve as concession of no liability due Mrs. Montana.

Please contact my office or cell phone with any concerns or questions,

Kind regards,
Michael Brewster
Attorney at Law

Olivia read the letter over and over. Was Champion blackmailing Curtis? The letter said "Mrs. Montana." It was certainly the date, as close as she could remember, of the hit-and-run.

Lou stumbled over the front landing on his way in, cursed, and leaning in the office doorway, quietly joked, "Not enough beds in this place?"

Olivia had lain down to think about the letter and drifted into a strange sleep. She jumped up and, hurriedly shoving the letter in her pocket, started scooping up the papers and putting them back in the drawer. "Just trying to organize a few things," she mumbled. "Congrats on Verde's win."

Laying down his gear, Lou spoke seriously. "Last night was tough for me, too, though nothing can compare to what you must be feeling. You can come to me any time. I think what you're doing is good."

She hugged him, and they left the office. "Let's have breakfast—after we sleep a little. I have questions. I must say there's nothing like experiencing things in the flesh."

*

By the time Olivia looked at her phone the next morning, she had eight voicemails—two from Amanda, one from Bart, one from Gabe, one from David Rogers and three from Sophie.

My God, doesn't anyone sleep? she wondered, then noticed it was already 10:00 AM.

Lou's door was still closed. Tyson was lying outside the kitchen door watching Marco lead the horses to pasture. Luisa was folding laundry in the sun.

Olivia closed herself in Curtis's office and dialed Brewster. "Thanks for taking my call on a Sunday," she said. "This is important."

"I heard you're working with the Commission." He sounded like he was trying to be extra sensitive, like he could hear her anxiety. "I think it's a win for both sides."

She ignored his spiel. "I saw the letter." She could hear the hardness in her voice, but she couldn't change it.

There was no response.

"I know who Bernard Champion is."

"Olivia, I don't understand."

"Sure you do," she said abruptly. "We're entrusted with carrying out Curtis's wishes. He asked me to make sure Bernard Champion continues to extort money—Curtis's money. He's the kid Curt ran over, right? Will you finally answer?"

"You misunderstand the situation entirely."

"Then explain," she replied angrily.

"I'll be more than willing to go over everything. I need to ask you to do me one favor first."

"What?"

"Talk to your mother. Then I can answer any additional questions."

"I'm asking you, Michael."

There was a silence. Then, "Talk to your mother, Olivia."

•

Her mother was the last person in the world she wanted to talk to, especially about this. All the old anger welled up in her. Her mother was a person who wrecked everything. She had wrecked their family life, she had wrecked her husband, she had wrecked Curtis. Olivia had always thought of herself as the one who got away, but now she saw that her mother was still in control of her too, and that she would continue to be until Olivia finally stood up to her.

She fretfully debated how to approach her. She hadn't spoken to her since last week, though she was front and center at the fight, courtesy of Ed Rappaport. Olivia couldn't seem to push the anger aside, to think clearly. Shouting had always gotten partial information from her mother, but it always made Olivia want to murder her. The woman was a conniver and a liar.

Leaving a note for Lou for a rain check on breakfast and ignoring a text from Amanda, she got in the car and drove over to Sophie's.

Before exiting the car, she checked her face in the rearview mirror—an old habit still necessary because her mother never missed a chance to mention her appearance, good or bad. Break one tyranny, maybe others follow, she suddenly thought, looking down at her sweat pants, torn sweatshirt and worn sneakers and realizing there was nothing she could do about them. What if she marched in there regardless of what her mother might criticize? Did she really care, in her mid-thirties, what her mother thought?

She laughed at herself ruefully. She had never cared what her mother thought of her, but somehow the woman got to her anyway.

Sophie opened the door and smiled her sweetest. "Dear, come have breakfast with Lucy and me."

Seeing her still in her red brocade bathrobe and hair in curlers, Olivia snipped, "Going somewhere, later?"

Lucy greeted her from the kitchen. "Come and have a biscuit, hot out of the oven," she called.

Olivia followed her mother into the kitchen and kissed Lucy hello. She poured herself a cup of French pressed coffee and leaned against the counter, across from both women, as they helped themselves to biscuits and fresh berries.

"Mother, we have something important to discuss."

Sophie held out her cup and asked for a refill. "I know dear," she said, as if they were talking about the weather. "Michael called this morning very concerned."

Lucy rose to go, but Sophie flagged her to remain seated.

"Mother, it's better if we talk in private," Olivia said, turning to her aunt and clutching her hand. "Lucy, please."

Once alone, Sophie said brightly, "Why don't I change, and we can chat."

"We can chat just as you are."

"I know why you're upset—"

"I don't think you have a clue why I'm upset." Her tone escalated. "I'm kept in the dark all these years while you're being blackmailed by some guy Curtis evidently hit on a dark and stormy night way back in 1997—a guy, by the way, who you told me Curtis had killed and left dead by the side of the road. Why is Mirabelle working for Rappaport? And more important, why was she on Curtis's payroll?"

Realizing that no response was forthcoming, Olivia shouted, "Mother, I'm not leaving until you tell me the entire story. Since Brewster was kind enough to give you a heads-up, I'm assuming you've prepared a response."

But Sophie only launched into an elaborate speech about how family secrets need to remain buried. Olivia need not worry, everything was taken care of, and she, too, was carrying out Curtis's wishes.

Olivia took another tack. She moved next to her mother and lowered her tone. "Let's start with the letter I discovered."

Sophie stared straight ahead. Olivia saw those same brown eyes that used to placate her father in the very early days, before they divorced. She handed Sophie the letter. "I promise to be calm. Tell me what this is."

Sophie took one glance at the letter and clutched her face. "I never wanted you to know," she sobbed. "It's ancient history. Thank God for your brother."

Angry outbursts typically made Sophie manufacture wild stories. Olivia considered bringing Lucy back but had no idea if her aunt knew the truth. Instead, Olivia chose silence—the one thing she knew her mother couldn't withstand. Sophie lived in a world where conversation, even her own idle chatter, created peace and comfort, especially during trying times.

After a 15-minute harangue about how she knew she had ruined everyone's life, Sophie blurted out, "It was me!"

Those words...they were Curtis's words: "mom, not me."

"Olivia, my darling, it was a confusing time. No one was more thoughtful than Curtis. You lost a lifetime of wonderful experiences—things a brother and sister should share. You held everything against him for something—"

Olivia slammed her cup on the table. "Stop it, Mother," she shouted. "You're turning this on me? If you ever loved your son, you'll tell me the rest." She had to stop herself from grabbing some part of her mother and really hurting her. "A few minutes before Curtis died, he said—"

Sophie shrieked, "You never told me he spoke." She started pulling the curlers from her hair with both fists and hurling them across the room. "I should've died first. My son, my poor son, I made so many mistakes," she moaned, dropping her head in her hands.

Furious at how little she had yet learned about the matter at hand, Olivia took hold of her mother's tear-soaked hands and pulled them away from her face. She knew something bad lay ahead. She detested her mother's histrionics, but this was the only way she knew to get some answers.

"We can't heal unless we put this behind us," she said in a carefully even tone. "I need the truth, now."

Sophie wiped her eyes and took a deep breath. Straightening her robe, she murmured, "I'd do things differently. I swear to you I would. Once you claim a path—"

"Mother, this isn't *The Bold and the Beautiful*," Olivia calmly chided her. "Go on, please."

Sophie was holding her crucifix tight. "I pray you can forgive me and understand—"

"Enough."

Violently shaking her head, Sophie rubbed her hands together, as if she was cold. She had a glazed look in her eyes. "It was so dark. The streets were icy. I should've never let Curtis train so late. Or he should have stayed overnight with Vinnie. I got it in my head that I had to pick him up. You weren't here. You know how I detest staying alone."

Olivia barely dared breathe. Something was coming.

Her mother shuddered. "Lake Shore Drive was closed. I lost my way going through Cabrini Green. It was close to midnight so I sped up. I took another shortcut and then..."

Olivia grabbed her chair. "What then?"

"You tell me, first. What did Curtis say? How could you betray me like this?"

"Betray you?" Olivia hissed. All these years she couldn't bring herself to forgive her mother or Curtis for the hit-and-run. This was worse. Sophie was driving. Sophie hit the kid, not Curtis. Was Curt even in the car at the time? The words he had scribbled, right before he died, "Mom, not me"...Why couldn't he have told her before? Those events had changed her life, too. They were each victims of their mother's negligence and deceit.

How was she going to keep it together? She looked at her mother, suffering away, as she was so good at doing. Olivia was completely immune to that; she didn't care how hateful it made her feel. She could find not one iota of love or emotion for her mother at this moment. She couldn't even remember when her heart had been filled with anything but anger toward her.

Sophie pleaded, "There're things you can't take back."

"Some place between your house and Cabrini, at midnight, you ran someone over. But he didn't die, like you said. He survived, and he's been blackmailing you ever since, right?"

"Livy, listen to me." She took hold of Olivia's hands and looked her in the eye. "Bernard was 14. He was leaving a friend's house. He didn't see me, and I—"

"He didn't see you? It wasn't his responsibility to see you! You left him to die in the snow. His father blackmailed you, then."

"Livy, will you stop about the blackmail. It wasn't like that."

"I'm listening," she shouted.

"I'm not saying another word until you stop shouting at me."

That was it. Olivia turned to leave. As she was reaching for the kitchen doorknob, Lucy returned.

"Livy, you need to hear your mother."

"Aunt Lucy, what else is there to tell? Can this get worse?"

Hysterical, Sophie muttered incoherently to herself.

"Let me tell this," said Lucy, handing her sister a box of Kleenex. "Curtis and your mother scoured the newspaper and listened to the radio that day. They called all the nearby hospitals. There were no reports until the following day when they saw a small article in *The Chicago Sun-Times* about a hit-and-run." Lucy went over to Olivia and led her by the hand to a chair.

Olivia flinched. How had she failed to see that report? She too had scoured the newspapers.

"Your mother decided to contact the police. Curtis talked her out of it. It was right before the Olympic trials. There were endorsements and sponsors. The newspaper set up a fund where you could donate money to cover hospital expenses. Bernard—"

"'You knew about this the entire time? You were an accessory to a crime."

"As were you," Lucy said very quietly. Then she continued with the story. "We would have told you. Curtis demanded we spare you in case the authorities found out. Yes, we should have gone to the police. Yes, maybe your mother should have served time. Bernard and Mirabelle were wards of the state living in a foster home. Curtis paid Bernie's medical bills, and he supported him and Mira through college. Bernie recovered from his injuries. He teaches English at Northwestern." Lucy's eyes were shining, as if she was talking about a child of her own. "He loved your brother," she added.

Olivia waited for the anger to pass, but it didn't. She couldn't get past it. It made her feel like a monster, like the person she feared she truly was. She scowled at her aunt.

"Let me get this right," she said, her voice cutting the air. "Bernard and Mirabelle knew Mom ran him over…Or, did they believe Curtis was driving? Did my mother ever own up to her actions?"

"Livy, you know the answer to that," Lucy barked, out of character. "You weren't around, and they protected you. You never asked any more questions, did you?"

Again on her way to the door, Olivia shouted, "You both secretly blame me."

"Olivia, we love you. However, you aren't being rational."

She turned back. "My life changed that night, too. You were all protecting yourselves. Mom should have faced charges. You dragged a 15-year-old boy into this process. I believe Mother—and Curtis—were concerned I would turn her in to the police. That's why they didn't tell me any of this. And in the process I lost my family—I lost my brother *twice*! I missed having a mother, too. Now, I don't know if I can ever look at her again."

"Your mother protected her family," Lucy said evenly, not backing down. "You need to consider that. Your entire life, you've judged others. My darling, sometimes we have to look to ourselves for the way things turn out."

Lucy wrapped her arm around her sister and stood her on her feet. "I know you don't want to face it," she said, turning and speaking over Sophie's shoulder as she led her out of the room, "but you had a role in this too."

Olivia sat paralyzed, wondering what sort of mother lets her son take blame for something she did. Did Curtis understand how his and their mother's actions made Olivia mistrust everyone? Now she had to face her own truth—that she had based her life on a lie. The inescapable emptiness took her breath away.

Eventually she left the house and drove to Duffy's. When she called home to say she'd be late, Luisa mentioned that Bart had stopped by. Olivia was glad she had missed him.

Devoid of customers at 2:00 PM, Duffy's musty wood smell welcomed Olivia. She dropped her Platinum card on the bar and waved to the bartender, who recognized her from the week before. "Yoichi," was all she said.

"You know your whiskies," he responded, smiling appreciatively and reaching for a glass.

Sliding into the far booth she said, "Bottle, please."

"Sure, Doc, coming right up."

Olivia checked Western's emergency call schedule. She wasn't taking calls for another two days. Seeing two voicemails from Sophie, one from Lucy and a recent one from Bart, she powered off her cell.

Admiring the Steuben whiskey glass in the afternoon sunlight, she sighed, thankful for the hot comforting sensation Yoichi provided.

No more regrets. No more bullshit. What Curtis went through? She wanted to hurt Sophie like she'd been hurt. She poured another hit. She wasn't sufficiently anesthetized.

*

She looked around for a wall clock, as an arm reached over her shoulder and lifted the Yoichi bottle.

"Norris, you're full of surprises," Bart said. "Mind if I sit? I'm meeting someone from Caesar's." She looked at his watch. It was 6:00 PM. She had been here for several hours, evidently.

She had learned to pace her drinking in college. She was nowhere near intoxicated, though it had been over a year since she'd spent an afternoon slowly sucking down whiskey.

Straightening her slouch and replacing her shoes, she smiled up at Bart. "My pleasure, Rossi. Ever had this stuff? A wealthy boyfriend turned me onto it in med school. I don't know much about coffee, but whiskey is another story."

She couldn't tidy her makeup or risk toppling over by going to the ladies—or take the chance of Bart leaving. Today it was the alcohol making her light-headed and not him—though maybe not.

Draping his camel hair jacket over the seatback, he slid to the back of the booth and swung his feet up. Just that little action of his, so familiar to her already, lifted her out of all her self-pity. She blinked, taking her first free breath all day.

"To what does Duffy's owe your honorable presence on a Sunday afternoon?" he asked. "Duffy happened to mention you've been here since noon."

"I got here after two," Olivia snapped, brushing her hair off her face and adjusting her sweatshirt.

Infatuated with her, he changed tacks. "Everything went great last night. You showed everyone that you're here to stay."

"Terrific," she muttered.

"Can I get you kids anything?" Duffy interrupted.

"An extra glass," Bart requested. "Think I might stay a while."

Duffy came over with the glass. "What about your dinner?"

"Nah, this is much more interesting. Besides, Dr. Norris and I have important things to discuss."

The phone rang and Duffy wandered off to take the call.

Olivia poured a modest drink for herself.

"Don't hold back because of me," he said. "Here, let me help you."

He took the bottle and poured them each four fingers. "Now, you want to tell me what's troubling you?"

She stared at his in-need-of-a-shave face. He blushed at her directness, or perhaps it was from the whiskey.

"Eaten anything today?" he asked her.

She shook her head, proudly raising her glass.

Bart motioned to a waiter and ordered some cheese fries. "You need something in your stomach. Everyone will tell you I'm not particularly empathetic, and the last thing I want to do is hear your problems. With that said, what can I do to cheer you up?" He couldn't help grinning.

She wanted to smile. He was cute and sweet—everything she fantasized about, except he belonged to someone else.

Looking around the now overflowing bar, Bart said, "I guarantee everyone here is in worse shape than you. My advice is drink up. If you need to get shit-faced, I'll make sure you get home safe. Here, try some of the finest fries you'll ever taste."

"Jesus Christ, these are good," she exclaimed, wolfing down the fries. She looked at him, mid-bite. "I don't need babysitting."

"Hey, I'm here for the fries and whiskey. Doesn't bother me that you eat like a goddamn bird. Means more for me…Let me distract you. I got a story to tell you. I have this friend in New York—"

"A girl, no doubt."

"No, a 70-year-old guy—one of the best card players I've ever known. He taught me poker. And this guy is wealthy—Forbes 400 wealthy. Still, he plays the New York lottery. Even though he has a chauffeur, every day he leaves Park Avenue and takes the subway to a Brooklyn drug store near where he grew up and buys a lottery ticket. It's a place where you can pick your numbers."

She waved him off. "I'm not in the mood—"

"Shut up for a minute and listen. He plays these same numbers. When I'm in Manhattan, he drags me along."

Giggling, she said, "I can't imagine you lining up in a drug store for a lottery ticket."

"You'll like this," he promised, swallowing some whiskey and taking a moment to appreciate it going down. "This is strong stuff." He took a look at the bottle. "I bet you can drink me under the table."

She snickered. "Today wouldn't be fair. I got too much of a head start."

"So listen, last night leaving the Event Center, I was looking for a piece of paper in my wallet when my lucky numbers must have fallen out."

"You carry them in your wallet? Why not in your phone? How many years is this story going to take?" She was laughing by now. She couldn't help it. "Anyway, if you play the same numbers every time, how come you haven't memorized them by now?" She tapped her head with her finger, as if to say he maybe wasn't too swift.

"You're getting your sense of humor back…and that smile." Frankly admiring her, he briefly lost the thread of what he was trying to say. "Oh, so I was walking to my car," he resumed, "and one of the fighters ran up behind me and handed me my paper. You know what he said after reading the numbers?"

She waited.

"He said, '*Tienes un amigo en Mexico?*'"

"He asked if you have a friend in Mexico?"

"Let me show you my numbers," he said, reaching for his wallet and pulling out the rumpled paper that read 10-12-58.

"And this has significance?"

"Think, Norris, think. Pull out *your* numbers."

"Christ, Rossi. I'm not a gambler."

"The numbers Curtis left you."

"10-25-68?"

"If you place an 001 in front, it becomes a telephone number in Mexico."

She had to think about this. She got up to use the ladies room and her legs slightly buckled.

"Seabiscuit," he said, putting out a hand to steady her, "stay put."

Scowling, she regained her seat. "You believe these belong to some place in Mexico?"

"Don't you ever listen to your voicemail? Or just not ones from me? When I didn't hear from you this morning, I dialed this number. It goes to a clinic in Tecate."

"What kind of clinic?"

"A medical clinic. When I went by your house this morning—looking for you, I might add—I spoke to Chui and Marco. This clinic performs prefight blood tests, physical exams and scans on boxers. And it's owned by Dr. Juan Alejandro Santiago Fernandez, the brother of Santiago, the head of the UBA. If that weren't enough, Fernandez owns gyms in Tecate, Ensenada and Mexico City. Remember Curtis trained in Mexico City and Tecate? This could be the key..." Suddenly aware of Olivia's pallor, he whispered, "You're looking green."

She fled to the ladies room.

A few minutes later overhearing groans, Bart knocked on the door. "Norris, you okay?"

Before he could come in after her, she came out. "How humiliating," she mumbled.

"Don't be silly. It's happened to me plenty of times." He led her back to the booth. "Let's sit down. At least this gives me hope I can outdrink you the next time."

"That's one of the kindest things you've said to me. Look, your friend must be here by now. I'm calling a cab."

"While you were—shall I say, indisposed—I canceled my dinner. I'll drive you home."

He paid the bill and put her credit card in her wallet.

"Thanks," she said sheepishly. Searching for a mirror in her purse, "I must look a sight."

"True, you have looked better." It sounded tender, coming from him right now.

They stood without speaking as they waited for the valet to bring his Porsche.

He helped her in, went around and slid in under the wheel and reached over her to lock her seatbelt.

"That's so s-w-e-e-t," she said, with a slur that was adorable to his ears. "What about my car?"

Admiring her coif obscuring her left eye, he said, "The boys can pick it up in the morning."

"I wanna go to your house," she demanded.

"Not a good idea."

"I don't want to go to Curtis's house. Please," she said with a sweet pout that made him want to kiss her.

Turning into his driveway, he saw that she had fallen asleep. Carefully he unbuckled her seat belt and leaned in to scoop her up out of the car. Dreamily she put her arms around his neck and nestled her head against his chest.

Locking the car with the remote, he buried his nose in her thick sweet-smelling locks. Inside, he reluctantly laid her on the living room couch and went into the dressing room closet to get a pillow and blanket. Coming back out, he tripped over her Nikes. He followed a trail of clothes on the floor and flicked on the hall light. Admiring her discarded black La Perla bra, he shook his head. This ain't good, he said to himself.

"Norris," he called out, "we need to get you home," as he bent to pick up matching La Perla panties in the bedroom doorway.

He turned on the bedroom light. Unconscious, Olivia lay curled up under the duvet, her sumptuous red hair rising across her mouth with every exhale.

Bart perched on the edge of the bed quietly laughing. He gently jiggled her shoulder. It was hopeless.

He gazed at the nape of her neck flowing perfectly into the slope of her shoulder but then stopped himself. Bad idea, he said to himself. Actually unforgiveable. He stood, and bent over her, tucking the duvet around her shoulders, averting his eyes from her generous breasts. He went back out in the hall and picked up her clothes, then went back and left them on the bed.

Picking up the pillow and blanket he had gotten out for her, he went back down the hall and tucked himself in on the living room sofa, with Sarah Vaughan singing in the background.

•

What seemed like minutes later, Bart woke up with a start, hearing a cup shatter.

"Sorry," Olivia said, peeking in from the kitchen. "I made coffee. I didn't want to wake you. I have to get home to change before work."

He sat up, fully clothed except for his shoes, and rubbed his day-old beard. She handed him a cup of coffee and said, "Don't expect much. This might be the worst you've ever tasted." He grabbed her wrist. "No, it's fine. Let me throw some water on my face, and I'll drive you to Duffy's."

She gently pulled her hand away. "Thank you for taking care of me last night," she said, failing to look at him. "It could take a lifetime to explain."

"By the way, you look surprisingly good after last night," he said.

"Good?"

"I mean, no one would believe you spent the afternoon wrapped around that bottle."

Years of periodic practice, she wished to blurt out.

He examined her expression intently. There was something important here. Something neither could yet admit.

She looked at her phone. "I should call Amanda."

Amanda. He had thought of her off and on last night. More than once when he caught himself gazing at Olivia, Amanda's image would appear in his mind. She had texted him, but he had ignored it. He knew he couldn't continue to ignore it, but what was happening with Olivia, as yet unspoken...just what was he going to do?

"I should phone her," said Olivia again.

Then, suddenly, it hit him. His phone. Amanda had borrowed it. She had passed it back to him while Gabe was castigating him for leaking to the press.

How could he have been so naïve? She had gone through his messages. That's how she found out about Stewart treating Vasquez, which she then told Rush about at the HBO table. He thought about all the times before when Mandy had innocently asked him to lend her his phone for a few minutes. How had it taken him so long to figure out what she was up to, for God's sake? For a split second he was furious, then just as quickly he was not. Amanda had played him, had played them both. But even though that burned him, it also meant she had done him a favor. This released him. And they—Olivia and he—could use her as she was using them. Everyone would get something out of it. So yes, he was still mad, as it turned out, but that just made it easier.

There was a feeling of time off the clock between him and Olivia, time that moment by moment was coming to an end. Driving to Duffy's flew by. The quiet was more erotic to Bart than seeing her naked in his bed.

"Are you sure about the clinic number?" Olivia asked.

"Let me make a few more calls," he said. He pulled into Duffy's empty lot and drove over next to her car.

Reluctantly she got out of his car. She could feel his eyes tracking her as she moved toward the Range Rover. Every move. She turned and asked quietly, "So, what now?"

"We go to Tecate."

Right away she felt less fragile. "Tecate?"

He winked, rolled up his window and sped off, practically tasting the deliciousness of a weekend with Olivia now that there was no loyalty issue. And he had no intention of confronting Mandy, either. Let her wonder why he wasn't calling her to task. He bet she would figure it out all by herself. When they met that evening for the usual session at the ranch house, he would see right away how she was going to play it. If she was greedy, she would fight for him *and* the story, but he wasn't interested in her anymore. She would figure that out, too, and also how not to lose face.

He put on Dr. John and Etta James and turned up the stereo to its fullest as he drove over to take punishment from Gabe about the leak Saturday night.

Twenty-Six

OLIVIA DROVE STRAIGHT to work for her 7:30 AM patient, her white coat hiding her sweats.

Donna, in a green scrub set of her own making, handed her a message that Senator McAllen needed to reschedule. She had completely forgotten about McAllen. She asked Donna to show the patient to the exam room when he arrived. She was going to call the senator's office right now and would be with them in a minute.

Once in her office, with a big mug of steaming coffee next to her, Olivia tried not to fantasize about a trip to Mexico with Bart. She ruminated on Curtis's leaving her the phone number for the clinic in Tecate. Was Bart seriously thinking they would go there? She wasn't at all sure she wanted to risk getting killed—even if it meant being with Bart. And what kind of cover could they use?

She dialed McAllen's number, thanked Elena for her call and asked her to have the Senator call whenever he had a chance.

"Do you speak with your brother often?" she asked.

"Yes, his wife Esme and I are very close. Their son, Rodrigo Jr., already loves boxing."

"I've been thinking about a little midweek getaway," Olivia said nervously.

Elena laughed conspiratorially. "Ah, I understand, you need privacy," she said. "I think Rancho Cielo Azul would be the perfect place."

"Yes, that's what I was thinking."

"I think it will not be possible to get a place there on short notice," Elena said hesitantly. "May I call Esme to find accommodations for you? She would love to meet Curtis's much-talked-of sister."

"Oh Elena, I'm not sure it would be good that she knows who I am...because I'll be with—"

"Don't worry, Esme is very discreet. She has to be, in her line of work. You know she is not even going to tell me who is with you." Elena was bubbling. She sounded like she couldn't wait to call her sister-in-law. "It would be a good time to go, before it gets too hot."

If she only knew how hot it already was, Olivia thought. Would Bart go along with her having taken his idea and run with it?

"Perhaps let Esme know we would like to arrive this Tuesday."

They re-rescheduled the call with the Senator for the following week, and Olivia was off the phone and texting Bart the details of her call.

Her phone vibrated. It was Amanda. Should she tell her about last night? Nothing happened, but would Amanda she see it that way? Do we bring her to Tecate? No, everyone knows she's press.

At four o'clock she stopped to take a breath as her office manager handed her another chart. It had been a productive day for a new-to-town practitioner. At the very least, her Las Vegas move was professionally successful.

•

Returning home, she discovered Bart perched on a barn grain barrel, tossing Tyson a tennis ball while he chatted with Marco and Chui. For the first time, the Golden ran to her, tail wagging. She dropped the ball at Olivia's feet. Thrilled, Olivia pitched the ball as far as she could and watched the dog's beautiful loping run as she went after it.

She went over to Bart, who was grinning at her.

"Fast move on Tecate. That's good work," he said.

"Curtis loved Mount Cuchama—the holy mountain," Chui said. "He would run up there for hours."

"Let's not forget the beer," Bart sighed.

"Chui and I took advantage of the local *cerveza*," added Marco. "Curtis never drank."

Bart asked the boys, "Did you ever visit Rancho Cielo Azul?"

"No, but Rodrigo's wife, Esme Escalone works there. We trained at the gym."

Olivia said, "You mean the gym owned by Juan Fernandez?"

Marco and Chui cryptically glanced at each other, then excused themselves to finish chores.

"Was that odd or is it me?" Olivia asked.

"I noticed it too." Bart called Marco back. "Is it Fernandez or the gym?"

Marco hesitated because of the nonverbal admonishments of his brother, then mumbled, "Chui and I enjoyed being with Curtis…Something was not good at the gym…or *la clinica*."

"You mean the medical clinic run by Fernandez?" Olivia asked.

"*Sí, la clinica.* It is part of the gym."

Bart looked askance.

"Tecate is very small," Marco said. "It has the beer factory and El Rancho Cielo Azul. The gym and the clinic are owned by Dr. Fernandez. He owns most of the city, with his brother."

"You mean Santiago?" said Olivia.

"*Sí. Señor Santiago* and his brother control boxing in Mexico. They control other things like horse racing and gambling, too. Chui and I worried it was the wrong place for Curtis and Vinnie. Lou will agree. There were things going on..."

Bart went a few steps deeper into the barn and petted Sweetpea Won. Olivia was pacing up and down the barn aisle as Marco went on to explain how Tecate was the perfect place to train: peaceful and surrounded by mountains. But the gym made them uncomfortable. On several occasions they told Curtis this, but he disregarded their worries, saying they were imagining things. It was the same in Santiago's Mexico City and Ensenada gyms. After a month in Tecate, Vinnie sent Lou and the boys home, saying Curtis needed fewer distractions. Believing Vincent must know best, they returned to Las Vegas.

Chui glumly added, "Maybe things would be different if we stayed."

Bart thanked the brothers and shepherded Olivia into the house. He grabbed two bottles of Evian and made his way toward the living room.

"Water?" she protested.

"We need clear heads," he replied, wondering why Olivia looked so damn together wearing those old disorderly clothes and after all she had had to drink. It meant one of two things: this broad was different—real different, or she'd traveled this road before. He relished the idea of finding out which.

Lying on the living room couch admiring the Botero, he was asking her if she had gotten coverage at the ED for the days they would be gone when the doorbell rang and Olivia went to let Amanda in. Giving her a hug, she called out "Yes," to Bart's question.

"Is he giving you trouble?" Amanda sighed, handing her a huge bag of Chinese take-out. In the living room, she plopped down next to Bart and grabbed a giant swig of his Evian.

"Back off, Mandy," he barked. "I'm getting in shape for the spa." He grabbed the bottle back from her and sat up.

Amanda took half a second's hesitation, then jumped right in. "Yeah, I thought about tagging along to Tecate," she said, "except next week I'm subbing for the main anchor."

He could see her calculating, trying to get one of them to tell her when they were going.

She met his eyes. "Guess they felt bad about cutting my stories," she added.

"I bet there's nothing stronger than fruit juice at this establishment," he said, "even though the biggest brewery in Mexico is down the road."

Olivia tossed him a printout she had run of the spa's fitness activities, menu and treatments. She was afraid to think about what Amanda had just said and passed over it with talk about the food she was unpacking.

Bart perused the lists. "This place is almost all vegetarian, perfect for me. But there's no way I'm climbing this goddamn Mount Chucamunga at six in the morning—or maybe any other time, either."

"Mount Cuchama," Olivia said, and they all laughed. "You'd better be in shape. We need to blend in as guests or exercise nuts. Esme will have her eye on us."

"Esme?" Amanda asked. "Rodrigo Escalone's wife, right? What's the connection between Esme, manager of the spa and wife of the former light-weight champ, and Senator McAllen, whose assistant happens to be Esme's sister-in-law?"

Bart and Olivia looked at her, and she laughed.

"Jesus Christ, I do my homework. Escalone was friends with two of the Mexican boxers who died. He went to Vincent about this drink concoction." Turning to Olivia, "Do you need me to do anything while you're gone? Bart, are there any fights I should attend—you know, to keep an eye on the Commission?"

Putting his hand on Amanda's knee, Bart grinned. "You need to keep your eyes open and relax, beautiful."

Amanda laughed off his sexist verbiage and removed his hand. "What are you hoping to uncover in Tecate?"

Olivia sucked on her Evian bottle. "Amanda's right. We need a plan," she said nervously. "If we're invading Fernandez and Santiago's playground, we'd better bring the right equipment."

"Ladies, relax!"

"The laws are different there," Olivia snapped.

"Look, we're staying at an exclusive fitness spa, not a hotel in Kabul. This is a fact-finding trip."

"Mexico can be dangerous these days."

Bart continued as if she hadn't said anything. "We were told Curtis had his prefight medical tests a week before the fight. We assumed they were done in the States. Do we know this for a fact?"

Blood drained from Olivia's face.

"That was insanely thoughtless," Amanda interjected. "Of course Curtis underwent his exams in the U.S. It makes no sense for him to test in Mexico, right?"

"We can't assume anything," Olivia said, jumping up and heading for Curtis's study. His passport would tell them, if they correlated the dates of his tests with when he left Mexico. She found the passport in the files under "Travel Documents" and smiled at how organized Curtis was. Going back with it to the living room, she found the other two bickering.

She threw the passport on the coffee table and started opening food containers. Amanda went to the kitchen and got plates.

"Curtis visited Mexico six times last year," Amanda said, perusing the passport. "Must be when he was in training for the Mexico City fight. He then stayed in Tecate before his last fight, and reentered the U.S. four days before the match."

"So if he had exams one week before that bout, they sure could have been completed in Tecate," Bart said, taking a big mouthful of sesame noodles with his chopsticks. "I can check in the Commission office. Have to figure out how to be discreet about it. The last thing we want is Gabe suspicious. It makes no sense for me to review Curtis's medicals. You think we should ask Lou?"

Olivia buzzed Lou on the intercom. "Chinese!" she exclaimed. "And can you come help us for a minute?"

Lou was still rubbing his eyes when he appeared in the living room. "I was napping," he grumbled as Amanda handed him her notes, the brochure for El Rancho Cielo Azul and Curtis' passport. "What the hell are you folks plotting?" he said. "These people play for keeps." He dabbed his perspiring forehead with an embroidered handkerchief.

Bart dug into the Szechuan eggplant while Olivia and Amanda reassured Lou. He wouldn't concede.

"Bart, you know this sport. It's power more than money. Livy, your brother was a great fighter, and Vinnie was a good man. I'll go to my grave believing he didn't die from natural causes."

Offering Lou some vegetable fried rice, Bart said, "Then you must know why we think something happened in Mexico. You love these kids. We owe it to them. Olivia and I want to—"

"That's enough," Lou interrupted, pounding the table. "Santiago controls Mexican boxing—hell, he controls all boxing. Sure, guys like Rappaport and Davolo funnel opponents to the States. That may not mean anything except that it's a shit sport."

"I don't understand," Olivia broke in.

Bart looked from Lou to her. "A boxer needs someone to fight. Promoters and managers chose opponents carefully, especially when they have a hot prospect." He made a face. "You know this, I've told you this," he said, frustrated by Lou's caution. "Curtis was a name when he turned pro, but there were lots of fighters out there who might have beaten him. Vincent approved opponents who helped Curtis develop his skills against boxers unlikely to win."

"Vinnie turned down lots of guys," Lou put in. "Don't get me wrong. Curtis fought no tomato-cans! Mexico has a constant supply of opponents and tons of gyms. For a poor kid with hardly any education, it's a good career."

Tyson chose this moment to grab the rather large piece of eggplant Bart was holding in his chopsticks as he waited to make another point. "What?" he shouted as Tyson moved away to eat her spoils. "You sneaky dog!"

Turning right back to Olivia, Bart said, "Santiago is boxing's Don Corleone. He wanted to see Curtis win, but..."

"But what?"

"I'm not sure if boxing attracts people searching for power or people who get a taste and want more. Santiago controls who fights for a title in a specific weight class. People—especially promoters and managers—owe him."

"Are you saying Curtis or Vincent owed Santiago," she replied, exasperated, "and that's how Curtis died?"

"None of us knows why Curtis died. You need to prepare yourself that it might turn out that it was just from a tough fight."

"You guys said the fight wasn't tough," she snapped.

"Livy, any time you're sparring, you take risks," Lou said. "I'll tell you what worries me to death:, your Tecate fact-finding mission. These are not people you fool around with. God damn it, Bart. You shouldn't be risking anyone's life down there, especially not Livy's."

Bart took a deep breath, sensing that Lou knew more than he was saying. "Didn't you live there for a while?"

Lou started shouting. "I've been trying to tell you. You shouldn't put your noses where they don't belong. Boxing has operated like this for a hundred years. You think you're gonna change this sport? If you do, you need to know it may cost too much."

Bart looked at Amanda, who was suddenly silent. He saw that she was listening intently, taking in everything. Olivia nervously twisted her hair, listening more to their voices and paying attention to their actions to try to read how dangerous it actually might be.

"I know you have a few years on me," Bart shouted over Lou's words. Lou stopped talking and Bart continued. "But I've worked in boxing for over 30 years. Like you, I've seen kids die. This trip may only prove that boxing occasionally takes a life. On the other hand, if we find a link to something more, I'll also be responsible because I walked away, too. The path I chose—hiding my head in the sand—isn't cutting it."

Lou grunted and ambled out to the kitchen. He came back with a beer in hand and stood leaning in the doorway, quietly fuming as he sipped it. The two women brought out more of the take-out containers while Bart answered his phone.

"Okay, okay," he growled, "what do you want from me?"

Amanda hugged Lou so hard his cigar fell to the floor and beer spilled down his shirt.

"Jesus, woman. See what you made me do?"

Bart put down his chopsticks and leaned back in his seat. "Describe the layout," he said. "Do the boxers rotate in from Mexico City and Ensenada, or are these all Tecate kids? Who's training them, and where does Fernandez come into play? Are fighters his only patients?"

"Hold on, damn it. Let me catch my breath. Where are Marco and Chui? They spent more time there than me."

Olivia called the brothers on the intercom, and they came right over. Amanda was madly taking notes. Bart warned her the information couldn't go any further without his permission. She admonished him for giving her no credit for understanding when it was important to keep things to yourself and then had the good grace to blush.

Marco recounted memories of the Ensenada racetrack, the camaraderie among the fighters and riding horseback while Curtis ran in the mountains at dawn. He described brutal gym wars when one boxer demonstrated his prowess above another. Several times a week someone would be KO'd, unsuccessful in escaping a right hand.

"The clinic is attached to the gym, so Fernandez oversees both and treats the fighters?" Bart asked.

Marco nodded, clearly nervous.

Bart snatched one of Luisa's fresh sugar cookies from Olivia and grinned over his prize. "Well, Watson, looks like we're off to discover Tecate," he said goofily. "Bring your hiking boots and Lululemon yoga pants."

Amanda was looking through her notes. "I'll do a background check on Fernandez," she said. "I have a close friend who's the sports anchor for Univision. He's bound to know the good doctor. Are you driving or flying?"

"I think we should fly to San Diego, then rent a car so we can visit the local hot spots."

Olivia checked her phone and found a confirmation email from the spa. "We're booked," she said, holding up the phone excitedly, though there was a lot of fear in that excitement, too.

"Hot spots? You mean local bars," Amanda teased.

Lou started in again, ignoring Amanda and haranguing Bart about the dangers of what they were doing. "You could easily get killed," Lou said one last time, glaring at Bart, who maintained a stubborn obliviousness. Frustrated, Lou left the room.

Bart was aware that Amanda was watching him. He didn't let on, but he also didn't stop himself from tracking Olivia's every move. Was Amanda going to fight for her rights—which she had forfeited by stealing from him and using him?

At one point Olivia left the room and Mandy stared at him boldly. He looked over at her. "Something on your mind?" he challenged her.

She was fuming, but she didn't answer, and he went back to perusing fight factsheets and test results. Evidently she still thought she had something to lose, he thought. That annoyed him. He thought for a moment of letting her hear some bitter truths about herself but managed to hold himself back.

"I'll email you a detailed report before you leave," Amanda said with spirit. "Please tell me you know your life might be in danger."

He stood up and went to the doorway. "Yes, I know," he said as he walked away.

*

Bart went into the kitchen, just to get away for a few minutes. What he had said was true, but it wasn't going to Mexico that frightened him, it was going with Olivia. No, it was Olivia herself, the fact of her—it terrified him.

She brought up old feelings, feelings he hadn't felt for so long, not since that time in New Orleans so many years ago with Tatou. Just thinking of that name made him stop. He felt the friendship band in his pocket, the one he carried with him still, and he momentarily forgot where he was, caught in the grip of sensations he thought he had long since achieved control of.

He heard a soft knock on the kitchen door and wheeled around, startled.

Olivia chuckled. "Hey, it's dark in here," she said. "There's chocolate cake in the fridge," she told him, going to the refrigerator and pulling open the door.

He admired her silhouette, backlit by the refrigerator light in the darkened kitchen. She brought out what was left of a multilayered chocolate cake with fudge frosting and looked at it with fondness.

"I see you got a head start," he remarked, opening cupboard doors until he found where the plates were and taking out three of them. "Let's take this beauty out to the party."

She touched his hand, just touched it. "I'm traditionally unflappable, but I have to tell you, I'm frightened," she said.

He reached over and smoothed her hair off her forehead. "I think as long as we're careful and we get out if we feel at all worried, we'll be okay."

Olivia shook her head. "No, it's not that." She shrugged. "I think I don't know enough to be scared for my life. I'm frightened of finding out things about Curtis that I don't want to know. But I was a terrible sister. Curtis died from a sport he loved, and I never supported him. It would be easier to accept that he didn't die in vain. That's why I have to do this."

"Well, if you don't get yourselves killed, everyone will benefit," Amanda said acridly from the doorway.

Olivia jumped away from Bart.

"You want cake?" she blurted.

"This story," Amanda persisted, "if there is a story, will change my life." She looked from one to the other, glaring, then laughed it off. "Were you going to eat all that cake between yourselves?" she exclaimed.

Bart held up the three plates. "As you see, Sherlock Holmes, we were going to share," and he led the way back to the living room.

Twenty-Seven

IT WAS EASY TO forget how green Las Vegas wasn't, Olivia thought, until you drove from San Diego to Tecate. The undulating emerald knolls were lined with horse paddocks and grazing cattle on the outskirts of working ranches.

She felt at ease. It was good to laugh wholeheartedly as she and Bart shared personal and professional war stories in the Toyota FJ Cruiser they had rented at the airport.

Proudly offering him potato chips, diet Coke and a Snickers, she said, "I have a regular Coke if you prefer. Pig out now. It's a safe bet that low-fat and concealed fiber will be number one on your plate."

"How do you think I maintain my girlish figure?" he rejoined.

"I thought you did that by staying up late gambling, womanizing and drinking."

"Ha, that shows how much you know. I've been a vegetarian for 25 years." He flashed her a grin. "This place will suit me perfectly."

Olivia rolled her eyes. "Isn't it a contradiction to drink alcohol and not eat meat?"

"Alcohol is a vegetable," he said pointing to his T-shirt that read: "Grain Feels No Pain!"

For that moment she felt completely happy. She lowered her window and leaned back to enjoy the air on her face.

There was no wait at the border. After the Federales checked their passports, Olivia took a deep breath.

"Nervous?" Bart challenged her.

"A bit."

"Take that guilty look off your face. We're here for a rejuvenating vacation, not counter-espionage." He reached over and patted her thigh like a college basketball coach.

"Before you picked me up, Lou was waiting by the door with a duffle bag, looking like he was heading off to summer camp. When I explained why he shouldn't go, I thought he'd cry. I said we needed him to keep an eye on things in Vegas and promised to call twice a day."

"Lou is a loyal friend and a good man. Not too many of those around these days."

When they reached Tecate, Olivia was like a kid, looking at and exclaiming about everything. Bart watched her as she took in the colorful *zócalo*, the town square, crammed with vendors and children playing. Her eyes were alight, her face intent, but he could see that some part of her was far from here.

He wondered why she and Curtis were estranged. He wouldn't ask her, he would wait for her to tell him. She would explain when she was ready. He wasn't in a hurry for that because it would mean he would have to share too.

She was looking at him inquiringly, and he realized she expected a response to something she had just said.

Embarrassed, he confessed, "Sorry. I wasn't paying attention."

She laughed at him, embarrassed too because she had been so open. "I just said Curtis must have seen all this hundreds of times."

Driving through the flourishing El Rancho Cielo Azul gardens, Olivia suggested ditching the junk food.

"You think they'll search your suitcase?" he mocked. "I sure hope not: I have two bottles of Stag's Leap and a bottle of Laphroaig."

They left the car with the very handsome valet, who also took charge of their bags while they went inside to register.

Manicured magenta bougainvillea and white roses lined the freshly painted adobe registration building. Inside, they were plied with papaya juice and fresh fruit skewers as they signed in. A clerk handed them cloth bags containing a refillable water bottle, a schedule of activities and a map of the premises, and they were met with their bags and escorted to Casita 15—a 10-minute walk from the main building.

The valet opened the seven-foot carved wooden door into a hacienda-style cottage surrounded by a lushly landscaped, wrap-around patio. A 20-foot ceiling fan circled warm air over a king-size poster bed. When the valet had left, Olivia made a giddy run for the bed and threw herself down to luxuriate.

"By the way," she said, pleased with herself, "so we don't argue later, I get the bed, and you can camp out on the sofa."

"We can trade off sleeping accommodations," he muttered.

It was three o'clock. There was a New Guests Orientation in an hour. They decided to unpack and go for a walk to look around the grounds and the main house. Olivia insisted they attend the orientation.

"We just arrived and already you're planning a hike?" Bart said. "Stop being so OCD."

"I plan to take advantage of our surroundings," she countered. She turned on the CD player, which was fully equipped with a wide selection of soundscapes and Mexican music. "I could get used to this place," she said, dancing to a meringue. "There's a stretch class we can take before orientation."

"The only stretching I'm doing is reaching for a wine glass."

·

Fifteen minutes later, on the cobblestone path that led through the sculpture gardens teeming with rabbits, butterflies and birds, they came upon a tall lanky gentleman in his early sixties with six pairs of binoculars around his neck. The man pulled a list with pictures of local birds out of his jacket pocket and handed it to Bart and Olivia.

"Already here for bird-watching—just what I like to see," he said, handing them a pair of binoculars. "I'm Mike. For future reference, you should keep your ranch bag and bottle with you at all times. Folks quickly dehydrate here, even in the winter. It's all the exercise and dry weather."

Over the next 45 minutes, Mike led them, along with four other guests, around the grounds identifying birds. Bart lagged behind, bored, but Olivia fell in love with the surroundings.

Ending up where they began, Mike carefully folded each pair of binoculars and said, "I'll be conducting the orientation. May I give you some words of advice? Folks overdo it while they're here and forget everything once they return home. Pick one thing you want to accomplish and can live with. It could be cutting out soda or incorporating some form of exercise daily. I'll lead a hike tomorrow, so hope to see you there."

Olivia asked, "There are other hikes?"

"Yes, they leave every 30 minutes."

"We're looking forward to catching up with Esme Escalone. Do you know when she'll be around?"

"You know Esme?"

"She's a relative of a friend, and we wanted to hook up," said Olivia.

"She should be around. Try the office." He started to turn away, then added, "She leads the 6:15 hike tomorrow morning, before going in to work."

·

The cuisine was excellent: grilled vegetable salad, roasted cauliflower soup, beet soufflé, eggplant quesadillas and flan. The chef had once run New York's Four Seasons.

Strolling back to their casita, Bart removed his jacket and wrapped it around Olivia's shivering shoulders.

"I had no idea it would get this cold at night," she said, grateful for the warmth.

"Even though three days in this fitness paradise will seem an eternity, the time will disappear if we don't prepare. By the way, check my pockets."

"Thank you," she laughed, gleefully pulling two carob cookies from Bart's jacket and giving him one of them.

Slowing in front of their cottage, both were apprehensive that it would be the first time they'd be together all night. Olivia inadvertently touched Bart's hand. Her heart raced.

To avoid a discussion, Bart turned on the CD player, which accidentally skipped from a salsa to a Luis Miguel ballad. He poured two glasses of wine and handed one to her. "I'm a bit on edge too," he said smoothly.

If he only knew. She looked at him surreptitiously. He looked good in those jeans. Was she going to be able to sleep here and not make a move?

She kept busy putting clothes in the drawers, poorly concealing her nervousness.

"Have a sip by the fire," he suggested, indicating the loveseat. "I promise to be a perfect gentleman."

"You mean like the other night when you kissed me?" she said sharply.

He didn't respond, unsure which direction to take. He took a generous swallow of wine and challenged her to a game of poker.

"Strip?"

"What would you do if I said *yes*? Actually I was thinking about a friendly game of Texas Hold'em."

"Sure—even though the deck is stacked," she replied, grinning.

As they played, Bart recounted gambling tales from New Orleans, Vegas and from a cruise he had taken to Istanbul.

"Some résumé," she said. "Before we get too tired, let's form a plan for our time here."

Grabbing his Partagas cigar, he offered her his warmest jacket and suggested they step outside. He threw a few logs on the outdoor fireplace and pulled over two chaises. He considered admonishing her for looking so good in his coat, but he was well past playing her, and she was too smart.

With fresh wine in their glasses, they started to concentrate on a plan. They would take the hike with Esme tomorrow morning, and Olivia would encourage Esme to hook them up with her husband, saying that she would love to see the gym where her brother had trained.

"Roberto takes us to the gym, where we check out Fernandez's operation," Bart continued, making it sound like a Girl Scout picnic. "Once we get a better idea of the layout, we can nail down our angle."

Olivia nodded, fixated on Bart's hands, imagining them against her skin. Flushed from the wine, she said, "I think I need some rest." She stood. "You coming?" She couldn't help smiling, noticing his eyes memorizing her contour.

"I can look, can't I?" he grinned. "You go on ahead. I'll be inside in a few. This cigar is too good to waste."

She left him a blanket and pillow on the sofa. Something—guilt?—prompted her to text Amanda, who immediately responded telling her to have a good time. Relieved, Olivia took a deep breath and turned out the light. "Bet she means not too good," she murmured as she drifted into a deep sleep.

·

Hearing the 5:30 alarm, Bart flew off the sofa. Olivia was gone already. "Who gets up before they absolutely have to?" he groaned. He found a scribbled note on the toilet seat. "Time to breathe some fresh air, Norris," he said half out loud. He read the note through bleary eyes: "Don't forget hiking boots, sleepy head."

Crammed into the folk art lounge, 30 chatty guests remarked on one another's footwear. Some would head up Mt. Cuchama for a three-mile medium-to-difficult climb while others waited for a brisk walk through the sprawling ranch acres.

"Olivia," Mike called across the room, "where's Bart?"

"He's on his way, I hope, though I wouldn't be surprised if he—"

"Someone looking for *moi*?" Bart roared. "Bet you thought I'd still be asleep."

She looked at his boots. "Hmm, you might remove the REI tag, Mr. Outdoors."

"I needed new ones."

"Sure you did. By the way, let me introduce you to Esme."

An ebullient thirtyish woman in a green sweatshirt, black fitted leggings and hiking boots ran over to shake Bart's hand. Bart felt her in his solar plexus. Straight black shoulder-length hair framed deep olive skin with bright black eyes and a generous mouth the color of burgundy.

Esme smiled. "*Mi esposo* and I have been expecting you," she said. He's at the brewery until 1:00. He wanted to invite you to the Hidalgo gym. Then, if you're not too tired, you're welcome at our home for dinner. I promise not to stray too far from ranch food." She giggled.

"Esme, let's get going," Mike yelled. "Everyone here for the mountain trail, follow me. Esme will be at the back if anyone needs to stay behind or go slow." Eyeing Bart, reticent at the back of the crowd, he added, "Bart, I see you back there. FYI, the meadow walk is leaving in 15."

Bart considered bailing until he assessed the meadow hike attendees—plus-size females in their sixties. His fate was sealed.

Ninety minutes later, Olivia waved Bart to her outdoor dining table, where she was already halfway through a gigantic bowl of granola.

"Jesus, you barely broke a sweat," he sighed, putting down his tray of breakfast food and collapsing into the chair. He pulled off one of his boots to expose a fresh blister on his big toe. "Guess I should've broken these in beforehand."

"You do look a little pooped."

He wiped the sweat off his forehead. "This tortoise may be slow, but hanging back with Esme has its benefits." He put fresh yogurt and mango into his bowl of granola and took a bite. A beatific look came over his face, and she laughed.

"I know. Isn't it the best? They make it fresh." She reached over and removed a small drop of yogurt that had strayed from his spoon to his cheek. "Tell me about Esme."

"Some of these women are Amazons," he said with his mouth full. "They'll shove you down the mountain to get ahead. One Manhattan broad actually—"

"Can we dispense with your hiking adventure and move on? We have yoga in 30 minutes."

"Yoga, Norris? I thought you were joking." He scowled for a moment, then went on. "Esme and I are tight. She's picking us up at 3:00 to go to the Hidalgo gym with Rodrigo."

"She doesn't know why we're here, right?" Olivia hesitantly asked.

"No, though I think the fighters will enjoy meeting you—El Toro Blanco's sister."

"Will Fernandez be there?" She couldn't help it. She was suspicious. Now that they were about to do something, everything worried her.

Bart said, "Think fact-finding, not *Syriana*."

Full bellies and the feeling of physical accomplishment fueled their climb to Casita 15.

"You shower first," Bart said, blushing despite himself. "I'll wait on the patio."

"Been a long time since you took call, has it? I've shared many an on-call room with male residents. You won't bother me one bit. On the other hand, if you're afraid to be alone with me…Not to fear, I've found it's a common occurrence." She smiled demurely and headed for the shower.

Clean and wrapped in the largest bath towel she had ever seen, she leaned out the terrace door and asked, "Did you take a tumble up there?"

"Why do you ask?" he said cagily.

"I was curious about all the dirt on your hiking shorts."

"I was trying to tell you. These Medicare-eligible broads shoved me aside on that first hill and I slipped. I could have taken them down like wildebeest…" He chuckled. "Then I thought it might draw too much attention," he added, sadly rubbing his scraped knees.

While Olivia changed, Bart reclined on a chaise with Michael Chabon's new book, slyly peering over the top every now and then. With no makeup and her hair in a ponytail, Olivia was captivating. He fantasized throwing open the door and taking her right there, wondering if she would want it as much as he. Yeah, she'd deck me, he thought. Or would she?

After 90 minutes of Anusara yoga, followed by another 90 minutes of mat Pilates and a hearty barley soup, Bart declared naptime. Olivia opted to take a walk.

A golden wildflower blanket hovered at the base of Mt. Cuchama. Natives of Tecate called the mountain "The Exalted One." That it was. Meandering, Olivia examined the footprints in the copper sand, wondering where Curtis had stepped.

"Olivia!"

She hesitated to turn.

"Didn't get enough exercise this morning?" Mike asked, loping up to her. "Be careful, folks have a tendency to overdo it the first day, then spend their second and third in bed recuperating."

"I can see that," she smiled. "It's so peaceful here—if this mountain could talk…"

"We always enjoyed Curtis running laps up and down the mountain."

She felt a shiver run up her spine, then realized that, of course, everyone who worked here would know she was Curtis's sister.

"It's a small town, and to have a celebrity here, especially an athlete, is something," Mike said.

She would have gone on by herself, but he stayed with her, naming the foliage varieties.

"You've worked here a long time?"

"Fifteen years. I have a small place in San Diego where I go for breaks. This can be a tough place to leave," he muttered. "Hope I didn't make you uncomfortable mentioning your brother. Esme told me who you are. I imagine this trip is difficult."

"It's a trip I probably should've taken sooner."

She searched Mike's eyes. Although genuine, they harbored something she couldn't decipher.

"Did you know Curtis—I mean, were you acquaintances?"

Picking up a broken off daffodil from the ground, he said, "Yes. Not well. I love to hike." He took off his ranger hat and carefully tucked the daffodil into the band. "We met a few times up on the mountain. I guess you might say I planned some of those times." He put the hat back on and turned to her as if to ask how he looked. "I never witnessed the level of training a boxer endures. I've done triathlons and a couple Iron Man marathons. Your brother was the most disciplined athlete I've ever seen."

"Did you see him spar?"

"Once."

"At the Hidalgo gym?"

"Before this last fight, he invited me to a sparring session."

So he had seen Curtis shortly before he died. What questions could she ask without raising suspicion?

They continued their leisurely walk as Mike elaborated on how the Ranch foliage had changed over the last decade.

"Sorry to pontificate. Do you have any questions for me?"

"About El Rancho?"

Hesitating, he stopped and turned to search her eyes. "No, about your brother. There're many fitness spas, so I guess it's safe to assume you're not here because of the yoga."

Olivia stammered. "I wanted to be where he spent so much time. I wanted to—I don't know, find more of him by coming here."

Mike pointed at the gulley, commenting on the decrease in rains over the years. "It's become so arid," he said, carefully dissecting her expression. "Do you wonder about Curtis' health before the fight?"

She just looked at him, afraid if she moved or said anything she would cry.

"Many boxers come through the Hidalgo gym. The clinic is attached. Fernandez owns both."

"Have you met him?"

"He owns a lot of the town, and what he doesn't own, he controls."

"This place, too?"

"No, although the El Rancho owner maintains a good relationship with him.

Fernandez isn't Tony Soprano, but there is some resemblance. He's got to be in his early seventies—a big man. Reminds me of Anthony Quinn." He laughed.

Olivia couldn't stop herself from quizzing him. He made it easy, guessing her questions. "What more do you know about the gym?"

"He has the only boxing gym in Tecate and one in Ensenada. Both have clinics attached. I don't know about the gym in Mexico City. That one might be overseen by his brother Raul Santiago—actually his half-brother."

Why was he telling her all this? Which side was he on? There was something about him that made her hesitant, but she felt such a need to know more, she just kept going. "What about the brewery?"

"That's privately owned. Santiago and Fernandez are on the board. Both men are also involved in Ensenada thoroughbred racing."

"Were you impressed by the gym?"

"I've visited a few American boxing gyms. This seems comparable. If a fighter is hurt, there's simple access to medical care."

She stopped, needing to take in more air. It must be the elevation. Mike suggested they head back, but she motioned for him to give her a moment.

He offered her a small peanut butter sandwich, which she gratefully gobbled down. His tanned, weathered skin covered sturdy arms that became enthusiastically animated whenever he identified anything feathered.

"No wife?" she asked in a friendly way as they turned to begin their descent. "With all the well-to-do ladies coming through this place? You're quite the catch."

He shrugged. "I was married in my twenties. Not a lifestyle for me." He looked around. "I enjoy wildlife, hiking and training. Women are too much damn trouble."

They were silent for a moment. She was behind him on the trail. "Tell me something," she ventured. "What about the gym struck you as odd?"

"Guess I wondered why Curtis trained here. With all the gyms, why Tecate or Ensenada?"

Olivia explained why boxers prefer out of the way places and discussed Marquessa's training Mexican fighters.

"Curtis introduced me to Vincent," Mike said. "Very knowledgeable. Is he still in Tecate?"

She sighed. "No, he died," she said. Looking into the valley, she saw some men on horseback. "Who are they?" she asked, not wanting to have to answer questions about Curtis.

"I'm so sorry." Mike turned to follow her gaze. "They work for the Mexican border patrol. This is a place where people try to sneak into the States."

Now she realized what made her wonder about Mike—it was that he was too ready, somehow, with answers.

He resumed walking and she followed. After a few moments, he stopped again and turned to her. "This place is like any small town, too many folks are likely to know your business," he said, then added hurriedly, "Forgive me if I'm getting personal. Your presence here will not go unnoticed. Fernandez is not someone to toy with. If I might ask, did Curtis die from his fight?"

"That's the way it appears."

They had reached the garden at the back of the main house. She extended her hand. "Thank you for accompanying me," she said.

"By the way, I didn't see anything unusual that day at the gym—except an exceptional boxer. One piece of advice..."

"I bet you're going to tell me to not ask too many questions."

Mike lowered his bush hat brim. "No, only consider who you're speaking to in Tecate," he said emphatically.

Twenty-Eight

A DIAMOND BLACK Dodge Ram 3500 pulled up in front of the main house promptly at three o'clock, and Esme hopped down from the driver's seat.

"I'll be right back," she said. "Please, get in," and she loped off toward the office.

They both turned and watched her go—Bart admiring her body's movement, Olivia envying her leather Gucci jacket and her Ferragamo knee-high boots and matching purse.

"Hey, Lover Boy," Olivia said, pulling Bart by the sleeve toward the car. He climbed in the front, and she slid to the middle of the back seat.

"What's she doing driving this vehicular sore thumb?" Bart wondered aloud.

Esme waved as she hurried back to the car and jumped in behind the wheel.

"Thank you for chauffeuring," Olivia said.

"This is one hell of a truck," Bart grunted. "Did you buy it in San Diego?"

Speeding down the main drag, Esme laughed and said in pretty good English, "Hang on, you two. I'm a speed demon!"

"Guess you don't have to worry about the cops," Olivia giggled.

"No, my brother is the *jefe*." She laughed. "To answer your question, the truck was a gift to my husband. We'll pick him up at work, then head to Hidalgo."

Bart pulled down his sun visor and glared at Olivia in the mirror. "These are gorgeous leather seats, too."

"The stereo is the best," Esme yelled, turning up a *cumbia*.

Coming to a screeching halt in front of the brewery, Esme bounded out of the driver's seat and got in behind, next to Olivia, as a striking man in his mid-thirties with mahogany eyes approached the car.

"I am honored to meet you both," Rodrigo said when he had introduced himself. "The entire city was very sad about Curtis. Vinnie worked with several Tecate fighters. We were devastated to hear he passed."

Rodrigo's eye caught Olivia's in the rear-view mirror, and he expressed his sadness. Then regrouping, he suggested, "Would you prefer to come directly to our home? We can share an early dinner?'

"We'd like to tour the gym first," Bart said.

"Many are gone," Rodrigo somberly whispered, barely acknowledging Bart's answer. He pulled out of the brewery's parking lot and headed down the road, seeming distracted.

Olivia awkwardly changed the subject, asking him when he had retired from boxing.

"It's been two years," he responded.

"You were the UBA lightweight champion with 32 fights. How were you smart enough to retire when so many others fight too long?" she prodded, unable to keep the envy out of her voice.

"I had my wife and children to think about. It was the right thing to do, but I'd be lying if I said I didn't miss the ring and the excitement."

"Rodrigo loved training," Esme piped up. "I think you also miss your friends," she said, putting a hand on his shoulder. "Plus, things were not the same after Antonio and Miguel died."

"Esme!" Rodrigo said harshly. Calmly turning to Bart, he said, "You may not remember that you worked my second title defense at the MGM."

"Of course, that was five years ago. You were very talented. If my memory serves me, Noguiera and Madrid were on that card?"

"I've enjoyed two years of my wife's excellent cooking," Rodrigo said, "and some truly delicious wines." He laughed. "So you see there are compensations."

The rest of the short ride was spent in talk of food and drink. At the gym, Esme again got behind the wheel, waved goodbye and took off with a screech.

•

The Hidalgo gym walls were plastered with fight posters stretching back 50 years. A row of speed bags—several broken—hung over cracked cement along-side worn heavy bags. Gym lockers, many missing a door, lined the opposite wall. There were three elevated boxing rings. Young Mexican boxers with loose-fitting headgear were sparring inside each of them while Burgess Meredith types shouted instructions in garbled Spanish. Twenty wanna-be fighters, some amateur and some professional, looked on, debating how they'd handle the action.

This was not what Olivia had expected. It looked like the stereotypical Mexican gym in a B movie. Plus, there was nothing at all sinister about the place.

Rodrigo floated through the building like a local hero, introducing her and Bart as he went.

"Dr. Norris and Dr. Rossi, to what do we owe this unexpected pleasure?" bellowed a towering gentleman in an overly fitted black suit. "Your brother is sorely missed. I know you're in my humble city on vacation. We're honored to have you visit the Hidalgo."

It was Fernandez. Olivia couldn't help noticing his resemblance to Wayne Newton.

Bart was thinking Elvis—sideburns, weight and build in the idol's final years—minus the sequined white jumpsuit.

"Juan Alejandro Santiago Fernandez," Fernandez announced, beaming. He wrapped an arm around Rodrigo while proudly displaying his liberal belly compressing a gigantic gold buckle.

"Did Rodrigo show you our meager establishment?" he asked them.

Rodrigo grinned along with his boss until Fernandez's grasp tightened. The former champion nervously scanned the ground and declared, "*Sí, Doctor.*"

"You must tour the clinic," Fernandez declared, "after you watch some sparring. I'm always surprised Las Vegas doesn't offer this type of set-up. Fighters that are so full of ambition don't have the resources to take care of their physical well-being. If a fighter injures his hand or is cut, I have a medical staff available no matter the time of day or night."

Fernandez introduced the trainers and pointed out two fighters who had bouts scheduled in the U.S. Olivia was looking everywhere, trying to take it all in, wondering what lurked. Searching the faces of the athletes when they heard who she was—some sorrowful, others embarrassed—her mind raced. Was this where Curtis was injured? Did he go into the bout with a cerebral bleed? Would anyone tell her the truth? Why was Fernandez so hospitable?

Bart took her by the elbow in a proprietorial way and then empathetically clenched his fingers as Fernandez eyed them.

"Please, come tour the clinic," the large man said abruptly, standing aside and ushering them out.

The clinic was the antithesis of the gym. The alabaster tiled flooring and walls were clean enough to eat off of. The contemporary chrome-rimmed sofas and chairs were filled with young mothers and children.

"They are here for what I think you call wellness checks," boasted Fernandez. He explained that Tecate had a small eight-bed hospital. "I do my best to help the people that live here. Some of the ticket sales from local fights pay for the medical care of our citizens."

Bart and Olivia examined everything, including the radiographic equipment. Fernandez told them there was a portable CT scanner and MRI machine that traveled twice a week between Tecate and the Ensenada clinic. The hospital had its own CT in case of emergencies.

Fernandez introduced the staff—a perfectly matched set of five pretty young women dressed in pressed white uniforms. The exam rooms were equally impressive, with exam tables covered with perfectly preserved leather and gray upholstered chairs. The walls displayed images of local landscapes.

"These were painted by Tecate artists. Aren't they beautiful?" Fernandez cooed.

"Lovely, simply lovely," Olivia agreed.

"My office will interest you." He escorted them through hand-carved ceiling-to-floor walnut doors.

A six-foot black marble-topped desk in the middle of a brightly colored Indian carpet dominated the room.

"I brought these chairs from Spain. They're rumored to have been in the castle of King Ferdinand."

While Olivia humored the king in his office-castle, Bart inspected the framed photographs of Fernandez posing with celebrities and U.S. politicians—including an autographed picture with Senator Harry Reid of Nevada. Bart pointed at one with Curtis and Raul Santiago.

"Your brother, I believe," he said.

"Actually, he's my half-brother."

"If I may, Doctor, you speak impeccable English," Olivia commented.

"Please, no formalities, call me Juan," the large man said beaming. I completed much of my training in San Antonio."

"How long ago was the photo taken?" Bart asked, eyeing it more carefully.

"To tell you the truth, I am not sure—maybe a year or so ago? I think it was before Curtis fought in Mexico City."

Rodrigo probably would have known when the photo was taken, Bart thought, but he had left them. A medical assistant came in with refreshments on a silver tray, and Fernandez handed them each a fresh churro dipped in caramel and a café con leche.

He bowed slightly to Olivia. "Curtis was very proud of you," he said. "Our mothers are Castilian—mine unfortunately died when I was 12. My father remarried into a wealthy Chilean family from Guadalajara. My half-brother Raul became an attorney, while I pursued medicine. He boxed for a while—unsuccessfully. We are both working to make boxing as safe as possible. I'm familiar with some of your work, from the Internet. You must know Dr. Rivers?"

"Not personally, though I'm familiar with his research on the mechanics of cerebral trauma."

Rodrigo quietly knocked on the doorframe, and Fernandez excused himself to attend a meeting. "You will be my guests at tomorrow's races in Ensenada," he said. "I'll send a car at 4:00." They shook hands. "I am certain you share Curtis's love for horses," he said to Olivia. "He came with me several times."

*

Esme's mother, with the two children in tow, came out to greet them as they entered the beautiful 3,000-square-foot Escalone home—a house that, while not extravagant, clearly surpassed the means of managers of a brewery and a spa. Folk art, colorful rugs and furnishings filled the house. Olivia was enchanted by the place. She asked to be shown around, and Esme gave her a tour of the hacienda-style living room and the beautifully landscaped terrace and gardens out the back. The dinner, too, was superb—a tortilla soup the likes of which she had never tasted, piquant tamales and the perfect white cake to balance the savory tastes of the meal.

After dinner, as they were moving out to the terrace for coffee and brandy, Olivia excused herself to use the rest room.

Bart and Rodrigo talked about baseball as they enjoyed their excellent cigars and cognac. Esme came out with coffee and sat with them, but she seemed nervous. Bart wondered how close Curtis had been to these two. Whatever it was they didn't want him to know, he figured that was only part of the story. Were they afraid of Fernandez—or Santiago, or under threat from the brothers? Or were they on the other side? Either way, he could see that he and Olivia would be a danger to them. There was a lifestyle here, they had enviable things, their children were precious to them. He was just wondering if he could learn something from Rodrigo—if only his wife weren't there—when she jumped up and went inside, saying something about the children.

He decided to take a chance and prod the former fighter, see if he could learn anything without giving too much away. "You have a beautiful home here," he said, leaning back in his chair and showing he was feeling relaxed and contented. "And your children are adorable—really smart, too."

"Thank you," Rodrigo said, smiling broadly. But he didn't quite relax into his identical chair. "You have children?"

"No. Boxing is my life. I don't see how you could give it up. You were in the ring. You were good—"

Rodrigo said nothing for a moment. He looked over at Bart, as if he were deciding something. "I think you know why I stopped," he said.

Was it a challenge? Was it an overture? Bart's instinct told him to beware. He met the man's eyes, wondering what was required of him. There was a long silence, and then the door burst open and Esme was saying she would give them a ride back to El Rancho. She had an errand to run there. They were out of the house within minutes.

•

Back at the casita, Olivia went to use the bathroom as Bart teased her about her tiny bladder. He went out, started the fire on the terrace, set up two glasses and opened the bottle of Domecq's Presidente they had been given by Fernandez.

When she joined him, he told her about the partial exchange he had with Rodrigo.

"Why did he say that?" she asked. "What's obvious about it?"

"I don't know. I suspect he suspects we're here for more than a pilgrimage to Curtis's stomping grounds." He lifted his glass to her and took a swallow of the smooth, smoky liquor. "What happened with you and Esme? She hustled us out of there pretty abruptly."

"I saw that one of the children had gone into the guest bathroom, so I excused myself to use it and conveniently found it occupied. I wanted to see if I could see more of the house."

He laughed, looking at her face lit up with intent. "Boy Norris, don't ever think you can play poker," he said, adoring her.

She forced herself to ignore him. "I opened a huge carved double door that turned out to be to the master bedroom. There, hanging over the bed, was a Goya."

He leaned toward her. "Are you sure? How can you be sure?"

"It was just hanging there, a painting of a beautiful woman in a white dress lying on a chaise, her arms behind her head."

"Bah," he said, annoyed. "You don't know it was genuine."

"True, and that does worry me. But when Esme found me looking at it, she was visibly distressed. She grabbed my arm. I said, 'Has it been in your family for generations?' and she said, 'A gift from a friend of the family. It's a copy, of course,' which I don't believe. She was too upset. And there's something completely fishy about those two, driving around in that car, living in that house filled with beautiful things."

"Maybe she was just upset because she found you in her bedroom," he suggested.

"I told her I was looking for a bathroom because the guest one was busy."

"And she was supposed to buy that?" he said harshly.

She gave him a look—halfway between saucy and disgusted. "Who cares?"

"And the bathroom?"

"Yes, and there's another thing. She said the bathroom hadn't been cleaned today and she would rather I didn't use it. Then she hustled me out of there, and you know the rest."

Twenty-Nine

BART FELL ASLEEP in the chaise out on the terrace. Olivia had gone in for a sweater and when she came out, he was out cold. She watched him for a while, sorry not to have more of his company tonight, but relieved, too. There would be no drama, and she would be safe for one more night. It felt strange, to be so detached and at the same time completely filled with this person. She went in and got a blanket to put over him, then got into bed with her laptop and got lost in her research.

Sometime toward morning, she woke up and heard him groaning. He had come inside at some point, and he was lying on the couch, crying out in his sleep. She put a hand on his arm, gently stroked his cheek.

"Rossi, wake up. You're having a nightmare."

His eyes half-opened and he made a pitiful sound.

She shook him slightly. "It's okay, it's just a dream," she said.

His eyes shot open, and he looked at her for a moment with real anguish. Then it subsided. "Norris," he said, finally recognizing her.

"You had a bad dream," she said.

He pushed himself to a sitting position, giving her room to sit.

She turned, saying, "I'll get you some water," but he caught her by the wrist and asked her to stay with him, just for a little while.

She sat.

He pushed the tears off his face with the heels of his hands. "It's been a long while since I had that dream," he said, taking a few deep breaths and wiping his eyes again with his shirtsleeve. He looked at her with a look she didn't understand. "It's because of you," he said. "You're the first one. Since her."

"Please don't be cryptic," she pleaded. "I never do well with cryptic."

He touched her arm. "I want to tell you about her," he said. "I have a feeling you should know what happened."

"What happened to you, you mean? What made you guarded and remote and hard-shelled?" She didn't say it in a harsh way, but she needed to understand what he was trying to tell her.

He was about to say *no, not that*, but he shrugged. "You're right."

"Let me get us some water."

Reluctantly he let her go. She came back and sat down on the chair right next to the sofa. Handing him a bottle, she opened her own and took a long swallow.

"You want to tell me the dream?" she asked.

"The dream is irrelevant. I know where it comes from. I want to tell you what happened."

She waited, listening.

"New Orleans Jazz Fest was a small event in the late 1970s, when I was doing my internship at Big Charity," he began. "One late Friday afternoon, I wandered to Louis Armstrong Park with a couple of college buddies to hear Clarence 'Frogman' Henry and Irma Thomas. It was a typical stifling hot May evening, heavy with humidity. The grounds were soaked from the morning's rain, so no chairs had been put out. Everyone just stood around enjoying it all."

He paused to swallow more water and then settled in to tell her the story, quietly and slowly dragging it out of himself sentence by sentence.

Off-call for the next 12 hours, he wasted no time that day downing a few Jax beers as his friends scoured the crowd for eligible ladies. Fats Domino was just finishing "Blueberry Hill" when a torrential downpour began. Fats didn't miss a note as the listeners ran for cover under the trees.

Bart collided with someone and they both went down. When he had helped her up, the Audrey Hepburn look-alike pushed back her slicker hood and brushed wet leaves from her shorts. "You like Fats?" she said in a refreshing, off-the-boat French accent. "I'm more of a Pete Fountain fan."

He could barely catch his breath. Who was she? The eyes were mischievous, but warm. The mouth was pert, plump and ready to smile.

Before he could propose marriage, the wind swirled into the rainy mist, and she vanished into a sea of drenched folks seeking shelter.

He ran to catch up, but he couldn't find her. He climbed onto a trolley heading to the Quarter, and there she was, on a bicycle, at a stoplight on the corner of St. Charles. Unlatching the window, he called out, "How about a café au lait?" and got a face-full of rain. The trolley, passing her, ran across a giant puddle, and she got drenched.

He saw her pull to the corner and dismount, and he jumped off the trolley and ran back to her. "Looks like I'm not your good-luck charm," he said, with a grin he couldn't conceal.

"Are you responsible for this, too?"

Handing her his Saints cap, he stammered, "Please take this."

She laughed—a lovely, surprising peal of laughter coming out of her French throat. "Isn't it a little late for a hat?"

Another woman would have looked like a drowned rat, he thought. This one looked like an angel.

"Can I offer you a beignet while we dry off?" he proposed.

She stared. Was she enthralled, or did she just think he was crazy? "I have a class," she stammered. "I don't...I have a test coming up next week and..." Seemingly amused that there was no escape, she asked, "You aren't a serial killer, are you?"

He shook his head ardently. "Not today. A beignet is the least I can do. Plus, if you run away again, who knows what other accidents I might cause trying to find you. Don't you believe in fate?" He gently extended his hand and introduced himself.

"I guess I can spare an hour," she said, vaguely taking his hand but forgetting to tell him her name. "Then I have to get back and study. I have one request."

"What's that?"

"You must not fall in love with me."

He looked at her, not sure she had really said what he thought she had said. She didn't smile. Her sweet pretty face was completely serious. Then he came to her eyes, her black, laughing eyes.

"Ha," he said, "So you're the enchanted princess." He handed her a rumpled Kleenex from inside his jacket to wipe her face. "And what will happen to me if I do fall in love with you?" He took her book bag from her and walked her bike as they headed for the Café Du Monde.

She frowned at him. "You mustn't."

He laughed. She was adorable. "Well, I don't promise," he said boldly.

"You might be sorry," she scolded, shaking a lovely slender finger at him and barely controlling a smile that flickered at the corners of her plump little mouth.

The café's ample awning sheltered a crowd of people taking refuge from the rain. Bart dropped five dollars into the instrument case of the resident street saxophonist, a guy he had listened to for years.

"Thanks, man, any requests?" the fiftyish bearded musician asked.

"How about 'La Vie en Rose' in honor of my new French friend?"

Delicately grasping the girl's wet hand, he guided her through the sea of outdoor wrought-iron tables to a spot with a view of Jackson Square.

He pulled out a chair for her, murmuring, "May I ask your name?"

She turned her head toward him as he bent over to push in her chair. She was very close. "Mathilde," she murmured back. "Mathilde Tatou."

Bart ordered a basket of beignets and café au lait and listened to Mathilde happily telling him that her mother was born in New Orleans and had traveled to Paris to study art. She had died when Mathilde was 10. Wanting to live where her mother grew up, she had come over here and enrolled in communications at Newcomb. She intended to return to France as a newscaster.

An eternity passed while he blissfully memorized her face and demeanor. Her ears and eyes were too big but fit together perfectly and gave her a gamine look. Her strong convictions contrasted with her diminutive frame. In the past, he had sought after lust. This chest-tightening feeling he could only think must be love.

Finishing another beignet and seriously gazing at him she scolded, "I told you not to fall in love. I warned you."

He laughed. The whole episode was absurd, and he felt how lucky he was to have discovered this treasure.

They spent as much time as they could together during the following months. He called her Tatou. Mathilde seemed less whimsical. After much resistance, she moved into his French Quarter residence, though she knew her father would kill her if he found out she was living with a man.

Something indefinable existed between them. His heart ached without her. At the same time he had a feeling that if he blinked, she might disappear.

The sweltering New Orleans summer folded into a tempestuous, golden fall. Bart was forced to spend more and more time in the emergency department, which pained him greatly. There were fewer and fewer moments with Tatou, his enchanted one, his mermaid.

They both clung to the time they had together. On the weekends, whenever he wasn't on call, there was nothing as dear to them as the Audubon Zoo. They talked for hours about their hopes and dreams, sitting on Monkey Hill. He told her everything he wanted, the whole future he saw so clearly. She clung to every word.

One Sunday as it came time to leave the Zoo, Tatou suddenly became very pale. He asked her what was wrong. She had been studying hard, she said, not getting much sleep.

As she rose to leave, she collapsed into his arms.

"Tatou, Tatou, Christ! Are you alright? You haven't been eating. We're close to Charity. Let me run some tests."

Waving him off, she insisted she was fine.

"Give me a break. Nearly passing out is not fine."

She persuaded him that this was an occasional fainting spell that she'd experienced since childhood. Despite his doubts, he dropped the subject. Why, he didn't know, except that he couldn't bear the idea of anything being wrong with her.

From that day on, her demeanor changed. She became more and more distant. He tried to bring her back to him. She picked fights with him over the least little thing, which he despised.

One day after a 36-hour call, he came home to find her gone. She had left a note saying she needed more space and that she was moving back to the dorms. Alongside the note was the colorful Mardi Gras Indian wristband he had given her shortly after they met.

Try though he might, he couldn't convince her to return to him. She wouldn't even see him. He had no idea what he had done or how to bring her back. Devastated, he resumed his lifestyle of bedding willing nurses and sitting in on an occasional coronet set at Tipitina's on Saturday nights.

Months later he was on his way out of the place at the end of a 4:00 AM set when the hostess ran to catch him. "There's a call for you. It's Kyle," she said. "He says it's urgent."

A bit drunk, he shook his head. "I'm off-call."

She grabbed his arm as he tried to walk away. "Bart, he said something about Tatou."

He rushed to Big Charity.

"Bart, over here," Kyle shouted.

At the back of the ED was a quiet, curtained-off bed for seriously ill patients. As Bart slowly parted the white drape, he saw two blood-filled IV bags running wide open. His chest caved in and he lost his breath.

"Tatou!" he cried out. "My God, Kyle, what happened? Can you bring me her chart? When did she come in?"

Kyle left the cubicle while Bart pulled up a stool and gently clasped Tatou's hand. He whispered the words he meant to say before she left. Never losing hope for reconciliation, he replaced the Indian wristband on her arm.

Instead of the typical emergency clipboard, Kyle proffered a two-volume chart and handed it to Bart.

"Dr. Rossi, I need to put her in a gown," an elderly nurse interrupted squeezing Bart's arm. "I promise to call you if there's any change."

Bart carried the records to the on-call room and locked the door. When he emerged an hour later, Kyle called to him.

"She's awake after the second unit and the platelets. We took her for a head CT. It's normal, no bleeding."

Reentering the cubicle, Bart sat close to the head of the bed.

"How could you not tell me?" he whispered. "How could I have not seen it?" He sighed, wiping his eyes.

At first he thought she was not going to talk to him or that maybe she couldn't talk, but then a little voice came out of her. "I've had leukemia since I was 5. Can you imagine what my life has been like with all the chemo, transfusions and doctors? I should have told you…I wanted to so many times. I prayed for a future with you."

"So you chose to desert me? That wasn't your decision to make."

"I didn't want you to see me die."

"Oh God," he wept, "we lost months we could have had together, all because of a cliché."

She looked at him, wide-eyed, and suddenly she started to laugh. It started like a cough, but he saw that it wasn't that: she was laughing, and he had to laugh too.

"Love is a cliché, my darling Bart," she said, quieting down, exhausted by the effort.

"I won't let you leave me."

Six weeks later, latching the wristband on his arm on Christmas morning, she died. But not before she told him she was glad he had fallen in love with her.

*

When Bart finished telling this story, one he had not even told himself all these years, he fell into a silence, as if to say one more word would be to break the spell. He knew it needed to be broken, but he didn't have the heart for it just at this moment, and Olivia seemed to sense that. She remained silent and still.

After a while she got up, and he could hear her go into the bathroom and close the door.

Olivia felt like she could barely breathe. It had been years since she had wanted anyone this much. She turned on the water and doused her face a few times, then buried her face in his towel, breathing in the smell of him as she dried off. Quietly, she opened the door, wondering how she would be able to go back and sit demurely next to him after hearing his soul's most cherished secret.

Coming out of the bathroom, she practically walked right into him. He was standing in the dark, leaning against the archway that led into the living room area. She could just see his outline in the grey light of dawn creeping in around the curtains.

She had never felt this way until now. She didn't care that she might be one more conquest for this womanizer. She didn't care about Amanda. She just wanted. All of her—body, mind, and soul—wanted. She moved closer to him, and he turned, brushing her breasts with his shoulder. She was so close to him. She gently jostled him against the wall and fell upon him with a deep kiss.

For an instant he held her at arm's length. "Are you sure?"

She murmured "yes," nuzzling his neck, and slowly placed his hand against the small of her back while she shifted closer. He unbuttoned the pajama top and pushed it off her shoulders, and she let it fall to the floor. He put his hands on her hips and pushed the pajama bottoms down until they fell to her ankles. Then taking hold of her buttocks, he lifted her and she wrapped her legs around his waist as he carried her to the bed. He was on his knees over her, his velvet mouth traveling along the inside of her thighs. The roughness of his unshaven face increased the intensity of every kiss.

He stood in front of her, the hint of a smile on his delicious mouth as he carefully unbuttoned his shirt, taking pleasure in the view of her body.

Suddenly self-conscious, she said, "How long are you going to leave me here like this?" She meant to bark it, but it came out soft and hoarse. He was beside her in a second, tenderly caressing her hair and face.

"Happy?"

She nodded and kissed his hand, pushing a few of his fingers inside her mouth, then moving them across her breast. His breath caught at the sensation.

As they kissed and fondled every inch of each other, she whispered, "This is right, isn't it?"

He held her face in his hands. "My only regret—"

"Regret?"

"Is that it took us so long." He was licking her ear, whispering. "God, you're beautiful." Then he paused. "This is important to me," he said into her ear.

"...That makes it even more significant. I only wonder if we should have..."

"Called Mandy?"

"She's been a real friend."

"Wanna call now?"

Hitting him over the head with a pillow, she giggled. "Don't be a jerk."

He rolled over and pulled her on top of him. "I need to say something."

Placing her fingers softly over his mouth she said, "Shhhh, you don't need to say anything else."

"No, I do." He turned over and they lay on their sides facing each other. "I've been closed off for years and years and spent my life successfully playing at many things," he said, brushing her hair softly off her cheek. "Then you came along."

"And I've been angry my whole life," she said, her heart pounding with fear. She forced herself to say more. "No matter who I met, and no matter how much I thought I wanted to be in love and told myself I was loved, the truth is I never got over my parents splitting up. My world fell apart, and I never understood that only I could put it back together, until I lost Curtis. And now, you come along." She was thinking maybe that was why this might work, because by some elaborate twist of fate, they were both there at the same moment.

They kissed and explored each other for a long time, slowly and blissfully.

"This is certainly better than hiking Mt. Cuchama," she quipped after a while.

"I did enjoy looking at your ass."

"And I enjoyed flaunting it." Throwing his body back on the pillow and straddling his hips, she sensually sighed, "Tell me again how much you liked my ass?"

Suddenly the door flew open. Bart jumped out of bed, throwing the duvet over her, and stood between the bed and the intruder shouting as loud as he could, "Get out or I'll kill you." He was just reaching for the nearest thing he could use as a weapon when Olivia pulled him back.

"Wait," she said, seeing that it was Rodrigo. "What's wrong?" she asked Rodrigo. "Is something wrong?"

Rodrigo retreated out the door, and Bart, hurriedly getting into his pants, ran after him.

"Wait," he called as softly as he could. "Come back. What's wrong?"

When Rodrigo was back inside the casita, Bart put the "Do Not Disturb" sign on the doorknob and locked the door.

"It wasn't closed," Rodrigo mumbled apologetically. "When I knocked, it opened. I'm so very sorry. Please forgive me."

Olivia had gotten her robe on, and she beckoned Rodrigo to sit as she sat down on the sofa. Bart moved over a chair and handed Rodrigo a bottle of water. The former fighter was perspiring profusely.

"Esme doesn't know I'm here," he said. "She would be very angry. I can no longer stay silent."

Olivia soothingly clutched Rodrigo's hand. He was like a small boy in terrible trouble. Bart closed all the curtains and then came over and sat down.

"Rodrigo, if we can help you in any way, we will," he said.

For several minutes Rodrigo stared at the ground.

Olivia let go of his hand and sat back. "It's something you know, right?" she guessed. "You have information." She waited but he didn't say anything. "Drugs," she ventured. "Are the boxers given drugs, *drogas?*"

The former champion vigorously said no, then admitted he wasn't sure.

"We heard there was a drink or supplement that builds muscle," Bart suggested, hoping to trigger Rodrigo's tongue. "Something illegal...or maybe injections?"

Rodrigo remained silent.

Olivia felt tears spring to her eyes. Were the tears for this ex-fighter? Or for Curtis? Maybe for herself? Mostly she wanted the truth. "You can tell us anything," she said tenderly. "We'll keep you out of it."

They were getting nowhere. She started talking. She said whatever came into her mind. She talked about her poor relationship with Curtis and how it was her fault, not his. She told Rodrigo she wanted to make amends, even though it was too late, by uncovering what was behind his death.

She saw that Rodrigo was listening, finally. After a moment he reached for his wallet and removed a torn photo of three teens—Miguel Noguiera, Antonio Madrid and himself. Handing her the picture he moaned, "*Todos mis amigos*—dead."

Showing Bart the picture, she sighed. "You all look about 15."

"*Sí.*"

"Let me tell you what I think is going on here," Bart said. "Maybe that will help. Just say yes or no, that might be easier."

Olivia glared at him to back off, but he continued. "I'm guessing you're here to tell us about illegal drug use. My guess is that these drugs are supplied by Dr. Fernandez."

Rodrigo looked at him but said nothing.

"Did Noguiera and Madrid die from something Fernandez gave them? Is that why Curtis died?"

The young man stood.

"Wait," Olivia said. "You came here to tell us something, and maybe you came because something has happened. Why come this far and then go no further?" She spoke as softly and kindly as she could, hoping she wouldn't sound like she was scolding him.

Rodrigo went over and peered outside the drapes, then resumed his seat and started to talk.

"It wasn't always this way. The clinic helped us. If we had a bad hand or cut, the doctor treated us. I have insurance through the factory. When I was a fighter, things were different. Fighting in America, the boxers must bring tests. They are very expensive."

"You mean all the prefight medical studies like brain scans, HIV and hepatitis screens and eye exams?"

He nodded, fretfully rubbing his hands.

Bart left them and returned with the envelope of medical records Amanda had gotten. He pulled them out and laid them on Rodrigo's lap.

Olivia watched Rodrigo as he cast his eyes over the records. "Do these tests have to do with why my brother died or why your friends are dead?" she asked.

He jumped out of his seat and turned toward the door, but he wasn't fast enough to get past her. She briefly embraced him, then stepped back, but she kept herself between him and the exit. "I know you want to help," she said. "I see it in your face. I believe Fernandez and Santiago bought your silence and that your children are in danger because of that. I think you came here because you can no longer live with the guilt. I'm guessing you understand what happened to Curtis—what happened to Madrid and Noguiera."

"There are many young men and women training. I don't want them in danger."

"Danger from what?" Bart asked.

"We understand every fight could be our last. We could end up like Muhammad Ali. There was a time...a time that if I had a medical problem that could stop me from boxing, I would have paid to have it covered up."

Rodrigo told them he didn't know why Curtis died. He wasn't even sure what happened to Noguiera, though he believed he was silenced. He described how a fighter underwent prefight testing at Fernandez's clinic and that no physical exams were ever done. "The boxer hands over a fee based on what he can afford," he said, his voice so low they could barely hear him. "He then comes back for the completed paperwork the following day."

Bart shuddered, disgusted. "I knew it. I always wondered, except I couldn't allow myself to believe it," he growled.

"These kids have never even undergone blood tests, right?" Olivia asked.

Rodrigo nodded.

"The boxers coming through any of these clinics submit medical records for licensure without ever having their blood drawn or a brain MRI. So who knows what problems they have," Bart elaborated. He had to stop himself from shouting. "Who else knows about this?" he asked Rodrigo.

There was no response.

Bart suddenly lost patience. "You've said too much to not tell us the rest," he demanded.

"I'm risking the life of my wife and children in coming here. There's nowhere for me to go. Esme will not understand."

Olivia pleaded. "We'll protect you." She turned to Bart. "Amanda can do a story; it will be too public for anyone to get silenced because it will be too obvious." She wasn't even thinking, she was just talking. Too much was going on inside her.

While the two argued, Rodrigo ran outside.

"You frightened him," she yelled accusingly.

"This isn't some TV show, Norris. Who do you think is going to testify? Do you think we can place Rodrigo and Esme in a witness-protection program? I told you boxing was a cesspool. Even if we have proof that Fernandez and his cronies are falsifying medical data on boxers or giving them drugs, who's going to care?"

Olivia slammed the casita door, which Rodrigo had left ajar in his hasty departure. Bart took her hand and led her to the couch. Attempting to reassure her, he gently passed his fingers over her cheek.

Olivia grabbed the medical forms that had scattered to the floor from Rodrigo's lap—test results that were prepared in Tecate and emailed to the Commission. It wasn't like the promoter or the fighter had altered them. Did everyone know about this?

"How can I sit there and do my job if the athletes' medicals were falsified?" she said, close to despair.

"These documents aren't sufficient proof, and we can't ask any more from Rodrigo," said Bart. Startled by a noise, he asked, "Do you hear that?"

"You're making me crazy," she said, pulling on her hair in fistfuls.

He went to the door and looked out the peephole. It was Rodrigo. He cautiously opened the door, and the young man strode in and sat down in front of Olivia.

"I do not know if Curtis was sick before he fought Samson Livingstone," he said somberly. "I do know he was asking questions about the supplements. And I know it made Santiago angry." Suddenly striking the coffee table with his fist, he shouted, "Miguel Noguiera stood beside me when I got married. I still visit his family every week."

"Why did Miguel die?" she asked.

Rodrigo's eyes pooled. "Two weeks before his final bout in Las Vegas, he was knocked out in the gym and shook."

"Shook? He had a seizure, and they let him fight?" Olivia exclaimed.

"In Santiago's Mexico City gym," Rodrigo whispered.

"Did he go to the hospital?"

Shaking his head Rodrigo mumbled, "He complained of headaches, so Santiago arranged for a scan through the clinic."

"What did the scan show, Rodrigo?"

"Miguel told me there was a bruise."

"A bruise on his brain," Olivia demanded. "And you didn't stop him from competing?"

"They told him he would be okay."

Bart interrupted. "Who told him?"

"Santiago...or Dr. Fernandez. Miguel never told me." He hung his head. "If I could change the past, I would. The only thing I can do now is tell the truth." He looked from one to the other of them and stood up. "I tried to think of a way to get you a sample of the vitamin cocktail, but I have no access to the gym. I will contact my wife's cousin who works in the clinic in Ensenada. If she can find a way to send you a sample, she will do it. She has personal reasons."

Olivia caught his eye, questioning him, and he nodded slightly.

"Something to do with my brother?" she asked.

"Yes. She was in love with him. He thought of her as just a kid—she is pretty young."

"Will you tell me her name?"

He shook his head, rose and shoved his hands into his pockets. "I have to go to work or they will miss me," he said nervously. "And you must leave now too. Now. Please do not think I am just saying this. You must leave. I know you have an invitation to the races, but you must get out of that and leave here as quickly as you can without attracting attention."

Bart started to protest, but Rodrigo interrupted him, reaching out and touching his arm. "With respect," he said, "you have no idea what you are in the middle of. *Escúcheme*, listen to me."

And then he was gone.

By that time it was morning. They had signed up for the 6:15 hike up the mountain, and they decided they had better show up for that, then get word to Fernandez that they had been called away by a family emergency. It was hard for either of them to imagine they were seriously in danger, but Rodrigo had put himself in harm's way for them—for Curtis—and they agreed that for his sake they would do as he had said.

They could find out who the young woman at the clinic was from Chui and Marco, but they had no way of getting in touch with her.

"They really will harm Rodrigo's children," Bart said as they headed for the start point of the hike. He was trying to make the danger feel real.

They didn't say much as they joined the hike and began to climb. After a while, though, Olivia stopped at the top of an incline and turned to Bart. He saw the sun glinting off her red hair as the wind caught it and tossed it out behind her. He saw her tanned athletic legs glistening from sweat and red mountain dust.

"I think…" she said, seeing two stragglers approaching and saying no more.

He waited for them to pass. "You think…"

"The painting could've been a bribe or a thank-you for loyalty. Or it could be a forgery and it's on its way to a buyer." They resumed the hike, now even farther behind. "I keep wondering what else the house has concealed in it. And yet, there's no alarm system."

"You checked?" He laughed in astonishment.

"Esme didn't want me seeing the painting—or any other part of the house."

"Let's keep hiking or we'll miss the granola," Bart insisted, surging ahead.

Frustrated, she jogged to catch up to his brisk clip. Passing him by she suddenly thought of something. She turned around, letting him catch up.

"They're untouchable," she said.

"You mean the house or the painting?"

"The Escalones," she breathed.

"Could it be you've seen *The Godfather* one too many times?"

She responded by elbowing him in the ribs, then pushed ahead of him for the last sprint—to the granola buffet.

They ate in a silence that bristled with questions, their eyes never meeting. When they were about to get up, Olivia reached over and picked an almond slice off his chin. "Cute," she said.

"What? I was hungry. That was a big hike."

She bent close to him and, in her most sultry voice, she said, "Hard not to appreciate a man with a healthy appetite." Her lips were within an inch of his.

Then she was up from the table, bussing her tray and off for the main desk to check them out of the spa.

Not taking his eyes off her as she disappeared down the cobblestone walkway, he said to himself, "She might be more than you want to handle." But he knew that wasn't true. He wanted her no matter how difficult that might be. He had passed the point of no return. She was not just another one of his conquests. This one took his breath away, but for a different reason. It scared him how shaken she made him feel. But she made him feel more alive than he had felt in many years.

*

The minute Bart pulled the car out onto the road, Olivia drifted into sleep. He indulged himself with admiring glances as he drove in the morning light. Her head rested against the headrest, long white neck exposed.

Looking at the road, driving with nothing coming in either direction, he began to feel a little uneasy. Every time there was a long slow curve in the road, he half expected to see a car come out of nowhere to stop them. He kept checking the rearview mirror. The emptiness worried him.

He tried thinking about how to put the pieces together. He was convinced Tecate was the key to unraveling not only Curtis' death but also the deaths and retirements of other fighters. He tried to figure out how he could visit the Hidalgo without an entourage or the gym's owner. What did Escalone, Noguiera and Madrid have in common? All had fought for the UBA—two were dead, and one was controlled by Fernandez.

*

Awakening as Bart stopped the car in the line to cross the border, Olivia opened her eyes and saw his hands on the wheel, slightly clenched. She hadn't thought about the border crossing. Were they in danger? Still looking at these hands she already loved, she saw Tatou's wristband where Bart's jacket and shirt were pulled away from his strong wrist. She was grateful that he trusted her with the story of this girl who had meant so much to him. She never understood why people didn't seem to appreciate her sensitivity. Maybe she covered her emotions too much. Bart hid his feelings too, she had noticed. It was hard for him to be kind to someone he had feelings for. And it was hard for him to be sincere.

She touched his hand, startling him.

"I never got around to telling you something Esme told me—before she caught me snooping in the backrooms. She said how happy she was when Rodrigo quit boxing. And..."

"And what?"

"She said she believes he's in better health."

"That's no surprise, getting hit in the head—"

"No, I'm pretty sure she was talking about the vitamins the clinic provided. She said he had headaches and nausea from them even though he looked fit. She said all the fighters used them."

He slammed his hand on the steering wheel. "Jesus, you could have let me know," he growled. "We might have asked him better questions."

"What?" she answered, for some reason so angry she raised her hand to slap his chest. He grabbed her arm to prevent the blow and pulled her inches from his face.

His grasp made her catch her breath. His breathing was warm and hypnotic, luscious to her. She yearned to kiss him so hard, she prayed he would maintain his unbreakable hold.

At the head of the line, they were waved through to the U.S. side. They held their breath for a few hundred feet, then both started laughing at the same time.

"Let's eat something that's really, really bad for us," she said.

Soon they were sitting at a Waffle House with pancakes and French fries and many napkins. All they wanted to do was joke around. All the severity of the last hours had evaporated. They were giddy, and neither of them wanted to discuss anything, not even their interrupted lovemaking. They were heading back to reality—a reality that included Amanda eagerly waiting to welcome her boyfriend.

On the drive to San Diego there were long silences as each of them mulled over what they had learned, and what they had found or might have found in each other.

The plane ride was comforting; they napped, leaning against each other.

Finally, after six hours of travel, Bart pulled his car up to Olivia's front door. He got out and carried her bag inside, then turned to leave.

Frustrated, she clutched his forearm. "Don't go. There's so much to say," she murmured, hoping he would take her in his arms and finish what they had started.

He leaned in and kissed her behind her ear. "I haven't forgotten. It's hard to think about anything else. This is an opportunity to clear the air with Amanda."

"Why did she even let us go on this trip together?"

He thought about what to answer. "Because the story is always the most important thing to her," he said. That was all he was going to say. His epiphany about Amanda, when he realized she was stealing information from his phone—and who knew where else—was something he didn't want to talk about. It made him feel stupid, like a sap.

Olivia was holding him by the shirt, shyly. He found it endearing. "If you were my boyfriend," she said, "I would have threatened to strangle her if she even looked sideways at you."

"If I were your boyfriend," he said, and he kissed her deep and long. Then he pulled away. "Now I'm going to be the mensch I seldom am and see her."

Olivia still held him. "She actually stopped sending me texts because I ignored them all."

Gently stroking her face, he half-smiled. "It's the right thing," he whispered.

It could have referred to anything, she thought, as she let him go.

She shut the door and leaned against it. She felt completely unsettled. Was it from wanting him so much? Was he going to sleep with Amanda tonight? How would she take it—if he really did tell her? And besides all that, there was what they had discovered in Tecate.

A sound startled her, and Tyson rushed in through the dog flap in the kitchen door and greeted her with kisses. It was the first time. Olivia knelt to hug the Golden and sobbed. Now she was home.

Thirty

S HE WIGGLED HER numb right foot free from the weight of Tyson's head. As soon as she stirred, the Golden climbed up and licked her face, reminding her that 6:00 AM was late enough to stay in bed. She rolled over and looked at her phone. Nothing from Bart, nothing from Amanda. Inhaling the aroma of Luisa's fresh corn muffins, Olivia headed for the shower.

Thirty-One

At her office, Olivia tried to concentrate on her work, but she still felt unsettled. She enjoyed seeing patients in her office. It was so different from working with inexperienced, overzealous residents. But part of her couldn't stop thinking about kissing Bart.

She was in the middle of explaining to a patient that it was unusual to develop headaches at his age, and that a brain MRI would help her determine the best treatment approach, when her assistant knocked on the door.

"There's a Carmen from the Commission on the phone," she said. "She said it's important."

What could they want? She asked the assistant to schedule an MRI for her patient, went into her office and picked up the phone.

Without preamble Carmen stated her business. "One of the docs has to leave town this weekend. Gabe moved you ringside at the MGM."

"At the MGM? Sure, sure, fine," she said in her best doctor manner. She wasn't going to let Carmen know how nervous the assignment made her.

"I'll email this afternoon's weigh-in time and tomorrow's report time."

Olivia frantically texted Bart, then sat musing about the feel of his hands on her skin as she waited to hear from him.

Her office manager knocked, startling her. "We have your other patients in rooms," she said.

Olivia rose, only to feel her phone vibrate. She waved that she would be right there and closed the office door. The call was from Bart.

"I've been a ring doctor for what—a month, and already they've assigned me ringside to an HBO card? I've never even worked the amateurs. I don't have the confidence. Why would the Commission put me in this position?"

"Congrats, they're dumping you into the big time," Bart said, chuckling. "Gabe thinks you're hot."

"Rossi," she complained.

"I'm only judging an undercard bout. I promise to sit next to you, and we can discuss everything. It'll be fun."

Olivia was barely able to listen as Bart explained that with three cards scheduled for Saturday—including one mixed martial arts event at the Eldorado in Reno—there weren't enough physicians to fill the positions. Gabe believed this would be the safest place for her, with him discreetly next to her and Atherton in charge.

"Babe, this is a great chance to demonstrate your ringside intuition in a protected setting."

What ringside intuition? she thought. But she went along with his enthusiasm, covering up her insecurities as she knew so well how to do, and agreed to meet him at Duffy's when she was finished with the weigh-in. Desperate to hear what had happened with Amanda, still she couldn't bring herself to ask, and she ended the call too nervous to think.

For a moment she lusted for a drink, chocolate ice cream, or both. Then she pulled herself together and went down the hall to her next patient.

*

Touching up her mascara and hair before heading out for the 3:30 weigh-in, Olivia felt her phone vibrate again. It was Elena from Senator McAllen's office, apologizing that it had been so difficult to get her together with the Senator.

Olivia was thinking she had heard this a few times already. The Senator always had to reschedule at the last minute. She waited to hear what Elena would propose.

"I told the Senator of your visit to Mexico and that you'll be working fights. He hopes you might have expanded views."

Olivia felt a quick panic. Too much was happening at once. "I was assigned to a fight card this weekend," she said, then suddenly wondered if the Senator already knew of her assignment.

"That's even better," Elena was saying. "The Senator will be in Las Vegas for the fight—a guest of HBO. Let's have you meet with him then. He flies into town Saturday morning to meet with donors. He has time Sunday before catching a morning flight back."

They set up the details, and Olivia ended the call without saying anything to Elena about her brother or Esme. Elena strangely hadn't brought it up, and Olivia wasn't sure whom to trust at this point. McAllen certainly didn't seem to have any real interest in Curtis's ideas. He must have been stringing Curtis along.

•

The weigh-in went without incident, and Olivia finished and headed for Duffy's to meet Bart. Duffy's patrons stood shoulder-to-shoulder at the bar, every table occupied.

"The most beautiful neurologist in Vegas," Duffy exclaimed, grabbing Olivia in a humongous bear hug. "He's in the back. I think he's trying to extricate himself from the MGM's CEO. I have strict instructions to point you in his direction before a younger, better looking stud—like me—gets to you first."

Olivia scooted between a number of handsome men in suits and ties to find Bart barely visible behind a bosomy platinum-haired waitress in a two-sizes-too-small Hofbrau blouse, taking his order.

"I don't see a CEO," Olivia said, grinning and moving the waitress aside as she slid in next to him. "Is this what I have to look forward to?"

Bart felt himself blush, a thing he seldom did. It wasn't getting caught in a seemingly precarious situation. It was Olivia's demeanor that confounded him. She was nothing like Tatou. Yet right now he felt the way he had felt that afternoon in the New Orleans rain.

"You okay?" she asked.

Hesitating for a moment he mumbled, "Uh, yeah…yeah."

"Rough day?"

Fighting the urge to kiss her and loving the anticipation, he channeled the discussion to her ringside debut while discreetly eyeing her mouth, eyes and the nape of her neck.

Managing sexual tension was one of Olivia's talents. There had been many men who wanted her. The difference this time was she wanted the man just as much—maybe even more so.

Following Duffy's fried zucchini and a pitcher of beer, she invited Bart over to watch fight DVDs.

"My Porsche is in the shop," he said. "It won't be ready until the morning. I can call a cab."

Batting her long lashes and throwing him the valet ticket, she stood up and said, "You drive."

•

In the car Olivia finally brought herself to ask him, "What happened with Amanda?" She blurted it, going against her desire just to be quiet and breathe him in.

"I didn't see her, she wasn't home." He glanced over at her. "Punishing me."

"Yeah, no communication—she's giving us both the silent treatment," Olivia said, thinking she should care but not concerned in the slightest. "I thought you said she was all about the story. Would she let a little thing like us get to her?"

"Now, now, sarcasm will get you nowhere," he pretended to admonish. "I'm sure she's hot on some trail right this moment," he added. "She'll call when she needs us again."

Reaching over to stroke his cheek with the backs of her fingers, she said, "Can you give me some pointers about tomorrow's fight?" She tried to feign aloofness as her breathing deepened with every second of silence.

As he started talking, his voice came out husky and he had to clear his throat. He reminded her of everything they had gone over, suggesting how she might make herself look tough if necessary. He spoke faster and faster, and his hands anxiously caressed the wheel. She loved that she unnerved him.

He pulled into the driveway and she jumped out of the car, tugging on her fitted skirt that had hiked up to her mid-thighs. Noticing he wasn't immediately following, she leaned inside the car.

"You aren't coming?" she asked in a teasing tone. Seeing no movement from him, she said, "It's okay if you have a game. You can have the car," and she headed for the front door. Let him decide. She wasn't going to force herself on him.

Bart sat behind the wheel with the engine idling and watched Olivia make her way toward the house. She had a way of walking that was womanly and childish at the same time. His heart flooded, watching her as she opened the big front door and disappeared inside.

This was the point of no return. He had always believed he would never travel this road again. He turned off the engine and followed her.

She was waiting just inside the door, in the dark entryway. He pushed her gently against the wall so he could close the door and bumped into Tyson, who was standing against her legs. He could hear her smile. He murmured an inch from her ear, "Let's go to your room."

Excitedly unsteady, she led the way, with Bart nuzzling her neck as he stumbled along behind her and the dog in contact with her legs at every step. Stopping at Lou's room, Olivia opened the door and Tyson went right in, jumped onto the bed and laid her head on the pillow. Lou never missed a snore.

Grasping Bart's hand, she pulled him inside her bedroom, quietly pressing the door shut. Removing his hand from the light switch, she placed it on her breast, then unzipped her skirt and let it fall to the floor.

"I want to see you," he charmingly protested.

"Another time—please," she whispered and kissed him so hard neither of them could breathe. Her mind raced with doubt and passion.

His advancing touch forced unrestrained exhalations as their mouths and tongues molded to each other. For the first time in so long, nothing else mattered except now. Her nipples hardened against his fingers, then his lips. Then he was inside her, every thrust causing her to moan and making her so wet she was momentarily embarrassed. She wanted to beg for more of this exquisite agony, but she bit her lip. Somehow this was beyond love or ecstasy. It culminated in peace.

Coming back to reality, she nuzzled his neck and whispered, "Thank you."

He held her close—so close she couldn't look into his eyes.

"Are you okay?" she asked.

She moved her lips along his face. She tasted tiny tears at the corner of each closed eye.

He kept holding her. He had no intention of letting go anytime soon.

"I believed I didn't need anyone—that I didn't need you—another mistake." His voice was comforting.

"I can't be everything Tatou was," she whispered, taking the chance of saying her name.

There was a silence. Then he said, "No, not what she was, what you are."

She longed to ask him what he meant. When he had told her the story of Tatou, the way he talked about her was rapturous. She couldn't compete with that even if she had wanted to. Was he saying she didn't have to? Was he saying she was someone to him? This smart, funny, egotistical, intuitive, gorgeous man—this man who was so much more than she had expected—could she deserve him?

And could she confide in him about her demons? Would he accept all the flawed decisions she had made, all the warring years with her mother, with Curtis? Would he understand her fears? Would he see that they were warranted?

He pulled away and looked at her with mischief in his eye.

"What?" she asked, smiling because she couldn't help smiling at him.

"Nothing," he said. "I was just remembering lighting a cigarette after sex, how delicious it was."

"Hmm, I never smoked. But I think I know what you mean." She disentangled herself, against his protests, and got out of bed. Throwing on her robe, she left the bedroom.

Bart lay suspended in time, filled with possibility.

She came back with two pints of ice cream, two spoons and a DVD. Handing him one of the ice creams, she climbed back into bed. He took the DVD from her and tried to make out what it was as he ate ice cream.

"It's Curtis's last fight," she whispered. "Maybe I'll be able to watch it now."

But something else was going on. She had thought she could watch it, but being in bed with him made her realize that wasn't what she wanted right now. She wanted him again. She let him know with a gentle touch. He obliged, hardening against her and moving her legs apart.

"You'll want to see him fight," he murmured, "but we'll have plenty of time for that." He nuzzled her neck, breathing in the scent of her. "Plenty of time," he repeated as he moved against her.

•

Sweetpea Won's whinnies and early morning sunlight soothingly roused her. She turned to a note on an empty pillow: "You looked too peaceful to wake. 8 AM shift at Western. See you at the MGM."

She couldn't stop grinning. The pulsating shower against her body let her relive his touch.

Thirty-Two

SITTING RINGSIDE at the MGM, Olivia couldn't think. There were so many things spinning in her head. As she looked around, she shivered. She would do this for Curtis—be the kind of sister he deserved. She would put the athlete's welfare above all else. She could be the advocate Bart described—at least she would try. Maybe in the process, she could find a way to let go of the self-doubt that always seemed to eat away at whatever she achieved.

Bart suddenly appeared out of the crowd.

"You okay?" he asked, taking care to leave a foot of space between them in this public place.

"I can barely hear myself think," she shouted. "It looks like all of Vegas is in the Grand Garden."

His eyes remained fixed on her face.

She shrugged. "Okay, I admit it, I'm jumping out of my skin. Don't go too far. I need you close."

He saluted and strolled to the other side of the ring to speak with Gabe.

Olivia adjusted her hair and secured the top button on her starched collar. She had one more bout tonight. She started pranayama relaxation breathing to distract her from her fear that all 16,800 fans were waiting for Curtis Montana's inexperienced sister to screw up. She looked around for Amanda, but the Girl Reporter hadn't showed up yet.

·

When Bart got to the other side of the ring, the commissioners were engaged in their usual meet-and-greet with politicians and celebrities. As a group, he thought, none of them looked particularly interested in boxing as they caught up on one another's business ventures and stock tips. Gabe fluttered among them, keeping peace with the press by answering last-minute questions about gloves and undercard judging decisions.

"Gabe, I need a minute," he said, waylaying her with his hand on her arm.

"No time. Rappaport is pissed that Markus lost by one point. He had the kid set up to defend the title next month at The Pearl. I haven't reviewed the scorecards. What the hell was Simon thinking? He gave the twelfth round to the other guy. I'm sure I'll hear about this Monday. They're already discussing filing a protest. When will those damn judges ever learn?"

Bart continued to tug on her jacket. "You and I must talk," he said quietly but with force.

She stopped talking and looked at him, finally seeming to understand that he wasn't moving. He led her to the other side of the ring—out of commissioner earshot.

"This main event is bullshit," he said with no preamble. "I'm not leaving until I get answers. What happened to Grover? Olivia examined him at the weigh-in, and now he's not fighting?"

"You read the *Review Journal* article."

"Let's skip over the sarcasm, okay? I spoke to Rappaport. Grover *suddenly* twists his ankle running last night? His biggest payday, and after making weight, he goes running as opposed to hitting the buffet? You're talking to me, not some flunky salivating journalist. Plus, I can't believe HBO is accepting Viceroy as a substitute. He fights 10 pounds heavier. Viceroy is gonna assassinate the network's golden goose. HBO is making money with Higgins—handsome Irish white middleweight. We both know Higgins can't punch his way out of a paper bag."

Gabe took hold of his lapel and pulled him close to her. With her best smile on her face for show, she said, "I'm trapped. Half the house is sold on seeing Higgins. Viceroy's opponent dropped out. And we have his medicals. Santiago approved it. The NBC and MGM are happy. HBO is more or less thrilled. Look around this place—all those Irish flags and banners. The hotel is expecting a big drop this weekend. It could even move the casino's Monday stock price."

Normally he would have kept his anger strictly under cover, but he wanted to shake her up. "You want me to believe that Higgins stands a chance against Viceroy?" he said, putting a growl into his voice and a frown on his face. "Drinking the Kool-Aid, are we? Or is someone taking a dive," he taunted her. "I know that ain't true, right? That would mean the end of many people's career, and jail time."

She dropped his lapel and tried to move away, but he caught her by the wrist.

"So, is it just a plain old bad substitution?" he pursued. "I promised Olivia we'd take care of her—"

Laughing, Gabe jumped in. "Ah, now I get it. You're afraid your little neurologist can't handle the heat."

"Fuck you." He let go of her wrist and straightened his jacket. "Let's at least switch physician corners."

"What? You want me to move Olivia to Viceroy's corner—put her over here?"

"The last thing you want is controversy."

A cameramen waiting in the ring to film the boxers' entrances covered his earpiece and leaned over the rope close to Gabe. "The director in the truck said there's some problem. Viceroy wants to enter the ring second."

Gabe hollered back, "That's ridiculous. Higgins has the title and Viceroy is the challenger. Christ, he went back and forth on the purse, demanded a suite upgrade and now he wants to enter as the champion?" Turning to Bart, "I've got to take care of this. It's holding up the telecast."

Waving to Craig Nelson, the chief deputy attorney general who handled legal discrepancies, Gabe said to Bart, "Olivia will be fine. She'll have you right next to her."

The crowd's taunts and cheers heightened as the arena's overhead illumination darkened into a kaleidoscope laser show. Jennifer Hudson, wearing a sparkling black beaded pants suit, began the *Star Spangled Banner*.

Bart looked across the ring to find Olivia.

•

Suddenly the empty chair next to Olivia disappeared. A firm, well-manicured hand touched her on the forearm. A pleasant, very familiar-looking seventy-ish countenance, proudly displaying an American flag on his lapel, presented himself.

"Senator McAllen," she said. "Of course. Elena said you'd be here."

"I've been wanting to meet you for some time—since long before you first called my office. Let's meet tomorrow morning. I'm staying at the Four Seasons. I hope an 8 AM call isn't too inconvenient? We have a great many things to discuss."

A secret service agent whispered in the senator's ear.

"They're asking me to take my seat," he told her. "My assistant will call you to confirm." He waved companionably as he trailed off with the secret service.

Birds took flight inside her chest as an unending trail of cornermen carrying buckets, stools and flags waved their arms and mounted the ring stairs. Viceroy stood in his corner as his cutman spread Vaseline on his face. Higgins waved his arms to "Danny Boy" blaring above cheers and boos. Reviewing Bart's reminders over and over, she flinched from a tap on her shoulder.

When she turned and saw that it was Bart, she almost hugged him.

"I'll be across the ring at the Commission table," he told her. "It's not what we planned, but things get moved around at big fights."

She urgently stuttered. "Not to be childish, but I'd feel better if you were next to me. And I don't understand why the fight wasn't canceled after Grover got hurt."

He squatted next to her chair. "Don't give it another thought," he said. "You know exactly what to do." Melting her heart with a wink, he added, "Don't question your instincts. You never wanted to come to Las Vegas, and you despised boxing. Curtis brought you here—to this moment. I wouldn't have allowed you to be in this chair if I didn't believe in your talent and feel for the boxers. Another wise boxing physician once told me, 'Treat your fighter as your patient. All the rest will fall into place.'"

She let the sound of his voice soothe her as he continued his pep talk.

"Work with Atherton across the ring. He's a good doc, and Frank is a talented ref—he's traveled this road a million times. Search his eyes at the end of each round. He'll nod if you need to check Higgins between rounds. Atherton will manage Viceroy."

He watched Higgins dancing around the ring as if he had already won, in St. Patrick's Day green satin trunks. This kid was going to get the shit kicked out of him.

"Keep it together, Norris," he said, and he left her to it.

Olivia confidently turned her chair to face the ring apron, shutting out the world with a stone-cold glare. For the next 50 minutes, two hopeful young men were her only responsibility. She owed them her absolute attention and allegiance. The boxers would dictate the outcome of the fight. She was there to help—if necessary. It hurt that Higgins resembled Curtis—handsome, with straight black hair framing bright green eyes.

"Seconds out, touch gloves and go to your corner," Frank yelled signaling the timekeeper to sound the bell for Round 1.

As Higgins repeatedly peppered Viceroy with his jab, Viceroy was setting up the Irishman. Viceroy knew he had the power. He was letting Higgins handle the action but waiting for an opening. Hastings and Rush, seated 20 feet from Olivia, urgently chatted about the two competitors—undoubtedly aware the fight would not last long.

"Lawrence, we're almost two minutes into the first round and no real punch has landed—lots of posturing."

"Tom, I can't say that's a bad thing for Higgins. Viceroy has heavy hands. He's a vulture waiting for Higgins to tire himself out."

"Lawrence, you're thinking what I'm thinking...Oh, that punch came out of nowhere," Tom shouted. "Another right, a left, and Higgins is down! Fifteen seconds left in the round. Will he make it to his feet? Even if he does, can he recover from that punch during the one-minute rest? Does his corner let him go back out? What does the physician do?"

The arena exploded—most screaming for Higgins to get up. Olivia's heart throttled her throat as the timekeeper stood and slapped the ring apron to assist the referee's count.

Standing close enough to grab Higgins should he collapse, Frank searched the rocked fighter's eyes for mental clarity, shouting, "Three, four, five..."

Higgins got up. His cornermen leaped into the ring with towels, hurling water in his direction to revive him. Barely making it, Higgins collapsed on the stool. The cutman took an ice-soaked sponge and clapped it onto Higgins's head.

"Shit, man, what the hell happened out there," hollered his trainer, who then signaled the cutman. "Get in there or gimme the fucking Enswell, or we're never gonna open that eye."

Olivia calmly entered the ring and stood quietly behind the trainer, aggressively monitoring every utterance by Higgins. Bart nodded to himself that he'd taught her well—complete a quick, non-interfering neuro exam by observing how the fighter responds to his trainer. Although shaken, Higgins was speaking clearly.

With the one-minute break about to end, Olivia forced the cutman to uncover Higgins's eye. Bart had taught her that a fighter could fight with one eye swollen shut if he still had unharmed eyesight in the closed eye and could properly defend himself. That had to be determined before the eye closed. Later it would be impossible to pry the eye open and assess whether the eyeball was normal and moving in all directions or there was an eye-socket/orbital fracture.

"Back off, little lady," the trainer commanded, elbowing Olivia out of the way.

She didn't budge. "Sorry, Murphy. I have to make sure Terry can see before I let him go back out."

Grumbling profanities, the trainer and cutman shifted their stances an inch. Olivia leaned in and whispered to the fighter. "You okay, Terry? Follow my finger," she requested, having him trace the direction of her digit to examine his eye muscles, pupils and alertness. After Higgins convinced her he was okay, she stepped back and said, "Thank you, gentlemen."

Stepping away from the corner, she took Frank aside. Her palm over the microphone on his lapel, she said simply, "This is not a good start. Keep him close. The eye is fine as long as he's not getting hit because of it and you think he's stable. Happy to take another look and recommend the fight stop if this keeps up."

"Okay, doc," Frank said eagerly. "We're on the same page."

Everyone seated at the Commission table eagerly watched this play out on the HBO monitor. Bart grinned to himself. She was professional, succinct and performed exactly as instructed.

He leaned in to Gabe. "Fantastic," he whispered.

"How'd you know I'd be watching her?" she protested. Then she rejected his comradely stance. "Yeah, I only hope Viceroy takes him out fast, or this could get ugly."

The bell signaled Round 2. Higgins sprang into the center of the ring to touch gloves.

"He's gotta be hoping right now that his altered depth perception won't be his downfall," Lawrence commented.

"So, Lawrence, the fighter can only be saved by the bell in the last round. Higgins barely made it to the corner. That eye is nasty, and he keeps pawing at it."

"It's either really bothering him, or he's looking for a nice place to land."

"Tom, you think Higgins wants to quit?"

"If he's smart," Tom laughed as Higgins ate a few more left hands that forced him against the ring ropes.

"We knew the change in opponents was going to be rough for Higgins. There are few fighters who know how to punch properly while backing up. Unfortunately for the fans, this kid isn't one of them," said Lawrence.

Olivia sat expressionless. Despite tightening every muscle in her body to remain still, she felt herself swaying with each crushing blow.

Inside, she was begging Higgins to land some punches, at least connect with Viceroy. His eyes—his eyes were so much like Curtis's. Shouldn't the referee stop this?

Higgins held on for the rest of the round. He avoided another shot from Viceroy like the one that had sent him down. He did the same in the third, and again in the fourth. But he was taking massive punishment and hanging on by a thread.

In the break after the fourth round, Frank, his eyes filled with worry, slyly motioned to Olivia to examine Higgins for the second time. Climbing into the ring, Olivia once again questioned the fighter and assessed his alertness. "I'm good, doc," Higgins said. "No worries." He was, in fact still completely alert and sounded clear as a bell. She had no medical grounds to stop the fight at that point, though she knew, and she knew Frank knew, that the slaughter should stop.

Round 5. Higgins came to the ring center more slowly. Frank advised the boxers to touch gloves and moved aside. Hastings and Rush continued to debate the mismatch. They considered bringing Olivia into the discussion—well aware this was her first big fight.

Viceroy connected with a right to Higgins's jaw that could have knocked over Michelangelo's David. To everyone's surprise, Higgins remained upright, but a cascade of blood splattered down his chest. Viceroy, stunned for a moment by the violent crimson eruption, looked to the referee to stop this ugly mess. Then he resumed his jabs to Higgins's bloodied face. Higgins managed to land two punches, staggering Viceroy.

"That kid can take a punch, and look, he's finally connecting," Tom shouted into his microphone.

"Tom, this fight is hard to watch. I came here to see a war, not an assassination," said Lawrence.

"He's the champion, he's been in this situation before. Matter of fact, this is how he won the welterweight championship."

Disheartened, Lawrence noted, "That was five years and many head shots ago."

The bell sounded to end the round while the commentators bickered about whether the fight should continue.

Olivia was in the ring in seconds as Higgins turned his head, spitting out a full cup of blood into the bucket. She tried to open his mouth. Blood gurgled in his throat forcing him to cough and spit out more. She called the referee, shaking her head.

"I'm sorry, Terry," she repeated over and over to the desolate fighter, who pleaded for her to change her recommendation.

The cameraman followed Olivia, with Higgins in his corner with his contentious cornermen. Ed Rappaport complained to Lawrence, who was already in the ring.

Bart had taught Olivia to remain close to a fighter if she stopped his bout—if they were that injured, they would need a doctor nearby. As Higgins's protests mounted—his arms waving furiously—she escaped for counsel.

Pushing through 50 high-spirited men—some happy, others furious—she leaned over the ring apron near Bart. He motioned for her to come down.

"I wish there was a way around this," he told her.

Astounded, heart racing, she whispered, "Around what?"

"We—everyone on the Commission—understands your actions. You had no choice. Higgins could have choked on his blood—explain it that way…Yeah, that works. He could have an open jaw fracture necessitating surgery…Make it clear a jaw fracture doesn't stop a fight. An open jaw fracture is a different story. Be succinct, direct, and speak in layman's terms."

Stunned, she grabbed Bart's arm, "Explain to whom?"

"Lawrence Hastings."

"Are you saying I need to be interviewed by HBO—my first big fight? You've got to be kidding."

Gently he pushed her to the ring step, as if she were a terrified soldier being led into combat. "Gather your thoughts," he said sternly and evenly. "Take a deep breath." He waited while she took breath. "Now go attend to Higgins. I saw Lawrence interview Frank, so be prepared."

For some reason she thought of Amanda. She looked around for her, wanting to see her familiar face—no matter how angry Amanda might be at the two of them. Strange, Olivia thought. It was unlike Amanda to miss a story like this, with all the innuendoes of the substitution and now this controversial call of hers.

She mounted the ring steps with deliberation and gracefully climbed between the ropes. Higgins continued arguing while his trainer removed his gloves and his cutman wiped his bloodied mouth. She wanted to flee hearing Rappaport rant about her ring inexperience.

But she didn't flee. She summoned everything she was made of and leaned over Higgins again. "I need you to sit another moment, Terry," she said soothingly, "so I can get a better look inside your mouth. Then you can be interviewed."

"Doc, this was my chance," he muttered, spraying tiny blood droplets in her face and hair. "I could've taken this guy. I've done it before. I had him where I wanted him. Why couldn't you have let me go one more round? I would've—"

Calmly shining her penlight into his mouth as he gagged on his bloody secretions, and wishing she had a tongue depressor, she asked, "How did you lacerate your tongue and mouth like that?" She moved someone out of the way so she could get a better angle. The cuts were severe. This couldn't be from a punch. Turning to the cutman, she asked to see Higgins's mouthpiece. Reluctantly, he reached into his pocket, and handed the mouthpiece to her.

Yes, it had jagged edges. Bart had told her sometimes they didn't have time to get new ones and they would cut one themselves.

Lawrence approached Olivia with a microphone and cameraman.

"Dr. Norris, could we have a moment," he asked smoothly.

She calmed herself and, turning to the commentator, smiled confidently. "Of course, Mr. Hastings."

"Dr. Norris, can you explain to the viewers why you stopped the fight?"

"Certainly," she said, nodding to the camera. "First let me clarify that I recommended to the referee that the fight stop. In Nevada—"

"Yes, I understand. What did you see that made you recommend…"

Succinctly and in her perfected doctor's manner, she regurgitated Bart's statements. They played well with her white collar splattered with Higgins' blood.

"Dr. Norris, I completely support the need to stop the fight. We all know you are Curtis Montana's sister and a new ring physician. How do you respond to those saying it was too soon to place you in this position?"

Purposely polite, Olivia smiled, melting the camera and her interviewer. "Mr. Hastings, I think the circumstances speak for themselves. I believe it's imperative for the fans to question what we do. The repercussions of a mistake are too great. I keep that in mind when I evaluate and treat every patient. Please, if you'll excuse me, I need to return to my fighter."

Hastings nodded, grinning with pleasure. "Of course, doctor," he said, letting her go and turning to the middle of the ring. "Tom, I'd like to add that the doctor saved Higgins from unnecessary punishment. She is what the sport needs—a doctor who cares and is not afraid to do the right thing."

Rush adjusted his earpiece and said,. "I get it, Lawrence. Now Higgins is ready to talk." He was holding the judges' scorecards up for Higgins to see. "You were way behind, losing every round except the last."

Trying to grab the microphone, Higgins shouted, "That's the point. I'm the champion. I'm the one that the fans came to see. You can see I'm okay. This doctor—let's face it, she doesn't know what she's doing. She took away my dream—my life. You can see I could've gone on." Blood was spraying out of his mouth, and Rush backed away a little as the fighter wiped his face with his towel. "Blood is a part of the sport," Higgins said, disgusted.

Rappaport leaned between Rush and Higgins and screamed, "Tom, let me say something here. Vegas is supposed to be the best. They're supposed to have the strongest officials. Tonight was a travesty. It's a sad day for Nevada boxing. You saw it, we all saw it. Terry won the last round on all three scorecards. He's the champion, and he should have been given the opportunity to come out for one more round. If he couldn't continue, then I have no problem. All I can say is that we are filing a protest Monday. We are going to suggest they send Dr. Norris to the minor leagues before they allow her to ruin someone else's career."

The two commentators allowed Rappaport to verbally punch himself out, and then allowed another tirade from Higgins, and then Lawrence turned the camera and grinned, "Back to you, Tom."

Olivia tuned out the catcalls as she climbed down the ring stairs. A frail-looking gray-haired hotel security guard reached for her hand at the bottom step.

"Dr. Norris, don't listen to these fools. They got nothing else to do and nowhere else to go. Most are drunk and others lost money. Let me help you down," he smiled. "I'm Maury—old Maury, most call me. It was an honor to be here when your brother fought. He mentioned you to me more than a few times. Yeah, he was real proud of his big sister—the doctor."

Olivia hugged him. "Thank you. I needed to hear that right about now."

Maury adjusted his tie and added, "I'm here if you need me."

Bart came up and put an arm around Maury. "Thanks, man. Watch over her. She's a keeper and did a terrific job tonight. Dr. Norris, let's have a seat," he said, taking her elbow and escorting her to a seat in the third row, where the officials were sitting. "Gabe is going to review the fights."

Olivia sat next to Frank, who wrapped his arm around her, laughing. "Trial under fire is what we face every night. You did great. No one should tell you otherwise."

As she listened to bravos from her fellow officials, she couldn't ignore Bart arguing with Gabe in the side aisle. Brusquely he extricated himself and moved to the row behind her.

Turning she mouthed, "What was that about? Am I in trouble?"

Pointing for her to listen to the discussion, he smiled. "We'll go over it later."

Her heart sank. Bart's troubled expression told her there was a problem. She barely heard Gabe or the others.

Thirty-Three

THE MINUTE THEY were out of the place, she nudged him. "Talk to me, Rossi," she demanded as they made their way to the parking structure.

"Not to worry," he said, "You did well. Focus on that."

How dare he not talk to her; how dare he not tell her what was going on. "I gave a great interview to Hastings," she said, her pulse racing. "He even supported my stopping the fight. Is it Rappaport? Doesn't the loser always launch an inquiry? Is the Commission upset?"

They were standing next to her car. Bart leaned over and kissed her softly, his mouth moving against hers as if he was saying something.

"I'll see you at the house," she said as she opened her car door. She slid in behind the wheel and closed the door, too angry to say more right now.

Bart was shaking his head.

She lowered her window and looked up at him.

With one hand on her door, he said, "This was a tough night—actually they're all tough. Get some rest. I promise to be by first thing in the morning."

She could not understand what he was doing. She desperately wanted him beside her tonight. She felt like she was in the middle of something, and she needed to know what it was. But his remoteness left her completely bewildered. She couldn't find a single word to say. She had spent her life running away from help, and she didn't know how to ask for it now.

He reached in and stroked her cheek with the backs of his fingers. "Don't take any calls, especially from press," he instructed her. "Let me do what I do best." His voice was soft and sweet to her, and she understood that whatever was going on, he wasn't deserting her after all.

"I've had years of experience in this business," he said. "I can prevent things from spiraling out of control. There's something more at play here. I need to investigate and make some calls."

She couldn't look at him. She sat there, unable to speak or move, afraid she would cry. He opened her door and, squatting down, put his arms around her.

"You'll be alright," he whispered, nuzzling her hair, then kissing her neck. His mouth on hers brought temporary calm.

Brushing her hair from her face, he kissed her again, this time on the forehead, then gently stroked her lips with his finger. "I'll be at your place first thing in the morning," he said, and he closed the door and turned from her to answer his phone.

·

She drove to the house without noticing where she was or what was going on around her. Safely inside, she poured herself a whiskey and took it into the shower. She stood with the hot water beating down on her and let the tears stream out of her. How was she going to get through this night?

When she was out of the shower, she pulled on her favorite torn Levi's and one of Curtis's T-shirts. She wiped the fogged bathroom mirror and saw a girl with bloodshot eyes, a Rudolph nose and no one to trust. No, she told herself, that wasn't fair. She would not, could not yield to the siren song of "This is who I am, discarded by yet another man."

But the self-blaming thoughts persisted: she was 36, living a carefully fashioned existence in her dead brother's home, insinuating herself into his life because she didn't have one of her own.

No! she thought again as she stared at her reflection. Bart was real, Amanda was real. They were in *her* life, not her brother's. No, she was not justifying being in Vegas by trying to find out why he died. She was here because this was where she should be. Maybe there would never be absolution for her, but something had changed since she moved into this life. She felt alive for the first time since she didn't know when. She must not yield to the old comfortable misery. Bart had promised her something. If she could trust him—If she could trust herself—there would be more.

She swallowed the whiskey, somewhat diluted with hot water from the shower. She had been living with guilt for as long as she could remember, disguising it to herself as righteousness. But guilt didn't just go away. She would have to work harder at it. But was that work real?

"Yes, yes," she forced herself to say. Even if her motives hadn't been pure when she started, something had changed now. Bart was not another illusion. Her feelings for him were different from anything she had ever felt.

And yet here she was, drink in hand, a near alcoholic with an eating disorder. Who was she fooling?

She wanted to scream. Would that question ever go away? It was a false question, she told herself, a question that pulled her back down into the swamp.

She shook her head against it, turning away from the mirror, and going into the bedroom.

Tyson was patiently waited for acknowledgment, carrying her stuffed Aflac goose.

Olivia smiled, wrapping her arms around the dog in an effort to keep from drowning in self-pity.

Lou cracked open the door, his eyes shining with sincerity. "Bet you could use a friend," he said. Then, groaning and shakily kneeling to stroke Olivia's wet hair, he mumbled, "Livy, sit beside me."

Tyson also accepted the invite and leapt onto the bed, licking each of their troubled faces.

"Did I ever tell you about my first major job as a cutman?" he said, unscrewing his silver flask. "I never made it as a boxer in the Navy. No chin. After Marilyn's funeral, I was at the L-station meeting her sister and nephew. They were collecting some of her things. Shouldn't be a surprise I was drinking heavy. She was my life. Vinnie tapped me on the shoulder. He was waiting for a friend. We knew each other from the Golden Gloves. He invited me to his gym...I never left."

Wiping his mouth following a hefty swig, he passed her the flask. "We had our first ESPN fight—one of our kids was fightin' for the championship. I must have repacked my case 20 times. I had my Q-tips lined up, the Avitene and Thrombin ready—this kid cuts bad. Vinnie must have repeated his instructions a hundred times."

Olivia could smell the old man's liquor and cigar breath and slept-in clothes as she sat quietly listening to his kind voice.

"End of the first round, the kid drops from a big right. He bounces up like a jack-in-the-box, barely making it to the stool. Vinnie screams to me, 'You get in there first; I'll stay on the outside.' In championship fights, only one person is allowed inside the ring to work on the fighter between rounds. I wiped the blood from his right eye. I swear to this day, he had the worst eye I'd ever worked on. Every inch of me was shaking—including my hands. I dropped the ball, my head emptied. I couldn't find the epinephrine or any of my stuff. Vinnie screamed to get my act together and shoved me aside. I can still feel that shove. He put pressure on the eye. The next two rounds I stopped the bleeding and kept the eye open."

She waited, but he didn't continue. "What am I missing?" she asked. Why did he tell her this story?

"You did the right thing tonight because you understand the sport. Our kid lost a decision. The only hands held to the fire were mine. It didn't matter one fucking bit that I got my act together and did the right thing later in the fight. All that mattered was that I let them see me sweat—I showed weakness. Tonight you were everything I should have been on my first night."

She looked at him. She had not seen that coming. It made tears come to her eyes again, but she brushed them away as Lou bear-hugged her. Tyson quickly pushed between the two, thinking it was playtime.

Lou tousled Tyson's ears. "I don't always say things right," he said. "You hardly ever see someone like you in boxing. Bart is the only other one I've known. You showed you have no fear in protecting a boxer in trouble no matter what anyone says. You did your brother proud by trusting your instincts." He pushed the dog out of the way and tweaked Olivia's nose in a nice, fatherly way. "What's more complicated is playing the game. Bart can better explain selling your call."

"Didn't I sell it, when I did the interview on HBO?"

"We'll see." He stood and headed for the door. "The promoter will use officials to barter a rematch," he said. "They'll make anyone who goes against them look incompetent. You hear a losing fighter call the judges—good judges—corrupt, blind or incompetent all the time. Promoters use an official's performance to force a rematch. They'll say the ref missed a low blow, or the judge screwed up the score, whether it's true or not." At the doorway, he turned. "The tough part is to stay out of the line of fire. Now get some rest." Then he and the dog were gone.

Funny, all this fuss, she thought. In a way it was for nothing. She hadn't thought about it, she hadn't summoned courage, she had just blithely forged ahead because she was sure she was right. Could she ever see herself as heroic, the way other people were evidently seeing her?

Olivia picked up her phone. There were three old voicemails from Amanda and a new one from her mother. "I'm so proud. I wouldn't have had the guts to do what you did...Of course you could have let the fight go a bit longer. The HBO commentators were very supportive too. The rest of the press argued you shouldn't have been in this position. Everyone has to start somewhere, so don't let their criticism get to you. We can't always be right. Things will get better."

She heard that mixed message her mother was so skilled at delivering, but right now it sounded more pathetic than stinging. Sophie had kept her and Curtis on a very short leash all these years, one way or another. With Curtis,

Sophie had clung to his financial security while using his dependence on her approval to keep him close. And with me? Olivia asked herself. It was the anger. She was attached to her mother by it; she couldn't let go of it. It was as old and true in her as her own name. Her mother knew how to use it, and she never failed to do so.

She deleted the message and went on to one from Bart, and it shocked her. "You have my heart…I like the sound of that, Norris. Be by in the morning. We're in this together."

With a sigh, she went out to the barn. She wrapped Sweetpea Won's blanket around her shoulders and handed the stallion a giant carrot. Forming a makeshift bed of hay in front of his stall, she searched the horse's all-knowing eyes.

Bart was the ultimate reason to clean up her act. Lying there, she confided every pent up fear to Sweetpea Won, who sporadically snorted like an expensive shrink saying, "And how does that make you feel?"

Finally on her way to sleep, she wondered again if she could ever tell Bart why she had brutally turned her back on her brother so many years ago. Would he understand or alter his opinion of her? Did she even understand it herself anymore?

•

Either the sun's heat or Tyson's weight on her legs woke her. Or maybe it was Sweetpea Won greeting Bart with a soft whinny.

"Don't move," Bart said, smiling and crouching beside her to rub Tyson's neck. "Don't tell me you were out here all night. Soul-searching, Norris?"

"You caught me." She sighed, stretching her arms.

He took her hand and pulled her to a standing position. "Let's grab some coffee," he said and raced Tyson to the kitchen.

Olivia slowly followed, lingering so she could watch him move.

Inside, Lou greeted them at the kitchen table as he ate Luisa's cinnamon rolls.

Bart grabbed a bun and poured himself some coffee, then handed it to Olivia and poured another.

He started describing his talks with Gabe, his press buddies and Lawrence Hastings. He had even cornered Stu.

"Gabe always plays dumb when it works to her advantage," he said. "She tells everyone what they want to hear. I should have known better—"

"Gabe said I did okay?"

He grabbed her and kissed her wherever he could reach as she struggled out of his grasp. "You did exactly what I would have done. It's harder—"

"Harder? You mean because I'm inexperienced or because I'm me?"

Lou interrupted. "It's like we discussed, Livy. It takes time for folks to trust you no matter what you do."

Sucking down his coffee, Bart interjected, "Let me tell you about Stu."

Lou's face turned sour. "His brother could be responsible for Curtis's death, and we know he's tied to Santiago and Fernandez."

"Let's all calm down. It wasn't until I spoke to Stu that I realized we're being set up."

"By whom?"

"I've known Gabe for 20 years, and I know when she's acquiescing. Stu made it clear that we're becoming a liability."

"That's total bullshit," Olivia spat out. "Gabe was the one that wanted me to see fighters—wanted me to work fights. You're saying they set me up to fail? It makes the Commission look bad. Unless something made them change their minds."

Firmly nodding, Bart grinned. "You got it. When everyone thought we were working to improve the NBC's image and put aside any concerns about Curtis, everything was okay. They wanted you there. They knew I'd keep my mouth shut while you were there."

Lou left the kitchen and returned with a fresh bottle of J & B.

"It's gotta be noon somewhere," he said without the slightest hint of a smile.

Olivia gently took the bottle away from him. "My sweet Lou, I know this brings up bad memories and questions."

"We've become a nuisance," Bart went on. "The only sure-fire way to get us out is to dishonor you. In the process, they disgrace me. After all, I was the one who brought you on board." He was positively chortling, as he continued.

"Stu confirmed that the NBC, the press and Ed loved having Olivia where they could keep an eye on her. Then Senator McAllen called Arnold Seine. Seine controls a large block of MGM stock. Maybe McAllen wanted a room upgrade or access to the high-roller baccarat tables. He mentioned Olivia's desire to carry out Curtis's wishes in forming a federal boxing commission. The last thing the NBC wants is to lose control and have the feds looking over their shoulder. The commissioners contribute heavily to the Senator's re-election. McAllen is never going to sponsor a boxing bill."

Olivia, still holding the bottle of whiskey, gasped. "I forgot all about my meeting with McAllen this morning," she squeaked, looking at the clock above the sink. It was already 10.30. "They were supposed to call to confirm." She checked her phone but there was nothing from the Senator's office.

"Do you think they didn't call me because of the MGM's concerns?" She felt like taking a swig herself. Instead she put the bottle away in a cupboard and poured herself more coffee. Then something occurred to her, something that had been there all along but that she had never noticed until this moment.

"What's that look on your face?" Bart asked her.

"I just realized," she said, "Curtis's instructions were that I should get in touch with Senator McAllen's office. He didn't actually write that I needed to work with the Senator—I was the one who read it that way."

"You think it was about—"

"It must have been about Elena," she interrupted. "Or rather, Rodrigo and the whole Tecate connection." The Senator had never had any intention of being in touch with her. Curtis was telling her something, not asking her to do something.

"And where the hell is your friend Amanda?" she asked, wishing for one second that something—anything—could turn out to be straightforward.

"Actually it's starting to worry me a little," Bart said a little sheepishly. "It's unlike her to be so silent, with this Higgins thing going on." He took out his phone and called Amanda, but the call went to voicemail.

Olivia was checking her call list. The last call she got from Amanda was Thursday night. She had let it go to voicemail, but there was no message. "Check your call list," she said to Bart.

He was ahead of her. There were missed calls from Amanda on Friday, which he had let go to voicemail. Why hadn't she left messages? Or why not text him?

Bart leaned back against the counter and crossed his arms. "Let's think this through," he said.

Luisa came in, dressed for church. She started anxiously putting churros on a plate.

Bart pulled up a chair for her and insisted she sit. Her hands were trembling.

"What's going on?" he asked in a calm voice.

Tearfully, she whispered, "You not got called by Diego?"

Olivia and Bart exchanged a look, and Olivia sat down next to the housekeeper and grasped her hand. "Please, Luisa," she said, "who is Diego? I'm not sure why he would be calling us."

Luisa looked from one to the other before she answered. "Diego called two days ago. He say he give the *información* to your friend, Miss Amanda."

"What information—"

"Wait," Bart said. "Luisa, who is Diego?"

The housekeeper looked down at her hands, too worried to answer.

"Don't be afraid," Olivia coaxed her. "We need to know what's going on so we can help."

"Miss Amanda come here Wednesday night," Luisa began, still looking down, and speaking so softly Bart had to move closer to hear her. "My uncle is a retired trainer. He lives in Ensenada. Miss Amanda ask me to contact him. She has a plan to get *información*. I call my uncle, then give her his number. That is all I know because she say it will be safer for me to know nothing about what was going on."

"And you said your uncle called you Friday?"

"*Sí, sí*...Friday. He sound very mad. I worry."

"Mad about what?"

"He say many bad things about Dr. Fernandez and his brother."

"Did he tell you anything about what was happening?"

She looked at him in great distress. "Did I do the wrong thing? Miss Amanda say you sent her to do this plan."

Bart couldn't help chuckling—frustrated, though, that he was not to have more information. Amanda had pulled off something really big, if his guess was correct. She must have set up the old trainer to somehow get some proof from the clinic.

"You didn't do anything wrong," Olivia said. "Is there anything else you can tell us that might help us find your uncle?"

"I do not want anyone to get in trouble." She was trembling. Bart filled a glass with cold water from the fridge door and handed it to her.

"No one will get in trouble," he said, "I promise."

Luisa took a small sip of the cold water, then another, and sat back in her chair. "The young brother of Chui's girlfriend is a boxer. He go with Diego. I do not know where they go, but I guess Mexico, maybe Ensenada. His name is Antonio Santos."

Olivia got up to call Chui on the intercom. She got Marco, who laughingly reassured her they were ready and would not make her late.

"Marco, this is Olivia," she said. "Luisa is here with us in the kitchen. Would you and Chui please come in for a minute?"

The brothers appeared moments later, dressed in their Sunday best, with their hair slicked back and freshly shaven cheeks. Luisa spoke to them in Spanish, asking them about Antonio.

"We have not heard from Antonio since they went to Ensenada," Chui said. "Is everything okay? What happened?"

"Can you tell us anything about the plan?" Olivia asked.

Both men shrugged. "She told us the less we know the better," Chui answered.

"She? Amanda?"

"*Sí*. I think she went with them."

"Yeah," Bart said, wishing he could put the pieces together better.

"We better go now," Marco said, looking at Luisa, who had not stirred.

"Okay, we don't want to make you late for church," Olivia said. "If you think of anything else or hear from anyone, let us know right away, okay?"

"He give money to the *clinica* after he say Antonio has problem getting a license," Luisa suddenly said, braver now, maybe, because her two cousins were there. "She take Antonio."

"She?"

"The *mujer*—the nurse at the *clinica*."

Olivia looked at Bart. He started pacing, then paused by Luisa's chair and put a hand on her shoulder.

"I do not know more than that," Luisa sobbed. "My uncle carries much anger. I fear he say things that make Fernandez not trust him." She stood up, took a lace handkerchief from her pocket and wiped her eyes.

Lou's voice from the doorway startled them.

"Now it comes back," he said.

All eyes turned to him, but he didn't go on.

Olivia smiled at him as if he were an exasperating child. "Lou, honey, what comes back?"

"I met Antonio Madrid when Vinnie, Curtis and I were in Ensenada. He trained with Diego, didn't he?"

Luisa nodded. "My uncle blamed the promoter and Sr. Santiago. He say many times, they kill Antonio Madrid."

Bart feverishly rubbed his jaw and excused himself to smoke the Partagas he'd carefully put in his pocket.

"Where are you going?" Olivia shouted.

"I need to think," he said, heading out the back door with Tyson.

"Am I in trouble, *Doctora*?" Luisa asked Olivia. "I thought you knew about... about—"

"You're not in trouble," Olivia said. "We'll figure this out."

"It is time to go to church," Luisa said.

•

Olivia went down to the paddock, where Bart was petting Sweetpea Won. He was on the phone with the cigar sticking out between two fingers at the side of his head.

Seeing Olivia, he hung up and waved smoke off to the side. "Can't have your horse subjected to second-hand smoke," he said with a laugh.

"How can you be so calm?" she demanded.

"There isn't much we can do except wait."

"Are you insane? We have to find Amanda." She was fuming, but all the time, she wanted to laugh with him.

Quietly, without a word, he gathered her into his arms. It was so unexpected, it confused her.

"I'm not a child," she retorted, pulling away.

Bart leaned back against the fence and made a show of setting the timer on his phone. "Let me know when you've finished. Aren't you going to ask who I was talking to?"

Stopping dead in front of him, unsuccessfully ignoring his sexy grin, she asked, "First, why the timer?"

"It took you 90 seconds to slow down. I'm not being condescending. I just want to know what to expect next time."

"You jerk," she said socking his gut.

He grabbed her fist and kissed her hand. "I called my FBI friend. He's placing a tracer on Amanda's phone. Now we wait."

"Isn't that illegal?"

"I told him what we were up to before we went to Mexico. He said we were nuts but that I absolutely must call him if we got in a tight spot. He'll get back to me within the hour. We shouldn't panic until then. Maybe she lost her phone." He thought again of the many times Amanda had borrowed his phone, and it burned him again that he had been so stupid he hadn't understood she was stealing information. "Or she ditched it," he added, "if she felt she'd raised suspicions."

He took Olivia's hand and led her to the side of the barn. Shifting his chilled hands underneath her sweatshirt, he drew her against his chest, his lips against hers as he fondled her breasts. His grasp intensified the kiss.

Gleefully shameless, she dragged him into a stall lined with bales of fresh hay, pushed him down, and straddled him, undoing his zipper.

He laughed lasciviously. "Ah, now I know why this hay is here."

When they had finished, they lay there smelling the delicious scent of hay. "I missed you last night," he said adoringly. "I won't leave you like that again."

It was what she longed to hear. She would wait to tell him how she felt, hoping this man would be different.

*

Bart's phone vibrated, and he motioned for silence as he listened. "That's not good," he said after a moment. "Okay, thanks for checking. Let me know if you hear more. I'll do the same. Be safe."

Olivia stirred, looking at him questioningly.

"Amanda checked into The Royal Hotel in Ensenada on Thursday night, then nothing," he said.

"What does that mean, 'then nothing'?" She found her panties and jeans and stood to shake some of the hay out of them, then put them on.

Bart watched her, torn between the sweet look of her body after sex and the information he had just gotten about Amanda—or the lack of information.

"There were no credit card charges or calls, according to my friend at the FBI," he continued. "Mandy stayed in a suite at The Royal, and the room was under a Nick Cappo. He's a cub reporter for the *San Diego Union-Tribune*. They had room service for one night. A hotel employee described an attractive female in her early thirties. They explained they were newly married. No one saw them check out, though the bill was paid Saturday morning with Cappo's credit card. The U.S. border has a record of her and Cappo coming back to the States through Tecate."

"You think it's a boyfriend?" Olivia gingerly asked.

Bart shrugged. "Knowing Amanda, it's more likely some kind of deal she made with someone who could help her."

"She told me someone had helped her get the test records, using the Freedom of Information Act," Olivia remembered.

"My guy said Cappo is working off book. He's been on leave from the *Union-Tribune* for at least a week."

"This is crazy. She can't just disappear." She was picturing the gym, and how closely they had been watched. The feeling made her shiver.

"I have to get this hay off me," she said. "It's making me itch. How about a shower?"

"You go warm it up for us. I want to check with the *Union-Trib* staff. I have someone in San Diego who can get to them."

She was too itchy to take his rebuff personally. "Your loss," she tossed over her shoulder as she headed for the house.

•

The shower felt delicious, and she lingered, imagining his wet touch, waiting to see his shape appear through the frosted glass shower wall. In a few minutes he was there, slithering into the steamy stall, pressing her against the tiles.

"My guy is going to ask a few questions," he said, assiduously licking water out of the hollow at the base of her neck. "He'll get back to me."

●

They were eating lunch when the guy called him back. Bart took the call, nervously swallowing a huge mouthful of quesadilla too fast and gulping coffee to wash it down.

It turned out that no one at the paper had heard from Cappo in 10 days. He signed out saying he was chasing a front-page story. He wasn't salaried.

"Did he tell his editor the angle?" Bart questioned, putting the call on speaker and laying the phone on the table.

"No. All they know is it was a boxing investigative piece. The paper gave him travel expenses. He told his boss it would 'blow the lid' off the sport."

"Well, it might crack the lid," Bart muttered. "It's going to take a lot more digging to get enough to actually change anything."

"That's all I have," his friend told him.

Thanking him, Bart ended the call, wandered over to the refrigerator and took out a beer. "This is all speculation," he said, frustrated and worried, despite himself, about Mandy.

His phone vibrated and he looked at it. "I'm on call at Western. Gotta take this...Stewart, I'm busy. Who? How much blood did she lose? I'll be right there."

He put down the beer and grabbed his jacket and ran, shouting as he went, "Come on, Mandy's in the ED."

Thirty-Four

ON THE WAY to the hospital, Bart told her what Stewart had told him. Mandy had been flown in by Flight-for-Life from somewhere between Bakersfield and Las Vegas. Before she was intubated, she asked them to contact Bart.

"She had an accident? When did this happen?"

"Not sure, but I would guess early today or late last night. Amazing they flew her here. There were certainly closer hospitals.

Olivia laughed. "She seems to have her ways," she said, briefly wondering if Amanda would find a way to get Bart back.

"Stewart said she has abdominal injuries."

"What happened to this Cappo?"

"I have no idea. Let's hope Mandy survives."

She looked at him. He returned her look. "Let's hope it for her sake, too," he added.

·

"Bart, over here," Stewart called out, hovering over the ventilator settings at Bed 1. He handed over the chart. "Flights said she was slumped over the wheel. She was muttering your name…and Olivia's."

"Why was she tubed?"

"Her PO2 was less than 80. She's got at least five rib fractures and a pneumo-thorax. On arrival, she could barely respond…I tubed her as a precaution."

"Her head CT?"

"Negative…Good thing though, her face could double as a Macy's Day Parade float. Took quite a beating. Must have pissed someone off big time."

So it wasn't just a car accident. Olivia was thinking that Amanda was lucky to be alive at all with Steward treating her.

Stewart continued. "Metro must have her belongings. Her hematocrit has dropped since admission. She has internal bleeding—maybe a ruptured spleen. We did chest/abdominal CT's—nothing. General Surgery is coming. How do you know her? Doesn't she work for Channel 8?"

All too familiar with Stewart's nosiness, Bart didn't bother to answer.

"Why would she ask for Olivia?" Stewart persisted.

"She was writing a follow-up on Montana—maybe commenting on Olivia becoming a ring physician."

Olivia asked sheepishly, "Do we know who made the 911 call?"

"Reportedly a hysterical woman with a thick Spanish accent. Might be the same one who called here about 30 minutes ago asking about her condition."

Olivia started going over Amanda's unconscious body for telltale symptoms, forcing Stewart to step away from the bed a bit.

"Oh, the passenger didn't make it."

She reeled on him, ready to wring his neck when she felt Bart's hands on her shoulders, massaging them to keep her still.

"The passenger?" he asked. "Do we have an ID?"

"The car was a mess. It turned over three times going down the ravine. Landed in a gully." Stewart seemed to be savoring each detail he spoon-fed them.

"Do they have an ID on the passenger?" Bart asked again, just as off-handedly as the first time.

"Nick Cappo. A kid. Twenty-three years old. He was some kind of reporter."

•

Olivia was stunned. Bart tenderly rubbed her trembling shoulders.

"Let's take a walk," he suggested, gingerly guiding her to an empty waiting area. "Gerald Handler is the surgeon—smart and good with his hands. He'll call after reviewing the scans. We need to get our story straight."

Irritated, Olivia muttered, "She's lying there because of us, and you're worried about our story?"

"No, she's lying there because she is either too good a reporter or too pig-headed to leave all the sleuthing to us," he said. "Or a bit of both."

She stamped her foot, but she knew he was right. Once Amanda got going, there was no stopping her. She had proved that more than once.

"We know she went through the Tijuana border crossing without showing a scratch," she said, thinking aloud. She was rarely this unnerved, and it made her twitchy and loud.

He gestured with his hands for her to lower her voice. "Put things in perspective," he said, and his phone vibrated.

He looked at the screen. "My friend at Metro," he told her and answered the call. "Yeah, I know…I'm also concerned about any media falling into this story, and where it might lead…"

"What fucking story?" Olivia demanded. Right now, she didn't like this man at all.

Bart continued to listen to the caller while firmly grasping Olivia's arm and ushering her out of the ED and into his car. He finished the call and slid in behind the wheel.

History had taught him that telling a woman to calm down was like throwing a match into gasoline. He opted to take a steady informative approach.

"Mandy was beaten up at a gas station, and so was Cappo. Their wallets and phones are missing. They were ID'd by facial recognition—evidently reporters are in the database. The 911 call came from a woman they think was local, from a pay phone at a truck stop outside San Diego. The police went over the car but they didn't find anything. They're not hauling it up the bank—too expensive."

"No paperwork or X-rays in the car?"

He shook his head.

"Could Cappo have turned on her?" she wondered.

He sighed, wishing he had more answers. "Probably not. It wouldn't make sense. He was beaten up too."

Olivia looked over at him. Why was he cutting her off? Why was he so remote? "Maybe Cappo set her up," she said. "Maybe he mistook her ardor for the story as cutthroat. Maybe it was worth more to him to turn her over to them than—"

"Listen to yourself," Bart insisted. He put his hand on her arm as his phone vibrated. The caller's ID was blocked. "Yes, this is Bart Rossi," he said. "Can you speak up? I didn't catch your name. Please don't hang up…No, I'm not tracing this call. Yes, they're taking her to surgery soon. Can we meet? Are you the one who called in the 911? I'm here with Dr. Norris…We'll come to you." He hung up and turned on the ignition. They were out of the parking lot at warp speed.

The look on his face was intense in the way Olivia had only seen when they were making love. She suddenly saw him clearly. He wasn't remote. He hadn't closed her off. He was expecting her to be with him, idea for idea, emotion for emotion.

"Okay Jeff Gordon," she said with more breath in her than she had felt for hours. "I take it that was the 911 caller." She hung onto the door handle as he made a very sharp turn.

He screeched into Denny's parking lot and slammed on his brakes. Sprinting out of the car, he looked back for her.

She jumped out and caught up with him. "You're paying for the chiropractor," she said.

He rolled his eyes. "I don't want her leaving."

They both saw her the minute they walked in—a slender brunette sipping from a mug in a rear booth. She looked up at them with almond-shaped, cinnamon-colored eyes. If it hadn't been for her disheveled clothing, Olivia thought, she could have been a dead-ringer for a bit older Selena Gomez.

"Linda?" Bart said, slowly approaching.

She nodded, looking beyond them anxiously. They slid into the booth, across from her.

"Don't be afraid," Olivia said, reaching out but not touching the woman's badly bruised arm.

Linda straightened her torn flower-print blouse and sat up. She looked at Olivia and her face changed. "You look just like him," she gasped, and tears welled up and ran down her cheeks.

"You're Esme's cousin, right?" Olivia said quietly, suddenly realizing this was the woman Rodrigo had mentioned would help them.

Linda nodded but didn't speak.

Olivia was shaking. She reached across and took hold of Linda's hand. "We want to make sure that what happened to my brother doesn't happen to anyone else," she said.

The young woman gave a little laugh of scorn and pulled her hand away. "He loved you," she said. "He was used to ignoring that you weren't there." She spoke in a low voice, barely audible, dense with Spanish pronunciation, but her words were the words Olivia already knew. They were incised in her heart. Linda met her eyes, blazing. "You were never there, Livy-the-doctor."

Olivia felt Bart's comforting hand on her leg under the table. "You're right," she whispered. "But he loved me just the same." She finally understood it. "That's my redemption."

A waitress came over and Linda ducked her head. Bart ordered them coffees, and there was silence at the table until she had put the two steaming mugs on the table and gone away again.

"Can you tell us anything about what happened to Amanda and the reporter from San Diego?" Bart asked.

Tears rolled down Linda's cheeks as she looked over at him. "Amanda never should have been there," she said with scorn in her voice. "How could she not have known how dangerous it was?" She bowed her head to hide her face, which was contorted with tears.

Olivia reached across again, smoothing the beautiful black hair away from the young woman's face. There was a bruise and a small laceration at her hairline that followed a trickle of blood onto her blouse.

"You need to let me look at that head-wound," she said.

Linda pulled away, wiping at her cheeks with both hands, in anguish. "She stuck her nose in, and now Nicky is dead," she whispered, holding back sobs.

"Cappo?" Bart asked. "The reporter was your boyfriend?"

She looked at him, her black eyes flashing. "We would have been married in three more weeks." She was shaking her head, as if she could shake away the loss. "He did this for me. No, the story would have gotten him status, but I was the one who wanted to get back at them for Curtis's death, and the deaths of the other boys."

"Can you tell us what happened?" Bart asked again.

"She happened," she hissed. "Amanda. She pushed her way into it. She insisted in going to Ensenada instead of staying in the States and waiting for Diego and young Tonio to return safely, like we planned. *Dios* knows where those two are right now."

Bart sipped his coffee and hated the taste of it, but it helped him think. If the plan was to send in someone who would need the tests faked in order to be licensed by the Commission, then this Antonio Santos kid must have an anomaly that would show up in a scan. "If the clinic supposedly scanned Santos and the film showed nothing..." he ventured.

"Then we would have at least some proof of their underhanded practices," Linda broke in. "Amanda has Tonio's original scans, done here." Eyeing the exit door at the back of the restaurant, she lifted her purse onto the table and started cleaning it out, as if she was looking for something. Bart watched fascinated as a beat-up *People Magazine*, two empty Chiclets boxes, crumpled up tissues, a torn bandanna and three pieces of a Hershey with almonds materialized and created a small heap on the table. "It's always about a story—some damn story," she was saying. "Nicky has to prove to that newspaper, to his dead father, to people who don't matter or care what happens to him that he's worth something. Now look!" She looked at the pile of trash as if there were some answer there.

"Please try to stay calm," Olivia said. "You need to have that wound looked at, and you should have a head CT."

"I have to go," she said.

"Please, not yet," Bart stammered, but she was already out of the booth.

"I FedExed the contents list to Amanda last night—that was the only address I had in Las Vegas. Guaranteed 8 AM delivery Monday—if it isn't intercepted." She pulled a messily folded FedEx receipt out of her bag and handed it to him, then took off. Bart went after her, trying to stop her as she headed to the back door. "Please tell me how I can get in touch with you," he pleaded.

With a stony expression, Linda said, "You and I both know I'm not safe here," and she was out the door.

Bart sat down at the edge of the banquette across from Olivia. "This is fucking great," he growled.

Olivia put her hand over his. "You're drawing attention," she whispered. "I'm going to get us some fresh coffee."

He watched her go over to the counter and order coffees, and he watched her come back toward him carrying them. He couldn't take his eyes off her; she distracted him from everything else that was going on.

"What?" she said, putting down the mugs and sliding in next to him.

He shook himself and took a deep breath. "I could use some Glenfiddich in this. Got any?"

She leaned in to kiss his cheek, but he quickly turned his head at the last second, and their lips met.

"She's right," she said, easing back against the booth wall. "Las Vegas wouldn't be the best place for her to be safe from Santiago and his brother."

Bart was looking at the mess the young woman had left on the table. He reached out and tentatively pushed aside some tissues, looking at the magazine.

"Did she mean she sent us the vitamin cocktail?" Olivia asked, looking at the FedEx receipt.

Bart slid the magazine toward him on the table, sweeping the other things off it. "She said, 'Now look,'" he said, picking it up and starting to thumb through it. There was something stiff in the pages. He turned the magazine upside down and shook it, but nothing fell out. He put it back down and turned to the stiffened part and there was a DVD—no case—taped between two pages. He pulled it out and turned it right side up. MRI: *Antonio Santos* was written in marker on a label with the clinic's logo and contact info printed on it. "What have we here?" he said gleefully, laying the DVD carefully on a clean napkin.

"They beat her up for this and didn't get it from her?" Olivia said, incredulous.

"They either didn't know she had anything and beat her as a warning, or they beat her and then she got it."

Olivia reached into the pocket Linda had made with the two pages and brought out medical records for Antonio, and also some receipts, in German, from a company in Bonn. Neither of them could read one word of German.

Tossing a twenty-dollar bill on the table, Bart pushed against Olivia to get her out of the booth. "Let's head back to Western. There's a laptop in the doctor's room."

As they got into the car, Bart's phone vibrated. It was the surgeon.

"Thanks, Gerald," Bart said, after listening for a moment. "Yeah, she's a fighter. Glad you were able to make it in so quickly...I know, they would have taken her to a Level 1 except she kept repeating my name. You think she'll be reasonably awake soon? Yeah, no, no game for me tonight."

Hanging up, he embraced Olivia joyously.

"Amanda's okay," he declared. "Minus her spleen. She should be fine." He couldn't help chuckling.

"Can we see her?"

"Gerald said to give her another hour. This gives us time to think."

Thirty-Five

CRANKY FROM TOO much coffee and too many unanswered questions, they ended up driving around, arguing about nothing until the hour was up. They were silent by the time Bart pulled the car into Olivia's parking slot at Western and they headed for Amanda's room.

"Labor and Delivery?" Olivia said. "This was the only place they could find a bed?"

A man in his late forties sat alone in the waiting area outside 3-North reading the newspaper. Bart saluted hello, then pulled Olivia inside the ward.

"Who was that?" she asked.

"Him?" Bart looked a little smug.

"Yeah, him," she said, pulling his ear.

"Ouch. That's Jack—retired FBI." He was chuckling and rubbing his ear. "He now works privately."

"Privately?'

"You can't be too careful. There's still no clue who got to Amanda. She may not remember—or ever have known."

Strolling by a row of rooms filled with newbie moms, babies in bassinettes, and celebrating relatives, Bart cracked open the door to 325 and bumped into a man in plain clothes.

"Thanks, Buddy," he said. "What's it been, five years?"

Hugging Bart, Buddy said, "Way too long. Been winning lately?"

"Don't I always?" he shrugged. "Thanks for keeping an eye on our gal. By the way, this is Dr. Norris."

"Very nice, Bart ol' man," Buddy said, poking him in the side.

Bart laughed. "This is business. Dr. Norris and I—"

"Whatever you say." He extended his hand, blushing, "Sorry, ma'am, I meant no disrespect. Bart and I go way back. We use to—"

Wrapping his arm around Buddy's neck in a playful chokehold, Bart interjected, "Me and my man Buddy spent many a lonely night together. That's what you were about to say, right?"

While they joked, a startling, pained groan came from behind the curtain that concealed the room's bed. Olivia quickly pulled the curtain back and went to Amanda.

"You okay?" she asked.

Amanda's face was badly bruised, with bandages covering facial and scalp lacerations. Buddy excused himself to wait outside.

Amanda was dazed and agitated. She ripped the oxygen mask off her face. Olivia tried to convince her to relax. Bart was ready to fire questions until Olivia mouthed for him to refrain. Reluctantly, he took a seat. "The police will want answers," he whispered. "We have no clue what she remembers or what she'll tell them."

Amanda had drifted back to sleep almost immediately.

The door cracked open. "Bart, you in there?"

Bart turned to see who it was. "Sullivan, come on in," he whispered. "It's my friend with the FBI," Bart said softly to Olivia. Sullivan—attractive, muscular, in his mid-forties—came quietly into the room. Adjusting his dark blue serge sport coat, which barely covered his leather gun holster, he extended his hand to Olivia.

"I wondered when you'd show," Bart said. "Did you speak to Metro?"

"Yeah. We're going to be handling things now, but we'll be keeping the police in the loop."

Bart stood up. "Sullivan and I are going to grab a cup of coffee," he said. "Stay here with Mandy in case she wakes up again."

He put an arm around Sullivan's shoulders, and the two of them went out. Olivia heard him saying, "They have this new espresso machine in the medical staff lounge—my treat."

She did not protest, but it perturbed her to have decisions made for her. Still, Amanda might wake up, and she would be able to ask her a few questions as long as she did it gently.

After a while, Amanda opened her eyes and looked around the room as if she was searching for something.

Olivia touched her arm. "Bart will be back in a bit."

"I'm sorry, I made a mess of it," Amanda said, her voice hoarse from the intubation. "Is Nick okay?"

"Sorry," Olivia said softly.

Amanda stirred anxiously. "What! He didn't make it?" she groaned. Suddenly she looked at Olivia as if she had just recognized her. "You slept with him, right?" she demanded. "I went after the story and you got the guy."

"What's that supposed to mean?" She was angry even though she had no right to be.

"Deny that you took advantage of my obsession to get this big story onto my résumé."

"I do deny it. You went rogue, disregarding all plans and completely without regard for Bart or me. You—"

"I made a choice. You two were off playing cops and robbers at the spa of your dreams."

"Mandy, this is crazy, you knew—"

"First of all, don't you dare call me Mandy. And second, I know I screwed up, so you don't have to tell me."

The two women eyed each other. Olivia had never been down this road before, facing her rival. She had never had a rival because she had never wanted anyone the way she wanted Bart. But looking at Amanda right now, with her bundled face and her eyes filled with anger, she found herself really liking her for the first time. She tried to figure out how to start again, to defuse the anger, but Amanda was ahead of her.

"It's because you're different," she said, and her expression changed. "I told myself nothing was more valuable to me than Bart. But it turned out it wasn't true, and he knew it."

"If it had been me," Olivia said, "I would have gone to your house and threatened to strangle you if you didn't stay away from him."

Amanda painfully shook her head slightly on the pillow. "You would never act like that in a million years," she said. "You have a serious rival, though, a French girl he never got over."

"Tatou?"

Wounded, she asked, "He told you about Tatou? It took me two years to hear her name, and that's all I ever heard…and that was by accident."

"Sorry." She knew the second she said the name that she shouldn't have. It was pulling a trump card. It was staking her claim. And it had worked.

A tremor passed through Amanda's body, and she pressed the pain medication button frantically a few times. "What happened to me?" she asked. "I was driving and then I blanked out."

"You went over the guard rail and…" Amanda had drifted back into unconsciousness.

•

Periodically a nurse came in to check the monitors and bandages. Olivia dozed off, and when Bart returned, she awoke with a start, surprised she had drifted.

"Where're your bodyguards?" she asked him sarcastically.

"Sullivan will be back. Now we can question Amanda without Metro—if she ever wakes up."

"Wait, aren't we missing the bigger picture? We still have no idea about Antonio and Diego."

"Oh yeah," he said shamefaced. "They decided it was best to stick around San Diego for a day when he didn't hear from Amanda. They're safe. I promise you," he added, embracing her.

"And you were going to tell me this when?" she snapped, amused at how deftly he assuaged her anger.

"I telephoned Lou just now. And no, you're not the last to know everything— well, perhaps in this one instance." He laughed, rising above her, soothingly rubbing her neck. "You drive me crazy."

In any normal situation, she would have slugged him or remained pissed off. On the other hand, how could she? She felt the same.

Amanda grunted, coming to. "Jesus, was I shot or something? My stomach is killing me." She pushed the PCA pump. "This thing isn't working."

Bart looked at it and said it was working. "You lost your spleen," he told her. "Can we call someone for you—your parents?"

"You can call my editor and tell him we have a damn story. Well, we have parts of a story. It depends who survived." She started to cry.

Bart tenderly wiped her tears with a tissue, but she pushed him away. "Don't be tender with me, Bart Rossi," she said. "I don't want to be the pathetic one. You chose her, stick by it."

Bart looked at Olivia. What had gone on between these two women?

"We—" Olivia stuttered.

"We had a little talk," Amanda interrupted. "Let's not linger over it. I take it Linda made it?"

Amanda's eyes looked wearily from one of her visitors' faces to the next. "There's so much more than fabricated MRIs and lab slips," she said. "Take a seat," and she punched the PCA pump button and started to talk.

•

Nick Cappo was the one who had helped her get the Freedom of Information Act records last week. Amanda, not good at waiting around for information to come to her, came up with a plan to send a fighter to one of the Mexican clinics to get tested. She needed someone with an anomaly that would show up on an MRI. She called Nick—he had the contacts; he was working on the story at his end.

"Why would he share with you?" Bart interrupted.

Amanda fixed him with her eyes. "Because I was his contact with you and Olivia," she said, her voice sharp with hoarseness.

"How pleasant to be a commodity," he said with disgust. "And you wonder why you and I didn't make it."

Olivia cleared her throat. "Let's keep this civilized," she demanded. "Keep going," she urged Amanda.

"Nick had come up with this kid, Antonio Santos, who was in excellent health but had a small abnormality on an MRI—a small cyst that couldn't be missed. It placed him at no increased danger."

"Ah, so if the clinic produced an MRI report with no cyst," said Olivia, "we would know it was false."

Amanda nodded. "He has also been immunized against hepatitis B. So, if the blood test showed no exposure or immunity, it's not his blood. That's how we prove the test results are not Antonio's."

"It's a good idea," Olivia said, "but I don't see why you went down there. Why take that kind of risk, when—"

"Why?" Bart butted in. "Because she didn't want Cappo getting the jump on her story."

"Rossi," Olivia warned him.

"He's right of course," Amanda said. "And I'd do it again. Only…I wish he hadn't gotten killed." The tears were rolling down her cheeks. She reached for the pain meds, but she had maxed out for the time being.

Olivia handed her the tissue box and suggested they stop for the moment and let her rest.

"No, let me get through it, in case something…else happens."

"You're okay," Olivia reassured her. "It was just your spleen."

"And we have security guards outside your door," Bart added, seeing Amanda's fear and feeling a little sheepish about having been harsh with her.

Blowing her nose gingerly, Amanda winced, then went on.

She said that Nick knew about a guy named Diego who was friends with Antonio's U.S. trainer. Diego knew the set up at the clinic and could take Antonio there. It turned out that Diego also knew and loved Curtis and that he was related to Luisa, Curtis's housekeeper, so Amanda had contacted him through her.

"Nick and I met Antonio at a motel diner about an hour north of Tijuana. We had arranged for Diego to meet us there too." She half-smiled. "'When we met, Diego said, '*Definitivamente* the tests will not be Antonio's—if you pay enough.' We gave him $2,000 and sent the two of them to Ensenada."

Amanda and Cappo had checked into the Royal in Ensenada as a honeymooning couple. They were able to watch Antonio live at the clinic, on Amanda's laptop, because he was wearing a camera; the footage was stored in her Dropbox. Linda was the nurse in charge at the clinic. They had told her everything, so she was in on the venture.

It had taken Linda about 20 minutes to perform a complete physical, and a technician then drew Antonio's blood. A middle-age woman came in and looked at the fighter's eyes for about 90 seconds with an ophthalmoscope, then checked off a full page of items on the form, signed and dated the page and put it with the rest of Antonio's papers. Antonio never even saw the doctor.

Fernandez then came in, and Linda told him they had blood, an EKG and a chest X-ray, which was untrue but was standard practice. Fernandez said he would do the MRI and take care of anything else that needed to be done.

"It was creepy," Amanda said. "He had his arm around her, and you could see him admiring her...curves."

She took another hit on the pain pump, and Olivia put her hand on her arm. "We can hear more tomorrow," she said. "Please rest."

"This can't wait," Bart intervened. "The FBI and Metro will want to hear at least part of the story, and we need to decide which part."

She quickly looked at him. "Can't it go through Sullivan?"

Amanda held up a hand, and they turned their attention back to her.

In the middle of the night, Linda had come to the hotel. She was a little frantic. She had an envelope in her hand, and she said they should get out right away. It was almost dawn by then, and they started throwing their things into bags. In the envelope were invoices. Linda told them this was something else, something worse than what Diego and Antonio were going to be able to give them. Fernandez had made her so mad with his constant fondling that she went into his office and started pulling out drawers. She didn't even care if he found her. She just started looking at everything. When she came to one drawer that was locked, she kicked really hard and it popped open.

"She said there were lots more receipts like the ones she gave us," Amanda said, "in an unlabeled file—all with this German letterhead. And she had a few packets of powder labeled in German. The receipts were for whatever was in the packets, soluble in water or juice. The promising fighters were given the so-called vitamin cocktail." She stopped talking suddenly, and there was a pause. Her eyelids lowered, and she seemed to have drifted off. She was breathing evenly but shallowly, as if the pain was immediate and she didn't want to disturb it even in her sleep. Suddenly she twitched, and her eyes flew open as she winced in pain.

Olivia touched her shoulder, hoping to comfort her. "Linda gave us some receipts," she said, "and Antonio's—"

Amanda let out a sob, then quickly put her hand to her mouth to keep herself quiet. "She's alive," she whispered.

"She's pretty beat up. It's been bothering me where she was," Olivia said, "that she called in the 911 from a pay phone when you and Cappo went off the road." She couldn't figure out how Linda could have been with them and not gone into the ravine with them.

"She was in the car with us. I was driving, no one around for long stretches. Suddenly there was a car and—I have no idea how it happened, but we were flying through space."

"Wait, Mandy, she was in the car?" Bart asked. "You're not confused by the head—"

"That must be why she was so beat up," Olivia interrupted, "she was in the car." But that would mean she got out of the car, climbed back up to the road, got a ride...it was too fantastic. It didn't seem possible.

"I don't know how she did it," Amanda said. "Except she really loves—loved Nick. She must have known how badly he needed help."

Olivia was thinking how frantic Linda must have been, and how dreadfully long it must have taken her, when Amanda let out another groan.

"There's one more thing," she said, holding her head with both hands. "God, my head hurts. Or maybe it's my stomach." She suddenly sat up and heaved several dry retches, then collapsed back onto the pillows.

Olivia went into the bathroom and came back with a damp washcloth. She handed the washcloth to Bart, and he wiped sweat off Amanda's face while Olivia poured her some water.

Amanda turned her head away from the accordion straw. "There's one more thing," she whispered. "Nick had the original bloodwork and scans Antonio had done before he went to Mexico."

"Can we access the lab work?" Bart asked.

"To save the kid money, we got a friend of yours to perform the MRI across the street. They scanned him as an excuse to check a machine upgrade. I have the disc."

"Where?"

"You're thinking they might have turned my place over." She was pushing her words past her constricted throat. She took a swallow of water and closed her eyes against the pain in her head. "Don't worry, it's in my Dropbox. It's all in the cloud."

"Do you—" Olivia began, starting to ask for the password, but Amanda had drifted off in a haze of meds.

•

They slipped into the ED and, unlocking the physicians' office, Bart pulled Olivia inside, shut the door and locked it. Brushing his lips against her ear, he reached for the lights.

"No one ever comes in here during the day," he said. "And the night guy is too busy. Sorry about the musty odor."

At any other time, Olivia would have been disdainful of the cramped, airless room with its creepy metal cot and chipped white walls. But right now, there was nowhere she would rather be.

Bart slid the Antonio disc into a laptop that had also seen better days.

"Will this thing work?" she joked.

"I used it last week to check labs."

There was only one chair, but some stacked filing cartons soon doubled as a seat for Olivia, and the two sat side by side waiting for the DVD to open.

There it was. Antonio Santos, full-screen.

Olivia breathlessly sorted through the medicals, and they both exclaimed at once, "I knew it!" The hepatitis screen was falsified. It should have showed positive for Hep B antibodies, but it didn't.

"Unfortunately we don't know if they ran the tests and falsified them, or just used someone else's," she said.

"I'd put a sizeable bet on the latter," Bart said. "Though the only way we're going to know is by finding Antonio. He started flipping through the MRI images on the disc.

Olivia looked at each image carefully. "No arachnoid cyst on these scans," she said.

Thirty-Six

DUFFY'S WAS A relief to Olivia. She felt less edgy the minute the Sunday night crowd closed around them. Bart took her hand and led her toward the back, where the Irishman himself was sitting doing some figures.

"Willing to share the booth?" Bart said, putting a hand on Duffy's shoulder.

"Ha, my favorite docs." Duffy looked up and smiled from ear to ear. "I'll leave you to it. Got to go take care of a few things." Jumping up he gestured for Olivia to sit. "What can I get you?"

They ordered Black Bottle and two glasses, and the drink appeared almost instantaneously.

"How does he do that?" Olivia said.

"Drink," Bart commanded her, and they drank. They made a rule they weren't going to talk about anything that had just happened.

They decided to play Truth or Dare as a diversion, with the ground rule that you had to make up everything you said; no reality allowed. They kept at it, both of them working on the liquor and on the game to keep the demons of the past few days at bay. Every now and then Curtis's name would come up and Olivia would shiver, but Bart was stern, forbidding her to veer toward anything real.

*

Eventually they went back to the ranch. Olivia couldn't shake the thought that they were going to be hunted down and killed. She kept deciding not to look over her shoulder. Bart reassured her, but it wasn't rational. The air around them, the very stillness out there, with the horses nickering in their stalls in the dark, seemed ominous to her. They got partway into making love and fell asleep.

All night Olivia clung to sleep, grateful to have Bart's arms around her and desperate to know nothing until morning.

•

Bart's phone buzzed at 7:00 AM.

"What is that?" she grumbled, putting her head under the pillow.

"I set my alarm. We have to get to Mandy's place. FedEx will deliver Linda's package at 8:00."

"Oh my God, I can't believe I completely forgot about that." She sat up, then groaned, but managed to get out of bed and head for the shower.

As she felt the hot water sluice over her body, all she could do was cry. She didn't know why. She felt like the whole weight of Curtis's death and the momentum it had given to her life had fallen down on her and was crushing her.

After a minute, she got hold of herself and started breathing again. Twenty minutes and three Advils later, she and Bart were in the car headed for Amanda's housing estate across town. Stupid idea to stop for Starbucks, but it was a necessity. She watched Bart clench and unclench his fists around the wheel.

Swallowing a gulp of coffee, she opened her mouth to suggest they take a back route, but tears betrayed her again, and she couldn't speak.

He glanced at her, then without a word he reached over and took hold of her hand. Monday morning rush hour traffic. Neither of them had to say it. They should have...

At 8:00 they were two long blocks away, praying out loud that the truck would be as late as they were in this traffic.

No FedEx truck was in sight as Bart pulled up to the entryway. They both jumped out, and Bart tossed his car key to the valet. "Back in a few minutes," he told him and sprinted off to catch up with Olivia as she rushed into the lobby.

Fortunately the doorman and the concierge both recognized Bart and greeted him warmly.

"I haven't seen Ms. Weekly for a few days," the concierge told them.

Bart made a quick decision. "She's in the hospital," he said in his best doctor manner. "Emergency spleen operation." He indicated Olivia, silent beside him. "This is Dr. Norris."

The concierge had heard of Dr. Norris, the sister of Curtis Montana. "Sorry to lose Montana," he said, sympathetically shaking his head.

Olivia was willing Bart to ask about the FedEx delivery. If they had any chance of intercepting this parcel, she knew she had to be quiet and let Bart do the talking, but she felt like she would explode waiting.

"You need to get something for Ms. Weekly? Go on up," the concierge told them.

"We're here to pick up a FedEx package or envelope that was supposed to be delivered by 8:00," Bart said, making a point of looking at his watch. It was already 8:20.

"Nah, they didn't get here yet. The traffic always delays the 8:00 delivery." The guy shrugged. "Go on up. I'll call you when he gets here."

They were still waiting at the elevator when the delivery came in with three boxes and some envelopes. Olivia started to hurry back to the desk, but Bart held her back and they sauntered over.

Bart pulled out the receipt Linda had given him and handed it to the concierge. They waited. Every nerve in Olivia's body was on edge as she stood watching the sorting and listening to the banter. Finally, Bart was signing the receipt form, and then they were on their way out of the lobby with a large envelope in hand.

•

Olivia sat in the car, barely breathing, clenching the envelope all the way home.

Bart put a hand on her knee as he drove, allowing the silence to keep them safe from whatever they were about to find out.

At the house, he turned to her and smiled in a way she hadn't seen before.

"Don't expect too much," he said, his voice so kind it started up the tears again. "We have no idea if anything in that envelope relates to Curtis."

"It's everything. I can feel it, she said."

He softly kissed her. "You want some privacy?"

Uttering three foreign words, she said, "I need you."

In Curtis's office, he shut the door and waited.

"You open it—I can't," she pleaded, handing him the envelope and crumbling into a nearby chair.

Quickly he cut the envelope along the top and took out the contents. There were the packets with German printing on them, and the clinic's name written in German handwriting on the lines provided. And there were more receipts in German, like the ones Linda had already given them. And there was Curtis's medical chart. He couldn't interpret some of the Spanish. "It's handwritten," he said. "Maybe by Fernandez—at least this looks like his name on the signature line."

Thumbing through the pages, he read aloud, "Toradol...Curtis had a torn shoulder muscle going into the fight. We knew that...He was injected 10 days and seven days before. He traveled to Vegas on Wednesday. That morning they injected a double dose. Incompetence—that would have killed his stomach and predisposed him to a subdural. No wonder his BUN and creatinine were rising."

"And it would have increased his tolerance to pain," she groaned.

Bart laid the chart on the table and went over to the window.

Olivia looked up, surprised not to hear more. "Why'd you stop?" she asked, jumping up and grabbing the chart. "There's more, isn't there."

Olivia read the rest of the chart and flung it to the floor, shouting. They had given Curtis steroids—testosterone. For a moment she felt as though she would have to explode in order to take one more breath.

Bart wrapped her in his arms and rocked her, speaking quietly next to her ear. "We should think about this. Curtis probably never understood what he was taking. There isn't a day you turn on the TV and don't see ads for Androgel. People don't understand that testosterone is a potent anabolic steroid. Fighters seldom ask questions—or at least the right questions. They're like trusting children."

She pushed him away. The rage inside her felt right, like it would help her.

Bart kept talking. "Look at all the NFL players suing for being given Toradol," he said, "and how it masked injuries."

She paced the room, her mind racing. "That doesn't excuse the steroids... Fernandez was brilliant. He even had Curtis sign a waiver for the testosterone. Did you see that? Curtis must have known it was illegal. How could he juice?"

"Norris, stop."

"My own brother was dirty," she sobbed. "If I'd been the sister he needed, could I have saved his life? I wish I didn't know any of this. What good does it do now?"

Bart grabbed her wrist as she paced past him, pulling her back. "You're so wrong."

"I can't listen to this anymore." She tried to pull away, but his hand held her firmly.

"Hear me out. I promise we can forget about all of this—even find a way to bury it if you choose. There's more here than what happened or didn't happen to Curtis. We have the goods on Fernandez, maybe Santiago as well. They're poisoning boxers, helping them cheat, committing malpractice and fabricating medical reports. Sure, it appears Curtis knew he was taking steroids. Maybe he did, but maybe he didn't. People sign all kinds of things without reading the language. The truth is, how many world-class athletes would refuse a little help if they thought it was the difference between greatness and mediocrity? This is what's wrong with all sports, not just boxing."

"Curtis was already great. He didn't need—"

"Look at Marion Jones, Lance Armstrong, Floyd Landis...The list goes on. If you were given the chance to win a Nobel Prize, what would you risk?"

Irate, she muttered, "That's not fair. I would never consider—"

"Okay, maybe you wouldn't..." He chuckled, pleased to the tips of his toes that she wouldn't. He knew she wouldn't. He led her to the couch and sat down next to her. "Let's take our minds off this for a few hours."

Olivia ignored him. "Do we wait for Amanda to be well enough to get the story out?" she asked, trying to think how to use the material, wanting vengeance so badly she felt it roar in her head.

"If we go forward, we have to do it with everything," he said. "How else can we protect other fighters from these monsters?"

"And what about Diego and Antonio? Are they safe?" she demanded, angry with herself that she had momentarily lost sight of two missing pieces to the picture.

Bart immediately took out his phone and called Sullivan. The agent told him they didn't know where the two were, but they had heard from Diego and they were safe. They were heading for Vegas. He had told them to go to the ranch.

"They'll have to go public," he said when he had ended the call. "Otherwise they can be killed anytime."

Olivia threw herself down on the sofa with a groan. "Are we really in this movie?" she murmured. She felt as scared and enraged as she had felt when she discovered Curtis had killed a kid on a dark night in the snow in Chicago. That had turned out not to be the truth, but this, now—there wasn't going to be any way out of this one.

Bart stretched out on the generous couch and pulled her down next to him where he could hold her and comfort her.

She sobbed against his chest for Curtis, and for herself.

Thirty-Seven

OUTSIDE THE Coffee Joint, Olivia straightened her gray stiletto skirt and loosely fitting sky-blue chiffon blouse. Bart had advised her how to dress for this meeting, and he made it obvious he loved the way she looked.

She muttered, "You think we should have met at the Commission office?"

"Nah, neutral ground is better." He pointed out that Tyler's and Gabe's cars were already in the lot, and he let her go ahead of him so he could admire her legs—long and shapely—as she negotiated the tarmac in four-inch steel gray pumps.

She pinched his side. "Are you Woodward or Bernstein? Will the attorney general be here?" she chided him. She felt giddy. Diego and Antonio had arrived safe and sound. There was something tangible to show. But her doubts about Curtis, and the sorrow they caused deep inside her, made her edgy.

"They would never come to this meeting without their attorney, especially since they aren't completely sure why we called them."

"Over here," Gabe called out, waving from a table in the back.

Gabe was effusive in her welcome—never a good sign, Bart knew. She introduced Craig Nelson, the deputy attorney general, to Olivia, who had sat down opposite her. Bart slid into a chair and assumed his usual slouch. When the espresso orders were in, he dismissed pleasantries and laid into Tyler about falsified medical records, the Fernandez clinic, stories of testosterone and Toradol. Expressionless, Gabe, Tyler and Nelson patiently listened. Tyler asked to review the documents, which Olivia was happy to display.

"The originals and the MRI?" Nelson inquired.

Olivia sat silent, astounded that the three invitees had so much restraint.

Nelson asked Bart, "Where do you foresee this going?"

"The fact that you're asking is not a good sign, Craig."

"My role is to protect the NBC—"

"And my role is to protect the Governor," Tyler butted in. "We appreciate you bringing this to us. Dr. Norris. No one should have to go through what you have. However, the events that either resulted in or contributed to Curtis's death are now apparent. At least now we know it was no fault of the Commission. And we can move on—"

Olivia abruptly started collecting the documents. "You people have no sense of decency. You dare to tell us your precious Commission, Nevada politicians, and people like Santiago and Fernandez take precedence over the lives of boxers?"

She stood up, scraping the chair back loudly on the floor. Bart grasped her hand. "Wait," he said, and it sounded to her more like an endearment than an order. "These folks have more to say, right, Jerry?"

"You're being unreasonable," Gabe said, looking at Bart.

"Am I?" he responded, full of indignation. "Commissioner Tyler, tell us all what happens, now that you know the truth. Dr. Norris is new to the way things work. So, enlighten us."

Tyler took a deep breath and mumbled, "We go on as before. I promise you both we'll look into this. It has to be carried out discreetly. No one wants litigation."

Olivia couldn't let it go at that. "Aren't you going to have a Commission hearing to discuss this? Bringing it out in the open will put a stop to it immediately."

"Not necessarily," Gabe cautiously responded.

Tyler was glaring. "All I ask," he said, "is that you let Gabe, Craig and I handle it. We'll figure out a way to make the necessary changes."

Olivia had sat back down tentatively, at the edge of the seat. She leaned toward Tyler, insistent. "Stop accepting medicals when they can't be corroborated. All testing should be completed at approved facilities under acceptable conditions. Drug testing—especially testing for performance-enhancing drugs—has to be ramped up, including random unannounced testing with blood and urine. Fighters need education on harmful substances like Toradol and recommendations on safe, efficient weight loss and preventing dehydration." She put the list she and Bart had prepared the night before, on the table in front of the three of them and pointed to it. "The rest is included here."

"Thank you," Tyler said smugly, smiling. He looked at his watch and rose to leave. "Sorry, my duties call me."

Bart and Olivia stood up at the same time, and Tyler took a step back, as if he thought they were going to attack him physically.

Bart couldn't help laughing, and Gabe joined him—as soon as Tyler was out of earshot. She looked up at Olivia.

"Carmen will be calling with your assignment for the MGM card," she said.

"You're in charge. Bart, you have the main event."

Bart dragged Olivia outside before she could yell, "Take this job and shove it."

"This is unreal," she said as they headed for his car. "A few days ago I was an incompetent ring physician, and now I'm in charge? They're not going to do a thing."

"Relax. Gabe's classic response to any problem is to dole out primo fight assignments." He pointed the remote and the car locks released. He shot her a conspiratorial look as they buckled their seat belts. "We started this, and we now have to finish it."

She was turning to say something, but he met her mouth with his in an intoxicating kiss. She finally pulled away to catch her breath. He took her chin in his hand.

"I walked away once before," he told her. "In fact, I think we've both walked away from many things in our lives. I'm not going anywhere this time."

"I know," was all she could say, but it seemed to say everything. He brushed her mouth with his lips, then started the car and drove her to her office.

"I'll bring dinner," he said, as she got out of the car. "We'll look over next weekend's card and prepare. Today was shock and awe. Unlike Iraq, we'll win the war on the ground."

•

Olivia worked her way through a day of patients, completely focused on each and equally fascinated by every case that presented itself. This was something she had always done, concentrated on work when everything else in her life was in chaos. This time, there was a difference. For the first time in her life, maybe, she felt connected to another human being. Loving Bart had shifted something. She took a call from her mother, and she wondered if even that anger had shifted a bit in her.

At the end of the day, there was Bart, teasing her and joking with her as they set up dinner in the den. Bart turned on the CBS Nightly News, just as he had done every day he could remember since he grew up and left home.

The news returned from commercial.

"Good evening, this is Amanda Weekly in front of the Nevada Boxing Commission office."

Bart reeled around and grabbed the remote to raise the volume. "Olivia, get in here," he yelled. There was Amanda, still wearing some bandages that she had tried to disguise under a large-brimmed hat and leaning stiffly against the wall of the building. How was she even standing up, with those broken ribs? Next to her stood a young Latino kid who kept grinning.

Olivia came in with a teasing word on her lips, then saw the TV. Bart turned up the volume a bit more. The turmoil inside him made him feel deaf.

Amanda was speaking with close to her usual gusto. "So far we've been unable to obtain comment from the Commission or the Governor's office regarding the evidence uncovered by this reporter about dangerous and illegal drugs forced on boxers, falsified medical records endangering fighters' lives and Commission negligence in improving safety standards."

Amanda went on, giving just enough detail to make the story tantalizing. She vowed they would cover this story until they got answers. She said the athletes deserved more. Curtis Montana deserved more. Then she introduced Antonio Santos, and it began.

The United Boxing Association Announcement

The UBA proudly invites you to attend an unprecedented weekend of seminars for officials and athletes on the hazards of performance enhancing drugs at Mandalay Bay on June 15.

The Agenda

Opening Remarks by
Jorge Santiago, UBA President and
Ms. Gabe Gunderson, NBC Executive Director

Role of Commissions by
Mr. Jerry Tyler, Newly Appointed NBC Chair

Understanding Performance Enhancing Drugs by
Dr. Mark Stewart

Opening Night Cocktail Party
Sponsored by Ed Rappaport

AWARDS Dinner
Sponsored by the Fernandez Clinic

When reserving your room, ask for the UBA discount rate.

A note from the author

B OXING, ONCE THE most highly respected athletic endeavor, has evolved into a niche sport due to insufficient regulations and a lack of unified standards. Commissions, promoters, networks, the media and politicians all bear equal responsibility. While repeatedly professing to care about fighter safety, none are willing to make the necessary changes. Instead they point fingers at one another. As a result, nothing changes, and the risks of acute and chronic brain injury accumulate.

The current federal regulations—the Boxing Safety Act and the Muhammad Ali Boxing Reform Act—were a start. Unfortunately neither stopped the existing corruption and lack of oversight. This is not to say that these bills didn't have the best intentions. However, they're not enforced on a state or federal level. Senator John McCain held two hearings and touted legislation that was never passed. He and Senator Harry Reid introduced another bill that to date has gone nowhere.

Commissions worry about losing control and their piece of the pie. A federal commission would make them finally have to answer to someone. It would stop the vicious cycle of jurisdiction and venue shopping so often used by many pro-moters to evade stringent regulations.

To this day, few commissions conduct routine MRI scans or neurological exams, and even fewer conduct performance-enhancing drug testing. Inadequate regula-tions regarding fighter weigh-ins and how much weight a boxer can gain after the weigh-in contribute to an unfair disadvantage over boxers who want to play by the rules.

Boxers with a history of brain injury as a result of boxing are too often allowed to compete—especially if they are known to the public and can sell tickets.

In the end, it is the boxers who suffer.

Most of the much-needed safety improvements involve little financial impact. They require that regulators have a conscience; use only highly trained referees, physicians and judges; have little fear in standing up to pressure from promoters; and accept the job they were hired to do—protect the fighters at all cost.

Acknowledgements

It would have been impossible to write this novel without chance events resulting in chance meetings.

First and foremost was the evening of a canceled HBO fight, when Jim Lampley stood outside Las Vegas' Valley hospital announcing that a neurologist would be called in to see a dizzy fighter. My phone rang, and I discovered a new purpose through Dr. Flip Homansky. Flip is so much more than my best friend; he is the love of my life as well as the finest ringside physician to ever grace the sport. It's tragic for the fighters, the sport and especially Nevada that they no longer utilize his expertise. Ringside medical procedures and many improved regulations were put in place by him. Many of this novel's behind-the-scenes details could not have been written without him.

So many years ago, while waiting to work a Vegas fight card, I met the incomparable Pulitzer-nominated author Thomas Hauser. I'm fortunate to call him my good friend. He encouraged me to write—especially about the inequities and countless problems boxers face. Tom taught me that if I'm not part of the solution, I'm part of the problem. I learned that if I cared about fighters, I needed to shed the blinders that so many in boxing rely upon—blinders that risk athletes' lives.

My gratitude goes to the boxers; their dedication and fearlessness captured my heart. I've known many great fighters—some succeeded, some failed, some succumbed to performance-enhancing drug use, while a select few tragically died. This book could not have been written without them. Although fiction, *Death in Vegas* is a way to give back—a vehicle to promote positive changes that might save the next boxer, encourage the federal government to look beyond Thoroughbred racing and major league baseball and help athletes who daily risk their lives.

No one can set out to write a novel without assistance. The finished product makes medical-school training look like kindergarten. Thank you first and foremost to my editor Melody Lawrence. Her immeasurable assistance and expertise can only be described as unselfish. She truly got it! Through Melody, I was able to meet the relentless Pamela Quinn and terrifically talented Christina Gruppuso, who probably never knew it would be so labor-intensive to design a cover juggling many strong opinions. Finally, thank you to Michael Smolinsky and to Adam Pollack and Win By KO publications.

Throughout my twenty years in boxing, I've worked with many caring commissioners, executive directors and talented officials who shaped my expertise and freely shared their expertise. They, too, played a part in developing this novel. Thank you.

Lastly, thank you to Steve Farhood, a true friend, great boxing analyst and writer. Your feedback and ideas were greatly appreciated.

My ultimate reward from *Death in Vegas* will be when the issues raised on these pages no longer exist. Until that time, we fight on.

CPSIA information can be obtained at www.ICGtesting.com
Printed in the USA
LVOW12s1626191114

414531LV00004B/805/P